MIRAGE

Tony Burnett

a Cash and Carrie novel

Mirage ©2026
Tony Burnett
Kallisto Gaia Press
All Rights Reserved

No part of this book may be used or reproduced in any manner whatsoever without permission except in the case of brief quotations embodied in critical essays or reviews.

This is a work of the poet's iumadination. Any references to historical events, real people, or real places are used fictitiously. Other names, characters, places, and events are products of the author's imagination, and any resemblance to actual events or places or persons, living or dead, is entirely coincidental.

Attention schools and businesses; for discounted copies on large orders please contact the publisher directly.

> Kallisto Gaia Press
> PO Box 220
> Davilla
> TX 76523

ISBN: 978-1-952224-44-7

First Edition

thriller / crime / human trafficing / serial killer

MIRAGE

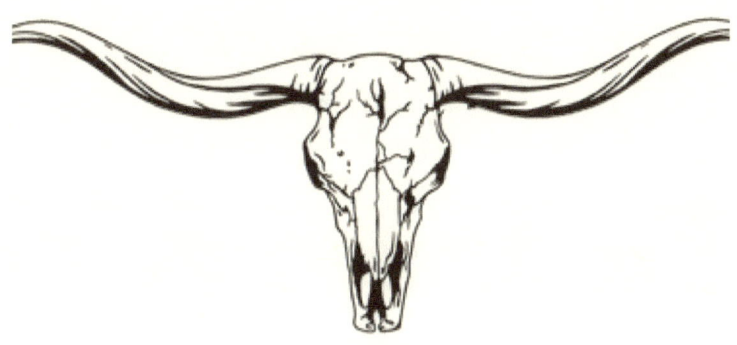

Tony Burnett

a Cash and Carrie novel

For Robin
who shared the meaning of life.

Revenge is sweet and not fattening.
—*Alfred Hitchcock*

Coyote

The searing August sun cooked the spirits from the desert landscape. The turkey vultures languishing on the bare branches of the madrone trees nodded, patiently waiting. Occasionally one would take wing to cool itself in the updrafts from the valley floor where a creek bed of fractured dirt and bleached bones meandered.

Had Carlos tried to verbalize his cursing of God, no sound would have escaped past his swollen tongue. Indeed his vocal chords had long since dried to the texture of dead smilax vines. Sweat no longer soaked through his denim shirt, only a greasy sheen where the fat of his once ample body oozed through his pores. Chasing the shade in a deep barranco, Carlos escaped the brutal midday sun, preferring to move by night.

So this was the path of least resistance? Easy money? Carlos realized now that Miguel conned him into compliance with the greedy scheme. The first two runs were uneventful. picking up two dozen obreros in Cuidad Acuna, letting them ride in the back of the refrigerated produce truck. They traversed the border at the tiny Amistad Dam crossing, manned by only two guards, one of which was Miguel's brother-in-law, virtually assuring an uneventful crossing. It was a chance to give a better life to men. The men would be safer and make enough money to send home to their families. In exchange for this altruism, Carlos received nine hundred dollars for ten hours' work. They dropped their charges off at a Dallas safe house where the money guys paid the balance and gave them their next assignment.

This last run was different. When they arrived at the pickup point 40 miles south of Acuna, the cargo was female. Eighteen young women awaited them. Several appeared to be dressed for a night on the town. Carlos knew he should have abandoned the project at this point. His experiences with women had been less than positive. His few attempts to relate to girls in high school left him stung and shamed. His mama's wisdom about respecting women hadn't served the plump little introvert well. These women they were transporting were flamboyant and teasing, several offering "favors" for the privilege of riding up front. Carlos understood that even hookers could make a better life in the U.S. but he suspected Miguel's fascination with the seedy side of culture was the real reason for his decision to carry the girls. Two of the women were out of place in the group. An older woman and a girl of about fourteen, who appeared to be her daughter, stood away from the group, their eyes averted. They dressed casually in the embroidered cotton dresses common to the working class of northern Mexico. Their calloused fingers lacked the painted nails of the other women. The older woman was beyond the age normally considered by men wanting to purchase companionship. She exuded a dark spirit that made her disturbing and unapproachable. Carlos was drawn to the distinctive Mayan features of the daughter, a girl with high cheekbones and full lips.

"Why women, Miguel? What are we to do with these women?" Carlos asked.

"Just a different kind of las trabajadora. Supply and demand, you know, land of opportunity and all that."

"Well I don't like it! Someone could take advantage of those two campesinas."

"It's not for us to say. The pay is good, no?"

"Sure but...."

"No buts, we take them. They've made the down payment."

"This is wrong!" Carlos said.

"No, this is life, same job, better environment, better pay, everybody wins."

"But what about the mother and child?"

"She doesn't look like a child to me. I wish she wanted to ride up front. I could work something out for her."

"You're a sick bastard."

"Why? You want her? I can make that happen."

"Let's just load up and go." Carlos briefly imagined himself on top of the naked girl but he saw only fear in her eyes. He shook his head violently to make the image fade. He helped the women into the truck, pulled down the overhead door, latched it and affixed a fictitious Department of Agriculture seal. Sliding his machete behind the seat, he climbed into the passenger side and they hit the road.

When they reached the border crossing Miguel pulled into the parking area and jumped out of the driver's seat.

"Ronaldo! My brother! Mi hermana treating you right? You don't look like you miss any meals." Miguel slapped the pudgy little man affectionately on his wide back.

"She's getting meaner every year but I can still outrun her," Ronaldo said, giving Miguel a hug. "What are you hauling today?"

"I've got a truckload of hookers headed for New Orleans."

"Yeah, right. Seriously, cunado?"

"Lettuce, already inspected and sealed." Miguel waved a hand toward the truck.

"So, are you ever going to settle down, start a family?"

"Not likely. I don't need some damn woman running my life. I'm doing fine on my own."

"Who's riding with you?" Renaldo asked, pulling a notepad from his pocket.

"Carlos, Maria's boy. He needed a summer job," Miguel replied. "He's only seventeen, but he has a license so we trade off at the wheel. More miles, more money, you know the story. Speaking of, I better head out."

Ronaldo put the notepad away. He went around and fingered the steel band threaded through the latch. "Don't let me hold you up. See you Thanksgiving if not sooner. Be careful!"

"You, too. Give Marissa my love."

Once back in the U.S., Miguel decided to stay to the back roads to avoid the checkpoints. One section of their route took them 40 miles through a hunting lease on a road that wasn't on a map. It saved 25 miles and avoided a checkpoint, a slow rough ride over a road that varied from a path to non-existent. By the tenth mile the women in the cargo box were yelling and beating on the walls. Miguel was trying to ignore them.

"Aren't you going to do something?" Carlos asked.

"Maybe you were right about hauling these women. They sure are a noisy bunch, They can make all the noise they want out here but I'll need to shut them up before we get back to civilization." Miguel said.

"I've never had anything but trouble with women," Carlos said. A minute later a loud thump emanated from the box followed by a blood curdling scream.

"Maybe this will shut them up." Miguel reached under the dash and flipped the cargo light switch, plunging the women into total darkness. After a couple of shrieks the voices became noticeably quieter. Soon a rhythmic thumping began and the truck began to rock back and forth.

"These God damned bitches are trying to flip the truck!" Miguel screamed. He stopped the truck, turned on the cargo light and reached into the glove box, pulling out a 9MM Berretta. "I've got to stop this shit!" He jumped out of the truck. "C'mon, bring your machete."

Carlos followed orders, popping the seal from the latch with the large knife. Miguel slung the overhead door open.

"What the hell is going on here?" Miguel screamed.

One of the women jumped out. "This old bruja conjures. See! Ants, all over me!"

"I don't see anything."

The mother of the young girl was laying, half-conscious, against the wall of the box, blood streaming from behind her ear. The frightened girl was kneeling over her.

"What happened to the campesina?" Carlos asked.

"She fell," the woman stated. The other women looked away.

"What's your name?" Miguel demanded.

"What do you care?"

"Give me your fucking name!" Miguel shouted and pointed the Berretta at her face.

"Rosa," she said.

"Take her around front of the truck. I'm going to see if I can help this woman."

Carlos motioned with the machete. Rosa slunk to the front of the truck. "I was just trying to give the chica some pointers, let her know what to expect. Her mama hexed me. I swear."

"Shut up! I didn't bring you up here for a conversation," Carlos said. He heard the door of the cargo box close.

Miguel came around the truck. "She's in pretty bad shape. The bleeding slowed. She might make it. This bitch beat the shit out of her, probably because she wanted to recruit the daughter."

"The witch has no clue to what's going on," Rosa said.

"Shut up! You're the problem!" Miguel barked. "Carlos, tie her up and put her in the truck."

"No," Rosa cried. "Don't put me back in there with her ... I can't..."

"Fine, Mexico is that way." Miguel pointed the gun south. "Del Rio is that way." He shifted the barrel slightly eastward. "Move it!"

"No, no, I'll die! Please let me ride up front with you. I won't be a problem."

"You're already a problem."

"I can make your journey very enjoyable."

"Yeah, so can anyone back there. You're not my type."

"But I'll die in the desert."

"Probably, but if you don't start walking I'll drop you with one shot and the buzzards can have you."

Rosa turned to leave then spun around and spit toward Miguel. The explosion from the Berretta echoed through the valley as Rosa dropped in a clump at Carlos' feet.

"God damn, Miguel! What the fuck! Are you ... you killed her!" Rage was causing Carlos to shake.

"Let's go." Miguel turned toward the truck. Carlos was unable to move. The machete fell from his hand, the handle dropping heavily against Rosa's lifeless cheek.

"I said, let's go," Miguel barked. Carlos bent down and picked up the machete. He lunged forward. Miguel raised the gun toward Carlos. "That's not a good plan," Miguel stated coldly. "We need to leave." Miguel latched the cargo door and climbed into the driver's seat. Carlos was still trembling when Miguel started the truck.

Soon they were bumping along the path. No one talked. Carlos was unable to reconcile the recent events with the cousin he grew up with, playing soccer and eating barbequed cabrito on the weekend. Miguel always organized the games and ruled them with his athletic prowess. When the other uncles and cousins were getting married and becoming tools of their women, Miguel drove a new pickup and restored a '72 Corvette, always flashed money and lived large. He was Carlos' favorite cousin. Now the man at the wheel seemed like a stranger with the arid landscape sliding past his gaunt features. The road was no longer visible. Only a crooked line on a handheld GPS kept them headed through the desolation. The truck began shuddering with the slightest acceleration. An ominous clicking sound was coming from somewhere underneath. Miguel stopped to inspect the problem. When he crawled from under the truck his expression radiated intense concern.

"U-joint. It's about to give out." He consulted the GPS. If we turn around, it's eleven miles back to the highway and another 10 or so to the closest town or it's 25 miles to the highway ahead but there's a town with a garage at the junction. I say we go for it. It's six of one , half a dozen of the other."

"Will we make it?" Carlos asked.

Miguel just shrugged. "We could lighten our load. It might help, but we wouldn't get the rest of our money."

"No! We're in the middle of the desert."

"Then let's move out."

After a half hour of creeping down the path with the noise getting no worse, the two men relaxed. Miguel decided to pick up the pace. As soon as he reached 20 miles per hour the u-joint gave way with a loud pop and the truck rolled to a stop.

"Shit!" Miguel shook his head and stared through the windshield. Carlos watched him, looking for some sign of action. Miguel just stared ahead. Finally he checked his cell phone. He climbed on top of the cargo box. After spinning a couple of 360-degree pirouettes with the phone held high, he flipped it closed with a resigned sigh. "No service."

"What are we going to do?" Carlos asked. Miguel pulled the pistol from the glove box.

"No!" Carlos screamed.

"What? I'm not going to shoot anyone but they aren't going to want to hear what I tell them. I may need backup. Bring your machete."

Miguel rolled open the door to the cargo box. When the women saw the pistol they huddled near the front of the box.

"Nobody is going to hurt you, but I need you to get out of the truck," Miguel insisted. The wary women kept their eyes on the men as they climbed down from the cargo box. Miguel stood aside holding the pistol while Carlos helped each woman negotiate the long step down. Only the injured woman and her daughter remained. The older woman appeared barely conscious and the girl glared defiantly, refusing to exit the vehicle. Carlos had one foot on the step when Miguel stopped him. "Let them be for now. Close the door." Carlos followed orders.

"Ladies, the truck is dead," Miguel said." It's going to take some time to get it fixed. We don't have enough food and water to keep you. If you follow the path back the way we came it's just over 10 miles to the paved highway. None of you pretty ladies should have any trouble getting a ride."

"What about our money? You were supposed to take us to New Orleans," one of the women asked.

"We got you across the border. That's the best we can do. You're on your own now. It's about a 4-hour walk. If you keep a good pace you should make it to the road well before dark. I suggest you girls get moving."

The women stood for a moment and consulted in hushed tones. Miguel cocked back the hammer on his pistol and the conversation died.

"Give us some water?" asked the woman who spoke earlier. Carlos took a jug from the cab of the truck and handed it to her. She turned to Miguel.

"Pendejo! You are the worst coyote in Texas, maybe the world! You should be ashamed taking advantage of us."

Miguel looked genuinely offended. "Look, it's the best we can do under the circumstances. I'm sure most of you will be fine. Consider it an adventure."

The women left in a group following the tire tracks back toward the horizon. The men watched them leave.

"What about the other two?" Carlos asked.

"I guess we'll keep them until help arrives."

"No one knows where we are except the women and I doubt they will say."

"We have a phone and a GPS, enough water for a couple of days and fuel to run the refrigeration system."

"Right. But we have no service and what about the campesinas?"

Miguel leaned against the truck and pinched the bridge of his nose. Carlos waited. Miguel was silent. Carlos needed a minute to think. He opened the cargo door.

"What are you doing?" Miguel asked.

"I'm going to check on the old woman." Carlos motioned the daughter out of the box, leaned the machete in the corner and kneeled by the prostrate woman. He held his fingers to her throat. Her heart was beating very rapidly. "What's your name?" He asked. She just stared. He repeated the question in Spanish. No answer. He felt her forehead. It was cool but clammy. He saw her lips move. He drew his ear close to her mouth. The words she uttered were clear but in a language that was unfamiliar. When he looked at her again, her eyes appeared to glow. They burned through him. A physical pain ignited in his arms and legs. He had to get away! He jumped down from the box just as Miguel grabbed the girl by the back of the head and pulled her to him.

"Miguel! Stop!" Carlos shouted.

"Hey, Cuz, we're going to be here for a while. We might as well have some fun."

"The old woman is dying! We need to get help. Leave her

alone."

Miguel released the girl and turned on Carlos. "I'm running this operation! You will not tell me what to do!"

"That doesn't seem to be working out too well," Carlos countered. Miguel took a step toward him and slammed the Berretta hard against Carlos' ear. Carlos saw an image of the old woman shimmer and fade as his knees buckled. When he regained consciousness Miguel was leaning over him with a damp rag pressed to his temple.

"Damn, Cuz, I guess you forgot the gun in my hand. Are you okay?"

Carlos wanted to strangle Miguel but his arms were limp sausages and his head throbbed. "Fuck you," he whispered.

Miguel grinned. "You're okay." When Carlos staggered to his feet he noticed the girl tending to her mother and Miguel studying the GPS, writing some numbers on a card from his wallet.

"See that rise?" Miguel pointed to an outcropping of rock about a mile away "I want you to take the phone and climb up there. Hopefully you can get a signal. Call this guy. His name is Julio. He lives in Beeville. We can trust him. Give him our coordinates from here on the back of this card. Tell him our situation. He'll pick us up."

"The women?"

"Fuck 'em, not my problem at this point."

"Why me? You go!"

"You need the exercise, fat boy. Now move!" Miguel waved the gun.

Carlos knew why he was selected to go but he didn't want to be a pile of dry bones. He took the phone and a canteen of water and began his trek toward the mountain. He was less than a quarter mile away when the muffled screams reached his ears. He tried to focus on the mountaintop through the tears and picked up his pace.

The mountain seemed to move away as he approached. It must have been an hour before he reached the foot of the incline. At least the screaming stopped. The climb proved rugged but Carlos knew his life was in the balance. As he ascended, he checked for a signal every few hundred yards. Nothing. The barren terrain began to level out when he finally got a signal. He pulled out the card and dialed. A woman's voice answered.

"Hello?"

"May I speak with Julio please?"

"Just a minute." A minute passed, then two.

"Hello?"

"Julio?"

"Yes." The phone beeped. The battery indicator was flashing.

"I'm Carlos, Miguel's cousin. We're broke down in the desert. We need help. I have coordinates."

"Let me get a pencil"

"Hurry, my battery is going dead!"

There was no further communication. When Carlos looked at the screen it was blank. He pressed the power button. The face of the old woman materialized on the black screen. His arms and legs felt the shooting pain again.

"Holy Christ! God Damn!" he screamed and threw the phone. He collapsed in the dust, balling up from the pain.

When he could move his limbs again, he began the torturous climb down. He didn't want to go back to the truck but there was nowhere else to go. At least, if Miguel shot him, it would be a quick death. The canteen was dry and his legs burned as he approached the truck. He saw the girl standing by the back of the truck with a blanket laid across the tailgate. Her dress was ripped down the front. She'd tied it closed with strings cut from the fabric.

"Is help coming?" she asked.

"No. Where's Miguel?"

She pointed into the cargo box. His cousin was lying face down in a puddle of blood, the machete buried in his rib cage.

"My God! What have you done?"

"My mother saved me. He raped me. He was going to kill me. It took her last breath, but she saved me. Now I will take her home."

Carlos just stared at his cousin's body. The girl climbed into the truck and lifted her mother's body, placing it gently on the blanket. Carlos saw the woman's eyes staring into nothingness. He reached for her face to close them. The girl grabbed him by the wrist. "No!" she said." She still sees. She's going to be my guide."

"She's dead. She can't help you. We can figure something out together."

"You don't know mi madre. She's with me. We're going home."

"You'll die in the desert."

"No, I'm from the desert. It's you who will die in the desert."

Carlos had heard stories of the native people of Mexico traveling hundreds of miles through barren terrain, but this child, carrying a body? "Please, leave her. Come with me. We can survive together."

"I owe her my life. We are going home."

"Wait!" Carlos filled his small canteen from the remaining gallon of water and handed it to the girl.

"Bless you," she said and turned to follow the tire tracks south, her mother's body draped over her shoulders.

Carlos left the refrigeration unit on. He covered Miguel's body with a blanket and sat in the corner of the cargo box to figure out his strategy. As the refrigerated air fell on him, he realized how tired he was. He would rest. Then decide.

While Carlos slept, dusk worked magic on the desert. He stepped from the box into the cool of the evening. The brightest stars pierced the purple sky. Unseen life produced whispers of sound in the still, dry air. Carlos gathered the GPS, the last blanket, and the rest of the water. He took almost eleven hundred dollars from Miguel's wallet leaving a single silver dollar he found behind the driver's license. Taking that would be stealing, he thought. He located the Barretta under the seat beside a Crown Royale bag containing two thousand dollars. The pistol was a foreign object to him, only bringing death and sorrow. He didn't see a problem with the money. It took him a few minutes to comprehend the technology of the GPS. After locating the map with the trail on it he proceeded. Twenty-six point eight miles to civilization, he should be there by sunup. There was barely a sliver of a moon but his eyes adjusted to the starlight as the amber glow receded over the horizon. He had learned his lesson from the phone. He checked the GPS and took his bearings. The moon over his right shoulder would keep him on track. He turned off the GPS. As the screen faded the old campesina's haunted face appeared and the burning pain shot through his extremities bringing him to his hands and knees in the dust. Slowly the pain left his body and he was able to stand. Moon to the right, he trudged on.

The still desert air grew cooler. Carlos draped the blanket around his shoulders. The moon rose higher in the sky. Soon he would have to check his bearings.

He turned on the GPS and brought up the map screen. There was no trail. He enlarged the coverage and found the trail off to his left about three quarters of a mile. He picked up his pace and left the unit on until he rejoined the trail. By the dim light he could make out what might be a set of wagon tracks snaking off into the distance. He decided to follow it. It seemed to be the road. Again, he turned off the GPS. This time he turned the screen away from him. Where the light from the screen shone, the sand formed a crystalline image of the old woman's face and pain shot up through the soles of his shoes, knocking him off his feet. He lost consciousness. When he woke, he noticed the water jug on its side. Most of the water had spilled out. The horizon was glowing to the east. Terrified, he gathered his things and began jogging down the wagon trail. Soon the trail became so faint he wasn't sure it was a trail or just lines of erosion in the sand. A deep barranco lay ahead that he knew no wagon or truck could cross. He would have to turn the GPS on again. Again, no trail. He expanded the map. Still no trail. He expanded again. At the edge of the screen was the trail, over two miles to his right. This wasn't working. He would leave the unit on and try to intersect the trail ahead. He turned slightly to the right and set a course. His legs were aching. The sun still touched the horizon but he was already sweating. He trudged ahead.

The sun was well into its searing arc when the GPS said he intersected the trail. He couldn't see any sign of vehicular traffic and the trail began a sharp incline. He shivered with the uncomfortable feeling someone watched him, toyed with him, like a rat in a maze, but there was no evidence of life in any direction. He began his ascent, paying close attention to the screen. He had no intention of turning it off. He enlarged the coverage until he saw where the trail intersected the main road. He still had thirteen miles to go. His heart sank. He forged ahead.

The climb was steep. Sweat dripped from his nose and sizzled in the sand. The battery indicator on the GPS said he was at one quarter. As he crested the rise he located a rock formation straight ahead to fix on. He got down on his knees and elbows facing the formation. He placed the screen of the GPS against the sand and pressed the power button. The pain was blistering. He vomited. He heard the old crone inside his head speaking the odd language just before he fainted. When he woke up sand and vomit were dried on his face. His neck and ears were stinging from ants. He cursed Miguel. He cursed God. He cursed the old woman that haunted him, whose strange language still gurgled in his brain. He sipped at the few ounces of water in his jug. It burned his swollen tongue. He tried to locate the rock formation he had fixed on. That one, maybe, or the one just to the left. He couldn't be sure. He set out for the formation on the right.

Time passed and the formation didn't seem to be getting any closer. His legs were shaking and he was soaked in sweat. There was a barranco a hundred yards to the left. He needed rest, and shade. He stumbled to the dry wash, curling in the shadows and sipping some water. He dozed lightly, repositioning out of the sun, until dusk was near. Before dark settled in, he crawled from his encampment like the other animals of the desert. He followed his footprints back to the trail.

He looked toward the rock formation that he used as his reference. He wasn't sure. The voices were silent. "Please, God, a sign," he prayed. A falling star dropped from the heavens straight toward one of the formations. That could not have been a coincidence. He was certain. He fixed his eyes on the mark and trudged across the vast desert plain. The night grew darker and cooler. He wrapped in the blanket and drank the last of the water. Surely he would reach the road by morning. The sky was growing lighter as the huge formation loomed before him. He must be close. Carlos activated the GPS. The battery meter began flashing as he pulled up the map screen. The trail was about a half mile to the left but no intersection. He expanded the map screen, twice. The intersection came into view just as the screen flashed "Low battery - Shutting down". It looked like about 3 miles, a little curve to the left. The tingling began in his hand and came up his arm. He dropped the dead GPS. It was too late. Pain racked his body but he maintained consciousness. The burning did not want to leave. The old crone's voice was screaming in his head, repeating the same phrase in the strange language. Carlos squeezed his hands to his ears and thrashed his head about trying to silence the demon woman. The pain was searing, cooking his bones to dust. Slowly the pain subsided. He was crying like a child.

That was the last he heard from the old woman, or God, or man. That was yesterday. He tried to use the sun as a compass but he never found the trail again, or the road. He could barely move. He wandered by night, generally north, he hoped.

The sun is up. The turkey vultures advance. He tries to raise his arm to shoo them away but only his fingers move. A vulture lunges and rips one free. The pain barely registers. Another hops onto his chest. It stares into his eyes, cocking its head to one side. Those eyes, those same eyes as the old woman. He tries to laugh but his last breath is only a sigh as the vulture's beak steals his vision.

GIRL

The temperature in the sticky neon shadows of night hovered around 100°. Her nylon blouse adhered to her body as she crushed out her last cigarette. For over an hour she'd killed time leaning against the green minivan. Caricatures of three girls and the name of a local cheerleading school adorned the back glass. The van's owner had yet to appear. As she kicked her cigarette butt under the vehicle the door to the strip club opened. Out stumbled a rotund man sporting khaki slacks. As he approached, the girl gouged her eyes with her fists and slumped against the bumper of the van.

"Are you okay?" the man asked.

" I'm fine," the girl said. "No need to worry about me."

"You don't look fine. Have you been crying? You must be in some kind of trouble. Anything I can do?"

She sighed. "This dude told me I could pick up work here but when I showed he wasn't here. If I come home without any money my boyfriend will kick me out, or worse. So I'm borderline stranded."

"I can give you a ride somewhere. What was your gig here? How much cash do you need? I might be able to help you a little."

"I'm a dancer, mainly. The guy, Jimmy, that wanted me to work, said I could make $500 a night in tips."

"So what else do you do? I mean if you've got skills maybe we could work a deal."

The girl smiled. "I don't do windows if that's what you mean. I'm in the pleasure business. I'm really good at it. I make a grand on a good night but right now I really just need $500."

"Tell you what, I'll give you a ride home. If we can stop at an ATM, then get a room, I'll make sure you get home with $500."

The girl flung her arms around his neck. "You're such a sweetie. I could just eat you up. You really are saving my life."

It wasn't a fancy hotel but it was nicer than some she'd seen. The man was already breaking a sweat before he unlocked the room, the girl giggling like it was prom night. She carried a purse the size of an overnight bag that rattled when she dropped it on the bed. "I have toys if you want to play. I'm really good at being the boss. Of course, if you want to be the boss that's cool too."

"No, you can be the boss. My wife and I hardly touch anymore. When we do it's like she's not even there. It'll be nice to have somebody at least pretend to be interested."

The girl was manic with excitement. "I am interested! We'll have so much fun. You'll remember this the rest of your life. Next time you're fucking your wife just think of me and rock her socks off!." She cranked the air conditioner down to 60 degrees. "Let's take a shower. It's really hot out and I've been sweating something fierce. Besides, we can slide our soapy bodies together. That'll be fun, right?"

"You're the boss."

"That's right I am. Get your ass in the shower, Boy. I'll be checking to make sure you wash behind your ears."

After the shower she posed like Aphrodite's statue while insisting he pat her dry and sprinkle her with baby powder. "Stay in here until I call you," she said. While he waited in the residual steam she arranged the bedroom.

"Don't touch me!" the girl said, once she allowed him in. She slinked toward him causing him to back up against the bed. They were so close you couldn't pull a thread between them when she grabbed his shoulders and pushed him onto the mattress. She was on him like an animal, handcuffing him to the rope she'd run under the bed, then tying his feet to the bed's legs. Once he was secure, she kissed and licked his knees. Ever so slowly, she kissed her way toward his crotch. By the time her hair caressed his inner thighs, his massive erection was dancing in the tutu of his black pubic hair. "Holy Jesus! That's the biggest one I've ever seen. I'm not sure I can take it. You might split me apart."

She rolled off. He was beginning to sweat again. He became a little nervous when he realized she was going to gag him. "Wait. What's that for?"

"It's just a little something to keep you quiet. Maybe there's a family in the next room. You wouldn't want their kids to hear this, would you?"

"I'm not really comfortable with the gag thing," he said.

"It's not up to you anymore, now is it?" She forced a golf ball into his mouth and tied it with a red bandana. "Now, let's see if we can get this baby any bigger." She massaged his erection (he dealt with the gag, considering). She licked it, put the head in her mouth and swirled her tongue around it. Satisfied it had reached its maximum, she straddled it and forced it in. The size did make her gasp. He moaned, or she thought he did. It was hard to tell. She grabbed a handful of his chest hair and slowly rode him, scrubbing her clit against his course pubes. She enjoyed the thick mass inside her, but that wasn't the point. She felt the twitching start and knew he was about to come. She jumped off, grabbed a wire guitar string from her bag, wrapped it around the base of his erection and yanked. His penis dropped onto the mattress and blood gushed. He screamed, but not so you could hear it.

"Don't worry," she said. "You won't feel this for very long. It only takes about 8 minutes to bleed out like this. I'll wait with you, okay?" Rifling through his pants she confiscated his keys and wallet then sat beside him and caressed his forehead. "I'm sorry I had to do this," she said. "Good daddies don't hang out in strip clubs though. Maybe the next daddy your girls get will treat them better." As the fountain of blood slowed she reached between her legs and felt for the spot that gave her pleasure. She held it between her fingers and massaged it. As the last inkling of life faded from his eyes her orgasm shuddered through her body.

She dressed in a hoodie from her bag. After making sure the motel room was locked, she took his minivan back to the strip club and walked two blocks to where her Honda Civic waited. Setting her satellite radio to a smooth jazz station she drove home.

PARTY TIME

Nadine applied the final touches of her makeup as the front door opened. "Carrie, is that you? Where the hell have you been? We're supposed to go to Chris's party."

"At the library. Sorry, I forgot. Why don't you go on without me? I really don't feel like going back out tonight."

"Damn it, you never go anywhere. You practicing to be a cat lady? Come on it'll be fun. A lot of guys I know will be there."

"You know I'm not into that. I'd just as soon have my teeth cleaned as go to one of your keggers. Those boys get a few beers in them and they turn into assholes."

"Carrie please, I need you to go. Bryan's friend is in from out of town. I told him I'd find him somebody to talk to. That would be you by the way. So it's like I kind of promised him you'd be there."

Carrie hated that she'd depended on Nadine way too many times."Fine. Can you give me a half-hour to get ready? I at least need a shower."

"Thanks, babe, you're the best. I guarantee you won't regret it."

"I already regret it." Carrie tossed her bloated handbag on the bed. She took a quick shower, pulled on a sundress and grabbed a pocketbook. "Alright, let's go. We can take my car. It's already gassed up and that way I can leave when I'm ready."

"Aren't you going to put on any makeup?"

"Hell no. The last thing I want is to churn up any interest from those hunks of Neanderthal meat."

"When did you stop liking guys?"

"I like guys. I just don't like those guys. I don't know where to go to find the kind of guys I want, but it damn sure isn't here." Carrie grabbed a beer out of the fridge, pulled the tab, and sucked down half of it. "Maybe this will get me in the mood. If you can't beat 'em, don't let 'em beat you."

Nadine gave her roommate a confused look. "For a sociology major, you're pretty damned antisocial."

"Honestly Nadine, it's been seven years, I'm getting tired of school. I don't have the credits or desire to produce a master's thesis. Even if I did, what's out there for me? Listening to people whine? That sounds like big fun, don't it? I picked a fucked up career path and I'm not sure what to do."

"The best thing for now is to have a good time, worry about it later. We're going to rock this party. Let's show them how it's done."

The rhythmic thump of the bass could have pulverized gall stones had it been medically necessary. Nadine bounced into the crowd like a helium-filled balloon with Carrie attached to the end of the string. "Try to be nice," Nadine said.

"I am nice, too nice to be here."

"Cool, more bitches," came through the sound system as they walked in. A stocky guy with a shaved head and a Fu Manchu waved from behind the turntables. Nadine waved. Carrie shot him the bird. "Bitches be feisty here in Tejas. We all here to party. Kegs are lined up out back like terrorists. Let's assassinate those fuckers."

Carrie flashed on this jerk hanging from an elm tree somewhere in East Texas; too good to be true. He was pasty white.

"I'm DJ Cash and we're gonna keep thumpin' 'til you all start humpin'. We got Eminem, Snoop, and Tupac coming right up. Stick around 'cause later we gonna break out the hard stuff."

Nadine had Carrie in a pinkie lock dragging her through a crowd intent on what could be termed sexual harassment; a garden of groping appendages. Nadine didn't seem to notice. She was on the hunt for Bryan. Carrie steamed. The slapping away of hands brought only jeers and catcalls.

Upstairs things were quieter, at least physically. Most people were paired off, maybe tripled off; some grouping where they concentrated on each other in isolation. Still no Bryan, though numerous partiers said he was around.

Finally, Nadine found him. She opened the last bedroom door on the right and recognized his creamy white ass with the kite-shaped birthmark. She couldn't see his dick as it was buried to the hilt in another woman's vagina. Words failed her, so after throwing her purse at his balls, she jumped on his back, grabbing his ears. She began smashing his face into the face of the woman under him. You - piece - of - fucking - shit!" One word, one down stroke.

Carrie stepped back into the hall and looked at the couple waiting their turn in the hall. "Go figure," she said, and started down the stairs. She noticed the music was on autopilot, no annoying DJ, as she was leaving; enough anthropology for one night. The night had cooled to a bearable level. Leaves fluttered down in a light breeze.

"Hey, girl, where you going? This party just be startin'." It was that jerk standing alone by the parking lot.

She laced her car keys between her fingers like she'd been taught in self-defense class. "I'm going home. This really isn't my thing. By the way, in case you haven't noticed, your hat's on crooked, looks really stupid."

"Bitches don't be telling me how to dress!"

"Yeah, that's fairly obvious."

"What you sayin', bitch. I don't got style?"

"Style, grammar, IQ, and if you call me bitch again I'll be wearing your testicles for earrings."

"My what?"

"Your nuts, comprende'? Now leave me the fuck alone."

"Damn, girl, you got a mouth on you. Can it do anything but talk trash?"

Carrie shook her head and started for the car, keeping a wary eye on the jerk.

"Look, girl. I'm sorry. Let me talk to you a minute. See, I put my cap on straight. I'm sorry about the 'bitch' thing. It's my DJ persona."

Carrie put two fingers between her eyes, thinking he sounded like some kid who'd been caught stealing candy. She took an aggressive stance. "So, talk."

He looked shocked, like this wasn't supposed to happen. "Well, I, of, I ..."

"Start with your name," she suggested.

"DJ Cash."

"Bullshit."

"Okay, it's Kevin, Kevin Cash. The Cash is real, honest to God. Want to see my license?"

"No." Her advanced abnormal psychology courses were paying off. "So, Kevin, what do you do?"

"I'm a DJ."

"So you're a trust fund baby?"

"Yeah, busted I guess. What about you?"

"Superhero," Carrie said. She eased the grip on the keychain burrowing into the palm of her hand.

"So you're a trust fund baby too?"

"Sort of. I'm studying sociology."

"Wow, me too, but not here. I was anyway. Now I'm in criminal justice. I didn't see much future in just sitting around listening to sad stories every day. Fuck 'em, lock 'em up!"

Carrie caught herself smiling at this asshole. She looked around for something to bang her head against.

"I'm here visiting my buddy; we went to high school together. He was going to hook me up with his girlfriend's hot roommate, but they never showed up."

Carrie could barely keep a straight face. "Your buddy's name happen to be Bryan?"

"Yeah, you know him?"

"He may be indisposed for a bit. Seems his little head led him astray. I'm Carrie by the way, his now ex-girlfriend's hot roommate."

Two police cars spun into the parking lot, lights flashing. "Looks like it's going to be a short party," Kevin said.

"You can thank your buddy and my roommate for that. I hope you aren't getting paid by the hour."

"Nope, tips, but I'm a trust fund baby remember? As long as I can get my equipment out I'll be fine."

"We'll probably have to bail them out of jail."

"What the hell happened in there?"

"Nadine caught Bryan in the act with some bimbo. She tends to get a bit emotional. There was some bloodshed."

"You were just going to leave her?"

"Like I said, this really isn't my thing."

People were beginning to file out when the ambulance arrived. Many seemed in a hurry to leave. Others stayed for the show. "I wish we'd met under different circumstances," Kevin said. "I think Bryan misrepresented you."

"I'm not hot enough for you?"

"I didn't mean that. It's just you're not Bryan's idea of hot. I expected, well, I don't know, somebody…"

"More passive?"

"Maybe. I will say, not many women can pull off that natural look and retain your elegance."

Carrie glanced past him on both sides of his head and stepped around to look behind him.

"What?" Kevin asked.

"I was looking for that thug I met a minute ago. That last sentence had a smidgen of intelligence and appreciation I wouldn't have expected from DJ Cash."

Kevin's face was burning.

"Oh my god! You're blushing. You're just a regular white bread guy!"

"Busted again. You're good. How about we get some coffee?"

"I'm blocked in. Tell you what, I'll help you load out then we'll see."

"You're sweet, thanks."

"Don't push it."

Before they finished packing up the sound system, the cops led Nadine and Bryan out in handcuffs. Bryan's bloody nose was a little off center. A stretcher followed with the poor unsuspecting "hot girl" that had been on the bottom.

"Carrie, you've got to help me." Nadine called as they escorted her out.

"Do you have an attorney.?"

"No."

"You should have an attorney if you're going to do stupid shit. I'll see if I can find one."

"I'm so tired of school I could puke. I get up every day and it's all I can do to show up for class. I haven't the slightest idea of what to do with my life." Carrie was looking across the table at Kevin. He no longer wore his cap at all. His hairline showed the slightest tendency towards recession and the stocky build came with a slight paunch. Not a pretty man, Carrie thought, but not repulsive.

"I'm studying to be a warden at a women's prison but there's a long waiting list for that job," He winked so she would be certain he was joking. That line had already backfired a couple of times.

She took a sip from her coffee while never taking her eyes off him. She didn't react. She was toying with him now, seeing how far into a corner he could paint himself. Cheap entertainment, she figured, making him squirm.

"Actually crime is fascinating. You'd be surprised how many people get away with it. Only the really stupid people get caught."

"So, have you pulled off any capers?" She deadpanned.

"No, but I've planned some just for fun. Bank robberies are probably the safest. Less than 50% get solved and it's rare for anyone to get hurt. Kidnapping is probably the hardest, at least in this country. The Somalis are doing pretty well with piracy."

"My great uncles would agree with you on bank robbery."

"They robbed banks?"

"Yeah, you may have heard of them, Frank James and his little brother Jesse? I'm a direct descendant."

"I'm remotely kin to Johnny Cash but I can't sing a lick."

"I didn't say I was a criminal, or even wanted to be. I just need to do something with my life, make a difference. Besides, my trust fund is small and shrinking by the day."

"So, let's rob a bank," Kevin said.

"You're out of your fucking mind!" She glanced around at the crowd and realized she was making a scene, whispering ensued. "First thing, if you were going to pull off a cockamamie stunt like that, you wouldn't plan it in a coffee shop. Just shut up, okay?"

"Whoa, girl. I wasn't even considering it. I was just messin'."

Carrie rubbed her eyes. "Look, this is crazy. It's getting late. I need to get home."

"Sorry. I didn't mean to freak you out, really. I'm not some criminal. I just, I don't know, maybe I'm bored, too."

"I never said I was bored, just stuck. Anyway, I'll see you."

"I'm going back tomorrow, University of Arkansas, but here's my card. Can I walk you to your car?"

"Yeah, sure. Pay the bill first, you're buying."

The heat had finally become bearable with the stroke of midnight. The city produced too much light pollution to see the stars but Kevin looked up anyway. "Cigarette?" he asked.

"No thanks, not one of my habits. I try to avoid deadly shit whenever possible."

He put the pack away. "Strange how we met. I mean, since we were going to be introduced anyway."

"I guess; statistics, coincidence, whatever, I don't buy that divine intervention crap if that's where you're headed."

"It's just,… Never mind. I find you interesting, that's all. We had a cool talk. You're not even my type. You're kind of scary actually, but I'd like to hang out with you again sometime."

"I'd hang out with Kevin. DJ can take a flying fuck at the moon. If Kevin wants to chat, here's my number." She took his hand and wrote her number on the inside of his forearm with a permanent marker, and started to get in her Civic. He leaned out to kiss her cheek but she dodged it. "No!" She said, "Not like that. Don't even think it." She drove off.

YOUNG KEVIN

Shit! **I flicked off the TV** *just as the doorknob began to turn. My game controller was safely ensconced behind my calculus textbook.* "Doris, damn it. Can't you least knock. I could have been masturbating in here."

"Jesus, Kevin! Do you have to talk to your mother that way? Speaking of, when are you going to start calling me Mom again?"

"Maybe when you start acting like one."

"Look, I'm busting my butt putting you through this fancy ass prep school. It's not like you need a lot of nurturing. You're fourteen for Christ sake."

"Cut to the chase, Doris. What do you want?"

"I'm going to the airport to pick up Ron. I just let Kay-9 out back. Can you let her in later?"

"Sure. When will you be home?"

"Don't know, probably late. Ron has to fly back to LA tomorrow."

"Ron, let's see, is he the writer or the software dude. Oh wait, isn't he the guy who owns the trucking company?"

"The writer, as you well know."

"I don't keep up with your booty calls, Doris."

"You little shit. I..." She started toward me so I raised my arms in mock defense, as if she would ever actually hit me.

"We'll talk later." She turned and slammed the door behind her. Sure we will. I tossed the calculus book aside and broke out my borrowed copy of "Grand Theft Auto". Time to off some hookers.

OOPS!

Apologies spewed from Nadine like foam from an empty keg. "Carrie, I don't know what happened. I just lost it. Thanks so much for bailing me out."

"All I did was Google '24 hour criminal attorneys' and pass on your info. No problem."

"I am a criminal, that's gross. What does it mean? Will they kick me out of school? I feel so dirty from jail. That place is nasty." Nadine was still pumping adrenaline, pacing like a caged meerkat, eyes wide with tight pupils. Her outfit looked disposable. "I don't feel like a criminal."

"Two counts of aggravated assault with bodily injury pretty much makes you a member of the club. Not like the Tri Deltas is it?" Carrie was having a little too much fun at Nadine's expense. It was only fair. Carrie had played the sidekick role since they pledged during their freshman year. "Why don't you clean up. You look like you've been cluster-fucked. A hot bubble bath, sleep all afternoon, anything to shut you up."

"Wow, Carrie. You don't have to be so mean. I know I messed up. I bet Bryan won't even talk to me now."

Carrie slapped her own forehead with the palm of her hand, "Jesus!" and sequestered herself in her room. It had been an eventful night for her too.

YOUNG CARRIE

*I*can't believe this. This stuff doesn't happen to me. It was only a word. I've managed to sail under the radar all the way through middle school (well, almost) without saying more than six words to Ms. Prudhomme on any given day. That, alone, says something. She's like this touchy-feely woman that's trying to, like, get all up in your head. Now here I am, sitting outside her office waiting for an "encounter".

"Come on in now, Carrie. Let's see if we can figure this out."

I'd never been inside Ms. Prudhomme's office. I didn't expect it to look like an art gallery. I'd figured more like a kindergarten classroom but, well, there you go.

"So, what's going on between you and Jessica?"

"She doesn't like me, I guess. The feeling is mutual."

"You know you can't use language like that here."

"She started it. She called me a bean pole. We just, like, exchanged descriptive terms."

"I know you, Carrie. You are too literate to resort to such base language."

"It was the most accurate term I could think of."

"Do you know what it really means?"

"A female dog, a breeder."

Ms. Prudhomme caught her breath at the second part of that statement. It seems you can learn something from your students. "That doesn't describe Jessica."

"I was going for the slang connotation."

"Here's what has to happen. I can't allow vulgarities to run rampant across my campus. I need to discuss this with your parents. Can you have one of them come in?"

"They both work." I'm not telling her that Dad works at home. I'd much rather have Mom deal with this. Anyway, Dad hates to be bothered while he's working. "I'll have to wait here and take the bus. Can you get my homework? I don't want to miss anything." I really do like school. It beats home. I can just hear Ms. Prudhomme as she walked into my house. "Oh my! So much negative energy here." Probably because Mom and Dad fight like badgers. "You know what," I said, reconsidering three and a half hours in captivity. "I bet I can get Maria to pick me up."

"As long as she's on your contact list."

"She would be. She's been our housekeeper since I was, like, two years old. She lives on the property." It was her day off but she really likes me. It sure beats sitting on display here all day staring at the clock.

DINING OUT

If luck took human form it would be Nadine's identical twin. Not only did Bryan talk to her again but they resumed their relationship. The hot girl on the bottom turned out to be Q P Stephens, a sophomore Tri-Delta who refused to testify against her sorority sister even though they had never spoken, as Nadine was a full four years ahead of her. Without the complainant the prosecutor had no choice but to drop the charges. Nadine took the news in a typical overstated manner. "Carrie, isn't that amazing. Let's get dolled up and go out for margaritas. It's a beautiful day."

"Why don't you take Bryan. I'm studying."

"You're always studying."

"I want to get out of this hell hole some day."

"Lighten up, babe. C'mon, pretty please. You haven't been out in weeks."

"Since the night you were arrested," Carrie hinted.

"See, too long. It's Friday. Let's cut loose a little."

After 2 hours of plucking, powdering and painting the sorority sisters could have passed for $2000 a night call girls. They stood together in front of the mirror admiring their reflections. "We are effing gorgeous," Nadine said. All that work didn't get the "deer in the headlights" out of Carrie's eyes.

After Nadine's Daddy Warbucks paid for Bryan's new nose and Q P's new face he picked out a red Mercedes convertible to haul Nadine through her emotional crisis. "I wish he would have let me pick the color," Nadine said. "I would have chosen black."

Carrie had a little trouble with Nadine's sense of entitlement. "I wish that too, Nadine. This is Texas. Every time you slipped your perfect ass into that leather seat, blisters the size of almonds would've popped up." Nadine laughed it off. They took the red Mercedes with the white leather interior. Nadine drove with conviction.

"I take it you have a plan?" Carrie asked.

"I was thinking Baby A's. We did say margaritas, right?"

It was official. Carrie had regained her sidekick status. Baby A's was loud. It was always loud on weekends, full of Greeks full of tequila trying to out shout, out laugh and generally impress each other with their lot in life. As if this wasn't enough, sitting with Bryan in a corner booth was none other than Kevin "DJ" Cash. Carrie yanked Nadine's hand hard enough to dislodge the strap of Nadine's Louis Vitton purse from her shoulder. "God damn it Nadine, you fucking slut. I can't believe—after all that—just, just fuck you!"

"Hey, you said he was interesting."

"That doesn't mean I want to party with his punk ass!"

They'd been made. The boys waved at them, even stood up. Nadine waved back and trotted over dragging a sulking Carrie behind.

"Good to see you, too," Kevin said. To his credit he wasn't wearing a cap and his tee shirt had a collar. "What happened to the earth mother thing. You look like a sorority clone."

"Keep digging, DJ. There is a bottom there somewhere. I was coerced by the way." She turned to Nadine., "blatantly lied to."

"Hey, I said 'let's go for margaritas'. They have margaritas here. Good ones."

"By omission, Bitch. You know what I mean."

"I didn't think you'd like that word," Kevin interjected.

"It's appropriate in this case." Carrie plopped down beside Kevin. "Bring me a large blue frozen. I might as well do this," she told the goofy little waiter who had tailed them to the table.

"Are you hungry?" Kevin asked.

"Lip gloss," she replied, still overwhelmed.

"Does not compute."

Carrie looked at him like he had a third eye and pointed to her face. "This took over an hour. One taco could ruin it. You want that on your conscience?"

Kevin busted into a belly laugh. "Now I remember why I drove down from Fayetteville. Seriously, though Carrie, eat if you're hungry. You're very pretty but that's not why I came."

"I hope you're not looking for a partner in crime. You would be shit out of luck."

Nadine and Bryan were engaged in a tongue infested lip lock. "See she's not worried about her lip gloss," Kevin said.

"Fine, I'll have a crispy taco plate with a side of pico de gallo. So why are you here? Don't you have gigs on the weekends?"

"I gave that up, packed away the equipment."

"Why?"

"It didn't feel right anymore. I got an internship with the federal probation office."

"Wow, federal, so you, like, replace batteries in ankle bracelets?"

"Yeah, well, it is pretty mild mostly. The Feds don't cut loose any really bad guys."

"I'm proud of you, Kevin. It beats calling innocent little girls 'bitch'."

"I hoped you would think so."

"Don't put that on me."

"No, it was my choice but you helped me see it. I'll graduate in another semester with enough credits that I could be within a thesis of a masters. I still have no idea what to do with it."

"You're ahead of me, although lately I've thought about the women's prison thing, not as warden, but some kind of prisoners' rights activist."

"Those girls would be hitting on you constantly as pretty as you are."

"Jesus! Would you just shut up? I wish the tacos would hurry up."

"You like guys, don't you?"

"Actually, I've been thinking about coming out, but I don't know if asexuals have a closet to come out of. Seems like a lot of bother."

"You don't have a sex drive?"

"Nothing I can't handle."

The tequila flowed. The heat between Bryan and Nadine escalated to the point that they excused themselves, leaving Carrie with the keys to a red Mercedes convertible.

"That's a very trusting friend," Kevin observed.

Carrie rolled her eyes. "Not really. She's just in heat and drunk on daddy's money. She doesn't even like the car."

"I'll take it."

"Get in line behind me. I'm stuck in the Civic I got for graduating high school. It wasn't new then."

"Think anyone can hear us here?" Kevin asked.

"We can't even hear us here, why?"

"I had something I wanted to talk to you about."

"Not interested."

"I drove all the way from Little Rock, at least listen."

"Fine, let's eat, I'll listen. Straight up though, no offense, but I can't imagine what you would say that I would care much about. You're nice guy and all, but I'm not looking for a relationship."

Kevin hiccupped a subdued laugh. "Me either, at least not

with you. It's complicated. For now, how about another margarita?"

"Trying to get me drunk?"

"I doubt it would matter."

They ate, drank and made merry, talking about classes and the similarity in their degree programs. Finally, Carrie delivered a man-sized belch and patted her stomach. "Pay up, Kevin. We'll take my car." She dangled Nadine's keys in his face.

"It's your turn to buy," Kevin said.

"Coffee doesn't count. You're the salesman. You buy."

Kevin sighed and pulled out his Visa card. "You drive a hard bargain."

"Tonight, I drive a little red Mercedes."

YOUNG KEVIN

My stomach moans. I look at the clock; 9:30. *I turn off my Xbox and roll off the bed, nearly face planting, not realizing that my foot's asleep. In the kitchen I find that my loving mother has failed to prepare anything remotely resembling dinner. Sometimes I think she forgets she has a kid. I'd go live with Dad but it would be the same story, except there I'd have to put up with that gold-digging bimbo he lives with. To her credit, Mom isolates me from the stable of guys she keeps. Still, it would be nice if she fed me. "You're old enough to cook for yourself, figure it out, it's a great creative outlet," she says. Bullshit, I'm fourteen. She's supposed to take care of me. That's what Dad's paying her for. Let's see, cans of fucking soup or mac and cheese. What a choice. Microwave, here I come.*

Staring at the timer I remember, Kay-9, Mom's dog. Stupid name. Supposed to be a reference to some book by a guy named Vonnegut. Maybe. Still stupid. She actually fought for her in the divorce, a fucking dog, can you believe that? Poor old girl, she seems lost without Dad around. He's the one who played and wrestled with her. She's a little old for that now though, gray around the muzzle. She just seems melancholy without Dad; seems that way to me anyway.

She's not in the backyard but she's got to be nearby. I've never seen any animal control trucks out this late. Besides she has a collar with an ID tag and a chip. I call out. I'm getting a little worried. I've been scouring the subdivision for over an hour, nothing. She always comes when I call. I hope no one stole her. As a gorgeous Afgan hound, her hair is a long wavy gold, like Mom's. Another one of those dog and owner look-alike deals. Mom even has a straight thin nose and a thin build, though she can put away a 12 ounce Porterhouse and have room for dessert. Men love her. I don't see what Dad's problem is.

I should probably call Mom and let her know but I'd rather Kay-9 magically appear and Mom not know she fucked up and left the gate unhooked. She's got a lot on her plate right now. I may not be in the mix but still, I think one of these guys proposed to her. I'm pretty sure it wasn't Ron. He's the only one I'm sure she would have said yes to. That wouldn't have been a problem. I met him briefly once, pretty cool dude, a bit younger than she is but nothing like that extreme shit Dad's pulling. That girl's still in college.

Okay, I'm checking the boulevard that runs between the subdivisions real quick but I doubt she's come this far. The traffic's heavy and moving fast as I jog down the esplanade; five blocks south, nothing. Just when I pass our entrance coming back north, I implode. I run full on now. She's near the curb. Still. Splayed in an unnatural position. I drop to my knees and try to pick up her head. She's cold and already beginning to stiffen up. Those bastards! Nobody even stopped. The fuckheads that hit her just left her there. How could they? God damn bastards! Doesn't anyone give a fuck about anything anymore. I feel my face get hot. Things are getting blurry. I've got to get her home. Mom's just going to die. I cradle her in my arms and start walking. Brakes squeal. A horn honks. I shoot the bird. "Why don't you just kill me, too, you son of a bitch! Slow the fuck down! Traffic stops and I walk across the lanes. I see a mom shield the eyes of her youngest child. I don't know why this pisses me off. "Yeah, y'all killed her!" I scream. The woman's face shows pity. I'm okay with that. Kay-9 deserves it. I have no idea what to do. I think I'll wait 'til Mom gets home to tell her. I don't even know what to say.

The whole subdivision seems dead as I walk through it, like an empty architectural rendering. The mist becomes a drizzle. The closer I get to home the harder it rains.

TOP DOWN

It took Carrie a minute to figure out the controls for putting the top down; another minute to adjust all the mirrors. She was almost 8 inches taller than Nadine. Having the top down made the car less claustrophobic. "So what's the deal, DJ?"

"It's about making the world a better place and getting rich in the process," Kevin said.

"I think the drug companies already have a lock on that."

"Okay, maybe that's a place to start but I was thinking of something with a bit less overhead. How many times have you watched a news story about some Ponzi schemer or insurance company ripping off billions and just getting a slap on the hands, if that?"

"Too often, but I'm not degenerated enough, morally, to do that. It always seems to hurt folks that have the most to lose."

"I'm not saying that we do that, but every time one of those pyramids crumble, who loses the least? The one most responsible. They come out smelling like a rose. That's our target."

"Target? I'm no assassin. I could never kill anybody."

"No, no, me either. I'm talking about hitting them where it hurts, in the pocketbook and shaming their name at the same time. We just need to dig around until we figure out who the money man is."

"This is crazy talk. Even if we could figure it out, we couldn't infiltrate their system. They didn't get there by being stupid."

"We don't infiltrate. That's the thing. I know you learned in Sociology, people with power have secrets. We come at them through their personal lives. We become their secrets. We don't want to bring down the empire, they just bounce back from that. We bring down their social network; their family, their friends. We break them."

"You're sick! That's sick! No, I couldn't be a part of that. No way. You've got me figured wrong. Besides, what if it backfires? This is a bad idea."

"Okay then forget I mentioned it. So how about we just rob a bank? Good odds of pulling it off."

"Not good enough. I'd rather be poor and free than rich and incarcerated."

"Alright, fine, it was just a thought, something I'd been working on. Forget I mentioned it."

"No worries. I already knew you were a flake. How about some ice cream?"

"Only if you're buying this time."

YOUNG CARRIE

Ms. Prudhomme's recent proclamation *combined with the brutal South Texas heat cause a massive systemic failure of my antiperspirant. The air conditioning in Maria's minivan gives a slight relief to the sticky pits. "Thanks for picking me up, Maria."*

"No bueno. What's wrong Chiquita?"

"Cramps. I think I'm fixing to start."

"We're going to take you home. You go to bed. I'll go get my special ingredients and, make a soup. You'll be better by morning."

When Maria drops me off at the house, Roxanne's car is in the driveway. Dad works at home. No one is allowed to disturb him in his study, except Roxanne. She shuttles paperwork from his office in Corpus. "We're free to be together," Mama says, but Dad is never included in that. I'm not even sure what he does for a living. He makes a damn good one though. I like Roxanne, well more like, I like her clothes. She has this quirky retro thing going. Maybe I can just take a peek, "Go forth and conquer," I read somewhere. It's not like I'm a wallflower, far from it, but I've suffered dad's wrath before. It can last for days.

The door isn't quite closed. Maybe I can check out Roxanne without being noticed, "Go forth…" like they say, right? The thing is though, she's wearing very little, neither is Dad. Usually he dresses in a suit. "Very dapper," Mom would say, though she doesn't understand why he doesn't just dress comfortably since he's home. What I see is dad reared back in his chair in only a shirt, tie and socks. Roxanne kneels between his legs, butt ass naked. Well, she is wearing a porkpie hat. "Damn!" I catch my breath. "That bitch." She's licking his erection. I feel my stomach start to dance as Dad starts making this weird animal sound.

Roxanne grabs his erection and begins pumping it with her fist. I'm not totally clueless about what's going to happen so I'm surprised when Roxanne opens her mouth really wide right near the head of his penis. When the stuff shoots out Dad is grunting like a pig. She catches it in her mouth and spits it out slowly so it runs down her chin. Then she takes the end of his penis and smears it all over her nose and cheeks. "Oh Daddy! So hot and tasty," she moans.

My tummy can't handle watching this. I mean, "Daddy!" Really? I try to run so they won't see me, but I leave a trail of vomit on the stairs.

<>

LISTENING IN

Awkward didn't even begin to describe it, staring at Kevin from across the coffee table while Bryan and Nadine were in the next room going at it like hot-wired ferrets. Kevin blushed at every grunt, yelp and squeal. Carrie envisioned her security deposit dwindling every time the headboard crashed into the wall.

"How about a beer while you wait?" Carrie asked.

"Can I get it in a glass. It sounds like they may be awhile."

Carrie glared momentarily then fetched the brew in a SOLO cup. "To go, just in case."

"The hostess with the mostest."

"Shut up." Carrie flashed a brief but effective sorority smile. "So, are you going to pursue a life of crime on your own?"

"Haven't decided. I need to set myself some ground rules. People get caught when they get stupid or greedy."

"People get caught because they break the law!"

"Everyone breaks the law. It's a matter of degree. Most people do it on a daily basis."

"I don't."

"Bullshit! You did it today. How many margaritas did you have before we hopped in Nadine's little red convertible?"

"Everybody does that."

"Don't make it legal."

Carrie began smoldering. This punk-ass kid was starting again on her nerves. "So you're big desire in life is to be a thug?"

"Ah contraire! My desire is to live the good life. I want to take down the thugs and steal their money. The only people I want to see get hurt need hurting."

"Vigilante justice?"

"Yeah, for a price."

"Better stock up on life insurance."

The animal noises from the bedroom wound down. The argument erupted almost immediately. "So it's wham-bam-thank you ma'am. Is that it?" Nadine screamed. "Can't even hang out for a minute or two? You piece of shit!" Something glass broke against the bedroom door as Bryan ducked out in his skivvies carrying the rest of his clothes. Carrie toasted his terrified look with her beer bottle. "You're a real piece of work. I can see why you and Kevin are buds."

"Hey," Kevin said. "You don't even know me that way."

"Don't hold your breath," Carrie said. Nadine began wailing from behind the bedroom door.

"You should go comfort her," Kevin told Bryan. "I'm not in a hurry. I'm having a lovely conversation with Carrie."

Carrie swatted her forehead and rolled her eyes. "He's right, as much as I hate to admit it, about Nadine anyway. There's got to be a limit to how much abuse she'll take, though I'm beginning to wonder."

"She's kind of scary right now." Bryan turned then hesitated with his hand on the bedroom doorknob. He steeled himself. "Nadine, sweetie? Can we talk? How about we plan a picnic for next weekend?"

The wail became a low moan punctuated by sniffles. Nadine's face appeared through a crack in the door. It appeared to have been left out in the rain. "Just a minute." The water ran in the bathroom. The toilet flushed. The reconstituted sorority sister appeared in a white cotton robe. The corners of her mouth twitched as if considering a smile.

Bryan occupied the leather recliner. "How about some lap time, Baby?" Nadine curled up in his arms. She looked smaller than normal, but content.

"I'm going to change into some real clothes." Carrie said. She took her beer with her.

"You guys have fun?" Nadine asked.

"Y'all abandoned us. That was bullshit!" Kevin chugged the rest of his beer. "Let's go Romeo."

"Don't you want to say goodbye to Carrie?" Nadine asked.

"I doubt she'd give a shit one way or the other."

"You got it wrong. She's… well… interesting. I mean, really headstrong, but sweet as she can be."

"Yeah, well, I think I annoy her."

Nadine giggled. "So what? Bryan annoys the shit out of me but we still have fun."

"Hey!" Bryan said.

Carrie came back in jeans and a Tri-Delta tee shirt. "Shut up, Nadine. Your twisted vision of this imaginary hook-up ain't going to happen. No offense, Kevin, but I'm not interested in a relationship… of any kind."

"I get it," Kevin said. "Tell her."

Bryan sat quietly observing the banter, intoxicated by the

scent of Nadine 's hard loved body. Her hair drifting across his shoulder created a desire to follow through on the romantic picnic he had so spontaneously proposed. "So how about tomorrow?" He blurted.

"What?" Nadine realized he was not just lumpy furniture.

"The picnic. Should we invite Kevin and Carrie?"

"Have you been on the earth? Carrie got up and headed back toward her room. "Leave me out of it."

"Wait," Nadine said. "Your mom called. There was a message on the machine."

"I'll call her in the morning. I'm done. Goodnight."

YOUNG KEVIN

I lay Kay-9 on the hearth *and turn on the gas logs, like it's going to matter. It's not like the heat will bring her back, or even keep her from being stiff. She looks unnatural so I get a blanket to swaddle her in. This is just going to devastate Mom. My face is still hot and wet. Anger is steeling my muscles. I want to lash out; to take somebody down, but who? I should have checked on her sooner. Mom should've locked the gate. Kay-9 should've stayed close to home. "Damn it!" I scream. "Fuck, fuck, fuck!" I can't leave her. I grab a blanket and curl up on the couch, pulling it over my head to hide the tears.*

<>

CALL HOME

Bright sunlight blasted through the windows when Carrie pulled the covers back. It had to be midmorning. A brief panic burned up her spine before she realized it was Saturday. She pulled on the jeans she'd left on the floor, unlocked the bedroom door and stepped out into the kitchen. Except for empty beer bottles and the pile of dirty dishes she was alone. She peeked out the curtains and saw that Bryan's jeep was gone. Thank God! She started coffee.

She noticed the light on the answering machine blinking the numeral 8. She put in the code. Message 1: *"Hi Carrie it's Kevin. I hope you'll come on the picnic. We really shouldn't let these two run around loose together. Call me."* Carrie shook her head and stared at the coffee pot as if that would speed up the process. *No! No! No!* Her brain said. *What is this guy's problem.*

Message 2: *"Carrie, didn't you get my message? Call home, please, as soon as you get this. It's important."* Important? What an odd word for her. It's usually "emergency" which constitutes anything from a canceled yoga class to an unwanted call from an ex-boyfriend. Important, that might mean something.

The coffee was ready. She picked up the phone. Nadine stumbled in. Carrie set the receiver down as Nadine shifted bloodshot eyes in her direction.

"Good morning," Carrie said.

Nadine grunted and rinsed out a dirty coffee cup. "Calling Kevin?"

"No. My Mom."

"I think Kevin has a thing for you."

"His 'thing' will fit nicely into anyone who doesn't have a thing. He should look elsewhere."

"He's so sweet, though. He's like a little puppy."

"Nadine! Jesus! He has a burning desire to pursue a life of crime. Forget it! Not gonna be a part of that."

"Hey, at least it's a plan, more than you have."

Carrie felt the heat rising from her chest. She grabbed the cup she'd pulled from the cabinet. The target on Nadine his face began to pulse. That was it. This bitch is going down, now! The phone rang. Carrie slammed the coffee cup on the counter and seized the phone.

"What!" she screamed into the receiver.

"Is this a bad time?" her mother asked.

"No, Mom. It's okay. What's up." The heat melted away. Carrie's being was subdued by her Mom's voice, as always.

"Carlos went missing. They may have found his body. Marie's nephew, Miguel, remember him? He's missing too." Carrie heard the tremor in her mother's voice. "Poor Maria, she can hardly speak." Carrie felt her energy drain away. She had to sit down. At the table, she laid her head in the crook of her elbow and listened as her mother rambled. Nadine brought her coffee and a tissue to soak up the tears.

"I'll be there, Mom. I'll see you tonight. Give Maria my love." She hung up the phone and slumped into a wail. Nadine massaged her shoulders.

"Bad news?" Nadine asked.

"I used to babysit him," Carrie mumbled into the tabletop. "He died in the desert. It doesn't make sense. He was only 300 yards off the road. His cousin's missing too. He'd hired Carlos to help him for the summer. They were supposed to be hauling produce but now I wonder. I can see him getting into trouble, but Carlos? He was a good kid. Always so sweet. This chubby little guy, loved to read, always smiling. He would never do anything against the law. Shit, he was a fucking Boy Scout. His mama's our housekeeper. She almost raised me. My dad was always working. Mom was always somewhere else, volunteering, or some shit to avoid Dad. When they were both home it was battle royale. They hated each other. I hung out with Maria and Carlos most of the time." Carrie jumped up and paced around the table. She pulled her auburn hair back into a long tight ponytail and grabbed her purse. "I've got to go." She looked down and realized she was still wearing yesterday's jeans. "Damn I've got to get out of here." She went to her room.

"When will you be back?" Nadine called through the door.

"Don't know."

"What about class?"

"Don't care. I need to be there for Maria."

"Maria? What about your mom?"

"Fuck her. If it wasn't for the drama she wouldn't even care." Carrie came out in jeans and a t-shirt, a fat gym bag over her shoulder.

"Aren't you going to pack?" Nadine asked.

"I've got clothes at home. I'll be fine." She was out the door.

YOUNG CARRIE

I know it's coming, the knock on the door. *It's been a while. Maybe he didn't see, or hear. He was preoccupied. I hear Roxanne drive off, still nothing. I pull up the covers and pretend to sleep but I can't stop gritting my teeth. I can't release the image, too twisted. I have nothing for reference. He's my dad. That isn't supposed to happen. I hear that place on the stairs squeak.*

"Carrie?"

I stop holding my breath. It's Maria. She sits on the side of the bed. I peek out. She has the sweetest smile. Little Carlos is straining to look above the edge of the mattress, eyes like toasted almonds melt me. I sit up. "I brought some special tea. The soup will be ready in about an hour. You're so pale, Chica." Her smile fades when she touches my forehead. She jerks her hand back. "You've been hurt! Your spirit, it sizzles in you. What happened?"

I glance at Carlos. "Can I come over after he goes to bed? I've done something terrible and I don't know what will happen."

"Of course, Carrie, after eight. Can you come down for dinner now though? Your mama will be home soon."

I'll come down when she gets here."

Maria took Carlos by the hand and led him out. When he glanced back at me a tear slid down my cheek. I had to hide away. Maria will know what to do. Until then just pretend - pretend everything is normal.

R.I.P.

Grief thickened the air in Maria's small kitchen. The two women leaned across the same drop-leaf table where Carrie made PB&J sandwiches for little Carlos while Maria attended Bible study years before. In the eight months since Carrie last saw Maria the matron aged a decade. Maria's silken black hair had dulled and lost the perfect frame around her prominent features. A jagged border outlined the tiny veins around her eyes and mouth. Her high sloped forehead no longer appeared regal but echoed an air of confusion and frustration.

"He would have graduated with honors, one more year. St. Mary's already offered a scholarship. I can't believe, I mean, how could he? Why?" Maria let Carrie take her hand allowing the tears to flood "Why not come to his mama? I gave him everything he needed, ever wanted!"

"What was he doing out in the desert?"

"Smuggling they say, but I can't imagine. That's not my Carlos."

"It happens though. There's money in it."

"I can't see my boy hurting people for money."

"After the funeral we'll figure it out. If he was tricked into it we'll find out who."

"It would be Miguel. That sleazebag would do anything for a quick buck, always causing trouble."

"Yeah, he's an asshole. He tried to pull some shit with me once, strutting around in his fancy ass car, thinking he was God's gift to girls." Carrie felt her skin tighten remembering his rough hands where they weren't supposed to be. "I shouldn't speak ill of the dead, but him I wouldn't miss. I know he was your nephew but still."

"No harm." Maria got up to refill the coffee cups. "I have to plan for the gathering after the funeral. There's a lot to do."

"Let's have it at the main house. Carlos had so many friends. I'll handle the details. You have a lot on your mind."

"Will that be okay with Lois?"

"Mom loved Carlos, more than me I think, sometimes. Besides, I'm not giving her a choice. It's my house too."

Carlos' enlarged yearbook photograph stood on an easel, a black and white picture of a smiling baby-faced teenager. The mild acne not quite touched up. The casket was draped with flowers. Flowers were piled everywhere. The sanctuary brimmed with family and friends. Carrie fidgeted in her heavy black dress as the Spanish language service stopped periodically to allow the English translation. Carrie stood next to her mom who resembled a peacock amid a flock of blue herons. By the time the eulogy ended they'd yet to see Carrie's father. It became a bit easier to breathe.

Carrie saw her father maybe Christmas. She received an occasional phone call on her birthday when periods of silence outweighed snippets of casual conversation. Her dad never mentioned "the incident" with Roxanne. Carrie had no proof she had been observed but within a week she had been enrolled in a high-dollar boarding school three states away with the excuse that she wasn't being properly challenged by her public-school instructors. She'd become a discipline problem at school (and possibly a liability at home).

Dinner that night had been pork roast spiced with cumin and cayenne, one of Maria's specialties. Normally Carrie would have wolfed down several helpings. She was anticipating an underhanded comment. Deciding to take the bit in her teeth, she sliced across the top of a dinner roll or two, laying them open like steaming vaginas. "Pass that butter will you please, Daddy?" She hadn't referred to her father by that name since she was seven or eight years old. She took a hefty glob of butter on the tip of her knife and pushed it around on top of the warm rolls. "Oh my God, these look so hot and tasty don't they, Daddy. I can't wait to gobble them down."

The color drained from her father's face except for his ears which were almost magenta. "Let's just eat, Carrie. Of course it's good but take time and enjoy them," as if it could be her last supper.

Carrie caught herself snorting under her breath. Her father gave her a brutal glance, eyes flashing electric black. He knew she knew. There was no doubt. What to make of the information was the question in both of their minds. They had reached a stalemate.

That was a time when her parents still communicated occasionally about issues beyond custody and property rights. Ten days later she was in a Colorado preparatory academy with no further discussion of "the incident".

May Day, how appropriate. The afternoon sun was searing a pale cloudless sky, temperature hovering in the high nineties. Carrie could feel the sweat soaking her black dress, making it even heavier. She was evaporating, disappearing in the heat. She was standing with the younger folks, letting the elders sit. Across the gaping hole in

Just before the preacher began speaking, a long, charcoal-gray BMW pulled up and a man got out, the man she despised most in the world, the man who donated his sperm to her very existence. God knows where else he'd sprayed it. No one else noticed his arrival but she did, and he saw her. He stood in the shade of a nearby tree and watched her sweat. At least that's how she imagined it because she didn't look back in his direction.

PICNIC?

Kevin stared across **Lake Travis at** a rolling hill that was considering the sun as an evening meal. "So, I'm just a third wheel here?"

"DJ, dude, don't be like that. You're cool," Bryan said.

"Yeah, seriously, at this point you're better off without her. She's not your type?" Nadine said. She's not anybody's type. Who bails on school with just two weeks left? Far as I know she was passing everything, not that she was loaded down. She was only taking like 12 hours."

"Shame, she was interesting. I think we had something going on," Kevin said. "Think she'll be coming back?"

Nadine pulled a strand of wet hair behind her ear and leaned against Bryan's bare chest. "Trust me, she won't and you didn't. I'm not sure she even likes men. She definitely doesn't do sex, not as far as I know and we've been roommates for like six years."

"That's not it. I like her. She's feisty."

"That she is, but she's fucked in the head. Just so you know."

"Know where she went?"

"Home, far as I know. South Texas, a little town called Alice."

"Weird name for a town."

"There you go. It all fits."

YOUNG KEVIN

I just begin to doze when I hear the key in the front lock. *That's weird. Mom's home early. I jump up and fold the blanket. "What are you doing still up?" She says. She looks rough like she's been crying. She spots Kay-9 by the fireplace and the little color left in her face drains away. "What happened?"*

I kneel beside Kay-9 trying to find words. She stands next to me, her hand on my shoulder. "She got out. The gate was unlocked. I found her over on Hester Avenue. Somebody ran over her, Mom. They just left her there." My voice slurs. "Mom I'm so sorry."

She drops to her knees beside me. She just stares at Kay-9. "It figures."

"What?" Now I'm confused. She reaches down and pulls the sheet over Kay-9's head, gets up and collapses on the couch. After dragging the blanket across her lap, she motions for me to sit beside her. "Let's talk."

Normally I would have rolled my eyes, maybe raised some kind of stink, but this is scary. Kay-9's death barely fazes her.

"Jerry asked me to marry him." She looked like there was more but the words got stuck.

"Jerry? What about Ron? I thought you liked Ron."

"Yeah, well, you know what you said about the booty call? You were right. When I told Ron he didn't even ask if I'd said yes. He just ask if we can still hook up. 'Hook up', his words. He didn't even try to talk me out of it."

"But Mom, Jerry? Really? The trucker dude?"

"He's not a trucker. He owns the trucking company. He can take good care of us."

"Aw, Mom. That's not what it's supposed to be about. You always said 'love is the most important thing'. You don't even like Jerry that much."

"He's okay. He loves me and he's... stable."

"Stable? Mom, really? Stable?"

"I'm not in a position to be choosy. I'm getting older. You know what that means and besides I kind of screwed up the money thing. I've painted myself into a corner."

"But ... we'll be okay. You don't have to marry Jerry. We can figure something out. You haven't said yes yet have you?"

"No, but I'm going to. I was hoping Ron would step up, steal me away, but well. It didn't happen."

"Oh, Mom!"

"We'll be fine. We might be moving though. I'll call a pet memorial park tomorrow for Kay-9. I guess we can leave her here for now. She looks comfortable."

Mom usually has a glass of wine or two when she gets home from a date. Tonight, she goes straight for the brandy.

MIRAGE AUTO REPAIR

Lupe Moreno has a lot of free time. Back before the state condemned his fuel storage tanks, he had maybe 50 customers a day. Now he's lucky to have 10. Still, a few locals bring their old junkers to get them patched up, try to squeeze out a few thousand more miles. Lupe can usually oblige. He can't retire even though age 65 has long passed by. It isn't just the money. His kids are grown but the old lady gets meaner every day. Better to lean against the shady side of the building and sip a can of Tecate than to go home and listen to her hounding him to move in with the kids. Hell, no! The kids weren't even his idea. He can't remember for sure if the wife was either. Today is even slow for Wednesday. Two customers and it's already afternoon. One really, since the family that stopped to use the bathroom only bought two bottled waters and a pack of Twizzlers.

Lupe rolls a cigarette; pops open a beer and grabs his cane chair. As he drags it to the shady side he notices over a dozen buzzards and a couple of caracaras flying low and lazy circles, dipping down below the ridge line behind the shop. There are too many for a rabbit or a coyote. He decides he'll check after closing. Whatever it is isn't going anywhere. The last cow skull he found in the desert brought $50.00 from the tourists. Even a goat's skull is worth $20 or more if it has the horns, well worth a quarter mile walk.

The heat waves distorting the desert air had subsided. A rare breeze was driving a line of thunderstorms in from the west. They were still a good hour away if they held together. Lupe tossed his beer can in the wire basket and stuffed his jeans into the top of his boots. The first 100 yards were uphill. At the top he saw the caracara bouncing in and out of the arroyo. Great. Whatever it was turned out to be closer than he'd figured. He continued his slow steady pace until he was almost there, then he began trotting and yelling "Aléjate aves apestosos!"

The body was human, hard to tell much else about it now. Judging by the clothes it was male and fairly hefty. The gold high school ring on the left hand was easy to remove as there was little left of the finger but bone. Lupe slipped it in his pocket. While shooing away the birds he grabbed the corpse's belt to roll it over in search of an identification, though he didn't expect to find one. He was surprised at the fat wallet and the $3000 it contained. The money went in his pocket with the ring; the wallet he slid back in the corpse's jeans. He knew he had to call the authorities, but which one; the border patrol, the state police, the county. When he got back to the shop he called 911 and let them sort it out.

DEAD SAND

Distance morphed into time and silence as the SUV sliced the shimmering asphalt, caressing the voluptuous hills like grimy fingerprints stroked across a reclining woman's naked body. The smell of flowers filled the air, sweet, strong, malicious flowers, not quite wilted from the recent funeral. The women fixed on their destination, the arroyo where Carlos took his final breath. As the aroma choked casual conversation both Maria and Carrie prepared prayers to recite to the desert spirits; Maria's forgiving, Carrie's laced with rage.

Dressed for the sun in large hats, shades, and loose white blouses, they were prepared for an undetermined hike in the sun. As they crested a rise on the endless blacktop, Mirage Auto Repair came into view. The dusty beige building stood out from the desert only by its angles. It appeared to have been abandoned for years. An old Ford pickup roughly Carrie's age rusted in the brutal sun. They pulled to a stop in front of the building and noticed a faded plastic "Open" sign suspended from the doorknob with a piece of baling wire. Carrie checked her purse to make sure her .45 was accessible.

The door to the station opened and a shriveled man appeared. His bushy hair and mustache, the color of the cirrus clouds haunting the horizon, was offset by his caramel skin. Tobacco stains on his mustache blurred the line between his hair and lips. Ignoring Carrie, he ambled slowly toward Maria.

"I'm Lupe. How can I help you today, Senora?" His raspy voice a breath away from a cough.

"You found my son," Maria said.

"Si, is a sad day. If I only could've found him sooner." His ancient eyes peered towards the horizon behind the shop.

"Can you show us?"

"Let me get my hat."

Carrie grabbed as many flowers as she could hold leaving only a couple of bouquets for Maria to tote. Lupe seemed very agile in the desert considering his age. It was difficult for the women to keep up with the sand sliding around under their shoes. By the time they reached the site the women were as wilted as the flowers. They laid the flowers in a circle around the depression where a few ants still lingered.

"Should we say something?" Carrie asked.

Maria sighed. "I've prayed until my soul is raw. He's still dead." She turned and stumbled back towards the building, leaving the others in her wake. No one spoke on the hike back. Somewhere in a nearby canyon an eagle screamed.

Back at the shop Lupe stood for a moment as if lost, then seemed to get his wits about him. "Would you like to come in and cool off? Have some water, a beer? It's a long drive back to town."

Carrie glanced at Maria. "Sounds good. I'll have the beer."

"Just water for me," Maria said. When they stepped inside the shop everything was just as dusty and colorless as the outside except for a brand-new mini fridge with a tag still on it, and that blessed window unit air conditioner quietly humming above the door, still gleaming with a fresh out of the box shine. Carrie couldn't help but notice these items and wondered where this man had acquired his windfall. Something to investigate.

The lines on the road ticked by hypnotically as the women traveled in silence, the blast from the AC vents blowing strands of hair away from their faces. "Maria, I hate to ask, but when you claimed Carlos' things was there any cash?"

A look of confusion swirled over Maria's countenance. "No, why?"

"It just seems odd that he wouldn't be carrying any cash at all."

Silence resumed. The SUV continued to soak up the road.

CHANGES

Somewhere in the overly dressed mob of spectators perched in the stands of Walton field, Doris and Jerry waited for her son to approach the podium. He should be excited. He should be happy. Instead, he was stuck in a deep blue funk, unable to even pack to move out of his dorm room. Seriously, who lives in a dorm for five fucking years. The satin regalia was making him sweat, buckets of sweat, enough to saturate the restrictive material. Contrary to his step-dad's predictions he'd managed to graduate in five years, two summer sessions included. He even had a couple of definite maybes as job prospects. Still, he couldn't shake the doldrums since he'd lost contact with Carrie. Somewhere there was a partnership, a common goal, something anyway that he'd never experienced before.

"Carlton, Carnales, Carnegie." The names were called. Soon he'd have to respond. He wasn't sure he could move, make his legs hold him up. Mudstuck with nowhere to go.

"Kevin Cash" came over the PA. He stood, wandered to the podium and went through the motions. He shook the appropriate hands, made the appropriate gestures, took the prize and wandered back towards the seat. A familiar voice yelling brought him out of his hypnotic state.

"Yo! DJ, what the fuck!" Carrie was leaning over the railing at the bottom of the stands dressed in blue jeans and a University of Texas t-shirt, the middle finger of each hand focused directly on him. He smiled and returned the salute. Not in a million years had he expected her to be here.

"Look, I know you've got to do your Mommy and Daddy stuff. Holler at me later. I'm over at the Motel Sucks on College Avenue. Here's my number." Carrie grabbed his hand and wrote her cell number on his palm with a permanent marker. "You may be right. Sometimes you have to step out and take stuff in your own hands. A good friend of mine was murdered, and I'm pissed. I'm pretty sure there's a lot of money involved somewhere and if you still want to, we can get it and hurt some assholes along the way. It's not a bank. It won't be easy, but it will be very, very rewarding."

"Yeah, sure," Kevin said. "It's not-like I have a lot going on right now. Even the jobs I have lined up won't start until fall. Plus, I can always use help with the student loans."

"Keep it under your hat for now. Don't tell anyone you're meeting me." Carrie held out her hand. Kevin shook it and leaned in for a quick kiss. Carrie dodged. "No! If we're going to be partners, you have to get over that shit."

When Kevin entered La Huerta, Carrie sat at the rear table looking like she'd slept in the burnt orange T-shirt and jeans from the previous day. Her buoyancy was gone as were the contents of the margarita goblet in front of her.

"Sorry," Kevin said, "parents and all, you know." There was a second of dead air while Carrie slipped back into the present.

"Yeah, sure. No sweat. I probably should have just called. It was stupid of me to drive all this way."

"No, no! I'm cool. I'm glad you're here. You eat yet?"

"Not since yesterday. This place any good?"

"-ish. You're in a Mexican food restaurant in northern Arkansas. The bar isn't set very high. Let's eat anyway. I'm starving. " Kevin motioned for the waitress. "So fill me in."

"It's just a feeling. When something like this happens down where I live it's like chickens on a Junebug. This time nobody's doing much. I could go busting in and stir up some shit but since I'm a woman, they would either ignore me or make my life a holy hell. Besides, I told Maria I would leave it alone."

"But you're not?"

"Hell no! Here's the deal. It's a county over from where I live but Mom volunteers for every lost cause in the area and my dad throws money at any politico that she has a beef with."

"Seriously? That's kind of fucked up."

"You have no idea. Anyway, there's an opening for a dispatcher at the Sheriff's office. With my name and my sociology background I'm almost a shoe-in. It's a start. I put my ear to the ground until I get some idea of what's going on."

Kevin holds a finger to his lips indicating silence. The waitress steps up from behind Carrie.

"What can I get you?" She asks.

"Menus," Carrie says, "and another Margarita. Can you maybe put some tequila in this one?"

You'll have to order a specialty. The house drinks are premade."

"El Petron, a double."

"Me too," Kevin added.

"You know those are eight bucks a pop, right?" The waitress asked. Carrie locked eyes with her and kept her face void of expression for the number of seconds necessary to make the girl melt away. "I'll have those right out."

"You don't much care for people in general, do you?" Kevin asked once the girl was out of earshot.

"Too many stupid people in the world."

"So, how's this about making money?"

"It's about money because it's about human smuggling. For me it's about fucking up the people who killed a guy that was like a little brother to me. But, yeah, I'll take the money too. I want to make sure you know though, these are not nice people and it probably involves at least some law enforcement folks."

The waitress bought menus and glasses of ice water. "I'll have those ritas right out."

"Thanks," Carrie said. "Sorry I was rude. I've had a weird week so far." She really didn't want to drink margaritas laced with waitress spit.

"It's okay, sweetie, we all have bad days. I'll be back to take your orders."

Kevin stared at the highway beyond the windows. His first thought was to bail on the whole ordeal and if it had been anyone else across the table from him he wouldn't have paused an instant. It was plain Carrie was damaged by this incident, not like she wasn't damaged before, but this hit her hard. He also knew that she'd go through with it with or without him. She needed backup. He needed something to do. Why not an adventure? Maybe he'd even have a chance to show her how he felt, that he was real.

"Okay, I'm in," Kevin said, "but we don't make a move until we know exactly what's going on and have a detailed plan. You need to keep your emotions out of it. Can you do that?"

"As needed."

"No, I mean completely cold. You can do that."

"What are you saying?"

"You know exactly what I'm saying. We don't bullshit each other."

"Cool," Carrie said.

Two margaritas appeared in frosted glasses along with plates containing a wilted crispy taco and two enchiladas bleeding orange grease into a lake of lukewarm yellow queso. Carrie looked at the platter of goo and pushed it to the center of the table. She grabbed the goblet and took a long draw on the straw. "That's more like it," she said.

Kevin began winding long strips of cheese around the forkful of bleeding enchilada wondering if his stomach could take it. He made it through one enchilada and scraped the innards from the limp taco while he watched Carrie vacuum down the margarita and order another.

"You want to help me pack up my dorm room when we're done here?" Kevin asked.

The giggle that bubbled from Carrie was attached to a brief snort. "You did your entire college in the dorm? Are you serious?"

"Well, yeah."

"No, dude, you're on your own on in this one. Besides I need my beauty rest. I'm driving back to South Texas tomorrow."

"What about me?"

"Sounds like you'll be busy for a couple days. I'll holler at you as soon as I know something."

Daylight began to fade as Carrie drove the few blocks back to the Motel 6, feeling fortunate that the drive was short as margaritas and coffee had been her only sustenance for over 24 hours. The two double Petron's had worked their evil spell. As she locked the Civic, a Navigator pulled up next to her with a well-dressed man behind the wheel, too well dressed for the Motel 6. When the man handed his young female companion a wad of money, Carrie couldn't help but notice a gold band embedded in his fat ring finger. The taste of bile entered her throat. She checked her hatch, remembered her tool bag was back home. She watched the unlikely couple climb to the room directly above hers, the girl hanging on the man like a drunk prom date. A bumper sticker on the back of the Navigator bragged "my son is an Eagle Scout". Carrie's brain shifted gears; tunnel vision and ringing ears, a dull throbbing at the base of her skull. She stumbled to the convenience store next door and bought some aspirin and a pack of Marlboro's, smoking two while standing at the edge of the parking lot fingering her keys. The headache subsided to a dull burn. She thrust a key between each finger of her left fist. The keys ground deep grooves down the length of the Navigator as she stomped back to her room. Once inside she peeled off her clothes, turned off the lights and made the shower ten degrees hotter than bearable. Hanging by the showerhead with one hand, her back against the cool tile wall, she imagined the water to be the blood draining from the man in the room above. With her free hand she brutally twisted and scrubbed her clit until the pulsing wore off. Blood and water and tears soaked through her skin and drained her. A subhuman moan burst forth from the depths of her rage.

  She awoke on the tile floor when the shower turned cold. Her skin was red and tender. She turned off the water and, without toweling off, jumped into the bed. Pulling the covers over her head, she trembled to sleep.

Kevin left the restaurant with more energy and focus than he'd known for weeks. Even if he had to stay with his mom and Jerry for a couple of weeks, he could handle it with the light glowing brightly at the end of the tunnel. Jerry had even backed off with his snarky remarks once he realized the college education was imminent. The only problem was Jerry wanting to put him in a truck until he scored a job. Jerry had encouraged him to get his Class A commercial drivers license as soon as he turned 21, more like insisted actually. Kevin had driven trucks over a couple of summer breaks. It was long hours with low pay, but the worst part was the boredom, mile after mile of gray interstate highway and endless desert two lanes. Thank God for satellite radio. If he could skate for a couple of weeks he'd be gone, hanging out with Carrie on a real adventure. He only had to figure out how to package this to satisfy his mom.

  He grabbed some boxes from the liquor store. If it took up too much space he could always throw stuff away or take it to Goodwill. He could even get a box van from Jerry if he had to, a plan he wanted to bypass if possible.

  Kevin's newfound energy kept him sorting and packing until it was done. It looked like everything he couldn't live without would cram into his pickup, weather permitting. Everything was packed except the sheets and alarm clock. It now read 4 am. Oh well it was done. He set an alarm for 10 am, rinsed off in the shower and crawled in bed. He caught himself chuckling as he dozed off.

Kevin was sleeping so hard at 8:30 in the morning that first he only thought he dreamed a cell phone ringing. Eventually he responded, "Hello?"

"I got the job." Carrie sounded flat.

"Great, I mean, right? Are you okay?"

"Yeah, just a little hung over I guess; but yeah, it's good. I start Monday."

"Want to get together later and celebrate before I head back to Little Rock?" Kevin asked.

Carrie looked at her tender pink skin and the mess she had to deal with. "No, I need to be getting back, but in the meantime check the job boards for Bee County, Texas and see if there's something in law enforcement, courts, probation or even County jail that you're qualified for. I can get my mom to put in a word if you find something. Let me know."

"Cool, I may not even have to unpack when I get home."

"Stay in touch," Carrie said.

"I will. I hope you feel better."

"I just need to get home. I'm still not sure why I came here in person."

"It worked out."

Carrie thought of the weird night, most of which seemed like a vague dream that kept slipping farther away the more she tried to grasp it. "Yeah, I guess. I'll call you in a couple of days."

YOUNG CARRIE

The thing I thought I'd like most about Sterling Academy is the distance from Mom and Dad's meltdown. Being in Colorado is also a plus, although when I got here I found that Durango is not what I think of when I think of Colorado. Still not bad though: a small student body of only 45, all who live on campus, no supposed religious affiliation, a plus for me. The truth of the matter, though, I'm seeing more crosses than an Episcopalian seminary. The place is run by Hal and Dorothea Sterling who could be poster children for right-wing Christian fanaticism. We have to wear fucking uniforms, no makeup, dresses to the knees. It feels like an episode of Leave It To Beaver. Dorothea runs the joint using her Masters in Business Administration and her chrome-plated personality. Hal has a Bachelor's in Psychology which in his mind makes him a guidance counselor, and every other kind of counselor he can think of including gym teacher. I find out only after I arrive that it's an all-girls school and most of the girls are here because they have "behavioral problems". It's more than a finishing school. It's a fixing and finishing school. Apparently my record of acting out arrived before I did. It turns out Hal has a program designed especially for me.

It's my second day here. I've been introduced to the half-dozen students in my grade level including Violet, the Goth girl from upstate New York who I'm rooming with. I'm sitting across the shiny mahogany desk from Hal. He peers at me over the top of his reading glasses while the florescent light reflects off his polished pate.

"So, Carrie James, it says here you're sexually active at 14?" He asks.

"I don't know where you got your information, but no. I've never even kissed a boy, or girl for that matter."

"What's this about the public nudity here?"

"I have no idea what you're talking about."

"Last semester, in class, you disrobed."

"Oh, that. It was nothing."

"Care to explain what you mean?"

"More like freedom of expression. This little bitch was harassing me about a gold lame' top my mom made me wear. Sure, it was ugly, and I'm too skinny for gold lame'. I realize that, but it wasn't her place. I dropped my linen and told her to kiss my ass. They wanted to make a big deal of it. It's not like I didn't pull them back up almost immediately. The teacher just had it in for me. She blew everything out of proportion."

"We don't use the 'B' word at this institution."

"Really? That's what you got out of this entire conversation? Holy Jesus!"

"I see we've got our work cut out for us,"

I don't think Hal's buying it. I'm getting a strange vibe from him like he wants me to be more dysfunctional than I am. I'm pretty normal except I don't put up with a lot of bullshit and I don't like to be touched, not just the way you think, but any way. I have to grit my teeth just to shake hands.

<>

When your school only has 40 some odd students, everybody has to go out for everything. Because I'm 5'11" and only 14 they're really excited about my going out for basketball. They don't get that I can barely walk without tripping and the slightest exertion makes me sweat like a pig.

I really want this to work. The last thing I need is to be sent back to the hell hole at home. I agree to the basketball team, not like I have a choice if I want to pass PE. I seriously never even held a basketball so we're looking at a pretty steep learning curve here. The worst part, it turns out, basketball is a contact sport and some of these girls can be aggressive.

Sheila Woodrow is the team captain. She's the only girl as tall as I am, a gorgeous blonde with a full-blown rack that looks custom crafted. She doesn't seem to care for me, or anyone else for that matter with the exception of a couple of her "BFFs" from the senior class. I'm sitting out the first day of practice using the menstruation excuse. It's a total lie but I want to see how this works before I get all up in it, at least try to figure out what the point of the game is. As I watch the team divide in half and scrimmage I notice that Sheila likes to get physical with the other girls, physically pushing, rubbing and shoving even when it's not necessary. By the look on her face she seems to get some sort of rush from it. I'm not looking forward to that.

I'm back in my dorm room before I realize Violet didn't go out for basketball. I can see why, she's barely 5 foot tall, maybe 90 pounds, but there were other small girls who went out. Without her Goth makeup and facial studs she looks like a normal 14-year-old girl, a little plain and thin like me.

"No sports?" I ask.

"Disability," she says, a girl of few words. We're going to get along fine.

"Really?" I don't see anything physically amiss here that shows. She notices me looking her over.

"I have a steel plate in my head," she confesses. "I can't play rough but it does keep the aliens from reading my mind." Her straight face makes me wonder. Either way though, I'm cool. I kind of hope she is a nutcase. It will make my stay here a little more interesting.

I don't usually buddy up with people. I figure it's because I'm an only child and a little strange looking. I've always been taller than my classmates, at least the girls. Oddly, Violet and I hit it off quite well. She has a way of communicating that doesn't waste many words. Somehow though, through her two and three word exclamations I find out that we both like psycho thrillers, thrash metal and red meat. When we talk she focuses on my face, her oversized eyes intense as if she's trying to look between what I'm saying. She hardly ever smiles but when she does only the tiny end corner of her mouth, left side, raises slightly.

"So if you don't mind me asking, how did you end up with a plate in your head?" I ask.

"Motorcycle wreck." She just stares at me as if it's an interrogation.

"You don't mind talking about it?" I ask. She shrugs. "So you had a motorcycle?"

"My boyfriend's."

I wasn't sure how deep I wanted to go into this but she just continues to stare at me with that inquisitive look on her face. "So you were riding with him?"

"Yeah."

"Was he hurt?"

"Killed."

My stomach does a little dance. I look to see if she's having any reaction. Still nothing. "I'm sorry. That's terrible. How long ago?"

"Shit happens. It was last year." She drops her eyes from mine and looks over at the mini fridge. I get the feeling the interview is over. That's the way we learned to communicate, mostly nonverbal. Later I found out she had a brother older than her. Her dad and mom were divorced but both of them were still in her life. The boyfriend she had been riding with was 19, she was 13. They couldn't prosecute a dead guy but they could send her away to school. They referred to it as "rehabilitation". We're both glad to be here because the shit back home is just too much to handle.

Violet and I have all but one class together, not surprising since there are only 7 freshmen. I'm in the liberal arts track. Violet is some kind of math phenom so she's in the engineering track although she says she prefers pure science, the theoretical stuff that I completely get lost in. She swears as soon as she learns the language for it she will prove that the speed of light is not constant. Maybe she can, who knows? PE is our last class, when we practice basketball. Although Violet isn't on the team she still has to show up for class. Most of the other girls hate her. You can almost smell the venom in their sweat. Since I'm her friend they hate me by association. Fuck 'em! I'll take one Violet over all their candy asses.

By the time we finish stretching and make a lap around the track I'm *sweating so profusely that I'm dripping like I just stepped out of the pool. Hal throws me a towel to put around my neck and we start passing the basketball back and forth in a circle. I figure out that anytime Sheila gets it she's going to throw at me as hard as possible. So far I haven't failed to catch it, which pisses her off something fierce. We line up for three free throws each. I miss all but one. Sheila hits all hers and gives me a little smirk. I silently mouth "FU" in her direction.*

When Hal divides us up to scrimmage, instead of considering talent, he goes by height, putting Sheila and me on opposite teams. Every time I get the ball, which is way too often, Sheila is all over me putting her hands in my face and sliding that perfect rack all down the side of my body making me want to puke. I nudge her briskly in her rib cage with my elbow making her grunt like the pig she is. She retaliates by "accidentally" stomping on my foot. "Get off me!" I scream. She slides her sweaty body down the front of me like she wants to fuck me or something. My knee finds her crotch, she doubles over and I bounce the basketball off her head. "Bitch!" Hal blows his whistle. She's on the ground. I'm not. I offer my hand to help her up. She offers me her single middle finger. I glance over at Violet and see the corner of her mouth, left side, twitch slightly. Apparently that's going to be it for basketball today. Hal points at me motioning me into his office. I dry my face with my towel and toss it over my shoulder.

Once again I'm sitting across the desk from Hal. This time the desk is metal and the room smells like dirty socks. "So why isn't Sheila in here," I ask.

"I'll deal with her later. She's an ongoing problem. I'm hoping you won't be."

I look at him in a way that I've learned from Violet, flat but curious. "She's my problem. Solve that, I'm good." I continue looking directly into his eyes. I find that he cannot hold the gaze. Seems I make him a little nervous.

"We're a small family here," Hal says. "We all have to get along. We all have the same goals, getting a good education, getting into a good college and becoming well-rounded young women." I have to restrain myself from giggling, thinking of Hal as a well-rounded young woman and wondering what he means by that. He adjusts himself in his chair and catches my gaze again. "You seem to have a lot of pent-up hostility. I don't know much about your history but it appears you have intimacy issues and a lot of rage. We're going to try some exercises that are designed to help you release some of the energy behind that rage. I want you to try to get in touch with yourself and your inner feelings so you can understand what drives you and adjust it accordingly."

I doubt Hal's bachelor's degree gives him credibility as a psychotherapist but I'm not in a position to argue. I hear the other girls finishing up their showers, talking, laughing. The energy in the dressing room is winding down. I just want to get out of my soggy uniform. "So what's the deal?

Hal rubs his chin as if pulling a nonexistent beard. "It's an exercise in cleansing and relaxation." So far so good. "Have you ever masturbated?" Okay, now this is getting a little squirrely. I pull my knees up under my chin and nod my head yes. "I'd like you to try something. When you shower I want you to turn the water on as hot as you can stand it, soap yourself up thoroughly, I mean really scrub. As you're rinsing in the hot water touch yourself, in whatever way will make you orgasm. When the spasms begin, think of it as the anger flowing out of you." Now I'm totally creeped out. I guess my jaw dropped. I'm in total shock. "Okay, I see you're not completely comfortable with that. Maybe you can work up to it. One of the other girls can talk you through it or I can ask Dorothea to work with you." I can feel my breath starting to catch. I refuse to cry in front of this idiot. What have I gotten myself into?

"No, I can handle it." I say.

The locker room is empty. As I pull my soggy workout clothes off, the cold air in the room makes me shiver. I'm alone. Why I'm even willing to do this I don't know, lack of options, I guess. I turn the water on and adjust it hot enough that the stall fills up with steam. I stick my foot in the spray and immediately yank it back out. My instep is red. I add just enough cold water to the mix to make it bearable and step under. It does feel good to have the water running over my head, down my shoulders and trickling through my pubic hair. I wish I could get the image of Hal from my mind. I soap thoroughly, per instructions, scrubbing my pits, my neck and ears, my crotch and my ass. I hang the wash rag on the faucet handle and lean against the cool tile. My fingers find my clit. It feels good all soapy and warm. It only takes a couple of minutes and I'm where I want to be. I didn't realize how much I needed this. As the waves rush over me a moan escapes and echoes off the tile walls. It startles me back to reality and I finish rinsing before the orgasm has completely left my body. An odd feeling of guilt has set in, so without even drying off I wrap in a towel and head for the locker room. As I round the corner I find Hal sitting, waiting, staring. "See, that wasn't so bad, was it?" He says.
Terrified, I wanted to scream but realize it would be pointless. I taste the bile rising in my throat. I shrink behind a locker. "Please leave," I mumble. He gets up and strolls out of the dressing room.

"See you tomorrow," he calls over his shoulder.

"Okay?" Violet asks when I return to the dorm.

"No." I don't even know how to talk to her about this. "I'm hungry. Let's go out to eat. I have some cash. I'll buy." God, I wish I could get drunk, get stoned, out of my head somehow. Violet's radar picks up on my mood.

"What happened, after I left I mean?" Her big eyes burn right through me. There's absolutely no way to lie to this girl.

"Hal gave me a spiel about anger management. Suggested rather emphatically that I masturbate."

"Report him."

"And what, where would I end up then? I've got nowhere else. I'm damn sure not going back home."

"Did you do it?"

"Yeah, I did. I thought I was alone but when I got out of the shower he was right there in the locker room listening. I thought I was going to puke." Violet just looked at me. It wasn't in any judgmental way, more like pity which pissed me off even more. "Look, this is my problem. I don't even know why I'm telling you. It's not like you can do anything. He better not touch me though, I'll kill him." We finished our hamburgers in silence. Every bite I swallowed did a little dance in my stomach. I felt like I needed to cry but couldn't.

I guess I become Hal's private project. "We've got to get some meat on those bones," he said. He bought me protein powders and let me into the weight room after hours. Every day after basketball practice I have to run a dozen laps around the track. I begin to put on a little weight. I develope thighs and a butt. My arms become more than just elbows and wrists. Some of the weight training builds up my chest to where I almost looked like I have breasts. Every day I'm the last to leave the gym. Every day I masturbate in the shower. Every day Hal sits out on the bench and listens. He never touches me. He never looks at me until I at least have a towel around me. It becomes performance art. Sometimes I make it long and loud. Sometimes I whimper like a little girl. Once, just to fuck with him, I even call out his name. The look he gives me when I come around the corner makes me decide that it is probably a bad idea. I never do it again. Several times, if I dry off quickly, I come around the corner to find him sweating with a towel in his lap. "Perv!" I say. "You're a sick bastard you know that?" For a couple of days he doesn't come by and I'd have the locker room to myself.

COP SHOP

Carrie arrived with a half hour to spare, dressed conservatively, though a bit wilted from the hour-long drive from home. She took the elevator to the top floor of the courthouse. After sending her resume she'd interviewed over the phone. "Hi, I'm the new dispatcher," she told the uniformed woman behind the desk. "Can you direct me to a supervisor?"

The woman behind the desk proffered a friendly smile. "Well, honey, the Sheriff's not in yet so I guess that would be me. I'm Gina. I run the show while the boys are out playing. I'll get you set up. Give me a minute." Gina wrestled her ample body free from the wooden chair and motioned Carrie to follow. "You'll have your own little office back here, a phone, a radio and your very own coffee pot. Pretty sweet deal. Rosie will be in to train you soon. She's retiring and since it's her last two weeks she's more or less keeping her own hours. I mean, what are we going to do? Fire her?" Gina waddled over to set up the coffee pot. "Just make yourself at home 'til Rosie gets here. There's not a lot going on Mondays during the day. Answer the phone if it rings. Holler at me if you need anything. I've been here since the dawn of time."

Carrie settled in, turned on the police radio and explored her new office. It was pretty basic, other accoutrements included a computer that was still running Windows 7, a carbonless pad for taking messages, a printer, a telephone and something that wasn't quite a fax machine. The radio squawked chatter constantly in a seemingly unrelated noise. "You can change that to channel 6," Gina said. "That's the channel the Sheriff uses. Rosie keeps it tuned in to channel 11. That's the Garza unit, the state jail. Her husband works there." Carrie turned the dial to channel 6 and the radio fell virtually silent. I hope this isn't as boring as it appears, Carrie thought.

She dug through the drawers for something to do. Time slowed to a crawl. She found a yellowed ten code sheet with a few of the more common codes highlighted. Most of them she'd heard on TV cop shows but she decided to try to memorize the whole sheet if possible. Boredom had set in. She'd lost herself in her project when a bubbly grandmotherly woman came in carrying several cardboard boxes. Holding the door for her was a living work of art. He was at least

6'3", shoulders as broad as a Brahma bull, dark hair, thin mustache and brown eyes with tiny flecks of gold that glistened when the light hit them just right.

"Oh, you must be the new dispatcher," the woman said. "This is Sheriff Carranza."

"You can call me Ross," the Adonis said. Carrie was still trying to catch her breath. It wasn't so much that she was sexually attracted to him, but she appreciated art as much as the next woman.

Carrie froze, stunned for a moment, then responded, "I'm Carrie James and I'm a lost ball in the high weeds here." She stood up and relinquished the chair. The room was much too small for the three of them, especially with Sheriff Carranza filling up so much space.
The woman threw the boxes over in the corner. "Hi Carrie, I'm Rosie. We'll get you all fixed up here in a minute."
"I'll let you two get acquainted," the sheriff said. "Carrie, stop in my office after you get settled in please. I'd like to give you the rundown on what we do here."

YOUNG KEVIN

We're standing in the backyard under the elm tree. *The smell of freshly mowed grass permeates the air and the flower beds have been tinkered with until you can smell the mulch. Mom's pastel green dress brings out the color in her eyes but it doesn't hide the sorrow. Oh, the smile is there, but everything else in her demeanor hints at resignation. I can't help but feel she needs my help. "Mom, you don't have to do this. I can get a part-time job. We can figure out something." She gives me a look like I'm three years old again, the situation beyond my understanding.*

"Honey, you'll get used to this. It's not so bad. Jerry is a really nice man. He loves me and he has a lot of respect for you." She takes another gulp from her wine goblet, puts her hand around my shoulder gives me a brief hug. "Just think, moving to his ranch, how much room you'll have to run and explore."

"I don't care about that. I want you to be happy and I don't see that happening there. You love this house. This is our home, I don't want to leave." The new puppy Jerry bought her has his teeth tangled in the tablecloth where the wedding cake is displayed. She rushes over to shoo him away and I'm standing alone. I look around and see a lot of people that I don't know. Jerry's surrounded by men with more creases in their skin than in their slacks. They look overdressed and out of place, similar to the way I feel. I walk toward them.

Jerry takes note and motions me over. "I want you guys to meet my new stepson, Kevin Cash. He'll be joining you on the big rigs before you know it." I shake a few hands and hear a few names that I will immediately forget. I know if I stand around and focus on Jerry long enough these guys will wander away. So I do.

"What's on your mind, Kevin?"

"You know mama doesn't love you, right?" I fix my eyes on him until he glances away beyond the privacy fence.

"Maybe, I don't know. We can learn to love each other. We're good for each other. Sometimes there are other reasons to be together."

An old Conway Twitty tearjerker blasts from the stereo. I look at the ground, back up at his face. I can feel my ears red from the blood pumping through my temples. "You're fucking up our lives. We were doing just fine until you came along. You need to find a way to make this not happen."

I observed his fists tighten. He turns full frontal on me. "Let me explain something to you, son." He lets this last word linger. "If you were me talking to my dad like that you would be peeling yourself off that privacy fence. I'm not going to ruin this by doing that right now, but don't think I'm not capable." He steps toward me, but I hold my ground. *"You need to deal with this however you have to. It's happening. Get over it."*

YOUNG CARRIE

It isn't easy but I manage to drag Violet *to another basketball game. We're halfway through the season and this is only the second one she's attended. I play the second half, actually score eight points, not bad for a newbie. After the game we're walking back to the dorm and her phone rings, actually rings, not a text. Nobody ever calls Violet. Nobody ever calls me either for that matter, except Mom on Saturday. Almost as soon as she answers she stops walking, just stands there like she's melting. Though her face shows no expression as always, water begins to trickle from her eyes. She says few words but I can tell something horrible has happened.*

"Is everything all right?" I ask after she hangs up.

"It's my brother, car wreck. I'll be flying out in the morning."

"Is he okay?"

"He's dead."

I'm at a loss. She's my only friend at the school. I think I'm probably hers and I don't know what to say, or do. Nothing like this is ever happened to me. I can't help but think about her parents. After piecing her together from her motorcycle wreck and now to lose their son. I feel my own tears burning in my eyes. We walk in silence.

Back in our room she curls up on her bed in the fetal position. "Can I make you some coffee, or anything, help you pack?" I get no response. I'm at a loss. I know what I should do but it's just not me. Still, I lay down beside her and wrap my arm around her shoulders. She snuggles into me as the sobs begin to rack her body. Finally, after several minutes she cries herself to sleep. I just lay there. I'm not comfortable but it's not horrible either. Her head is on my arm and I don't want to wake her. Soon, I begin to doze as well.

I have no idea how long we've been lying here but I awake with a start, feeling someone's eyes on me.

"Well, isn't this sweet? Look at the two lovebirds." Sheila is standing in the doorway flanked by half the basketball team.

"Close the fucking door, bitch!" I scream.

Violet starts awake. "Get out of my room."

"Come on. Let's go," a voice from the back of the crowd suggests.

Sheila steps into the doorway. "What's wrong? You don't want to watch some hot girl on girl sex? Well, maybe not too hot, but there's obviously something going on here." She pulls the door closed but I can hear the girls giggling halfway down the hall.

I'm not really into basketball practice today. I keep missing simple shots. When I hit one I look over to the bleachers where Violet usually sits, and she's not there. I already miss her and wonder when she'll be back. Sheila seems unusually aggressive today. Not only is she sliding her sweaty body all over me, but it seems like her face is always right up in mine. A couple of times when we're sharing the same breath she runs her tongue around the edges of her lips seductively. It makes me want to puke right in her face. I could give her the knee in the crotch thing but I don't want to deal with Hal's shit. The workouts have been paying off though, so when she's all over me one too many times I spin with my back to her, put my foot on her sneaker and slam my butt into her, knocking her on her ass. When she holds up a hand for assistance to stand I just walk away. I have my back to her but I can sense her anger and hear her footsteps. She jumps me from behind. I grab her head and roll her over my shoulder slamming her down flat on her back. "You want to go? Come on bitch, I can take your candy ass now." I've had it. I know I'm screwed even before Hal blows the whistle, but it was worth it.

Hal is between us even before Sheila has a chance to stand. "I'm not going to have any of this," Hal says. "Everyone to the showers. No, Sheila, Carrie, you wait here." As much as they hate to, the other girls finally wander off. "Look," Hal says, "I know what this is about, but I'm not about to put up with it. You're going to learn to get along or you'll be running laps 'til midnight. Sheila, in the shower. Carrie, you wait here 'til this clears up." Hal goes over and sits in the bleachers expecting me to join him. I pick up a basketball and continue to shoot hoops. Suddenly, I'm not missing a shot. Hal is glaring at me. I can feel his anger but I don't know where it's coming from. Sheila deserved what she got.

The locker rooms clear out but I'm not playing the shower game with Hal tonight. I'm still energized from the confrontation. I hit the weight room and do a few sets on everything. Hal is in his office and I finally calm down. The anger leaves me drained and soaked in sweat. I consider just going back to my room but decide to shower in the gym. I'm afraid of how lonely my room will be without Violet.

The water is comfortably warm, not too hot. I have no guilt to purge, nothing that I didn't leave in the weight room. I'm not performing tonight, not for Hal, not for anyone. Fuck 'em. My hair is lathered up with shampoo and I'm enjoying the normal temperature of the water sliding down my body. Out of habit I start to touch myself then shake it off - no reason to.

The last of my shampoo spirals around the drain as I rinse the soap from my eyes. When I open them I see Hal standing in the doorway of the shower wearing nothing but a towel. Before I can respond he grabs me by the throat and slams me against the tile. Water is running in my eyes but I try to kick for his groin. He dodges and my knee glances off his hip. I try to scream but no sound will come out.

I grab his arms and dig my nails in causing him to tighten the grip on my throat. His face is so red it looks about to burst and I can feel his erection pulsing against my hip. His free hand grabs my wrist, twisting it up behind my back. He releases my throat and grabs a handful of hair from the back of my head spinning me and shoving me face first into the corner of the shower stall. "Go ahead, scream all you want," he hisses. "There's no one here but us." I try to squirm loose but there's nowhere to go. "I hear you've gone queer on me. We don't allow that here at Sterling Academy. I'm going to have to show you what it's like to be a real woman."

I felt split into three people; the terrified girl being raped, the angry girl wanting to kill him and a girl watching all this is laughing at him trying to be" like a real woman". That last girl doesn't hang around long. He kicks my feet out from under me and I slide down the wall. Now he has me on my knees with my face shoved into the corner of the floor. My shoulder feels like it's about to dislocate. I refuse to cry and continue to kick but it doesn't keep him from shoving that thing into me. It hurts so bad I want to chop it off and beat him to death with it. All I can do is take it, every thrust slamming my face into the wall. I try to find somewhere inside my head to go but I can't quite get there so I just kind of phase out. Eventually, and violently, he finishes. "See, that wasn't so bad," he says. "You'll probably need another shower though." I curl up in the corner until I hear him leave then I get dressed and go back to my dorm room.

"Hey, girl. Looks like I'm your new roommate. It turns out your little sweet cakes ain't coming back. Boss lady said it would be good for us to learn to get along." Sheila said, sneering like a cat that ate the canary.

I turn around and start walking, most of the night. I know I can't go home. I don't know how I can stay here. If there's a Hell, I've found it.

THE SHERIFF

Though it was unusual for Carrie to feel comfortable under the gaze of a man, Sheriff Carranza's warm brown eyes set her at ease. His was a gentle countenance but one that held secrets firmly. Rather than placing her across the desk from him he placed two chairs near the window where they sat and looked out over Beeville's town square. He offered her coffee and made himself a cup heavy with cream.

"Carrie, I have to say, you have more education in law enforcement than most of my deputies. What made you want the dispatcher position?" The tone of Carranza's voice made her realize this was more than a rhetorical question.

"It was available. If it works out I have no problem with climbing the ladder here"

"It's a pretty short ladder. We have six full-time deputies, Gina and me. Honestly, I had no intention of filling the dispatcher position. I figured Gina could handle it since hardly anybody stops buy in person anymore. You see, we're only a small cog in a big wheel. The Border Patrol has a strong presence here, then there's DPS, the Texas Rangers and even the City of Beeville has a larger police force than us. We're not going to solve all the crime in the County. My philosophy is just to contain it, to keep it in localized areas where it doesn't affect the general populace. That's about all we can do here. I hired you for two reasons, neither of which had anything to do with dispatching. Diversity had a lot to do with it. All our deputies are male. All but one is Hispanic. With your education and a two-week boot camp you could be a deputy. Is that something you would consider?

It took Carrie a moment to wrap her head around this. It would definitely give her more access to the information she needed. "So what was the other reason?"

"Political pressure. Apparently you have friends in high places."

It was all Carrie could do to keep from laughing out loud. "I don't know about high places. My mom has her hands in every political pie in a five-county area, in spite of my dad's protestations. If any strings were pulled I'm pretty sure she was doing the yanking. I appreciate the job, though, and the offer. It sounds interesting but I'll have to think about it."

Gina's round face appeared in the doorway. "Sheriff, sorry to bother you but I think you're going to want to take this phone call."

"Excuse me," the sheriff said. He walked behind his desk, sat in his leather chair and, before picking up the phone, propped his spit shined alligator boots on the corner of the desk. "Ross here." As he listened the level of concern on his face deepened. "I don't have anyone on my staff that speaks it. Why won't she just tell us in Spanish? I don't know anyone who still uses the Mayan or Aztec dialects."

Carrie had nothing to do but listen to the conversation. As soon as she realized what was happening she got Sheriff Carranza's attention. He put down the phone. "I know someone who speaks Huastecan," she offered.

"Let me call you back." Ross hung up the phone and shook his head. "Damned if you're not paying off already." He motioned Carrie over to the desk. "I don't know if you've heard about it but we recently found a young man's body in the desert. It was probably smuggling related; drugs, human, who knows. The Border Patrol just picked up an indigenous Mexican girl trying to sneak back into Mexico just south of Laredo. She was carrying her dead mother. Apparently she's connected in some way to this dead guy we found but she's terrified of the Border Patrol and cops in general. She speaks a little Spanish but won't tell her story without a translator."

Carrie was having trouble deciding how close to play her hand. She didn't want the Sheriff to know her trilingual friend was Carlos' mother." Let me give her a call. I'm sure she'll be happy to help."

Carrie turned onto Highway 359 just as her cell phone rang. Normally she didn't answer her phone while driving but highway 359 is flat, straight and unoccupied. Even if she left the road the only danger was getting sand on her tires. Checking the phone she saw it was Kevin. "Hey, what's up?"

"I got a job interview with Bee County probation. It looks good but if nothing else there's some openings at the prison for guards, not what I was hoping for but it's a start."

"You'll get it. Nobody applies for those jobs out here. The one I got had been open for 18 months. If you need a reference, though, a woman I work with has a husband who's in charge of the prison guards. I'll have her put in a good word. I doubt you'll need it though." Carrie's Civic drifted off the pavement slinging up a dust cloud behind her. "Oops. Maybe I'd better call you back when I get home. Do you have a place to stay lined up?"

"I'll have to get a room when I get there."

"Let me talk to my mom, maybe you can stay out at the ranch."

"With you?"

"Don't think about it that way, not going to happen, but we have plenty of room."

Carrie and Maria, jangled from too much morning coffee, waited at the intersection in downtown Alice for Sheriff Carranza to arrive. They piled in his police cruiser and headed for Laredo. Maria became pensive, insisting on sitting alone in the back. Carrie thought of the language she'd heard Maria try to teach Carlos while he was still just a toddler. It didn't take. Being bilingual was enough for Carlos so Maria abandoned the project. He didn't see the point in learning an obscure language. Carrie vaguely remembered the strange mouth sounds, grunts and gurgles from her childhood though.

Maria wasn't making any promises. "There are a number of indigenous languages," she said. "I know the dialects that are common in central Mexico and the East Coast. Some of the mountain languages are so different that I may not be able to help you."

"It's worth a try," Ross said." We've got nothing to lose but some windshield time." Carrie knew there was a lot more to lose than time but if it could give Maria some closure it would be worth it. Maria fidgeted and stared out the window. Carrie sat in the front seat like a statue, barely breathing.

Itzpa sat alone in a tiny room, terrified. She had not communicated to anyone in English, though she had some skill with the language. Her Spanish was minimal, so minimal she was uncomfortable communicating with the crowd of Hispanics who had tried to get her to talk. Sheriff Carranza brought Maria in the room and, by way of introduction, offered her a chair. He then left to stand out with Carrie and observe through the one-way mirror. Maria talked with the girl for over an hour. Both ended up crying, holding each other, shaking their heads, growing angry then hugging again. Finally Maria rose, gave the girl a final hug and came out of the interrogation room emotionally drained. "That poor child," Maria said. "She needs to be reunited with her mother's body. They need to go home, she is of no use here."

"What's her story," Ross asked.

The bitterness in Maria's eyes flashed a moment of rage. "Her story is my story." Carrie held her breath knowing what was coming. Maria faced the Sheriff squarely. "The young man in the desert, his name is Carlos. He is my son. According to this girl,, he was trying to save the lives of 18 women. There are at least two more bodies in the desert. One is my nephew, Miguel. The other is a brutal Mexican prostitute who killed this poor girl's mother. There could be more bodies depending on how many of these Mexican prostitutes made it back to civilization. They were stranded in the desert at least 10 miles from the nearest road. It was a human smuggling operation gone wrong and, as horrible as it was that my son was involved, he and Miguel were merely pawns. They were employees of a much larger organization working both sides of the border."

"Did you get any details?" Ross asked. "You were in there for over an hour."

Maria glared at him. "We were talking about our families. She doesn't know much. She's only 14. Her mother handled all the details. There's a broken-down produce truck out in the desert, not sure where. You'll find Miguel's body in it. The other body is in the desert between the truck and the border crossing at Lake Amistad dam. It looks like you have a big problem here."

Inside the police cruiser a dry silence hung in the chilled air. Ross held the bridge of his nose between the thumb and forefinger of his left hand while his right wrist hung over the steering wheel. Maria was dozing in the back seat. "I'll take it," Carrie said.

It took Sheriff Carranza a moment but he looked toward Carrie. "What?"

"The job, the deputy position. What do I need to do?"

"We put you through training at the Department of Public Safety Police Academy. I'll find out when the next one starts. You have to live on site. It's tough, like boot camp, but only two weeks. In the meantime I will go ahead and promote you so you can get the salary and benefits." He looked out over the vastness of the desert. It looked dead, the only green a few cacti. "You sure you want to do this? It could be dangerous. Sounds like a cartel might be involved."

"Maria is our housekeeper. I grew up with Carlos, he's like a brother to me. I need to do this."

"This has to be about the law, not vigilante justice. Just so you know, we play by the book here, we don't cross lines. It's important for you to remember that."

Carrie stared at Ross's profile; bronze, manicured, every hair in place. Something made her not want to disappoint him. "I'm okay with rules. But just so you know, for me this is a family matter."

"We'll work together on it.

THE TEAM

The Sheriff dropped Carrie and Maria back in Alice, giving her the rest of the day off. Cell service was sketchy in the area. Carrie checked her phone and realized a text message had come in from Kevin. He was in Beeville looking for her, not a good plan. She immediately dialed his number. "Dude, don't be spreading my name around town. I don't know you, you know what I mean? Drive over to Alice, it's about another hour. Come out to my house. I'll text you the address. We shouldn't be seen in public together. You see, I'm the new deputy sheriff."

"Holy crap, girl! You don't waste any time, do you?"

"Shit happens. We'll talk when you get here."

Maria made enchiladas for dinner. Lois made a special effort to attend as she wanted to meet Carrie's "friend from school". Whatever Lois read into this relationship was probably much closer to Kevin's imagination than to reality. Still, everyone was having a pleasant dinner and Kevin was treated to some high-quality Mexican food. Carrie had some important news to share. "Mom, you will never guess what happened. Tomorrow I get measured for my deputy sheriff's uniform."

It was as if a bubble burst. Lois got serious. "Honey, this is probably not the best part of the state to be taking that job. A lot goes on here that you don't know about. Hell, a lot goes on here that I don't know about and I keep my finger on the pulse. It's dangerous, not to mention you may have to compromise your ethics."

"You're accusing me of having ethics?" Carrie looked over at Kevin and winked.

After a moment or two of tense silence Kevin put down his fork and took a sip of sweet tea. "Ms. James, I wouldn't worry too much about Carrie if I were you. She's obviously been working out and even when she was skinny she scared the hell out of me. I pity the perp that crosses her."

"Don't worry, Mom, mostly we just chase loose livestock off the road. Once in a while we have to take some drunk guy to jail for slapping this old lady around or vice versa. If that happens I promise I'll call for backup."

Lois continued to look concerned. "What about all the drug runners and the illegals crossing the border?"

"The Border Patrol handles most of that. Seriously, I'm just the token white girl on the force. Sheriff Carranza even told me I was specifically hired to diversify the department."

"Ain't that some shit," Kevin spouted. All three women turned and glared at him. "Oops," he said. "My bad."

Carrie kicked him under the table. "Put DJ away," she said. "We're feeding Kevin, not some thug." She wanted to get her mom off the subject of the job. "Mom, I told Kevin he could stay in our guesthouse until he gets a place in town. It may be a while. He probably needs to get a couple of checks under his belt. I'm going to have to find a place to live in Bee county. It's a requirement of the job since they're going to give me a cruiser to drive." She grabbed the serving dish and served herself three more enchiladas. "I'll be out of here pretty quick but just think of Kevin as the son you never had."

After dinner Carrie showed Kevin to the little apartment above the garage. "It's small but probably bigger than the dorm room you lived in for five years. Stretch out, make yourself comfortable. When we need to talk, this will be a safe place to do it. And we probably need to talk now."

"I know, I need to lay off the DJ personality. I was just practicing. It's how I'm going to approach the job, better to get in with the lowlifes, but I promise I'll be respectful to your mom."

"It's not that. Play it however you need to. If you get the probation officer job, though, you'll be working right across the street from me. If we're going to make this work you've got to pretend you don't even know who I am. We can come out here if we need to compare notes or make plans. Just know this is a small community and everybody knows everybody's business. Not only that, my mom is smack dab in the middle of it. She considers herself a mover and shaker in local society. Whether that's true or not I don't know but she does have her fingers in a lot of pies around here."

She filled him in on the day's details. "I knew this Miguel guy. He was a small-town thug so there's probably information on him at the probation office. I'm going to try to get assigned the case but if not I'm going to need you to feed me that information. Cool?"

"Whatever you need. We're in this together. Where should we start?"

"Well, we should probably start by unloading all your shit and getting it up into this little room," Carrie said. She leaned on her hands against the doorway, stepped back and stretched. Kevin couldn't help but fix on the lean muscles rippling in her back and her perfectly formed buttocks. She didn't notice his attentions. "Let's do this," she said.

Kevin spent a few more seconds admiring her as she bounded down the stairs, then broke the spell and followed. "So, where's your dad in all this? I know you have one, not your favorite guy, but still?"

"He has an office in Corpus Christi. I'm not even sure exactly where he lives. He won't be an issue. You'll probably never even see him. Actually, he owns this ranch but it's just a tax write off for him. He didn't want to divorce mom so she told him as long as he takes care of us and lets us live here she won't raise a stink. It's worked pretty well for almost 10 years so far. I don't see anything changing."

Carrie had only carried a couple of boxes and she was already drenched in sweat. "I can get this," Kevin said. "I didn't mean to get you out here and work you to death."

"Bullshit, I'm not even breathing hard. This sweating thing is just a curse, always been like that. One of the many reasons I don't date or have sex. So you see? Now you know." They unloaded the rest of his possessions in silence. Kevin made it a point to follow her up the stairs to enjoy the view. She didn't seem to notice. It only took about 15 minutes to complete the project. "Okay, I'm done here," Carrie said. "The unpacking part, that's your baby. I'm gonna go take a shower."

Kevin sat down on the plastic Art Deco couch and spent a heavenly moment visualizing Carrie in the shower. Little did he know.

GETTING IN

After again filling out the 10-page application he had already filled out online, Kevin finally got to meet his interviewer, a young woman probably two or three years his junior by the name of Betty Lou Spencer. She stared at him over the top of reading glasses that she probably didn't need as if she had been trained to intimidate. It wasn't working. Kevin leaned back in a swivel chair and placed his left ankle on top of his right knee. Betty Lou removed her glasses, folded them neatly and crossed her hands on top of them. "So, you have a bachelors in criminal justice from the U of A and you interned with the Western District Court. That's the Feds, ain't it?"

"Yes ma'am, it is."

"What brings you to our neck of the woods?"

"Wide-open spaces, adventure, job availability. If you want to know the truth, I needed to put a little distance between me and my stepdad. I have all this education and he wants me to be a truck driver. It's not in the cards." He could see Betty Lou trying to suppress a smile.

"Well, here's the deal. It's not my decision. I'm just here to weed out the deadbeats. The judge makes the final decision but with your qualifications I'm pretty sure you have the job, if you want it. First, though, let me tell you what you're looking at. We have two state jails right down the street. They're holding jails, which means the inmates are either awaiting trial or they've been convicted but sentenced to two years or less. What happens is these guys get out of jail after their sentence is up and they don't have anywhere to go. They hang out here in Beeville but there aren't any jobs so they end up back in the system. It's pretty frustrating. We do have a couple of small local manufacturing and trucking businesses that hire a few of them but most either wander off or end up back in jail."

Kevin let his foot slide off onto the floor and leaned forward in his chair, staring straight into Betty's eyes. "I guess I would consider that a challenge then. I'd like to take the job if it's available. What's the next step?"

"Let me run this by Judge Kendrick. She'll want to talk to you. She's free after lunch. Can you come back then?"

"Cool. Why don't you show me where there's a good place to

eat around here?"

"I brought my lunch."

"I'm buying."

"Let me get my purse."

Kevin and Betty Lou walked two blocks toward the courthouse to a little diner just off the square. Betty seemed to have lost track of most of her well-practiced composure. When she stumbled at the curb Kevin caught her by the arm. "Are you okay?" He asked. She nodded and brushed a twisted strand of pale blonde hair behind her ear with her ring finger, a finger that bore no ring.

Betty smiled shyly as Kevin pulled the chair out for her. Several of the patrons took note of his action. "Tell me about yourself, Betty, or do you go by Betty Lou?"

"Either is fine."

"Come on, girl, you must have a preference." Kevin removed his tie, stuck it in his shirt pocket and unbuttoned his collar.

"My mom calls me Betty Lou, so I guess that's okay."

"My stepdad calls me a punk-ass thug but my friends call me DJ. I'd rather you use that."

"You mean like a music guy?"

"Yeah, it's a sideline when I'm not too busy saving the world from crime."

When Betty Lou finally cut loose with a full-fledged smile sunshine filled the room. "So did you come to rock this town? Little old Beeville never gonna be the same, huh?"

"I might need some help with that. You game?"

"Sad news, DJ, but this town ain't never gonna change."

After a brief conversation with Judge Kendrick, Kevin found himself an employee of the 156th District Court of Texas whose offices were actually two and a half blocks from the courthouse. He couldn't wait to share the news with Carrie so maybe he was driving a little fast out on the highway toward Alice. When the police car came screaming up behind him with the siren on and the headlights flashing his heart went into his throat. He slowed and pulled off the shoulder well clear of the traffic lane. A voice crackled through the cruiser's PA. "Step out of the car and put your hands against the fender." He complied. A tall woman in a crisp tan uniform strutted towards him slapping her nightstick against the palm of her hand. "Son, we don't take kindly to city folk burning up our roads." The voice was steady and harsh from behind the mirrored shades, yet it was a voice he recognized. He dropped his hands from the fender and turned to face the officer.

"What the hell, Carrie. You scared the shit out of me. I think you have the intimidation thing down." He leaned back against his truck. "Looking good with the uniform and shades though, kind of makes my putter flutter."

Carrie slapped her hand with the baton a couple more times. "Boy, show some respect. You're talking to an officer of the law." She slipped her baton in her belt, took off her shades and leaned next to him against the pickup. "They're not wasting any time getting me up to speed. Next week they're shipping me off to Corpus for two weeks at the police academy and they've already given me this car."

"So they're going to just cut you loose patrolling in the meantime?"

"Nah, I'm not officially on duty until I get back. But I am getting paid like a deputy, plus the car, which is a turd by the way."

"Looks pretty good to me."

"It's got 250,000 miles on it, smells like sweat and cigars and the springs in the front seat are so blown out I have to put a pillow under my ass. But yeah, it feels awesome to drive it. I can't wait to see Mom's face when a cop car drives up to the house." Carrie slipped her shades back on and they took a walk around the cruiser. "When we get home can you drive me back to town to pick up my Civic?"

"Sure. By the way, I got the job with probation. It probably cost me lunch but that's okay."

Carrie raised an eyebrow. "Already working the angles?"

"Keeping my options open."

WORKING FOR THE MAN

Kevin arrived **15 minutes early for work** on Monday only to find the door to the building locked. Just as he turned to wait in his truck he saw Betty Lou step to the curb at the corner. When she looked up and saw him that sunshine smile brightened her face and she gave him a little parade wave. As she paused on the step in front of him digging through her purse for the key, the smell of strawberries wafted from her hair. She found the key, pushed a strand of hair behind her ear and opened the door. "Welcome to the salt mines," she said. "I'll help you get settled in but we've got to make it quick. Judge Kendrick left a list of things for you to start on. She won't be in 'til this afternoon. She has court this morning but she can be a real hard ass, so if you need any help getting oriented, let me know. My office is right next to yours."

"You didn't have anything to do with that, did you?"

She glanced at him sideways and gave a shy smile. "Maybe."

Kevin found his office well organized. In addition to the standard accoutrements he found a local newspaper, the daily from Corpus Christi and Betty Lou's business card with her personal cell number written on the back. He also found a rather extensive list of assignments from the judge. He was just beginning to read through them when Betty Lou appeared in the doorway.

"Do you drink coffee?" she asked.

He looked up, noticing her dress was a little feminine for typical business attire. "Yeah sure. I'll get it if you'll just tell me where it is."

"The break room is on the other end of the building, but I don't mind, just tell me how you like it. I'm getting a cup anyway."

"Sugar, no cream. Here, I have my own cup." He pulled a University of Arkansas Razorbacks cup from his backpack. "I might as well let everyone know. I'll probably get a lot of grief from you Texans anyway."

"Not from me. I'm a Hoosier. Us foreigners have to stick together." She took his cup and flipped her dreadlocks slightly as she exited.

This hair thing is going to drive me crazy, he thought, then concentrated on the list. It was quite a list, over 20 names of people who had not recently reported. At the bottom of the page, handwritten in red ink was a name that caught his attention, Miguel Arredondo. Beside it was a notation, "possibly deceased". Some of the names had listed places of employment, some had home addresses, most of this information had lines drawn through it as if it were no longer valid. Kevin decided to start at the bottom with Miguel. No home address was listed but he worked for Southwestern International Produce, a company with a local listing. Just as Kevin reached for the phone Betty Lou came in with the coffee. "Thanks," he said. "So what's the story on Miguel Arredondo and this produce company?"

All traces of a smile left Betty Lou's face. "He's reported dead, supposedly out in the desert in a produce truck, but the truck or the body haven't been found yet so that's just hearsay, officially. His partner's body was found though, probably a smuggling operation. It's complicated. That's one of the companies that hires a lot of our people so we're hoping this is just a fluke."

"So, he's one of ours?" Kevin asked.

"Yeah, got two years for forgery and possessing stolen property when they busted the chop shop just south of town. Did eight months then parole. We got him on with S. I. P. as a driver. He's never been a problem; makes his appointments, passes his tox screens. I met him once, kind of a jerk but harmless.

"I'm going to spend some time on this one. Probably need to check with the judge first. For now I'll see if I can run down some of these other guys."

Betty Lou raised her coffee cup in a toast. "Good luck with that. I should get back to work. But remember, I'm right next door." She spun gracefully and walked right into the door jamb, dribbling coffee on the carpet. "Oops," she said, looking over her shoulder, her cheeks burning pink.

By the end of the morning Kevin wanted to slam his head into the desk. He hadn't located a single person from the list. It looked like some legwork would be necessary, with the judge's approval of course.

Carrie found that the creased tan deputy's uniform fit her personality as well as it fit her slender body. It became her persona. She'd expected some harassment from the other deputies, but Sheriff Carranza's permission to carry her personal .45 caliber Colt SAA revolver previously owned by famous Texas Ranger Bobby Paul Doherty granted her a modicum of respect. The only kidding she got was about the tired old cruiser she'd been assigned. "It's not like I can chase down speeders in my Honda Civic," she quipped. That brought a laugh from the deputies hovering around the coffee pot.

"Boys, it's just a woman. I'm pretty sure most of you have seen one before." as Sheriff Carranza wandered into the break room. "Let's go round up some outlaws. Carrie, I'm afraid you're going to have to wait. We can't cut you loose without some training." The deputies grumbled but slunk away to their assignments. Carranza motioned Carrie into his office. "I know you have a certain special interest in this case, so I wanted you to know before you left for Corpus tomorrow, they located the missing produce truck.. A Border Patrol helicopter spotted it on the western edge of Jim Wells County. They have a unit on the way to check it out. You need to go home and pack but give me a call later and I'll fill you in on the details."

Carrie stood frozen. The Academy couldn't have happened at a worse time, but it wasn't like she had any choice. "I'll stay in touch. Please, Ross, don't let them screw this up. I know I didn't tell you, but the kid they found in the desert was like a brother to me."

"Don't worry, I've got this. I already knew you had a connection to this case. You forget I've been doing this a while. I tell you what, I'll manage this one personally."

Carrie smiled. Had she been a different person she might have given him a hug.

As it turns out Judge Kendrick was a little freer with the money than expected. She gave the go-ahead to Kevin's plan, even offered to pay him mileage. The large steel building out on County Road 202 seemed closed but it was hard to miss with a couple of company trucks in the yard. Set back behind the main building several travel trailers were permanently installed. One had a cherry red '72 Corvette parked in front. Kevin took the driveway up past that compound to the large limestone ranch house with Southwestern arches. He slapped the cast-iron knocker against the heavy oak door and waited. He knocked again. Finally he heard the deadbolt turn. Just inside the darkness stood a woman with tawny cinnamon skin. Gloss black ringlets burst from her scalp and cascaded down her shoulders. Though her vermilion lips lacked a smile they parted with the slightest anticipation as her coal eyes burned through him. He knew he needed to speak but words wouldn't form. She retreated into the darkness as if to avoid the light, her diaphanous gown dusting across the Saltillo tile. "Can I help you?" she asked. She held a paper towel against her wrist, blood just beginning to seep through.

"Are you okay?" he asked. She tilted her head slightly as if she didn't understand the question. "I'm with the 156th District Court. I'm looking for Miguel Arredondo. You know where I can locate him?"

"He works here, well, for my dad. He's living behind the shop. He borrowed one of our trucks to move his furniture from the Valley so he can get a place in town. I expected him back by now but you never know with him." She fostered the hint of a wistful smile. "Do you have a card or something? I can tell him you stopped by."

Kevin offered his card. "And you are..."

"I'm Lydia. My dad and I own this company. We hire a lot of your guys but I haven't seen you before."

"I'm new, just started today. Trying to get out and meet some of the folks."

Lydia looked at the card. "Come on in, Kevin. We have several of your guys working here. Good people. I'll fill you in."

Carrie entered the house and found her mother puttering around the kitchen. Though she needed to pack for the Academy there were a couple of things she needed to speak with Mom about, lie to Mom about actually, to avoid complications later.

"Hi, honey," Lois said."I'm glad I have a chance to talk to you. I don't mean to pry or anything, but what's the deal with Kevin? Are you guys dating, friends, what?" This was the opening Carrie was looking for.

"It's confidential," Carrie whispered, "but I need to tell you and I need you to keep it a secret. We're working together. We were recruited by the Feds, well, Kevin was but then I got involved because I'm from this area. I can't say what branch but it's international. There's a concern that several regional law enforcement agencies have been infiltrated by the cartels. It's our assignment to find out how deep it goes and report back. We're not to do anything but gather information so we should be safe as long as we're not discovered. We won't be making contact with each other except for here. This is our base but you can't tell anyone that we even know each other. Okay?"

Lois had stopped moving, stopped breathing, her jaw had gone slack. "I don't know. It's scary. Why you?"

"Like I said, I know the area. I wasn't even going to do it but then the thing with Carlos, well, I kind of had to. Don't worry, Mom. I know my way around here. I don't want you to be involved but if you hear anything that seems odd please let me know. I'm not saying go looking for trouble, just keep your ears open. Okay?"

Lois grabbed Carrie by the wrists, paused a moment then yanked her into her arms. Tears were beginning to form in the corner of her eyes. "This is such a bad idea. Can you get out of it?"

"I don't know, Mom, but I wouldn't if I could. This is important." Carrie had to pull free from her mom's embrace, afraid her mom might feel the lie somehow through her skin. "I've got to pack. One other thing, though, that girl Itzpa, the one found in Laredo, the police won't release her dead mother to her. They want to cremate her here. Itzpa is devastated. I want to pay to have the body transported to central Mexico, but I need your help with the money and the paperwork since I won't be here."

"Sure, honey. Whatever you need."

"I need you to handle it. Maria can help. She knows the girl."

Lydia moved like an apparition with Kevin tailing behind. "Have a seat," she said, motioning to one of the wooden chairs near the massive, rough cut oak dining table. She floated over to the kitchen sink, removed the paper towel and rinsed the blood from her wrist. She fashioned a bandage from gauze and tape before pulling the sleeve of her gown down over it. As Kevin's eyes adjusted to the light he noticed the hollowness in Lydia's face. The damp mascara gave her a wilted look. It was plain she'd been crying.

"So let me guess," Kevin said. "You already know the rumor about Miguel and you guys were pretty close." He saw her jaw tighten and when she turned to look at him her eyes flashed her rage.

"I don't know anything," she hissed. "Why don't you tell me if you're so damned smart?"

"I don't have all the facts. That's where I need your help. Like I say, I'm new at this. There's an unconfirmed rumor he was involved in a smuggling operation that went south. It's just a rumor. Why don't you tell me what you know?"

"I already told you, he went to the Valley to pick up his furniture. That's all I know. He should have been back yesterday. I haven't heard from him. I'm not surprised. He's kind of a free spirit."

"And that pisses you off?"

"What?"

"That he's a free spirit."

"Why should I care what he does? He works for my dad. I'm not allowed to consort with my dad's workers if you know what I mean."

"Yeah, sure, okay, and you do everything Daddy tells you, right? Sorry, Lydia, but you don't strike me as the type."

Lydia threw her head back causing her hair to whip away from her face. "You have no idea what you're talking about and no right to come in here and make accusations. You need to leave." She stomped toward the door and yanked it open pulling herself up to her full height. Kevin couldn't help but gasp at her beauty.

He had no choice but to exit. "I'll let you know if I hear anything."

"Don't waste your time," she said and slammed the door behind him.

Kevin walked back to his truck contemplating how he'd allowed the meeting to degenerate. He got in, took a deep breath and just before turning the key Lydia burst through the door waving her bandaged arm. "Wait," she yelled. Kevin stepped out of the truck. By the time she reached him she was breathless.

"I'm sorry. I didn't mean to be so rude. I'm just scared. Everything you said was right, I mean about me and Miguel being together, and about something being wrong. I don't know what Miguel was doing but my dad got a call that he was broken down in the desert. I don't know where and I don't think Daddy does either, but he left yesterday to search. He told me not to talk to anybody about it. So there you go, really, that's all I know. Please, please, please, if you hear anything call me."

"Sure, no problem. I hope everything is okay, but I'll let you know one way or the other as soon as I know."

"Thank you so much. I'm sorry I was mean." She leaned in and kissed him on the cheek then turned and ran back towards the house as if the sun would do her damage.

Carrie decided to take her Honda to Corpus Christi. Though Ross had the county paying for her hotel room she wouldn't take the cruiser. She liked the freedom of having her own car. The anxiety of being alone in her father's town, not to mention the stress from everything happening so fast turned her inside out. She needed to get her world back in sync, to at least balance her father's omnipresence in her own special way.

She rolled into town hours before check-in time. What's a girl to do? Shop. She drove into a semi-residential area and wandered aimlessly until she found the corner drugstore, one of those places with an abundance of makeup and hair accessories. It was all part of the plan. Carrie perused the aisle of hair barrettes, literally hundreds. She needed one with a strong spring-loaded clasp. One she could get a grip on. A round one caught her eye, a large oval with several dozen rhinestones, garish but suitable. She removed it from the cardboard backing and laid it across her palm. The rhinestone body filled her hand and the spring-loaded clasp tightly resisted closing. Rolling her fist around it she noted the bar didn't touch her skin. The clasp protruded a good 2 inches; chromed spring steel. She brought a finger to her throat and pressed against her jugular vein, gauging. It would easily penetrate. It wasn't her blood she needed to spill though. In fact, she couldn't afford to spare a drop. With more time to kill, Carrie drove to the beach. She spread a towel on the sand. With a file and a whetstone in her lap, she went about the task of turning the trinket into a razor sharp weapon.

FREE TIME

Carrie threw her overnight bag on the desk and splayed out on the super king-size bed. It was just for one night but Ross had set her up at the Hyatt in Corpus. He'd become almost a father figure to her, a real father not the douche bag that had donated his sperm to her existence. In one of the most elegant rooms she'd experienced away from home, she reveled in the isolation. Hotels gave her a sense of freedom, one that electrified and intensified her senses. She stripped off her jeans and T-shirt and rolled naked on top of the comforter, her skin soaking up the elegance. Tomorrow she had to move into the barracks at the police academy but tonight, tonight she was going to live it up. She laid out a short black mini dress, black panties and a black underwire bra from her bag, then picked up her scented soap and shampoo and headed for the shower. This is going to be special.

Take your time, she thought as she adjusted the water. She raised the showerhead as high as it would go, stepping under as if it were a rain cloud. Once her long auburn hair was saturated, the water cascaded down her thin tan shoulders wetting her body to her toes. She shut down the showerhead and thoroughly lathered her body with fragrant lavender gel. She squirted a generous amount of body lotion onto the handle of her favorite hairbrush and set it aside. As she slid the fingers of one hand up the inside of her thigh she teased at her pubic hair with the index finger of the other. Take your time. Cupping the orifice protectively she allowed her long middle finger to massage the rim of her anus. It was all she could do to hold off on the penetration. Reaching behind her to continue massaging her ass with her left hand, she used the right fingers to begin the same rhythmic rotation on her soapy clit. Her chest was beginning to heave. The air was permeated with the scent of lavender. Turning sideways and spreading her feet for balance she pressed her knot hard nipples against the cool tile wall. Take your time. It was all she could do not to rush things. She slowed the rotation, occasionally having to pinch her clit between two fingers to slow the buildup of energy. She felt a warm trickle on her breast and realized she was drooling down the wall. She slid down on her knees, the grout lines in the tile causing electrostatic impulses in her nipples. Her body was aflame with desire. She picked up the hairbrush and placed the perfectly phallic handle's tip at her anal opening. She thrust two fingers into her vagina as she slowly rotated the handle into her ass. She gasped. Slowing the process now was out of the question. With two slick fingers inside her she pounded her clit with the palm of her hand while squatting lower forcing the hilt of the brush into her anus. She was full and ready to burst. She stopped for a breath then she reached back and twisted the brush while the knuckles of her other hand mashed the engorged clit between her palm and the fingers inside her. Both hands trembled as a low moan began to echo from the tile walls. Her breathing became almost a bark. She sat on the brush, burying it in her ass as she pinched a nipple violently with her fingers. As the moan grew more guttural, the trembling throughout her body became a spasm of ecstasy. Torrential waves of orgasm engulfed her until she thought she would lose consciousness.

"You can be fucking hot when you need to be," she told herself as she admired the runway model in the mirror. She made some final adjustments to the rhinestone barrette holding the pile of wavy auburn curls in place, picked up a tiny black handbag and locked the door behind her. She'd advanced beyond needing any type of toolkit. Still glowing from her shower, she took a stool at the hotel bar and crossed her long legs above the knee, allowing observers to enjoy an unobstructed view of her well muscled hip. She ordered a margarita and checked the clock, 6:30 PM. She was fine drinking alone but had only a $20 bill in her handbag. She looked down at her smooth legs and stiletto heels deciding to give it 30 minutes. It took less than five. He was there before she'd even taken the first sip of her drink, not a gorgeous man, but tall. Leading with his chest he had an air of authority and arrogance. Typical, she thought. She didn't immediately notice his status. He had no wedding ring, but when he raised his hand to signal the bartender she saw the tan line. When he sat on the stool beside her she turned away from him, giving him the benefit of the doubt.

"I'm Lance Harrison," he said. "Can I buy you a drink?" She held up her untouched Margarita and gave him the blank stare she'd perfected. This guy was fake right down to his name. He wasn't getting many chances.

"I'm good," she said.

"I'll bet you are." He displayed several thousand dollars worth of dental work.

She pinched the bridge of her nose between her fingers leaning forward, letting the few loose ringlets of hair obscure her face. You're making this too easy, she thought. "Actually, I'm a fan of single malt scotch. I have no idea why I ordered this."

"I can fix that," he said and called the bartender over. "So what brings you to town?"

"How do you know I don't live here?"

"Well, let's see, it's a hotel?" She sensed a little attitude in his feistiness.

"Convention."

"At this hotel?" He asked, looking around.

"Nope." She gave him the blank stare again. Seriously, this is your last chance, buddy.

He was bound and determined to press on. "So what do you do?"

"Serial killer."

Lance, or whoever he was, broke into a wide grin. "Right. I can see that. Those are some killer legs."

That does it. "What about you? You married?"

Lance paused when he noticed her looking at his left hand. "Actually, yeah, but we have an arrangement."

"What a coincidence. That's what the last guy said."

When Kevin returned to the office he checked in on Betty Lou and noticed she was sporting a Hoosiers coffee mug. She didn't see him because she was writing a note with one hand and had the phone cradled on her other shoulder. As she reached into a lower drawer the phone took a tumble. Though she retrieved it just before it hit the floor, she bonked her head on the desk dislodging a few strands of hair. With the receiver in one hand, a pen in the other and hair in her face she finally noticed him. She deflated by trying to blow the strands of hair away through pursed lips. It didn't work. "Let me call you back," she spoke into the phone. She put her elbows on the table." What?" She asked, defeated.

"Nothing," he said. "I just wanted you to know I got back. Any messages?"

"As a matter of fact, yes. But I'm not your secretary so you have to bribe me. Get me a cup of coffee while I pull it together and I'll share all the world's secrets."

"In this?" He asked, holding up the Hoosier cup with two fingers.

"True test of friendship."

"The things I have to do around here."

"You haven't even been here," she said, using both hands to push her hair back. "Just do it."

He grabbed his cup from his office and filled them both. Returning, he pulled up a chair. "So what's up"

"Sheriff called. They found that truck, the one with Miguel's body in it. They're towing the truck but flying the body. Don't ask me why. He's got to be a little stinky by now."

"Crap. I was afraid of that. Lydia will be devastated."

"Lydia?"

"Long story."

"I bought a huge frozen lasagna. No way I could eat it all. Why don't you come over for dinner and you can tell me the whole story." She took a sip of coffee. "Bring a salad."

"A salad?"

"Yeah, DJ, a salad. You can buy it at the store. I'll text you the address."

"I know where the store is."

"No, goofball. My address, I'll text you my address."

It's all just some kind of sick game to these idiots, Carrie thought. She could play but she had to be careful, being in unfamiliar territory. She took a long slow look at Lance like a cold glass of water on a hot day, making sure he saw her do it. "I can be a lot of fun," she said. "But I'm not a cheap date."

Lance had already examined her carefully. He knew what he wanted. "How much are we talking about?"

Carrie feigned a look of shock. "Oh my God! You think I'm a hooker. I have never, ever in my life sold my body." She grabbed her handbag off the bar and stomped away. She moved quickly enough that he couldn't follow her without running. He wasn't the kind of guy who would stoop to that.

She exited the hotel and walked to the convenience store next door. As she was paying for her pack of Marlboros he caught up with her. "I'm sorry," he said. I didn't mean... I mean... Let me make it up to you."

She tilted her head back and, without smiling, looked down her nose at him. "I haven't eaten. I've always wanted to try the Executive Surf Club but I'm a bit overdressed."

Lance brightened. "I love that place. I don't get to Corpus very often but when I do it's one of my stops. I'd be happy to take you there."

She dropped the cigarettes in her purse. "Okay, fine. I'll meet you in the parking lot in 30 minutes."

"You're the boss. I'm in a silver BMW SUV. You can't miss it. It has Louisiana plates." Lance walked over and put his card in the ATM. Carrie took that opportunity to slip out the door. Over her shoulder she said, "You should empty that thing. It's going to be a big night."

Carrie slipped on a tight pair of jeans and a billowy silk shirt. She put on a straw cowboy hat to hide her face from the security cameras. When Lance finally found her she was at the far corner of the parking lot smoking a cigarette. She stomped it out, kicked it under his vehicle and hopped in. "Let's rock 'n roll," she said.

At the restaurant they ate, drank and snuggled in a secluded corner. When he tried to fondle her in any way she swatted his hands, but she leaned her elbow on his shoulder while she whispered in his ear. Meanwhile her other hand grazed along the inside of his thigh. "I get the feeling that you like to be in control," Lance said.

She slipped her hand up as high as she could without hitting home and gave a firm squeeze. "You are a very observant man," she said. "We should find somewhere more private."

"Back to the hotel?"

"Oh no, take me somewhere nasty. Some slutty place on the beach where we can open the windows and hear the surf, somewhere that smells like other people's sweat."

Lance's boner was about to bust his zipper. He paid the tab in cash, as she knew he would, and hustled her out to his SUV.

Lance had the perfect place in mind, a little drive from town but with all the requirements. He'd never been there but had driven by numerous times. Electricity between them kept them silent but occasionally Carrie would reach over and massage his crotch to make sure he hadn't lost interest. She let him put his hand on her knee, but for now that's as far as it went.

Outside of the city they reached the Ocean Breeze Cottages, the exact type of no-tell motel Carrie was hoping for. She waited in the car watching the foam on the breakers dance across the waves in the moonlight like tiny bolts of horizontal lightning. The salt air filled her nostrils and she relaxed, laying her hat on the dash. Lance returned and drove to the end of the lane, parking beside the last cottage. "I asked for the best view," he said. Carrie wrapped her arms around his neck and pressed her body close to his, allowing him to slip his leg between her thighs. He kissed her wet and deep. She nibbled his lower lip. While he fumbled with the door key she turned toward the ocean and inhaled deeply. "I've never done anything this crazy," she said. "This is going to be life-changing for me."

The room smelled musty; a darkness in the odor, a swamp-like dampness. The window wouldn't open so she turned the AC down as cold as it would go. "Why don't you get comfortable," she said. "I'm going to slip into the bathroom to do my girly stuff. I'll be right back." Lance was already taking off his shoes.

When she returned she found him on top of the covers in nothing but his boxer shorts. She still had on her black bra and panties. "I want to see you naked," she said as she unclasped the front of her bra and pulled it back like curtains revealing her dainty, perfectly formed, freckled breasts. He crawled out of his boxers without ever leaving the bed. She stood next to him. "Sit up," she demanded. He obliged. "Now, take off my panties." Again he obliged. She put a foot on the mattress next to him and pulled his face into her, guiding his lips to her clit. She straddled him and pushed him back on the bed. Knees beside his shoulders, she grabbed the headboard and stroked his face with her crotch. "You're pretty good at this," she said, "but don't finish me. I have a special treat for you." She reached behind her and grabbed his throbbing member. It was long and thin and for a moment made her think of her pink hairbrush. She gasped as he grabbed her ass and thrust his face deeper into her. No, she thought, keep your head about you. She rolled off him, laid beside him and gripped his bare chest. She put her lips against his ear. "You can come inside me if you have a condom." He rolled over and grabbed the wallet out of his pants. "No problem," he said and slipped one on. She began at his ear lobe and worked slowly down, kissing and licking, biting his nipple, kissing his naval all the while massaging his balls.

He tried guiding her mouth to his erection, but she kept avoiding it. "No, I can't," she said.

"But I did you."

"I know. You are really good too, but I can't. I'm sorry. I can make it good for you though." She put her hands on his chest and lowered herself slowly onto him then took his hands and arched backwards, placing his fingers on her nipples. "Pinch as hard as you want to.

I like it. I like the pain. It makes me hot. If you're a good boy you can fuck me in the ass. Not right now though, let's see how much of this you can take." She leaned back with her hands on his thighs and slowly stroked him with every dark wet muscle inside. He began to moan and she felt his hands trembling against her breasts. He was beginning to sweat. She stroked harder. She removed the rhinestone barrette and let her hair fall across her face. She leaned forward, dangling her auburn curls across his shoulders. Falling forward against his sweaty chest she squirmed, slipping against him, grinding her clit against his pubic hair. He grabbed her ass and shoved himself deeper inside her. She felt him begin to tremble. She grabbed his chin with one hand and, turning his head sideways, bit his earlobe. She licked the sweat from his throat, then, as the orgasm began to take him, she plunged the barrette into his jugular. He hardly noticed. He continued thrusting into her as his blood sprayed out into the musty mattress. It was hard to tell what ended first, his life or his orgasm. With his soft hot member still inside her she leaned her blood-soaked body back, reached down and finished herself. Standing up she saw that the condom had split. She flushed it and wiped down his flaccid member with a sterile towelette from her purse.

  That went well, she thought. What a mess. She found her barrette and cut open his nut sack, removing his balls and placing them in his mouth. She picked up her bra and underwear and took a hot shower. While showering she scrubbed the underwear thoroughly with the complimentary shampoo. After flushing the broken condom, it was difficult but not impossible to dress Lance in the wet panties. She shimmied into her clothes but left her hair down. Searching through his wallet, she found more than she'd expected. She'd expected the money, over $600. She'd expected that his real name wasn't Lance. It was Bernard. Figures. What she didn't expect was the badge. He was a federal agent, ATF. Shit! I have seriously fucked up, she thought. Oh well, he was still a dick. Serves him right. I'll just have to be very careful. She took the wallet and keys and left the mess, hanging the "do not disturb" sign on the door. She drove his SUV back toward town and found a rough neighborhood where she parked at the curb, leaving the keys in the ignition and the passenger side window down. She walked twelve blocks to the seawall, turned on her cell phone and called a cab. She had the cabbie drop her four blocks from her hotel and paid him with the agent's cash.

There was a point earlier in his life when Kevin "DJ" Cash thought he had women figured out. Thanks to Carrie, that point had long passed. He didn't know what to expect from Betty Lou. Was she just being friendly, making him feel comfortable in a new town? Was she lonely? Did she see him as competition, or a friend, or did she want more? The one thing he knew; he was comfortable around her. She made him laugh.

He drove through the large apartment complex until he found the right building where he parked, deciding to hoof it from there. Being mostly a meat and potatoes guy he had no idea how many kinds of salad were available. He'd made a random choice. The beverage had taken a little more thought; beer or wine, cheap or expensive, domestic or import. He bought a six pack of Fat Tire, a tasty but inexpensive domestic beer, though personally he would've preferred an upscale IPA. He held to the popular, though possibly misguided, belief that women preferred beverages without bold tastes. With the salad in one hand and the beer in the other he knocked on the door with his forehead.

"Damn, DJ, what's with the police knock? Trying to make me flush my stash?" Betty Lou flung the door open and stepped over to turn down the thumping music. "Just set that on the counter. I'll handle it from there." She saw the six-pack. "I didn't say BYOB. I had that covered."

Kevin set the salad on the counter and slipped the six-pack in the fridge right next to a six-pack of Torpedo, one of his favorite ales. He couldn't help but smile. "Is that The Charmers?"

"Yeah, I love ska. It makes you have to dance, but being a DJ you'd know that." Betty Lou had left all her office inhibitions at work. She wore blue jean cutoffs and a white tank top she'd pulled over her bathing suit. Each curly strand of her blond hair had made its own plan. "Grab me a beer will you? One of the good ones not the stuff you brought."

"Can I have one of yours?" Kevin asked.

"If you think you can handle it. It's pretty intense." She smiled and danced toward the patio door. She wasn't svelte or classically beautiful. She had one of those curvaceous muscular bodies one would see in a Sir Mixalot video. "We've got about 30 minutes before the lasagna is ready. How about we hit the pool?"

"I don't have a bathing suit."

"I have something you can use, I'm sure." She went into the bedroom and came back with a pair of board shorts roughly his size.

"Put these on. I'll find some plastic cups for our beer."

The pool was a few steps from her patio. Minutes later they were neck deep in the cool chlorinated water. "So, DJ, you have this long story to tell me, about the mysterious Lydia."

"Well I don't know how much Lydia has to do with it but I'm concerned about the Southwestern International Produce company. There are some indications that they're not what they seem. It could be just a couple of the employees but I'm afraid it may go deeper."

"That would suck," Betty Lou said." We have almost a dozen probationers and parolees working there."

"I'm not going to blow any whistles right now, but I'm going to do some investigating, see what I can come up with."

Betty Lou lost her flirtatiousness. "That's not our job. If you have evidence, you have to turn it over to the cops."

"That's the problem. I don't have any solid evidence, but I've got enough suspicion that I need to dig a little deeper."

"Don't take any chances, okay? Be careful."

"Don't worry, I'm a big boy I can manage it."

"Big boy, huh? We'll see about that." She dove under the water. Thousands of tiny bubbles escaped from her mass of hair. While he tried to figure out what she meant, they hung by their elbows on the edge of the pool sipping their beer from red Solo cups.

STILL LIFE WITH CACTUS

Though the heavy air baked the dirt, Kevin saw an occasional anemic dust devil spring from the surface of the vacant parking lot below. From inside the main ranch house, he observed a panoramic view of Julio's deserted trucking operation. The trucks that weren't in the shop were on deliveries, of what products Kevin could only surmise. The silence in the house, enhanced by guilt, distracted him.

Lydia slumbered in her bedroom exhausted by the trauma of knowing about Miguel's demise and her unusual reaction. The root of Kevin's guilt lie with her. He'd hoped to break the news to Julio and Lydia simultaneously but only the daughter was home. She'd been dressed in a nightie similar to the one she wore at their first encounter.

Lydia clutched his shoulder. "Tell me! You know something or you wouldn't be here."

"I talked to the Sheriff. They found the truck out in the desert southwest of Alice. Miguel's body was in the cargo box.

Lydia's jaw tensed. "What? How?"

"Stabbed, with a machete."

"Those bitches!" She screamed and began hammering Kevin's chest with her dainty fists. "I told that fucker. 'Stay away from those hoes!' I should have…." She fell into Kevin's arms wailing, "Why? Why? That motherfucker!" She broke free and grabbed a crystal table lamp. Swinging it like a major-league All-Star she smashed it against the stone fireplace, sending high velocity shards of glass ricocheting back into her face and body. The scant negligee did little to prevent injury. When she turned toward him she looked like a bombing victim. She collapsed to her knees, doing even more damage to her shins and feet. Kevin ran to her. Maybe he should've left. Maybe he should have called someone. He didn't.

He bent over her and wrapped his arms around her shoulders from behind. She resisted momentarily then melted into him, moaning even louder. "I'm so sorry," he said, feeling helpless but oddly enjoying the warmth of her body against his chest. "Go ahead, cry it out."

She pulled him tighter around her as her wails became sobs,

became sniffles. Little trickles of blood ran down her arms and face. One of her breasts left a sticky red patch on her negligee. Her legs made little blood puddles on the terrazzo.

"We need to get you patched up, stop this bleeding. Do you have a first aid kit?"

A look of confusion came over her then she noticed the blood and jumped up. "Shit! Fuck! Dad is going to kill me!" She started to run before realizing she was barefoot in a room littered with shards.

"I'll carry you," Kevin volunteered. "Show me."

She jumped into his arms. "Down the hall." She showed him into the bathroom. The sorrow had evaporated leaving a manic panic. She ripped off her gown before he had a chance to even turn away. "Medicine kit's on the top shelf of that closet." She pointed across the room and stepped into the shower. Kevin found the kit and stood stunned, staring at the wall, not knowing whether to go or stay.

After a brief rinse she toweled off. Though the towel was speckled red, most of the bleeding had subsided. A couple of places on her shins still oozed. "Can you bandage me up?" She asked and sat on the toilet lid. He began with the worst places on her legs. By the time he made it to the puncture on her breast she had leaned back and closed her eyes. The injury, though deep, covered little surface area. He found a small round Band-Aid to cover it. When he applied the antibiotic she shivered back to consciousness and smiled at his efforts. He placed the bandage and pressed it on with a fingertip. He lingered. She let him, then she took his finger and put it to her lips. "Thank you," she said and briefly took it into her mouth. "I'm cold."

Kevin found a beach towel in the cabinet and wrapped it around her shoulders.

"You're so good to me," she said. "I bet you're a really sweet guy."

Kevin shrugged.

Her gaze drifted down the hall toward the living room. "I can't deal with that mess right now. Can you just hang out for a while?"

"What about Julio?"

"What about him?"

"Wouldn't it be kind of weird if I was just hanging out when he got home?"

"He won't be home anytime soon. Please DJ?"

Kevin told himself he was concerned about her mental state after seeing her drastic mood shifts. Other parts of his psyche had other reasons, then there was the finger in the mouth thing, the warm dampness of her tongue, the fullness of her lips. He stayed. She took his hand and led him to the bedroom.

"Don't look. I'm going to change," she said, strange considering he'd just observed her naked from virtually every angle. He turned toward the wall. When she told him it was okay to turn around she was lying on the bed in another negligee, black this time with a red sash and collar. It appeared to be silk and wasn't see-through. She patted the unmade bed, "have a seat."

Kevin raised his eyebrows.

"What? I just want you to rub my back. I'm a little stressed out." She reached in the drawer of her nightstand and took a blue pill out of a prescription bottle, swallowing it without any water.

"I could've brought you something to drink," Kevin offered.

Lydia smiled seductively. "It's okay. I'm a good swallower." She curled around him as he sat on the side of the bed rubbing her back with his right hand while his left forearm hid his erection. Within minutes she was snoozing, her soft snore almost a purr.

He went downstairs and did his best to clean up the blood and broken glass. Now here he was watching the dust devils dance, trying to decide if he should leave or wait on Julio.

"I left," he told Betty Lou. It was just after dark and the pool lights illuminated the clear chlorinated water. He kicked back in the vinyl lounge chair working on his second cup of beer while he watched Betty Lou bouncing around flipping burgers in rhythm to The Paragons.

"Fucking Wuss! You should have banged her. Sounds like she was rubbing your face in it."

"That would have been taking advantage."

"And?"

"It just didn't seem right."

"It wasn't, but so fucking what? You're a guy. I'd have done it if I were you."

"You'd take advantage of someone who's incapacitated?"

Betty Lou leaned low over the grill emphasizing her ample posterior. "Have a couple more beers and find out."

It amazed Kevin how much more coordinated Betty Lou seemed when she had a little buzz on. She swatted her butt with a spatula. "Couple more and I'm going to take your keys anyway, for your own good." She danced over, took his cup, drank the last sip and licked her lips. "Looks like you're ready for a refill. Don't run off. I'll be right back."

Kevin stretched out with his hands behind his head. With Carrie at the Academy there was no reason to rush home. He figured he'd see how this played out. He wasn't sure about this new side of Betty Lou but ever since he told her about Lydia she'd taken on a different attitude. She strutted and danced in a most entertaining way, plus she was feeding him, a good sign in anybody's book.

Kevin arrived early and got his own coffee. Passing Betty Lou's office he noticed the door ajar. It didn't mean she was there. They needed to talk but he still had to sort out the issues; coworker, check; last night, bad plan. He glided by but her perfume floated in the air. Stopping and almost touching the knob, he heard the phone and waited; two rings, three, she answered. He began breathing and slunk to his office next door. He heard her voice, "You'll need to discuss that with Mr. Cash, she's his client. Let me see if he's in. Hold please."

Kevin scooted quickly into his chair and yanked out some random papers. A tap on the door, he looked up to see Betty, her blond dreads still unkempt, leaning against the door jamb. "Mornin' DJ. Your little squeeze screwed up again. Daddy's on the phone. He don't sound happy." She looked at his cup and the corners of her mouth drooped. "Are you okay? Last night, I mean, that doesn't have to mean anything."

Kevin grabbed his coffee and stood. "Let's talk later. How about lunch? I'll go fetch us another cup. Tell Julio I'll call him back."

Betty Lou handed him her empty Hoosiers mug. "Less cream this time, okay?" Her bounce returned. She pirouetted on the balls of her feet then grazed the edge of a file cabinet as she stepped back to her office.

As Kevin took the journey to the break room his brain spun. Betty Lou knew more about him than he was comfortable with and she wasn't someone he found it easy to tell a lie. Best to tone it down, keep his eye on the prize. He rinsed the cups and refilled them, one heavy with cream, one black with a touch of sugar. He flashed on the warmth of Betty Lou's full breasts against his chest, the lavender scented mass of blond tangles covering his face while they ground to the throbbing bass of the Skatelites. Even her sweat smelled clean, unlike the tart sheen and desperate violent lust of Lydia. Betty Lou was a vacation at the beach he decided, not something that should be incorporated into his work. He felt a thickness in his groin as his body's desire defied his brain's intentions.

In Betty Lou's office he took a seat to hide his enlargement and sat the creamed coffee on the desk. When she looked up they simultaneously realized he had switched their coffee cups.

Betty Lou shook her head causing her blond dreads to dance "Okay, Dude, after last night it's a little late to be concerned about catching your cooties but I'm not sure I can drink from the Razorbacks cup. My head might explode." Kevin's ears and cheeks glowed red "I'm.... Damn, sorry, I..... I guess I wasn't paying attention."

Betty came from behind the desk. Closing the door, she turned and massaged his shoulders. As she bent down to kiss his receding hairline, her perfumed locks cascaded around his ears "Don't sweat it okay?" She sighed. "None of it. You're right, we need to keep it simple. I think Lydia's trouble but you're a big boy. Maybe you have an agenda, I don't know and frankly, as long as your safe, I don't give a fuck." She sat back down. "So where are we with S I P?"

"The story I'm getting from Julio is that Miguel borrowed the truck to move some furniture. He swears he didn't know the Carlos kid. On the other hand, they found a woman's body in the desert that jives with the story from the girl they picked up at the border."

Betty Lou scribbled some notes. "What about Lydia?"

"Either she doesn't know anything or she's a real good liar."

"Hmm," Betty Lou grunted, leaning back in her chair. "Wasn't she hooked up with Miguel?"

"Nothing serious, according to her."

Betty Lou just stared, refusing to unlock her eyes from Kevin's. He squirmed and broke the gaze. "Okay, well, she did seem really desperate to know his whereabouts, I mean, before, you know, but that could just be her personality."

"What? Desperate?" She continued to stare but a corner of her lip was trying to break into that smile.

"Okay, I see where you're going with this. Maybe you're right. I've got to call Julio. I have a client in a few minutes. Maybe I'll know more by lunch." As he stood to leave she winked and puckered her lips. "Nice butt," she said.

"Careful," Kevin said. "That's sexual harassment."

"Prove it!"

Seated at his desk, Kevin picked up the phone, started to dial Julio then cradled the receiver, rubbed his forehead and picked the phone back up. Julio answered on the second ring.

"What the hell did you tell my daughter?" Came out first, no pleasantries.

"Nothing that wasn't common knowledge."

She went off the chain. She took Miguel's car and rammed it into the back of the funeral home at 2 AM. She's sitting in the Bee County jail right now."

"I didn't see that coming. When she asked me for the story, I told her she should talk to the sheriff. Call him."

"Can you get her out?"

"I'm sorry. I'm just a probation officer, Miguel's, not hers. Has she been charged? You probably need an attorney."

"Shit! Is there anything you can do? I need her home."

"Probably not, but I'll talk to the judge. I'm federal and that's probably a state charge. I can't make any promises but I'll make some calls."

Julio paused a long minute. "Well, you sure you didn't say anything?"

"About what?"

"I don't know. It doesn't make sense that she would do that." His tone lightened. "Anything you can do to help will be appreciated if you know what I mean."

"Let's talk later. I'll stop by."

Kevin ended the call and reared back in his chair. This was his inroad. Julio's daughter was his weak spot. If he could work some magic here he could gain trust. His intercom buzzed. "Your 10 o'clock is here."

Raul Garza only stood about 5'8" but he had to turn sideways to get his shoulders through the door. There wasn't an ounce of fat on his 260 pounds. Every exposed part of his body was tattooed with spider webs and barbed wire except his face which only sported three blue teardrops beneath the right eye. The guy obviously lived on steroids and protein, passing time pumping iron. "Where's Betty?" He said. "I usually see Betty."

Kevin motioned to a chair. "You got transferred." He stood to shake Raul's hand. "I'm DJ Cash."

"Fuck you, I want Betty." Raul crossed his arms in an ominous Mr. Clean pose.

Kevin stood to his full six-foot height. "Fuck you back, asshole. It's not your call. Now sit the fuck down."

Raul, stunned, unfolded his arms and sat.

"Now," Kevin said. "I see here where you passed most of your piss tests but I don't see where you were tested for steroids. I can add that or you can work with me. Comprende, bitch? Close the door!"

Raul obliged, still shaken from the confrontation, then sat back down. Kevin pulled a chrome 9MM from his drawer and set it on the desk. He unplugged the cord from the intercom. "Here's how it's going to work. I drive a piece of shit and live in a fucking efficiency while you punk-ass motherfuckers tool around in your black Escalades. That ain't right, not when I can pull your plug with one phone call. The deal is, I don't give a flying rat's ass about this job but it puts me in a certain place. We can have a conversation about that or you can walk your ass down the street to Medco and pee in a cup. Your call."

Raul had regained his composure. He rolled his head on the thick neck, popped his knuckles and folded his hands in his lap. "I'm listening."

"I know S I P hauls an occasional load of tomatoes. I also know that ain't all you move. I know this because I've already had this little talk with your boss man. I'm pretty sure there's some other shit happening that he don't know about. I'm about to find that out whether you tell me or not. So the question is, do you want to be the first kid on your block to be my buddy or does my information go to someone else?"

"What do you want?"

"First, where was Miguel taking that load of hookers?"

"New Orleans, I think."

"You think?"

"Yeah, I'm not sure. He took that job on his own. Julio wouldn't deal in women."

"Why not?"

"Just his code."

"So he didn't have any idea?"

"Not sure, but I doubt it."

"What about Lydia?"

Raul's eyes sparkled. "Miguel's girl, but Daddy didn't know. Used to be she played around, sneaky like, with all of us. I guess Miguel had something she liked."

"Julio okay with that?"

"Fuck no! He'd a killed Miguel if he knew. He thinks that little slut is the Virgin Mary, some angel or something. He's clueless. She's a meat hook."

Kevin felt his blood heating. "You know that how?"

"Talk mostly. I've never touched that. First, I like my job. Second, she's a twisted little bitch from what I hear, not kinky so much as a mindfucker. I don't need that shit."

"So you don't really know about Lydia? Just guy talk?" Kevin pulled a Ziploc bag of pale yellow liquid from his desk. "You clean right now?"

"For what?"

"Everything."

"Well, yeah, I've passed so far."

"Steroids? I'm adding it to the list."

"But Dude! I helped you. We're on the same team."

Kevin slid the baggy across the table. "Now I'm helping you. You know how this works right? In your crotch 'til it warms up, then pinch the corner in the stall."

"Cool, yeah. Why not just do like before?"

Street cred. You'll need it. Go pee, sign out, you're done. I'll catch you at S I P. Behave yourself but keep me in the loop. I need to know what Julio knows."

Sign in at Corpus Christi Police Academy coincided with dawn. Carrie showed early in jeans, motorcycle boots and an oversized T-shirt instead of her uniform. The hotel extravagance behind her, most of what she owned was stashed in the trunk of her Civic. After checking in early she took a desk in the middle of the classroom, her long legs crossed in the aisle. She watched the other cadets enter and judged them. Why not? Most had formed groups or cliques, but there were a few loners, like her. Several of the alpha males gave her a nod or smile. She shut them down with her deadpan. The lack of makeup and high ponytail dampened her allure anyway.

The class fidgeted for half an hour until an overweight uniformed officer sporting a gray handlebar mustache waddled in. He tossed a folder on the podium and ruffled through some papers before looking out over the class. "Good morning, I'm Detective Tolson. We were expecting agent Bernard Harrison from the ATF in New Orleans to open with the section on victim's rights versus alleged perpetrator's rights. He checked into his hotel last night but has since gone off the radar. Maybe he just had a big night. Until he shows up I'll be discussing how to maintain the integrity of a crime scene. At 10 o'clock we'll take a break and meet back on the R.O.P.E.S. course. Hopefully he'll be here this afternoon for his lecture."

Carrie's blood iced up. Knowing she had to be changing shades from pink, to pale, to red, to green like an aluminum Christmas tree, she wondered if anyone had the observational capabilities to finger her. She grabbed her new procedure manual and tried to casually peruse it. The knot in her stomach continued to tighten until she thought her breakfast might come up. She stood and headed for the door. "Officer Tolson? I need a minute, where's the bathroom?"

"Down the hall to the right, near the double doors. Hurry back. We're not going to wait."

"Yes sir." As she passed the front row, a Hispanic bodybuilder in a tight white T-shirt eyeballed her with a pearly white sneer. "Fucking bleeders," he said to his buddy, "need to get back in the kitchen."

Raul left the door open when he vamoosed. Betty Lou entered with the Razorbacks cup full of black coffee. "Trade you back," she said. "By the way you should know that Raul guy is rough trade. I heard you shut him down. Just know he hangs with a dangerous crowd."

"Don't worry. He's my bestest buddy now. He sure misses you though," Kevin said.

"Let him. He always creeped me out. I mean, I come from a family of outlaw wannabes but there's something really dark about that guy."

"I can deal with him. Don't sweat it."

"Anyway, thanks for taking him off my hands."

"Not a problem. I need him to help me figure out what's up out at S I P."

"Just be careful, make sure you're thinking with the right head."

"Get real."

"Bullshit, I see you."

"It's purely professional."

"Sure, okay. So, did you find an apartment?"

"I haven't had time to look, but I need to do something. The commute from Alice is getting tedious."

"There's a vacancy or two at my complex. It's really the only decent complex in town. The units are small but there's a pool, a weight room and tennis courts."

"Small doesn't bother me. I spent five years in a dorm room

and last summer sharing the sleeper of an 18 wheeler. Right now I'm in an efficiency above a garage. Having my own bedroom would be like a castle."

"Use me as a reference. We could be neighbors, with benefits." She plopped down in the chair, still warm from Raul, and put her elbows on the desk. "No strings, seriously. It's a big complex anyway. It would be more like living in the same city."

Bernard Harrison became a statistic, a warning to players and one night stand aficionados. His truck was never located. His body turned up late the next afternoon when the maid couldn't get anyone to answer the door on the third try.

Though Carrie knew the news was coming eventually, it didn't keep her from binding up. Her hair was still wet from showering after the R.O.P.E.S. course when a uniformed officer entered the classroom to make the announcement. Her mind jumped the track… "the victim of foul play…. put himself in a compromising position… gruesome details… due to circumstances the FBI… this class serve and participate in the investigation… with appropriate educational backgrounds…" The words jumbled and tumbled in her head. She felt a drop of liquid slide down the side of her face. Water? Sweat? Tear? Acid? Her hand automatically tried to wipe it away. She observed the trembling hand from outside her body then clasped it in her other hand and forced it back down to her lap. She shivered and glanced around to see if anyone was watching. Someone was.

She watched him with her peripheral vision. Those dark irises, giant pupils, giving him an owl like expression as he watched, never blinking, an intense expression of curiosity to his demeanor. It required measured movement and breathing to control her actions but with the new info about Harrison it was impossible. He was no one to me. She told herself. It was the same guy who made the "bitch" comment earlier. Screw him. He needed to keep his eyes to himself.

The officer at the podium said, "Can we bow our heads and pray for Lieutenant Harrison?" Everyone obliged as he prayed. It gave her a chance to control her breathing, let the tension flow from her neck and shoulders, regain control. When she opened her eyes he was standing at her left shoulder, those charcoal eyes still locked on her face. All her newfound composure evaporated.

"I'm Henrique, you can say Henry. You know something, yes?" he whispered.

"No, I don't, Henrique." She rolled the R in his name and put the appropriate inflection for a native speaker of the Mexican dialect. "Why would you think that?"

"Your reaction when you heard, too personal. Did you know him?"

"No. Just the way he died, it creeps me out. Plus, I'm one of the students with the 'appropriate education' to help with the investigation, but I've never seen a dead body," she lied.

"Maybe you could work for me on it. I lost two brothers to the cartel bullshit. I've seen too many dead bodies."

"What? You think I'll make you lunch while you go investigate? I'm supposed to stay in the kitchen with the other bleeders, right?"

"Kiss my ass, bitch. I'll nab the fucker myself. I thought you had an inside track. My bad." As he spun to walk away she stuck a biker boot between his legs and ripped his left foot from under him.

While he was yanked back facing her he fell backwards. She was on him as he hit the floor, her knee in his crotch and a forearm on his windpipe. "Don't ever call me bitch again?" She hissed through clenched teeth "Comprende, motherfucker?"

His expression changed from surprise to anger and he took a swing at her face. She blocked it with her shoulder while jabbing her free fist into his sternum. She leaned the full weight of her body into the arm across his throat. "I'll kill you if I have to. Are we clear?"

An understanding came over him and his body went limp. Classmates were tugging at her shoulders trying to dislodge her. She stood, forcing the last of the weight into the small soft package under her knee.

Lois and Maria began their trip home from the border in silence. What could be said had been. Though bonded by years under the same roof, the women were experiencing Itzpa's trauma from different perspectives. Maria, having lost her son, heard in her native tongue how he'd done everything possible to ensure the safety of the smuggler's victims. Her God and her heart tried to find the path to forgiveness. Lois, on the other hand, boiled at the thought of the place she called home being held in the evil fist of the cartels. Her sense of justice bordered on vengeance. It pleased her and terrified her to know her only child may be part of the solution. She only wondered how embedded the cartel was in the community. As the two-lane highway slipped by she doubted Carrie had the necessary resolve. Seven years of college hadn't produced a degree.

Maria consciously slowed her breathing as she fixated on the scrub cactus beyond the strands of barbed wire. "She was very brave, that Itzpa, and strong." Her voice was steady. Her eyes never shifted from the scenery.

"More like stubborn and stupid," Lois countered. "If she'd stayed with Carlos they might both be alive today."

Maria wiped her cheek with a finger then transferred the tear to her jeans. "She did what her heart told her. We can't second-guess. To her, Carlos could not be trusted. I am trying to see that."

Lois felt her gut tighten. How could this woman be so, so damn… at peace! It's an affront to decency.

Maria sensed Lois' anger as the SUV picked up speed. She leaned her seat back and closed her eyes. Seething quiet filled the cabin. At least Itzpa buried her mother in their family cemetery. Lois set the radio to a classic rock station and white knuckled the steering wheel with both hands.

The mist in the air lent an almost surreal density to the atmosphere surrounding the hacienda. Julio paced the veranda as Kevin advanced slowly up the driveway. For once the dust didn't boil up behind the Silverado. By the time the keys slipped from the ignition Julio stood outside the cab. He jerked the door so hard he nearly sprung the hinges.

"They wouldn't let me see her. Is she okay? I mean, thanks, thanks for coming." Julio held the door handle while extending his right hand. Kevin took it and eased himself from the truck.

"She's okay, a few scratches, but they're holding her for observation. She hasn't been arrested yet, probably won't be until the doctors sign off."

"What can I do?" Julio propped elbows on the hood of Kevin's pickup and sunk his face between gnarled hands.

"Get coffee? I've got some ideas." Kevin patted Julio's back like a brother.

"Yeah sure. Come on in. Where are my manners?"

Kevin headed straight for the kitchen table and sat down before realizing Julio may not know he'd been inside the house. Julio showed no surprise as he prepared a pot of rich dark brew. "Here are a couple of bondsman's numbers to call. I called the judge. He said if you pony up for the damages that she can probably get off with misdemeanor probation. They'll have to book her when she's arrested, but if you can get your ducks in a row she'll never see the inside of a jail cell." Kevin waited to continue until Julio sat across the table. He looked flustered by the situation. Finally, Kevin caught his eye. "Here's the thing, she could've been killed. What she did was extreme. I think she needs help. Is she using, drugs I mean?"

"No!" Julio whispered as if someone might hear "at least I don't think so. She's just high-strung, emotional. Her mother was like that. 'Crazy eyes' I called her. I can't believe she's doing drugs though."

"They'll do a tox screen," Kevin said. He locked eyes with Julio and shifted to a business demeanor. "The situation will be much worse if Miguel presses charges for stealing the car. I think we both know that won't happen. Dead men don't press charges, am I right?"

Julio's silence answered, as his jaw muscles tightened.

"Relax, Julio. This conversation is totally off the record. Just to be clear, I didn't take this PO job to be some high-minded crime fighter. I'm in it for the money, not the government paycheck either, get my drift? Something is going on here. You helped me. I help you."

Julio solidified. You could've bounced a quarter off his skin and discerned nary a ripple. Kevin chose to lighten up. "We can talk about that later. Right now we need to concentrate on keeping Lydia safe, okay?"

"Yeah, sure." Color returned to Julio's face

"You get her bonded out. I'll explain the situation to the judge, get the charges minimized. Be proactive. Offer to pay damages to the building. It's not too bad: the overhead door, a little sheet rock. It'll be good as new" Kevin got up to leave. "Great coffee, thanks. Don't worry. I've got your back. By the way, I know you're short a driver. I've got my Class A."

"Yeah, okay," Julio stared into his coffee. His color was draining away again. "Thanks, Kevin."

Carrie and Henrique sat a foot apart on metal folding chairs flanked by a rigid Lieutenant. Every adjustment in their posture caused a metallic squeak to echo in the barren room. Carrie did her best to remain motionless but every breath bounced the noise of metal off the walls. Across the expanse of gray steel desktop sat Capt. Carl Knox. Even seated the Captain towered above the two recruits. His gray crew cut crackled with electricity as did his steel blue eyes. He stood, palms flat, halfway across the desk, and leaned at the waist until the scent of Aqua

Velva and anger ripped through Carrie's olfactory receptors.

"What the hell, James? Have you lost your mind? Usually when I get a cadet with your qualifications they want to be a cop. Do you realize I can have you arrested for assault with bodily injury? I could probably make attempted murder stick from what I've been hearing from witnesses. You have 60 seconds to explain yourself or you're out of here!"

Carrie opened her mouth to explain about the "bleeder" comment and the "bitch" reaction but all she said was "I misinterpreted and overreacted,... Sir."

Capt. Knox tilted his head, pondered a moment and sat back down.

Carrie saw the direction this was taking and added, "I'm sorry. I'd like to apologize to Mr. ... to Henrique."

Capt. Knox turned to Henrique. "Garcia, I know she had some reason to react. I went over your military history. Seven years. Two tours in Iraq, one in Afghanistan, all as an MP. Honorable discharge. But, and this is where it gets squirrely, you didn't finish your final tour. Looks like you assaulted your superior officer."

Henrique tensed at this. The muscles in his jaw twitched. "No sir, I refused to obey orders, but I did not assault her."

"Her?" Capt. Knox asked and pulled Henrique Garcia's file from under Carrie's. He read it as Henrique stewed. "Hmm... I see...." He flipped through a couple of pages. Henrique began to visibly vibrate. Capt. Knox closed the file and slid all the paperwork into a drawer, leaving the gray desktop empty between him and the two recruits. He dismissed the Lieutenant. When the door clicked shut he stood again. "Here's my problem," he said. "There's too much talent in this room to send you home. James, you've got more education than most seasoned detectives. Garcia, you've got seven years experience under severe conditions. You both have a record of not being team players." He turned toward the back wall and ran his hand across the bristles of his flattop. "This is how it's going to work. The FBI is sending a team to investigate Harrison's murder. I've offered them a couple of assistants to do grunt work and show them around. You two will work with them. You will work together and you will get along. Do not let me hear of any problems from either of you. This is not open for discussion or negotiation. One screw-up and you're both out on your asses. Any classes you miss on this assignment you will make up during the next session. If you have a problem with this, pack up and leave.

Dismissed."

Carrie and Henrique stood and glared at each other. Henrique held the door as they left the office.

LIVING YELLOW BRUISES

In the short time he visited with Julio the mist had cleared and the sun was piercing the low hanging clouds. Kevin's dress shirt was soaked with sweat, liquefied by the sauna-like air of the Texas summer and yet he was pumped by the progress he'd made gaining Julio's trust. He'd figured right by judging Lydia as Julio's weakness. His foot was in the door. He drove out of the compound but had to stop at the pavement for an approaching pearl white Lincoln. As it turned in the driveway that Kevin was exiting the fat man behind the wheel gave the index finger salutation common to rural Texas. Other than that there was no acknowledgment from behind his dark shades. Kevin committed the license plate to memory until he was out of sight, then pulled over and wrote it down.

Betty Lou opened the office early and began making the coffee. While she was arranging the cinnamon rolls she bought for her coworkers she looked over and realized that she'd forgotten to put the pot under the drip. Coffee was running out all over the counter. She slipped it into place and grabbed some paper towels to clean up. Her mind wasn't on what she was doing. It was the second night DJ had stayed over and she wasn't sure she wanted it to happen this fast. She was okay with casual but she knew anything beyond that could get complicated. The fact that DJ was up to his ears in this mess with S. I. P. and Lydia didn't comfort her either. No sooner had she settled in at her desk than the phone rang.

"I need to speak with Kevin," Judge Kendrick demanded.

"He's not in yet. He was planning to do some visits before he came to the office this morning."

"Have him call me as soon as he arrives." She hung up without waiting for a response. It was unusual for the judge to be that brusque. It was undoubtedly related to the craziness surrounding the funeral home event but Betty Lou was curious to find out where the judge stood. She picked up a couple cinnamon rolls, popped them in the microwave and as soon as they were heated she headed for Kendrick's office. She found the door ajar but she tapped on it anyway.

" Come in."

"I went by the bakery and grabbed some rolls this morning. Would you like one?" Betty Lou asked. The judge looked at her for a minute and motioned for her to sit. Before sitting Betty Lou placed the rolls on the desk.

Kendrick picked up a roll, nibbled a bite and leaned back in her tall leather chair. "So what's our boy up to?"

"Our boy? Uh, you mean Kevin?"

The judge placed the roll back on the napkin and put both hands on the desk. "Let's get this straight. If I'm going to overlook this hanky-panky that's going on in my office I'm going to need to get some benefit from my leniency. We clear?"

"Okay, but first, we're just friends. I'm helping him look for an apartment, but all I know is he's got some idea that S. I. P. is involved in smuggling. I told him to leave it alone or turn it over to the Sheriff's Department. I don't know which he decided to do."

"I'm guessing neither," Judge Kendrick said. She picked up the roll, finished it in two bites and waved Betty Lou out of her office.

Betty Lou remained seated. Finally Judge Kendrick looked up. "What makes you think that," Betty Lou asked.

"I'm not at liberty to say."

"Look, Kevin and I are friends. I'm worried about him. He may be getting in over his head. I'll keep an eye on him for you but I need to know what's going on."

"This is just between us. No bullshit, if I find out you've told anybody you'll be out of a job. County Judge Carson Elders called me yesterday evening. Kevin contacted him on behalf of Lydia Ramirez trying to work out a plea bargain. He said he was working on a federal investigation and Lydia being incarcerated would gum up the works. That's way outside of Kevin's jurisdiction. I can't have my officers stepping out of bounds like this. If this accusation has any meat it needs to go to the FBI or the border patrol. If he's just trying to get his friend out of jail then it has cost him his job."

"He's fairly certain that somebody at S. I. P. is involved in smuggling but he doesn't know who or what."

"You should've come to me with this. I don't care how good of friends you are with Kevin. It's your job to let me know."

"I'm sorry, Your Honor, I just found out about it yesterday." Betty Lou felt the blood drain from her face. She needed this job; she liked it; she was good at it.

"Just keep me in the loop." Judge Kendrick pushed her reading glasses up on her nose, looked down at her paperwork and no longer acknowledged Betty Lou's presence.

Julio was still sitting at the kitchen table when the front door opened. There had not been a knock and the changing shadows startled him. The fat man's figure was silhouetted by the morning sun but Julio had no doubt who it was. This was the last thing he needed. "Morning Ronnie, come in. I didn't expect to see you out this way," Julio said.

"I don't expect so. We've got a problem." The wide man waddled over to the table and sat across from Julio.

"I know, I know, I'm on it. I can't believe my little girl went off the rails like that. I've got a guy from the probation office handling it. He'll make sure it's no big deal."

The fat man balled up his fists, placed them down in front of him and leaned over the table. It was all he could do not to scream. The words came out as a hiss. "I don't give a fuck about your little bitch of a daughter. I have people to handle issues like that and if you don't they will. I'm a numbers man. Here's the deal, this God damned fiasco that your boy, Miguel, pulled is bringing way too much attention to our neck of the woods, but that's not my problem. My problem is the $3000 that's missing. It should've been on the bodies or in the truck. It wasn't. We, meaning you, need to find out what happened to it."

"It should've been on Miguel. Otherwise I don't know, maybe the team that brought in the truck took it. Shit, Ronnie, it's just 3K. If it's a problem I'll cover it."

"It wasn't the team that brought in the truck. Those are my guys. It's not the amount of the money either. It's that somebody stole it from us. You need to find out who and you need to take care of the situation. Are we clear?"

"Yeah sure, boss. I have just the guy"

Ronnie stood up and brushed off his pants as if he'd been sitting in dirt. "You have 48 hours. I want restitution and I don't just mean the money. Comprende?"

Julio stood and offered his hand. "I'll take care of it, Commissioner."

Ronnie refused the hand but slapped Julio on the back. "I knew I could count on you. It's a pleasure doing business. By the way, Lydia seems like maybe she could use a vacation. Just a thought."

As the door closed behind Ronnie, Julio felt the bile rising up in his stomach. Ronnie Dahl wasn't a man who played games.

CHANGING THE STATION

Ross latched his office door and sat behind the wooden desk considering the call he was mentally preparing to make. His forehead throbbed. He brought a hand up and tried to push the pain to the back of his neck. It didn't work. It never did. He flipped through his old-school Rolodex and accessed an outside line. It took only one ring. "Jake, old buddy, how's it hanging?"

It took a moment for the voice to respond. "Never a dull moment, unlike out on the wide-open plains. Any cows escape their pasture lately?"

At the sound of his friend's voice, Ross relaxed and put his feet on the desk "I need a favor. I want you to open a can of worms for me. I know you've heard about the produce truck they found in the desert. It's owned by a local company and I'm guessing the owner may be involved. It's a small town. I don't want to open an investigation. I'm an elected official and I like my job.

On the other end of the line Jake Tosh heard the indecision in his buddy's voice. "Why not? What could happen in Beeville that you couldn't handle?"

"Let's just say it might hit too close to home. Besides, I don't have the manpower and the crime scene is out of my jurisdiction."

"Why not let the border Patrol handle it. It was obviously smuggling gone bad from what I've heard."

"I don't have a good feeling about this. If it's cartel the border guys won't be any help. You know the numbers. Half of them are on the Zeta's payroll. Far as I know only you guys are above board." Ross waited but only silence ensued. "I'll help where I can but ...."

"Okay, listen," Jake said. "You'll have to get a judge or state official to open the investigation and call us in. The Rangers don't want a turf war and we have to be brought in. That means somebody will have to admit defeat. I'm sorry , but that's the way the game's played."

"Yeah, I know. Thanks. I'll get to work on that."

No problem. I'll give you my cell number. Call me directly as soon as your ducks are in a row and I'll put my best team on it."

Lupe Moreno leaned back in the ragged office chair, propped his boots on the edge of his desk and pulled little balls of cotton from the cracked vinyl. He closed his eyes and let his head fall back, he felt like he'd been born tired. Every joint ached. The memory of the all-night argument with his wife still pumped in his head. A 12 pack of cheap beer. That set her off.

"You have money for beer every night but I can't see my grandbabies?" She was on him before he even shut the door.

"The road runs both ways. Let them come here."

"You heartless old bastard. They have jobs and commitments."

He pushed past her and loaded the beer into the bottom shelf of the fridge. "I have a job too. Who's going to run the station while I'm gone."

"What, run the station, you mean sit in your air-conditioned office guzzling beer all day? You barely clear enough to keep the electric on."

That's when he made his first mistake. Although he kept most of the cash he had squirreled hidden at the station, he'd become accustomed to the comfort of carrying a couple of hundred bucks in his wallet. He popped the pull tab and took a cool drag on the Tecate. Maybe he overplayed the gesture of pulling his wallet from his pants. Maybe it was the force he used to toss the pile of 20s on the counter. "So go, if that's what you want. Stay as long as you like." He underestimated her virulent reaction. Somewhere in his semi-inebriated mind he thought the offer would subdue her. It had the opposite effect.

She grabbed the money with one hand and picked up the beer can with the other. She threw the half full beer out the back screen door then turned on him. "Where'd you get this?" She shook the cash in his face. "What are you up to. The AC, and the little fridge, all this money, are you involved in something? You better tell me." Her voice was getting the gravel grinding grit she used when she was about to jump the rails. The night had gone downhill from there. He escaped with the dawn.

The condensation outside the plate glass storefront blurred the endless expanse of desert, slowing his thundering brain. Leathered eye lids fell like drapes over the morning. Time became fluid, the first morning in ages he hoped for no business. Somewhere between the soothing hum of the AC and the mini-fridge, the jingle of the door brought him back to life. The man silhouetted in the door allowed no light between his shoulders and the door jamb. He wore a wide brimmed cowboy hat. When he stomped his boots on the doormat Lupe swore he heard the jingle of Spanish spurs.

"Lupe Moreno?" The man asked. Lupe nodded still trying to decide if this was real. "Julio sent me?"

"Who?" Lupe still wasn't all there.

"You have something of ours. We want it back!"

Lupe shrugged and took his boots off the desk. Before he could stand the man had him by the throat in a rough-hewn grip, yanking him across the desk.

"What? What do you want? I'm a poor mechanic. I've got nothing." Lupe reached for his empty wallet. "See!"

The man twisted his arm behind his back and slammed his face into the door jamb. "Three thousand dollars. You took it off the dead kid."

"No, I…" Lupe felt his legs kicked out from under him. He was on his back, a boot on his chest, the spur at his throat. The man standing above him pointed a pistol at his forehead. "Hand it over and I might not kill you."

Lupe doubted that. Now that he could see the man clearly he noticed the three teardrops tattooed below his eye. Lupe knew what that meant. Maybe he could buy some time. "It's not here. Maybe I can get some of it." He felt the boot heel press harder on his collarbone. The tines of the spur against his neck felt like they might pierce the skin.

"Bullshit." Raul said. "You don't have anywhere else to put it. I've already chatted with your wife this morning."

Lupe felt the icy rage slice through his spine. What had this man done? He grabbed the boot on his chest and wrenched it with all his strength. It shifted slightly then he felt his collar bone snap. He wailed, more for his wife than his pain. Tears streamed.

Raul held the gun against Lupe's temple. He sneered. In his singsong voice he said, "Don't worry, I didn't kill her. I don't kill women. No need. There is much worse things you can do to them. I'm quite certain she doesn't know where the money is."

Lupe began to tremble. His bladder emptied, as did his stomach, all over Raul's boot.

"God dammit, you nasty old bastard!" He kicked Lupe in the ribs. "Get the fuck up and fetch that cash before I ventilate your fucking skull." He kicked again.

Lupe rolled on his side, defeated, crying like a car wash. "My

mirage

toolbox, pull out the bottom drawer of the top box. Behind there."

Raul grabbed Lupe by the foot, drug him into the shop and yanked out the drawer, slinging tools chiming across the concrete. He counted the money. "Where's the rest?"

"I spent it."

"Eight hundred dollars?" Raul gave Lupe another solid kick. "You owe me."

"I don't... What can I do?"

Raul looked around the shop. It was fairly well-equipped., Two bays, hydraulic lift, compressor, tire machines. "I'll take it." Raul said.

"What?"

"The shop."

"No, it's all I have."

"According to your wife you have a daughter and grandchildren in North Carolina. I could let you live if you gave me this place. Maybe."

"But..."

"Or I could drag your dead body out to the desert and go get your wife to join you."

" I'll go."

Raul bared $10,000 worth of premium orthodontic art complete with his only gold star. "I know you will." Raul looked around the floor until he found a 5/8 inch hex end wrench. He stepped on the back of Lupe's left-hand and slipped the wrench over his ring finger. "She begged me not to kill you, you know. I'll let her tell you what I was doing while she begged. You have one hell of an old lady." He twisted the wrench snapping Lupe's ring finger. "If I ever see either of you again, you're dead."

Lupe was balled in the fetal position on the greasy floor when he heard Raul click the door shut. The truck rumbled away. The AC and the fridge maintained the steady hum.

PLAN OF ACTION

Raul sat on the edge of the elevated platform that served as the stage at the VFW Hall. He raked his spurs down the edge of the rough-cut surface leaving little pock marks in the wood. Kevin paced around the stage locating electrical outlets and checking on the sound equipment. There were no turntables or microphones. The space was a large metal building with rows of picnic tables placed end-to-end around the perimeter. The center cleared for dancing, more suitable for polka party than rap or R&B. The only thing available, it would have to do.

"So the deal is," Kevin said, "you rent the equipment, pay me 300 bucks/ I'll bring my tunes and personality. Consider it a good deed, a bribe, I don't really give a fuck. That's not what this is about."

Raul rubbed his chin. "So what's the point, really?"

"I need in, you know what I mean? Plus, I'll give you one hell of a show."

"In?"

"Yeah, everybody sees me as the cop. I'm not. Fuck this. I need to score some cash. I hide my eyes, kind of a 'see no evil" thing. I'm going to get into your ears, though, your life. My music will alter your brain waves. I'm going to be your best buddy. Why? Because the alternative sucks for you."

"Sure man, I'm cool. It may be a tough sell. I'm not the guy that usually throws the party."

"Go to the kingdom of smuggling and tell the jester, or whoever your local party animal is, that I'm not only available but it's in everyone's best interest to hire me."

"That would be Lydia Ramirez. Word is, you're already all into that. You tell her."

"Dude, you're like a typewriter in Dell's front office. Clueless. I'm telling you, Lydia and me, that's straight up business, and it's my business. She don't know what we're into. Anyway, I want the gig." He booted a can off the edge of the stage like an all-pro field goal kicker. It bounced on the tables at the far end of the barn.

"But what about Julio? Can you see him allowing her to fraternize with the help?"

"Dude, let me worry about him. Even if he's against it, I'll convince him. Fuck it. Groceries get delivered. I'll get him on board."

"You think?"

"There's not going to be any doubt about it."

"Bullshit."

"Dude, I got this. I know, because you're going to help."

Due to the confrontation and resulting assist with the forensic investigation, Henrique and Carrie were deemed partners. They developed a strange cohesiveness. Henrique had no respect for women in general. Carrie had no respect for Henrique specifically. They were both in top physical condition so needed neither assistance or encouragement on the R.O.P.E.S. course. Their subcutaneous competitiveness drove them both to excel.

Since Henrique found Carrie intimidating, he made no advances. She let him stay alive. She even appreciated that he was unwilling to touch her in any way beyond what the training required. This unlikely pairing survived the two-week program. They smiled for the first time when told they finished at the top of their class.

Ross came to graduation. When Carrie spotted him in the front row he was sitting between a beautiful but ominous-looking redhead and Carrie's mom.

The brief ceremony held little pomp. The candidates walked across the stage, shook a few hands and received their badge from their sponsoring agency. Carrie felt a shift in her purpose. She had finally finished something. She was certified. The brief feeling evaporated as she knew it to be only a step toward a larger goal, but she took a moment to revel in it as Capt. Carl Knox pinned the badge on her crisp tan uniform. Henrique's badge was already attached to his green border patrol uniform. He gave her a nod from the edge of the stage. She nodded back. Both of their faces remained expression free.

After graduation Carrie found the only person in the world she wanted a hug from standing in the foyer with Ross and the redhead. Her mom obliged.

"This is Aurora, my wife," Ross said. "She's with the Justice Department - Homeland Security. It's part of the reason she's never around, always traveling."

Carrie took Aurora's manicured hand. "Glad to finally meet you. You're lucky to have Ross for a husband. Such a gentleman."

Aurora smiled. "You're all he talks about. You'd think he adopted a daughter to hear him go on about you, not to mention that famous sidearm."

Lois beamed as her little girl showed in the spotlight. Aurora continued. "We must have you over for dinner soon. Sometime when I'm in town. I make a mean stuffed flounder."

"I'd like that," Carrie said, trying to decipher the look of concern on Ross's face.

"Well," Ross interrupted, "we should be heading home. We have a drive ahead of us."

"See you soon," Aurora said as Ross pulled her away. Carrie couldn't help but notice Aurora's measured cordiality while her dull flat eyes betrayed no emotion. Carrie's body felt damp and dirty as if she'd just been caught stepping into the shower.

"Sure. I better go. I still have to pack." Carrie turned, giving her mom a quick hug. "I'll see you at home."

"Monday," Ross hollered over his shoulder as the group scattered in different directions.

Kevin paced the garage apartment. His cell phone sat on the counter, a time bomb that he had to diffuse. But how? He picked it up and read the message for the umpteenth time. It was from judge Kendrick: See me first thing Monday. Be early. I have court at nine. Kevin didn't have to guess, he knew he'd stepped in it. His conversation with the county judge would bite him in the ass. In a small-town word gets around. He had the weekend to stew. Fortunately, Carrie should be back today. Maybe she had a clue as to what to do. As he paced, he watched the long dusty driveway for her car.

Raul rolled into the driveway of S. I. P. and parked in front of Miguel's old pad, the only trailer that wasn't an RV, also the only one completely shaded by a grove of mesquite. He stepped down from his dually and rolled his head in a circle listening to the vertebrae in his thick neck crackle. His spurs kicked up little dust divots as he ambled to the door. He heard the phone ringing even before he went inside. Facing toward the main house he shook his head and stepped into the chilled air of the tiny living room. The phone continued ringing. He pulled off his boots and shirt, reached into the fridge and popped open a beer. He enjoyed having a fully equipped office on site even if it was only temporary. It made him feel in control. Taking a deep swallow, he sat on the barstool and picked up his cell. He took another swig of beer and answered.

"Well," said Julio's frantic voice.
"Hey boss," Raul replied.
"Is it done?"
"They'll never find the bodies."
"Bodies? What do you mean bodies?"
"The wife was involved."
"Shit!"
"Don't worry it's handled."
"I hate it when women die."

"Me too."

"The money?"

"Some. He spent $1200. I got the rest."

"God dammit!"

"We got the shop, too."

"So?"

"It's a good stash house; AC, fridge, full shop with tools. We can use it."

"Well, okay. I guess you did what you had to do."

"Yep. I'll go out tomorrow and change the locks, shut everything down and seal it up. What about the utilities? Can you get them switched over somehow?" The line was silent. "Boss?"

"Yeah, yeah. I'm thinking. I might know a kid who can work that. He wants a part of the action." Raul knew Julio meant Kevin but he remained silent. "Bring the money up."

"I'll stop by later. I need a shower and a beer."

"Now would be good."

"Later," Raul said, and hung up.

Julio stood. Cleared his lungs. Some folks you just can't push.

"Is everything all right?"

Julio startled at the sound of Lydia's voice. "You're up early." His daughter was dressed in a long-sleeved black robe, her hair tangled with rough sleep.

"It's 2:30 in the afternoon."

Julio checked the clock. "So it is."

"So is it?"

"What?"

"All right, is everything all right?"

"You mean aside from having a daughter that drives other people's cars into buildings?"

"I liked Miguel. I said I'm sorry."

"You didn't even know Miguel. Stay away from my drivers, you hear? These guys, they mostly come from prison. Not the type you need to hang with."

"So who? Who do I *hang* with? I'm stuck in this house, no friends. You don't let me see daylight. I'm 17 and I have no fucking life! That stupid Catholic school and this cage. I might as well kill myself."

"Don't talk like that. I'll get you some help."

"I don't need help! I need a life! I can't stand this anymore." Lydia crossed her arms to keep her hands from shaking. "I need out, one way or another."

"Please, baby girl, don't. You scare me when you talk like that. We can make it better."

"It worked for Mama. I don't see her moping around anymore."

"No honey! That's not the answer. Sit down. I'll make you breakfast."

Lydia ran to her room and slammed the door. Julio went to the kitchen. He felt helpless, just like before his wife took her own life. This time he would find an answer.

Betty Lou set the iPhone to a playlist titled "reggae – chopped and screwed". She dropped it in the dock and cranked the volume. The walls pulsed with slow lazy bass while cat-scratch guitar backbeat ripped the dense cold air. Through the window the heat waves shimmered on the asphalt parking lot. The smooth surface of the empty pool reflected glare from the brutal sun. She closed the drapes. The room went dark. The tumblers in the dish drainer rattled on the downbeat. She turned the sound down just enough to avoid breakage then stripped down to her white cotton panties and sports bra.

She pulled her tray from under the coffee table and kicked back on the couch. After dumping a fat bud from a pill bottle, she pinched it apart. It permeated the room with a sweet carnal smell like animal sex. The tips of her fingers were sticky. She slipped a single sheet from an orange pack of rolling papers and creased it into thirds. With one fluid motion she filled it, rolled it, licked it and sealed it. Again she peeked out the window. Four young kids were splashing about in the previously abandoned pool. Oh well. She lit the joint on the kitchen stove and lay down on the couch. She took a deep hit and held it, then slowly released through her nose. Cool air from the vents danced across her skin. Her tangled hair floated on her shoulders. Music was inside her body; the slow beat, synchronizing with her heart, bringing with it a deep relaxation. She let the cool leather of the couch support her as she fell under the spell. She thought of Kevin. She'd barely spoken with him since Thursday morning. He'd been in the field Thursday. Friday she'd been at the courthouse with Judge Kendrick, interviewing possible clients. Having him in her life added some depth to her day-to-day existence. He was comfortable to be around. She knew better than to ask too much of him. Experience had taught her enough to know slow and easy was the way.

Two or three hits in, the refrigerator began to beckon. She couldn't remember what it held, surely something. When she looked inside, the first thing she saw was the six pack of Fat Tire he brought on their first evening together. She opened one, grabbed her phone off the dock and sat back down on the couch. Halfway through the beer she dialed his number.

By mid afternoon Kevin's dread was replaced by boredom. Judge Kendrick would either terminate him or slap his hand. Anyway it would be Monday. Today he had to get Carrie up to speed on recent events. She was taking her own sweet time returning from Corpus. When he heard the dogs barking he ran to the window. It was just Lois returning home, but Carrie should be close behind. He continued to pace.

The phone rang. He grabbed it without checking the number. Had to be Carrie. "S'up?"

"Help me, please! I can't stand this anymore. I've got to get out of here. Please, DJ?" Lydia sounded frantic. "I'm dying in here. I think Daddy's going to send me away."

Kevin didn't immediately respond. It wasn't the call he'd expected. He hardly knew this woman, except that trouble stuck to her like sand burrs on a Texas beach. "Hey, Lydia. What's wrong?"

"I'm losing it. I told him I was sorry. Daddy wants to send me on a vacation to a treatment house, I think. Right now I'm trapped. He won't let me leave. I don't have any friends. Please DJ..."

"Okay, take a deep breath..."

"Stop it! Stop! I'm not a little kid. This is real!"

"All right, what can I do?" Kevin asked and sat perched on the edge of his futon.

"Come get me, please. I'm dying."

"No you're not. Calm down. Let's talk."

"Don't fucking tell me to calm down. Come *get* me!"

"Where's Julio?"

"He's here, but I'll sneak out. I don't care. Please!"

"You know I can't do that. Besides, where would you go?"

"I don't know, don't care. With you? I could stay with you, at least for a while. I'm a fun girl."

"No way. I live in an efficiency an hour away... and I rent from a cop who lives downstairs. Wouldn't work. I can talk to you though. Maybe we can figure something out."

"Okay." She was beginning to sound less frantic. "Can you come get me?"

"Not right now. You're not high are you? Have you been using?" Kevin waited for a response that didn't immediately come, usually a bad sign.

"Fuck you," Lydia screamed. The line went dead, a worse sign.

Kevin started to call her back but stopped in the middle of dialing. Instead he called Julio. Julio picked up on the first ring. Kevin knew to tread lightly. "Sir? I just got a weird call from your daughter."

"Why would she call you?" Julio asked.

"I don't know, but she sounded irrational like she might hurt herself. You should check on her. Maybe even call emergency services."

"Do you think she's serious? She thrives on drama."

"At least check on her." Kevin stood and paced the tiny space, feeling the pressure build between his ears.

"Thanks. I will."

"Let me know if there's anything I can do to help," Kevin said.

"I'll call you later."

Kevin hung up and turned his attention back to watching the long driveway while his mind slipped over the smooth caramel angles of Lydia's thin body. Even with the scars she was stunning; scary beautiful.

The phone rang, again, ripping him free from the fantasy. *Damn, what am I, the helpline?* He didn't check the number.

"Hey you hunka hunka burnin' love. How you holding up to the heat wave?"

The slow-motion spill of Betty Lou's voice made him think of waffle syrup, poured over guilt.

"You sound mellow," he said.

"You have no idea. Just thinking about you. Thought I'd invite you over for a midnight swim after it cools down."

"I thought the pool closed at ten?" Kevin thought he heard a slight giggle followed by a sigh, as if she were repositioning her body.

"It does, officially. If we can't sneak in we'll have to find some other way to get wet." She sighed again - a long slow exhale he found stimulating.

"I could probably stop by after dark. You want me to bring something for dinner?"

"No, I've got that covered. You can pick up something sweet and sticky if you want to. Toy food if you know what I mean. I like maraschino cherries, but feel free to use your imagination."

Kevin was getting warm just thinking about another evening with Betty Lou. Her passion, without the normal neediness common to his limited experience with women, was refreshing.

"Are you there?" She asked. He'd been lost in thought.

"Yeah, yeah it sounds like fun."

"Cool," she said. "I'm going to let you go. I'm touching myself down there and I'll need my free hand to pinch my nipples when it gets really good." She moaned low and long then the phone disconnected. Kevin forgot about the driveway and headed for the shower.

Julio stood outside his daughter's bedroom door. Tangible tension laced the air with the scent of electric gunpowder. He thought back to the many times he listened to his wife cry - breathe - sleep through a similar slab of wood until the day he heard nothing for too long; ten minutes, an hour. When he finally gathered the courage to enter it was over. The bathwater already cold, pink. Red nodules of coagulated blood tangled in her chocolate hair, adhered to her face below her empty staring eyes; a ghastly confection, failed by the man who never figured out how to properly worship her. Now he felt that ache twisting through him again. Behind her door he heard the muffled sobs proving her existence continued. He tapped on the door frame and jiggled the knob.

"Go away," she moaned. "Leave me alone."

He obliged, knowing no other recourse. As he strode down the hall, the various gears began falling into place like split shifting an old Brownlight transmission. She liked Kevin. Kevin wanted a job, a piece of the pie, something. He also seemed to care, or at least worry about Lydia. But best of all, Kevin had no criminal record.

Kevin exited the shower significantly more relaxed. So much so, in fact, that he put on shorts and a T-shirt before checking the window. Sure enough, Carrie was parked in the driveway with the hatch opened. Being cool from the shower he chose to let her get settled in before bombarding her with the local news. Why risk breaking a sweat?

This phone, again! It just wouldn't stop ringing. This time he checked the number. Julio. That was quick.

"Hello?"

"Mr. Cash," Julio began "I remember you mentioning you have a CDL?"

"Yeah, class A with tanker and hazardous material endorsements."

"I could use an extra driver part-time, nights and weekends mostly if you're interested."

"Sure, as long as it doesn't interfere with my regular job, assuming I still have one."

Julio paused a beat. "I hope I didn't cause a problem."

"It was my call, besides it's my first time screwing up. Maybe Judge Kendrick will just break one of my fingers or something."

"Why don't you stop by for dinner? We can talk. I'll have Lydia whip up something special. She's quite the cook you know."

Kevin didn't hesitate. "What time?"

"Around seven? By the way, I don't suppose you're trucking experience includes any mechanical abilities. Miguel did some of our maintenance, too."

"Not much; fan belts, alternators, lights, filter changes, I can handle. But not really any major stuff."

"No, I have a guy for that."

"See you tonight." Kevin kicked back on his futon absorbed in self satisfaction; his foot in the door and spending the evening enjoying Lydia's culinary favors, watching her float across the terrazzo like a delicious apparition.

"Shit!" He jumped up, leaned his head against the wall. Betty Lou, I can't miss that. It goes way beyond looking. Maybe I can do both.

Carrie threw her backpack over her shoulder and wheeled her suitcase into the house. Lois waited with a hug as soon as she dropped them in the front hall.

"I just saw you a couple of hours ago, Mom," Carrie said as she tried to wriggle free.

"I'm just so proud of you, though. I think maybe you finally found your calling."

"Yeah, we'll see. I have a long way to go. How was your trip with Maria?"

Lois picked up Carrie's pack and started toward the stairs. "Mission accomplished. The body made it back to the family plot." Lois didn't elaborate.

"And?" Carrie nudged.

"It was smuggling, you know, but Carlos was a gentleman to those girls. It still doesn't make sense."

"I know, Mom. The border situation is screwed up and dangerous. The cartels take the money but don't deliver safe passage. It should be easier."

"Or harder," Lois said. "So people wouldn't try."

Carrie pulled back her hair and slipped a rubber band from her wrist, leaving a wad of hair in a lopsided mass at the base of her head. "They'll always try, Mom. They have nothing. That's what needs to change."

Lois smiled at her daughter. Look, Honey, I don't want to argue. I'm glad you found a purpose."

The hyper-frosted air hissed from the Lincoln's vents in ripples of vapor. Still Ronnie wasn't comfortable. He wasn't comfortable about a lot of things. His armpits and neckline held residual moisture from the last time he had to step outside his premium pearlescent container. At 300 plus pounds a certain discomfort was unavoidable, but this heat, this God-damned heat. He more than needed a break from it. The car knifed its way down the two-lane in excess of 80 mph slowing to spin into the gravel parking lot of Southern International Produce, dragging a torrent of pebbles skittering in with the billowing dust. He found a shady spot near the metal building and dug into his jacket pocket. He had Julio on speed dial. "I'm here," he said.

"Come on up," Julio invited.

"You get your crazy-ass daughter shipped off yet?"

"No. I settled her down. We're going to work through this together."

"That's the stupidest God-damn thing I've ever heard. I'm not showing up there. You come down here to the shop," Ronnie said, "and leave her up there and don't fucking say where you're going. Bring my money."

"Yes, Sir." Julio took the keys to the four-wheeler. Before he left the house he stopped by Lydia's bedroom. "Sweetheart, I've invited a guy over for dinner tonight. I think you know him. Kevin Cash?"

"DJ?"

"Yeah, okay, maybe, anyway can you fix a nice dinner."

"Sure, Daddy. Thanks."

Julio bounced down the hill on his camo-painted four-wheeler and pulled up beside the driver's door of the long white Lincoln. Ronnie rolled the window halfway down, freeing a puff of frigid air. "So?" Ronnie asked.

"Is that really necessary?" Julio motioned towards the chrome nine mil poised on the leather passenger seat.

"Sorry, force of habit," Ronnie replied, dropping it in the console. "You got my money?"

"Some."

"God dammit, Julio!"

"I got what there was." He handed the fat man 12 one hundred dollar bills.

"I hope you got some restitution."

"You'll never find the bodies."

"Great," Ronnie peeled a couple of bills off the roll and handed them through the opening, "for your trouble?"

Julio put his hand on the throttle. "Fuck you, Ronnie. We're partners. You'll not own me and I'll damn sure not owe you. And another thing, if you ever insult my daughter again they won't find your body either." He cranked the throttle hard. The machine growled to life, fishtailing away and pinging gravel over the pearl Lincoln.

Kevin really did want to catch up with Carrie. At least that's what he told himself. But, he'd have to put on shoes and it being his day off and all. He sat back down. Two women were enough to think about for now, neither of them as scary as Carrie. She'd get around to him.

He dozed on the couch with his feet up on the arm, trying to work Lydia and Betty Lou into the same fantasy. It wouldn't happen, even in dreamland. There was a tap on the door. Carrie walked in.

"Jesus, Carrie, I could have been masturbating! What the fuck!"

Carrie looked at the bulge in his board shorts. "Eew! You sick puppy."

"Hey, you walked in on me. Don't blame my natural instincts."

Carrie turned to go. "Sorry."

"No wait, have a seat. You've ruined it anyway."

Carrie straddled the barstool. "So what's new?"

"I screwed up. The judge is pissed. I have an early meeting Monday."

"Think she'll fire you?"

"Don't know. The job was open for 18 months before I took it. Hopefully I'll just get a reprimand."

"What happened?"

Kevin sat up and hunched over his fading erection. "Not important."

"Bullshit. It's your job, our way in. Let me guess, you were thinking with the little head, right?

"Um, yeah, sort of, I guess. I was using my position to help out someone and get a foot in the door."

"At S. I. P.?"

"Yeah, but it's not like it sounds. I'm trying to build trust."

"... And get laid."

"One does what one can. How was your vacation?"

Carrie pulled up her T-shirt sleeve and flexed her bicep. "Added 4 pounds of muscle."

"So you worked out and tanned for two weeks?"

"We had class too. I even worked a federal investigation."

"No shit?"

"Yeah, one of our instructors got himself exsanguinated in some freak sex ritual."

"No way!"

"Way. Not only that, they don't have a suspect."

"Don't you mean 'we'?"

"I guess, I only worked with the forensics people. Not my best effort either. I did more damage than good."

"So you're a full-fledged Sheriff now?"

"I'll get sworn in Monday. Should we celebrate?"

"Can't tonight."

"What? You have a date?"

"Two actually."

"Damn DJ, I take my eyes off of you for a couple weeks and you become a man whore?"

"It's business. Trying to get my foot in the door. Like I said."

Carrie snort-laughed. "That's not your foot."

"Yo! What you say? You don't know how long it is."

"Just shut up."

"Anyway even if I get fired it looks like I can work at S I P. It's probably better in the long run. I'm absolutely positively sure they're at the center of the smuggling ring. I don't think the guy, Julio, that owns S. I. P. is the honcho though. I'm not certain, but I've got a plate number of a guy it might be."

Carrie tossed him a pen from the counter. "Write it down. I'll run it Monday and give you an ID."

"Cool. It might be random too. Don't get your hopes up. This is a process."

"We've got to put a stop to it."

"I thought it was about money and vengeance. We can do that. This 'save the world' shit isn't possible. That's a road to disaster, out here anyway."

Carrie walked to the window, looking toward the border just over the horizon. "What do you know about 'out here'? Let me tell you about 'out here'. You better suck up to that judge and watch your ass or you'll be buzzard shit."

Kevin saw the worry in Carrie's forehead, the glob of hair hanging at the base of her skull. She looked exhausted. "Thanks for caring. Get some rest. We'll talk on Monday." He walked toward her as if to give her a hug.

She shot out the door. "You be careful too," she hollered behind her.

After the golf ball size cast-iron knocker slammed against the oak, Kevin had a few seconds of self-conscious appraisal. It was entirely possible that his silk shirt and high-topped alligator shoes were over-done dress. A good first impression was desirable. Coming off like an arrogant poser, maybe not. When Lydia answered the door in a floor length embroidered navy gown accentuated by a pearl necklace and earrings he was relieved. She seemed much taller and more reserved in her heels. The length of her neck accentuated by carefully strayed hairs dangling from her complex up do made him jelly kneed. He needed to nibble that neck. The smile she gave him was equal parts innocence, fear, and hunger.

"Thanks for coming." She allowed him in and took his elbow. "This way. I hope you like cabrito." Her voice liquid, steady as a morning pond.

"I don't know. What is it?" Kevin heard the door latch clank closed. He was in an unfamiliar world. Tread carefully.

Lydia leaned into his shoulder, her dark words almost a whisper. "It's red meat with a wild edge. Very lean. Usually it's barbecued but I do something different. You'll see." She led him past the kitchen where he first met her. It was in a state of disarray. The formal dining room was expansive. Two black iron chandeliers hung over a heavy table that would easily seat twenty. Southwestern art in pastels hung low above the chair rails on walls textured to resemble adobe. At the head of the table sat Julio, integrated into the surroundings as if part of a Georgia O'Keeffe painting.

He stood. "Welcome, Mr. Cash. I'm so happy you could be here," his brief handshake extremely firm for his skeletal frame. "Have a seat. Would you like some wine before dinner or maybe something stronger?"

"Wine's okay," Kevin said.

Julio glanced at Lydia. She left. Julio drummed his fingers on the table and studied Kevin for a minute. Finally, he smiled. "So tell me about yourself."

"Not a lot to tell. Graduated University of Arkansas last spring with a Bachelors in Criminal Justice. Took five years because I started in Sociology then switched to Political Science then finally to C J. Only child, raised mostly by Mom. She remarried while I was in high school to a guy who owns a trucking company. I don't much care for him but he makes Mom happy."

"So that's where the driving experience comes in?"

"Yeah, I drove summers the last two years of college so I don't really have that many miles, but I have a spotless record."

"Passport?"

"Yeah, why?"

"We pick up loads in Mexico, produce mostly."

"Mostly?"

"Look around you, Mr. Cash. I move whatever pays. I've done all right. I know you know that or you wouldn't be here. There's a certain part of this business I like to distance myself from. I'm getting up in years, Mr. Cash."

"Call me Kevin."

"Fine, Kevin. Anyway, I'd hoped to turn this over to Lydia but she's not really cut out for it. Too much like her mother. I guess I'll run it till I keel over. I worry about her though. She's… well, let's say… fragile."

Lydia returned with two glasses and an unlabeled bottle. She sat a glass in front of each man, uncorked the bottle and put it in front of her father before taking her seat across the massive table from Kevin.

Kevin noticed no glass in front of Lydia. "You're not joining us?"

Lydia glanced toward her father. "I... can't, I don't..."

"She doesn't imbibe," Julio said and poured a small amount of blood red liquid in Kevin's glass. Kevin did what he'd seen on TV, swirled it around, sniffed it and took a sip. Julio suppressed a grin.

Kevin was pleasantly surprised by the complex fruitiness but lacked the proper vocabulary. "It's good," he said, and held out his class.

Carrie sat in the kitchen with a notepad and newspaper while Lois puttered around the cabinets. Several ads were circled in the classifieds. "Well at least rent's cheap out here. In Austin we were paying $1400 a month for a 60-year-old two-bedroom duplex. It looks like I can get one here for half that, if I can find one. About all there is here is trailers or ranches, nothing in between." Carrie refolded the newspaper.

"Why don't you just stay here?" Lois asked.

"You mean aside from the fact that I'm a little old to live with my mommy? My job requires me to live in Bee County if I bring the cruiser home and the Civic is on its last legs."

"So get a newer car."

"Mom, really? No. It's time to leave the nest, plus I'll be driving all day. I don't want to spend two more hours on the road."

"It's safe here." Lois's voice lacked conviction.

"It's not," Carrie replied. "It's not safe anywhere this close to the border if I'm involved. The uniform brings out the worst in some folks and I don't want you in danger." Carrie circled another ad. "Look, here's a restored Airstream five minutes from the station. Three hundred fifty dollars a month plus utilities and they maintain the yard."

"Where?" Lois asked.

"Daylily Courts off Rio de Muerte' Street."

"Sketchy neighborhood."

"Not after I move in. I'll call in the morning, see if they'll show it on Sunday."

"I hope you'll reconsider. I like having you around. I'm just getting used to it again."

"Sorry, Mom. I can't."

Lois pulled a link of venison sausage out of the fridge. "Hungry?"

"Sure." Carrie remained focused on the classifieds as she heard the sizzle of sausage hitting the pan.

Betty Lou grabbed her shades and purse. Stepping out into the fading sunlight was still a shock to her retinas. She pulled the beach towel off the driver's seat, tossed it in the back and crawled up into her lemon-yellow Jeep. Soon she'd have to put the doors back on but for now she took the ball cap off the stick shift and put it on backwards to keep her dreads under some semblance of control. After switching on the subwoofer she slipped a CD into the dash and treated the neighborhood to the Ramones.

Twenty minutes into her supermarket run she chastised herself for hitting the HEB with a buzz on. Her cart was half full. She scanned the contents to find the four items she came for and went to check out at register six. When the card reader ask if she wanted extra cash she hit $40.

The thin Latino with perfect skin who bagged her groceries asked, "Would you like help out with that, Ma'am?"

"Sure," she said and pulled her shades down over her eyes. The sun warmed her shoulders as she exited the store. The thin boy with her shopping cart stayed close behind. "Really, Hootie? 'Ma'am'?"

"I thought it was a nice touch," Hootie said. "What's up these days?"

"I need to re-up. You got any more of that sticky green?"

"Maybe. What are you needing?"

"Just a quarter right now. Payday's next week. I'm a little tight."

Hootie loaded the groceries into the back of the Jeep and then hopped up in the passenger seat. "Pull around to the back corner."

Betty Lou drove behind the loading dock where Hootie's gold Lexus was parked. Hootie hit the button on his keychain, got out, reached under the passenger seat of his car and shuffled through some letter sized envelopes until he found one with number four written in the corner. He handed her the envelope. She handed him the two twenties.

"I've got some peyote coming in tomorrow," Hootie said. "Supposed to be fresh from Baja."

"Cool," Betty Lou replied. "Save me a couple of buttons. I'll hit you up next week." Hootie saluted with two fingers to his brow and walked toward the loading dock.

That's how grocery shopping is supposed to work, Betty Lou thought as she pulled back onto the street.

Kevin watched the hall behind them as he followed Julio to the study, hoping Lydia had followed. He'd almost choked on a mouth full of cabrito when Lydia's silk-stockinged foot slid under his pants leg. He glanced over to see her seemingly hanging on her father's every word but two fingers of the hand she rested her head on gave him a tiny wave. Now she'd slipped out of sight. As he entered the dark-paneled space Julio pushed the door closed and motioned him to sit. He was absorbed by a cow hide chair that would accommodate a body twice his size.

"So is this the job interview portion of this evening's program?" He asked as Julio selected a bottle from the nearby bar.

Julio smiled. "Tequila?" Kevin nodded. "No," Julio said. "The job is yours, not that I have much choice. But we should discuss parameters, don't you think?"

"You're the boss."

"Right, and that's the first one."

"Sure, no problem. I drive the trucks. You make the rules."

"It's a start." Julio placed two shot glasses on the black walnut table between them and poured a generous shot of tequila in each class. "I need a little favor though." He picked up the glass and tossed back the shot.

"What? No salt or lime?" Kevin asked.

Julio shook his head. Kevin swore he heard the old man mutter "gringo" under his breath. "Lydia!" Julio hollered. Within seconds she appeared. "Our boy here needs some lime to choke down my top shelf tequila. Might as well bring the saltshaker too." Like an apparition she was gone.

"You were saying?" Kevin asked. He could feel his ears tinged pink from embarrassment.

"I've acquired a building, an old auto shop - gas station. The owner retired but before we could close the deal he passed away."

"I'm sorry to hear it," Kevin said.

"Yes, it complicates matters. I need the utilities transferred but I don't want my name on it, for reasons you know." Kevin raised an eyebrow. Julio continued "I'll pay the utilities, not a problem, just need another name on the paperwork."

"No problem I hope. I don't have an account in my name with the utility company yet but I have to find something soon. I'm stuck over in Alice right now. Too damn much commuting time."

"I have a space behind the shop. I need to clean it out but utilities are provided. It's small."

"I do small just fine. How much?"

Julio smiled, "We'll work something out."

UNDERBELLY

Daylily courts consisted of 400 yards; a single U-shaped gravel lane stuck to the end of a residential street in the southeast corner of Beeville. Older single wide mobile homes were packed on both sides of the street as tightly as city codes would allow. They seemed well-maintained. No junk or broken-down cars were evident, making the little community an oasis in this section of the city. Packs of young children pedaled around the circle on bicycles while their older siblings congregated in smaller groups staring at phones or skateboarding solo with earbuds in place.

Carrie's police cruiser made a slight ripple in the fabric of the neighborhood, but after she parked a few minutes in front of Number 42 without exiting the car the natural rhythm of the street returned. The Airstream was more compact than many of the other homes but featured a covered porch surrounded by ornate clay pots of tropical plants. A wrought iron chair resembling half of a large birdcage hung by a chain from a porch rafter.

Carrie waited until the appointed time of 11 o'clock. When the landlord still hadn't arrived she could no longer resist. She stepped up on the porch to try out the hanging chair. She fell in love. The scent of bougainvillea, honeysuckle and Texas hibiscus brought her a serenity she'd forgotten how to enjoy. A diesel-engine Ford with ladder racks hanging over a tool bed parked behind her cruiser. She continued to sit until the bearded man with the manila folder made it up the steps.

"Officer James?" He asked.

"Nope, just patrolman so far. Carrie is fine."

"I'm Ricky Bush. Want to see inside?"

She inhaled another lung full of the luscious aroma as Ricky fumbled with the keys. "Probably should."

Ricky opened the door and stood back. "We take care of the yard but the last tenant left the plants. I can get rid of them or you can keep 'em. Your call. The lady that lived here moved into a nursing home. She took a few but, well, small spaces and all, you know."

Carrie felt a pang of sadness catch her off guard. "Is she okay?"

"Just old as far as I know. Too old to get up and down the steps."

Upon entering the home the low ceilings and wood paneling gave the interior a claustrophobic feel. The windows were few and tiny. It would take a lot to brighten up the space. Just temporary, she thought. She glanced in the tiny bedroom, made sure the appliances worked and turned on the standup shower; all good, very basic. "How much?" though she already knew.

"Four-fifty a month," Ricky said, "but we like having a first responder on site so we'll cover the city utilities and gas bill. You just pay electric."

"Cool, let's do the deal." She had a new home. It even had furniture. She'd need to call Nadine and tell her she could have her furniture and stuff. It might save a trip to Austin if Nadine could ship her clothes.

<in. He drank socially and at parties without liquor having much effect. He found idiots who overindulged themselves to be entertaining and often an easy mark for some light scamming. As he conversed with Julio, the three hefty shots of tequila were more of a bonding experience. He spaced them out over the course of an hour, and on a full stomach. No problem, or so he thought.

The details of employment worked out with his convenience in mind. His first load would be solo; next weekend he'd bobtail to Brownsville Friday night, pick up a trailer load of produce and drop it at the brokerage in San Antonio. An empty trailer waited at the brokerage to bring home to Beeville Saturday afternoon. An easy $400 for days work, close to what he cleared a week as a PO. He also acquired the address of the auto shop and $200 upfront for the utility deposit. Something he could take care of on his lunch break. Everything legitimate, for now at least, on paper. Definitely low risk to him. His confidence at a peak, he bid Julio good night and stood. The tequila smacked him hard. He wobbled, considered sitting, thought he might stumble, then maintained a grip on reality. "Shit! Your tequila snuck up on me."

Julio smiled. "You can stay if you want. I don't need my new driver getting a DWI before the first run. Lydia can fix a spot on the couch."

"No, I'm cool. I'm supposed to be at a friend's tonight. It's only a couple miles."

"You sure? It's no trouble."

"I'm good."

"Well then, be careful. I'll have Lydia walk you out." Julio hollered for his daughter.

Outside the dry cool air brought him around. Though heat still radiated from the ground the dark sky appeared sprinkled with ice crystal stars.

"Thanks for coming," Lydia said. "I was having a really bad day until you showed up." She slipped her hand into his. The warmth of her long thin fingers cleared his head even more. He leaned against the truck. She stood close, putting a cheek on his shoulder. She'd let her hair down and the soft curls danced as she moved.

"I'm working part-time for your dad now," he said.

The edges of her smile turned conspiratorial. "I know. It's a shame."

"What? Why?"

She dropped his hand, turned and pressed against him, wrapping both arms over his shoulders. "Because now we aren't supposed to fraternize." She kissed him hungrily while digging her nails into the back of his neck. Her aggressive kiss finished clearing his head and his heart doubled its tempo. He wrapped an arm around her, feeling her lean hard body twisting into his grasp. He brought a hand to her firm butt and drove her pelvis into his now swollen crotch. She moaned and took his lower lip between her teeth while a perfectly manicured nail raked behind his ear.

She pulled tighter against him, letting his lip go and nuzzling into his collar. As he leaned to kiss the place on her neck he'd fantasized about earlier he felt a dampness at her hairline. She traced a line down his chest with a renegade fingernail. Just as she reached the zipper on his slacks the porch light came on. She jumped back startled. The door opened.

"Lydia, let the young man leave. He's supposed to be somewhere," Julio said. "Anyway, it's time for bed."

"God, don't I know it." She whispered and ran her moist palm over the bulge in his pants. In a heartbeat she transformed into the picture of virginal innocence. With her hands clasped behind her back she turned away. "I'm glad you're helping my daddy. Maybe I'll see you around," and glided toward the house.

Betty Lou flew low, the back beat in her backbone, almost to the edge of nodding. The green and the music mixed in her head. She'd long ago wrote off DJ for the night and made friends with her one-hitter. His loss, she mused. The soft silk baby doll nightie wrapped her in cumulus ecstasy as she considered leaving the couch for the comfort of her bedroom, alone but perfectly okay with it, she told herself. The song ended. The silence worked its way into her brain, reinvigorating her thoughts, thoughts she'd carefully and completely tamped down. She teetered on a precipice not knowing whether to jump or step back. God knows with her coordination she might just stumble in. No. It had to be her decision even if she wasn't sure where it would take her. DJ exuded a certain magnetic danger. He obviously had an agenda and she wasn't getting the whole story. Silence screamed at her.

She rolled off the couch and stood. Snatching her IPod from the dock, she pulled up the playlist of Béla Bartók's short piano pieces. The quirky melodies and dissonant harmonies scraped away the silence with a slightly insane blade. She turned down the volume, grabbed the three empty beer bottles off the table, trashed them and headed for bed. In the hall she glanced in the full length mirror, Damn, girl, you're a hot ass confection, she thought, good enough to eat. A brief tremor of disappointed anger rippled her heart. "Your loss, fucker." She started as the words actually flowed from her mouth. Crawling into bed she luxuriated in the fresh high count cotton sheets. The soft piano in the background closed her eyes with a sigh. She was sailing towards somnambulism when the doorbell interrupted.

Carrie stirred the pan of leftover carne guisada while alternately warming a flour tortilla on the grate over the burner's flame. Lois watched from the kitchen table leaning on crossed arms.

"Tomorrow," Carrie said. "Already paid the first month's rent. I have to work Monday, so I'm moving tomorrow."

Lois narrowed her eyes. "Don't you mean today?"

Carrie glanced at the clock. 1:45 AM. "Yeah, looks that way."

"You're not wasting any time. You could call you know, so I don't worry myself silly, instead of rolling in here at midnight."

"I had a lot to do today and I needed to get some work done."

"You're off today." Lois' fingers tightened around her biceps.

"I told you, there's more to it, okay? I needed to go by the office while I could have privacy for research. Also there was surveillance to be done after dark."

"Dammit, can you just do the job you hired on for and let Kevin work his angle. You've got enough on your plate." Lois brought a hand to the table in the shape of a fist. She pushed up and began pacing. "You're getting in way over your head."

Carrie watched her mom for a bit. "Don't worry. I'm careful." She turned back to the stove. "Shit!" Grabbing her spatula she tossed the flaming tortilla in the sink and turned on the water.

"I see that." Lois glanced at the sink. "How well do you know Kevin, anyway. He comes off as a little shady to me."

"I know enough. He's good at what he does." Carrie wasn't as sure of that as she wanted to be, but she did admire his dedication and focus. "You could help me, you know."

"I don't even know what you're doing."

"You don't have to. I ran a plate number for Kevin today. It came up as Ronald Dahl. The name sounds familiar. You know him?" Carrie knew the answer when she noticed Lois' anger turning back to concern. She lowered the flame and slipped a fresh tortilla on the grate. "What's his story?"

Lois shook her head and resumed her position at the table. "County Commissioner. Goes way back, more than a decade. Pretty much ever since the damn Republicans took over the County. He did a couple of terms in Austin as a state representative, then came home."

"Seems strange. Why would he do that?"

"Probably to be close to the local money. Just speculation on my part. He's done pretty well though, to be on a public servant's salary."

Carrie put the warm tortilla on a plate, spooned some carne guisada on top and sat down at the table. "Fill me in."

"His dad was a judge for the Fifth Circuit Court of Appeals back in the 80s. Family owns a large ranch in Jim Wells County. There's some old family money but they're not what you'd call rich. Little Ronnie though, he's got his hands in a lot of pies. Since he started in government he bought all the Valero franchises in Bee County. He bought another ranch in Jim Wells right next to his dad's. He has interest in some farms in the Valley through a corporation with some out-of-state people. It's hard to say what else. He keeps his cards pretty close to his chest."

"Sounds pretty successful for a County Commissioner," Carrie said between bites. "Think he has cartel connections?"

"I don't know. I can't imagine it's all legal, but cartel? That's a stretch."

"Why?"

"He's still alive."

"Mom, they don't kill everybody."

"He's white."

"That just makes him more valuable on this side of the border."

"Carrie! He's dangerous! That's all I know. Stay away from the slimy bastard!"

Carrie wrapped the tortilla around the remaining meat and swallowed it in three quick bites. "I wish I could, Mom. That's not how it works."

Kevin felt completely sober when he drove down the hill past SIP headquarters and turned toward town. Before he was even up to speed a pair of headlights came on a quarter mile behind him. His first thought was police. He drove 5 miles below the speed limit but the lights never got any closer. When he got to the turnoff to Betty Lou's apartment he continued past by a few blocks and turned left. The headlights followed, left again, still followed. He saw a streetlight near the back entrance to the apartments. He pulled in but stopped in the driveway. The car following sped up. As it whizzed by he recognized it. Damn Carrie! What the fuck are you up to?

He parked by the pool but couldn't see the light in Betty Lou's apartment. It was already after 11 PM but he'd told her he might be late. Something needed to be done about the nagging ache in his groin not to mention the hour drive home just to pull in behind Carrie. He checked his hair, put a stick of gum in his mouth and decided to go for it. Over a minute after he rang the doorbell a dim light came on. She answered the door looking up at him from a tattered cotton robe. Her stunning smile was nowhere to be found.

"What's up?" He asked.

"Not me." She stood at the door staring at him. He didn't know what to do, exactly.

"I'm sorry. Is it too late?"

She stepped back, letting him in. "Depends on what you want. You can crash here if you want but I'm already asleep."

"Can I use the couch?"

She shook her head as she wandered toward her bedroom. "Too much hassle. Come on back here. You know where everything is." She shed her robe and turned to make sure he saw what he'd missed before crawling into bed pulling the covers around her neck.

"Damn!" He whispered to himself before shucking his clothes and crawling in beside her. When he tried to cuddle up she turned her back to him.

"Not tonight. I'm tired," she said, and snuggled in to spoon. His groin ache returned with a vengeance.

Carrie had too much on her mind to sleep in, moving day and already a snag. The cruiser and her personal car were both at the ranch. On the one hand it meant she could load them both and make one trip. Unfortunately, she'd have to bow down and ask her mom for help. Mom would, but there was always a price. She really wanted to cut the cord cleanly.

She'd loaded the civic and only had a few things to put in the cruiser's trunk when she smelled bacon cooking. She followed her nose to the kitchen.

Lois had a butchers apron around her pajamas. "How about breakfast before we head out. I know you don't cook much, just that package health nut stuff. I'm making bacon, eggs and hash browns. Biscuits are in the oven."

"Sure, thanks. I'll miss this. And I guess you figured out I'll need help getting both cars to town."

"I figured Kevin would help you but he didn't show up last night."

"No, he stayed at his girlfriend's."

"He has a girlfriend already?"

"Two, apparently."

"See what I mean," Lois said. "Sleaze ball!"

"He's okay. Girls seem to go for the bad boy 'tude with the baby face. A winning combo."

Lois grabbed a sheet of biscuits from the oven. "I'm just glad you didn't buy into his BS."

Carrie finished setting the table for two. "You don't need to worry about that. I have no interest in any guys."

Lois paused mid-move. "What are you saying, honey?"

"Nothing. Just not interested."

"So you're gay? I mean, it's okay if you are, I guess. I just don't understand it."

"No mom. I think I'm what they call asexual. Being touched by people creeps me out, man or woman."

Lois continued making breakfast in silence. Carrie made orange juice. They were halfway through eating when Lois finally spoke. "That's not normal, you know. Don't you think you should talk to someone?"

"I've never met anyone who's normal. I'm fine. It works for me. Life is complicated enough without relationships and all the crap that goes with them."

"It's kind of sad you feel that way," Lois said, staring at her plate.

"I'm not sad," Carrie barked. She really needed to change the subject. Her stomach was tightening, not conducive to eating. "Anyway thanks for breakfast and helping with my cars. I know you're busy."

"No sweat." Silence resumed.

Kevin woke face down in the feather pillow. Betty Lou's lavender scent permeated by the rich smell of strong dark roast coffee. No hangover, good energy level, it must be late. He shifted as Betty Lou sat beside him.

"Mornin', Bruiser," Betty Lou said and ran her hand up from the small of his back. "You get in a fight last night?" She touched the scratches on the back of his neck.

Kevin lost himself in the tactile bliss of her caresses. The question only confused him. He grunted, then sighed. Betty Lou leaned in and kissed the little wound behind his ear. Then he felt her massage the warm oil into it. She whispered into his ear, "It's almond oil, high in vitamin E. You shouldn't let those nasty little girls mess up your skin. You have beautiful skin."

Kevin's eyes popped open like cartoon window shades. Betty Lou missed that. She was still behind him. How did she know? She didn't sound angry but he knew better than to trust his limited experience. "It's nothing," he said. "Just a little accident."

Betty Lou put her hand in the middle of his back. "Relax, DJ. We're cool." He felt the warm oil dribble down his spine. She began rubbing it in with a circular motion of her hands. "I'll fix you all up. This will keep you from scarring. Does it feel good?"

"Mmm, Hmm." He couldn't remember anything ever feeling this good.

"Better than getting scratched up, I'll bet?"

"Mmm, Hmm," he mumbled again, still too ecstatic to use his words.

She continued the massage, pressing her thumbs into the muscles down the edge of his spine, kneading his shoulders with her palms and rolling the heels of her hands into his buttocks. She finally leaned into him, pressing her knuckles in firmly starting at his thigh and tracing the firm musculature up to his neck. "I made coffee. Want some? I found a Razorbacks cup at a garage sale yesterday."

"Of course," he said and rolled over. He saw she was still wearing the nightie he'd gotten a glimpse of the previous evening. "Damn, you're hot." He was at a loss for further communication.

She pirouetted for him and gave him a shy smile. "Thanks, sweetie," and wiggled off to get the coffee, throwing in a little extra slinkiness for good measure.

When she returned with the coffee he'd reclined against the wrought iron headboard with the covers pulled around his waist. She handed him a cup and put hers on the nightstand beside a candle operated oil warmer to which she'd added additional almond oil.

"I got in," he said.

Betty Lou chuckled. "It appears so." She dabbed more oil on the scratch behind his ear.

"No. I mean I got hired at SIP part-time, weekends. I start next Friday, pick up a load in the Valley and deliver it to San Antonio."

Betty Lou stuck her lower lip out in a childlike pout.

"What?"

"Nothing really. I was just thinking we can go to Mustang Island some weekend. At least you're not crossing the border, right?"

"Not this time, and I won't be gone every weekend. I'm just doing this until I figure out who's running the show out there. Something's really screwed up over there."

"Like the girl who drives Corvettes through buildings?"

"She's got problems."

Betty Lou dipped her fingers in the warm oil and sprinkled it on Kevin's bare chest, massaging it in. She tweaked one of his little pink nipples with the tips of her fingers. "Sorry, I don't have long fingernails but I can make it hurt if that's what you like. I won't even leave a mark."

"No! Hell no! I don't like pain. Look, I'm sorry. Can we stop talking about her now? We have fun, right?"

Betty Lou straddled his lap in one quick bounce and hugged him with his face between her ample breasts. "That we do!"

Kevin decided right then to steer clear of Lydia as much as possible. Betty Lou was understanding but why jeopardize a real good thing.

She hopped back off to let him breathe. "Lay down flat. I'm going to finish your massage, then you can do me."

"I don't know anything about massage."

"Don't worry. I'll talk you through it. I'll bet you're a natural." She took a condom from the drawer and set it on the nightstand.

"I thought you were on The Pill," he said.

"I am, but if you're going to be fucking other women we'll be using condoms."

"But I didn't..."

"Shhh," she whispered, putting a finger to his lips. "Those are the rules."

He laid flat, per instructions, and sucked the delicious almond oil from the verb restraining finger.

Janet Kendrick anchored the Bee County criminal justice system. Born in nearby Tuleta, she'd spent most of her 60+ years slowly climbing the judicial ladder. "Sitting around waiting for someone to die," she said. Now younger, hungrier local stalwarts awaited her demise. Every year she threatened to retire. Every week she wondered what kept her in this rinky-dink outpost of inhumanity. Today would not be a good day.

She left the house early for the three-quarter mile walk from the two-bedroom frame house built by her late husband shortly before he keeled over dead at age 42. The whole point since that day had been to bring order and consistency wherever she could and banish or ignore the rest, not always an easy task. Like now.

In addition to keeping blood pumping through her crusty old veins, the walk gave her an opportunity to focus. She stepped off her porch not knowing whether to terminate Kevin Cash or make the effort to get him on track. The odds weren't in his favor. By the time she reached the courthouse she'd decided the easy way wasn't always the best. She traded her New Balance trainers for black leather pumps and pulled the ominous black robe over her sweats. At promptly 8 AM Kevin Cash knocked lightly on her door.

"Come in, Mr. Cash," she said. "Have a seat." She arranged a few papers on her desk while observing him. Dressed casually conservative in a pale blue dress shirt and jeans, his black Western boots polished to a mirror finish, he moved smoothly and deliberately into the subservient chair like a puppy caught shredding the Sunday Times. She locked him in her gaze. "You're new here," she stated the obvious. "I appreciate your enthusiasm."

"Yes ma'am. Thank you." He was the picture of submissiveness.

She waited a moment to let him anticipate the other shoe falling. "But we need to get a couple of things straight, boundaries and communication. First, this office works cases on the state level. We do not insert ourselves into the affairs of other departments unless requested through appropriate channels. Are we clear?"

"Yes, Your Honor," Kevin said.

Judge Kendrick clasped her hands to her face, parallel index fingers pointing at the ceiling, to hide her amusement at his blatant brown-nosing. "We have specific jobs to do. We're not in the investigating business. I understand that a parolee died while employed at SIP. Close out his file. Talk to other clients employed there if necessary, then move on. If you have suspicions of illegal activity, unless it directly involves one of your charges, report it to the proper authorities and move on. Are we clear?"

"Yes, Your Honor."

"This is a small town, Mr. Cash, and a very tight knit community. There is very little going on here that I don't know about. We have very few businesses willing to employ probationers and parolees. We need to keep the big picture in mind. If these businesses don't always follow best practices it's not in our best interest to get involved. Like I said, we are not investigators." She crossed her arms and leaned back in her chair. "I'll be honest with you. I came close to terminating you. I'm not, because you're dedicated and you take initiative. Use these boundaries to temper that initiative. Don't make me regret my decision."

"Yes, Your Honor."

Judge Kendrick pulled a manila folder from the stack, opened it and passed it to Kevin. "I covered for you this time. Ms. Ramirez is technically a juvenile. I got Judge Elders to agree to six months probation and restitution. I'm going to give you some free advice. It would behoove you to steer clear of Lydia Ramirez. Not just because she's a juvenile either."

"Thank you, judge."

"Besides," Judge Kendrick finally smiled, "I think you might have your hands full right here at home."

The color left Kevin's cheeks. The judge knew about Betty Lou. "We're just...."

Judge Kendrick raised her brows. "Remember, it's a small town." She dismissed him with a flick of her hand.

Carrie awoke in her tiny trailer elated by having her own space. Other than an occasional hotel room this was the first time she'd had a place totally to herself. She'd ended the previous exhausting day of moving with a scalding self-satisfying shower that required no vocal restraint, followed by 10 hours of deep dreamless sleep. Now she sat on her porch in flannel pajamas sipping coffee and inhaling the scent of hibiscus and honeysuckle while observing her little neighborhood come to life. Her Sheriff's cruiser in her driveway warranted attention and friendly greetings from most of her neighbors. She did note a sideways glance from a Latino bodybuilder in a crew-cab dually pickup. He made the extra effort to turn the iron behemoth around in the one lane road in order to leave by the far leg of the U-shaped street. Silly man, she thought, as she jotted down his plate number, *If not for your paranoia, I'd never have noticed you.*

On autopilot, Betty Lou traipsed up the sidewalk toward work. She knew Judge Kendrick well enough to be certain, barring any arrogant posturing on Kevin's part, that he was still employed by the state. She was slightly late on purpose, to let the dust settle from whatever Kevin's reaction had been. Besides, she needed the morning to revel in the massage and its rowdy aftermath. The boy was a natural at more than massage. He'd played an orgasmic encore with a heavy double bass downbeat on her willing body. She needed a moment to regroup and an extra cup of coffee to focus on her day. She liked what they had. It was easy and fun. She tried to suppress the little green demon dancing around the periphery of her consciousness by labeling it as a concern for his safety. That Lydia Ramirez was obviously bat-shit crazy.

After pulling instead of pushing on the building's entry door, the same one she'd passed through hundreds of times, her purse strap caught on the knob dumping a small portion of the contents on the marble floor. Fortunately, no one noticed except the ancient security guard who pretended not to. She piled her possessions back in the bag, snapping the protective cover back on her cell phone and checking the function. Down the hall her office door was open. Inside she found her Hoosiers cup brimming with perfectly prepared hot coffee and DJ sporting a sly grin. "I see you're not cleaning out your desk," she said.

"She knows," he replied.

Betty Lou considered the various things that statement might imply. "About what?"

"Us."

"And?"

"She seems cool with it."

"With what?"

"You and me, our thing."

"Thing?"

Kevin furrowed his brow and stood. "You know?"

Betty Lou kicked the door closed with her heel. "You told her we fucked like hot ferrets?"

Kevin hiccupped a laugh. "I didn't tell her anything. She figured it out somehow."

"Maybe you hound-dogging around my office half the day, you think?"

Kevin glanced at the door, grabbed Betty Lou by the waist and leaned in for a kiss.

"Nope!" Betty Lou dodged his lips. "We still have to be professional, besides, you'd look a bit strange wearing my lip gloss. Let's get to work."

"Speaking of, kinda, I scored a place to stay in town. There's an empty travel trailer out at SIP. I'm going to trade some truck maintenance for it. It cost me zilch!"

Betty Lou felt the jagged blade of dread twist in her stomach. "Is that a good idea?"

"What better way to keep an eye on the place. Keep it under your hat though, okay?"

Betty Lou sat down at her desk and wrapped both trembling hands around her coffee cup. "No, I won't say anything but don't you think for a minute this won't get back to Kendrick." She tried to maintain, but unexpected tears began to fill her eyes. Kevin stepped behind to comfort her. She motioned toward the door. "We've got work to do."

Carrie donned her crisp beige uniform and holstered the famous Peacemaker that gave her more credibility with her coworkers than all her postgraduate work in criminal justice combined. After pouring the rest of her morning coffee in an insulated travel mug she backed the clattering old police cruiser out of the driveway. She pulled away leaving a hint of oily blue haze. Five minutes later she parked at the County Courthouse Annex where her cubicle was waiting on the fourth floor. As she entered the office her six coworkers and the County judge congratulated her. Before the dozen celebratory doughnuts had disappeared she's been sworn in and the other uniforms were off on their respective assignments. Ross motioned her into his office.

Had Ross and Aurora's only attempt at progeny not failed in a terrifying and bloody late-term miscarriage the girl would have been about Carrie's age. Had Ross contemplated, which he didn't, he may have realized that to be the reason for his paternal instincts toward his recruit. He just assumed it was due to the lack of a father figure in her familial structure. Though they produced no offspring Ross felt fortunate to be wedded to Aurora as he considered her far more attractive and intelligent than he deserved. She also encompassed a focused determination for success that lifted her to the upper echelons of the National Security Agency, heading a multi-agency task force rooting out graft and corruption in federal law enforcement. It kept her on the road more than home but she relished her work.

Across the desk from each other Ross and Carrie assumed formal postures. "I know you want to jump in headfirst," Ross said, "but the first couple of weeks I'd like you to patrol the town square; get to know the lay of the land; meet folks. In the evening, say 4:00 to 730 you'll work booking on the fifth floor to get to know the judges and procedures. It's a way to understand how the wheels turn."

Carrie stifled her disappointment with the last remaining doughnut. "You're the boss," she mumbled around the glazed confection. "I'm planning to hit the firing range in the mornings. I passed my firearms test, but I still don't feel totally comfortable with my weapon."

"Yep. That's a heavy chunk of iron you wield."

Carrie washed the last bite of donut down with her coffee. "So, I should punch in around 10?"

"Works for me," Ross said. As Carrie stood to leave Ross held up a finger. "One more thing," Ross paused to catch her attention. "There is a Bar-B-Q Labor Day weekend, a big political event Commissioner Dahl does every election year. If you want I'll introduce you around. Aurora's out of town on business that weekend but I'm more or less obligated to appear. If you don't mind being arm candy...?"

Carrie felt the sweat melt her armpits. "Look, Ross, I don't want to get any rumors started. I like Aurora."

"Oh God, no! It's nothing like that. I just really want to show off the departmental diversity. Wear your uniform. As far as I know we've never had a female deputy. I know you'll want to network with the local honchos."

Carrie thought back to her chat with Mom about Ronald Dahl. "Sure, I'm game. Pick me up in time to get there before the brisket's all gone."

Lydia sat cross-legged on her canopy bed fondling the single edged razor blade she kept in in her mother's Bible. Her father had assigned her an ecstatic torture. A pickup load of cardboard liquor boxes were piled on the porch of the RV Miguel had inhabited. She had to pack away his belongings and clean the place so DJ could move in. Why her? She wondered. Was it a punishment? She could punish herself without any help from Daddy. He had no knowledge of the nights she'd slipped away under cover of darkness to have Miguel wrap her in his tattooed arms, tossing her around like a toy, loving her so hard it hurt both mind and body.

As she pulled the blade across her inner thigh, raising a tiny insignificant line that slowly flowed scarlet: up, angle down, angle up straight down. The M for Miguel, for Mama, for the mindfuck stupid assignment she'd rather die than do.

The sting of the blade against her skin brought forth tears. She used an index finger to wipe them from her cheek and press them into the glyph on her thigh, diluting the scarlet liquid while enhancing the pain. This may have been her final act if not for the image forming on the opposite side, the letters D and J. Her only hope throbbing just below the surface of her skin. She released them with the blade, then squeezed her mother's lace handkerchief between the wounds and buried her head away from the light so she could fully focus on the pain.

BULLET MUSIC

The dead air hanging in the steel building radiated Dog Day heat from every direction. Kevin's dress shirt glistened with sweat from the short walk downhill with the key to the RV Julio had just relinquished. They sat across from each other at the folding metal table in the expansive bay. Though opposing overhead doors were open not the slightest breeze stirred the scent of solvents and diesel fumes.

"Give me the weekend," Julio said. I'll have Miguel's belongings cleaned out and the place detailed. You can move in next week."

"No hurry. Just let me know, whenever." The heat drained all energy from Kevin. He didn't care if he ever moved again.

"Can you manage replacing a u-joint?" Julio asked.

Kevin looked around at the sparsely appointed shop. "Yeah, I've done a few." It had an air compressor and hydraulic press. A roll-around tool cabinet against the far wall surely held the basic hand tools needed for the simple repair. "You know, that auto shop you acquired out west of town is set up much better than this."

"Yeah, well, we may move some of the equipment here. I'll probably use that mostly to store cargo."

Kevin didn't have the energy to respond. He stared toward the highway and waited. Eventually he heard a dually pickup rumble up and stop behind the building. Dust wafted in through the opening and settled on the concrete floor, followed by the jingle of Raul's ridiculous omnipresent spurs.

"Here's the part you needed," Raul said, clanging a box down on the metal table. "They released the truck, finally. I paid the impound. Sonny said he'd tow it out this afternoon. Raul looked over Kevin's dress shirt and slacks. "Hell of an outfit for a mechanic."

"Tell it to your horse," Kevin replied, glancing down at Raul's spurs. When he noticed the thick man's jaw tighten he tilted back and stuck his thumbs in his skinny black belt. "Easy, Cowboy. I'm just fucking with you."

"We're cool. Sorry. It's just... Well, Miguel and me, we were buds since middle school. I can't, I mean, it just don't make no sense."

Kevin opened the box and unwrapped the U joint. He stared at it a moment thinking how one little piece of metal had changed so many lives. "This the right part?"

"Should be," Julio said. We changed one before on that truck. The numbers match."

"I'm a bit overdressed right now. Okay if I take care of it this weekend after I get back from San Antonio?"

Julio nodded.

Raul pulled out a chair and joined them. "How's the party coming?"

"What party?" Julio asked.

Kevin was in deep now. He'd yet to figure out how to approach the subject. He paused for breath. "Raul and I thought of maybe throwing a company party for Labor Day. I DJed for a while when I was in college, I still have some of the equipment. He figured after what went down with Miguel and Carlos maybe it would improve morale. We could rent the VFW Hall, have some food, a couple of kegs, invite the employees and their families, some local customers, and folks we want on our side. What do you think, Boss?"

Julio sat motionless except for his eyes shifting back and forth from Kevin to Raul. He reached up and stroked his chin. "Hmmm, sounds like you boys thought it out. How much will it cost?"

Raul and Kevin looked at each other. Neither spoke. Kevin shrugged.

"I'll put in a grand, maybe some beef. I'll see what's in the deep freeze. The rest is on y'all," Julio said. You'll have to invite the local constabulary. Most of 'em won't show up but they get invited or no party. Clear?"

Kevin and Raul grinned like they'd been handed the keys to their first car.?

"And I need that truck on the road no later than Monday morning," Julio added.

"No problem," Kevin replied.

Carrie contemplated the warmth of the iron against her outer thigh. The Peacemaker burned through two boxes of ammo in less than 45 minutes. Her control and accuracy improved to the point where the last 30 shots hit the kill zone at 40 yards. Her wrists and shoulders ached from the recoil but not to the point where the discomfort outweighed the elation of her accuracy. The session brought an intensity of power to her core and a confidence she'd rarely experienced. She cleaned her weapon and checked the time, ready to introduce herself around the town square.

After four hours of leapfrogging from business to business handing out generic sheriff's deputy business cards, the elation ground away. Whether they'd previously heard of her or not most citizens regarded her as Lois James' little girl. Her identity was only a shadow left from Mom's irrefutable presence.

Working in the jail during Monday afternoon doldrums did little to improve her mood. She ended the shift in a blue funk. She managed to exit the courthouse without having to interact with other deputies. The odd discourse with citizens sparked a desire for face time with her mom, but the two-hour road trip plus the freedom of inhabiting her own space quelled her aspiration. As soon as she reached her patrol car she put the Peacemaker in the glove box, let down her hair and reclined against the headrest. One deep breath and she startled to the chime of her cell phone, the number listed only as restricted. Normally she would have ignored it but curiosity, for once, got the better of her.

"James here."

"Hi Carrie, it's Aurora. Can we meet this weekend?"

"I guess. Should I stop by your house?" No immediate response. "Aurora? You there?"

"I'd rather we meet somewhere neutral. I'll just be passing through so Ross doesn't need to know I'm in town. It's about a case you're familiar with."

Carrie hit panic mode. There were only a couple of cases she had any knowledge of, none of which she wanted to share. Still, maybe she could get some new info. "Sure, I guess. When?"

"Is Sunday okay? I'll call when I get to town."

"Okay." Call ended. Carrie stared at her phone in disbelief, noticing her hand trembling ever so slightly.

Shades of stagnant brown August boredom ran on for miles of migraine inducing vibrational discomfort. Kevin had inadvertently reintroduced himself to the trucker's life. This better pay off, he thought, dragging his jarred body down from the Kenworth. More than money was involved here. Money alone wouldn't have coerced him into this madness.

He saw the box van parked on the incline behind the shop. He'd promised to repair it by Monday. He still had a few hours of daylight. What could take, maybe an hour, at most? Might as well save a trip back to town on Sunday. The U joint was still on the metal table where he'd left it. Even in an unfamiliar shop, it was mindless work repairing the drive shaft, though he'd have to crawl in the gravel under the truck to install it. He spotted grease-stained coveralls roughly his size hanging beside the toolbox. As he pulled them on he wondered if they belonged to Miguel. A shiver went through him when he zipped them up.

As he crawled under the box van, he heard an unearthly wail coming from the RV Camp across the parking lot, followed by breaking glass. Not my problem, he thought and focused on his work. He recognized the second wail as Lydia. He immediately thought of Betty Lou and decided to continue with his work. After more breaking glass, the noises subsided. His goal was to leave unnoticed. His pickup had spent the night inside the shop. Maybe she didn't even know he was here. He made quick work of installation. It was not the sort of repair requiring a road test.

Back in the shop he peeled off the greasy coveralls. Even the stagnant air felt cool on his sweaty arms. Tossing the garment on the workbench, he turned. Between him and his pickup stood a deflated Lydia, less than elegant in cut-off jeans and sweat soaked white T-shirt. Beads of perspiration lined the pile of curls on her head and trickled down that sensational neck. He could see the almond nipples beneath the soggy shirt. Her expression was unreadable. She stood ghostly still, as did he, two frozen sculptures disintegrating in the toxic oven of questionable lust. Several daylong seconds expired before Lydia lunged. The brutal sting of her hand singeing his face brought Kevin back to life.

"You don't even care, you fucker!" She wailed. "I could have been dying over there."

He tried backing away as the heels of her hands pummeled his chest. The workbench blocked his retreat. He wrapped her in his arms, his only option to spare her outrage. She melted into tears and sobs, all resistance drained away.

"I'm sorry," she said, burying her face in his chest and inhaling. She began moaning again. "It's never going to be okay, is it?"

Not knowing how to react, Kevin kept her in his arms as her fit subsided. Words didn't come. He feared making any promises but wouldn't release her either. Finally, she tilted her head up and kissed his cheek, thanking him and slipping away. When she reached the back door of the shop, she turned. "The little house is clean. I fixed it up really nice for you. Want to see it?"

A quarter mile from the highway the one lane road Julio navigated still featured a gray asphalt surface. Four-rail whitewashed oak fences bordered the lane. Behind the fences, melancholy Red Angus cattle dotted the lush green fields of irrigated grass. The whole storybook scene seemed lost in the drought-stricken plains of Southwest Texas where manicured clusters of elm and pecan trees replaced ocotillo and tumbleweed. Since passing through the architecturally rendered electric security gate, Julio became more angered and intimidated by the display of wealth. No wonder Commissioner Dahl wanted to meet on his own turf.

Julio crested a slight rise. An antebellum plantation house constructed of native limestone featured two verandas, the upper one supported by Roman columns. The Olympic size swimming pool was situated where a classic reflecting pool should have been. Julio's blood sizzled in his veins. Comfort is one thing; blatant excess had no place in this depressed rural economy. Money, however, makes the rules, the rules Julio must follow if he wished to maintain his level of comfort.

Considering the opulence, Julio was surprised when Ronnie Dahl personally opened the door. "Come in, my friend. Welcome to my humble abode."

Julio stomped his pristine boots on the horsehair mat. "Good to see you keeping up appearances. Must be a struggle." He shook Dahl's hand, a bit more firmly than usual. "What's up? Why'd you have me come way out here? You know you can stop by my place any time."

"I have a job for you, a lucrative one, but it's not something I want to discuss in the presence of your nutcase daughter, or your drivers either, for that matter."

Julio bristled at the mention of Lydia but followed Dahl to the study. Ronnie took two glasses from the cabinet and filled them half full of Glenlivet 20. "Get a taste of how the other half lives. Maybe you'll find it to your liking."

Julio took a sip, found it agreeable and reclined on the leather couch, propping his boots on the armrest. He held up his glass in a toast. "Too flagrant and unbridled wealth." He downed the elixir, passing the empty glass for a refill. "Don't be so fucking stingy. Top it off this time!"

Dahl filled the glass with Glenlivet. "Make yourself at home." Dahl waddled around the room trying to get his bearings, finally taking the chair behind the desk. "I need a load brought in from Mexico. I'm on a tight schedule," Dahl said. "I have an obligation to some folks."

Julio took a sip then ran his tongue across his upper lip causing his mustache to dance the tango. "No. I don't haul women, not for that." He put his feet back on the floor. "I don't appreciate you going behind my back either. Two men died, at least two women. My truck abandoned in the desert and the heat down on me." He stood and leaned across the desk. "I'll bring workers, even contraband, stuff that's coming here anyway, but you leave me out of the sex slave business."

"No can do." Dahl grinned, his sneer a dubious threat. "You're already in. Who can you trust? Raul?"

"Yeah, but no. For one, he can't get a passport. For two, I said I'm not fucking doing it!"

"The thing is... you don't have a choice. I have to make this work. I'm the Commissioner and your business is here. So that's one thing. The other thing? I have bosses too and all I have to do is snap my fingers and your daughter is buzzard snacks. Comprende?"

Julio's stomach did a little jig as all his blood rushed to his sphincter. He dropped back to the couch because his legs would no longer hold him up. "I have a guy. I need a week."

"Five days." Dahl said. "The pickup is set for next Friday."

Kevin drove with the windows of his pickup down hoping the desert air would dry his hair on the way to Betty Lou's apartment. Being late again bothered him but not as much as the reason. He should have waited to inspect his new living quarters until Julio gave him the key. He didn't want to hurt Lydia's feelings after she worked so hard cleaning the place. Now he wondered if he had been played.

His first clue: When she followed him in and closed the door, he noticed the AC was still pumping out frigid air. Lydia however, was anything but frigid. Two wineglasses sat on the tiny breakfast bar by an open bottle of rosé, already down a third.

"So what do you think?" Lydia asked, panning the room with her fingers.

He had to admit she'd done a tremendous job. Everything was spotless and polished. The only truckers smell came from his own clothes. "Wow, I like it. Who would have thought a little tin box could be so... so livable. It looks like the cover of one of those decor magazines you see at the checkout stand."

Lydia smiled and took a stool at the bar. "I've actually opened the cover of a few of those." She winked. "Let me know if you need a good housekeeper." She poured wine into the glasses and patted the other barstool. "We should celebrate your new home."

When the wineglass touched his lips a moment of trepidation fluttered through his brain, but he assumed he still had the situation under control. Two glasses later when Lydia pulled the barrette free and those curls cascaded down around that perfect neck he knew better. Her hand was resting on his thigh and he was certain her lips wanted to be kissed. What the hell, he thought. Who'll know?

She turned away, holding the thigh enticing hand in his face. "You smell like a trucker! Nothing personal but no, not now. Why don't you take a nice hot shower?"

"I don't have any clothes with me."

"I left some shorts and T-shirts from the last guy on the dresser."

"What? Wear a dead guy's clothes?"

"He won't need 'em. Besides, don't tell me you've never shopped at a thrift store. What did you think you were buying?"

He hesitated, then slid off the barstool. "They've been washed?"

"Smelled like it. Better than what you're wearing."

He still hadn't figured it out. She sat demurely on the stool with her legs crossed at the ankles sipping her wine.

Kevin enjoyed the shower with a high-pressure pulsating showerhead pounding out at a temperature barely below scalding. He would feel right at home here. Thoughts of tipsy little Lydia perched at the breakfast bar kept entering his mind. The tiny bathroom steamed like a sauna. He was rinsing the shampoo out of his hair when he felt the change in air pressure. A moment later the curtain pulled back.

"I can wash your back if you'd like," Lydia said stepping into the tub, not a tan line visible on her sleek amber body. The almond nipples of her teacup breasts dripped with suds he'd flung from his hair. "Turn around." She took the washcloth from his hand and, as much as he hated to relinquish the view, he obeyed, leaning his elbows against the wall, arms crossed above his head.

She slathered the cloth with liquid lavender soap and began at his shoulders in firm circular strokes using her free hand to massage the muscles along his spine. She hummed as she scrubbed until she worked down below his waist and the song lost its melody, becoming appreciative moans. He was covered in lather when she dropped the cloth and began rubbing his butt with both slick hands. He could feel her breath on his neck. A slender finger slipped between his cheeks, the tip resting on his anal aperture. Her foot slid up the inside of his calf, a suggestion. He hesitated only briefly before spreading his feet. When her finger entered his ass he flinched. "Damn girl! Fingernails! Easy."

"I thought you liked to play rough?"

"No way! Not there anyway."

"Sorry," she whispered and withdrew her hand. She wrapped around his waist, cheek against his shoulders and breasts writhing rhythmically against his back. Her left hand cradled his balls, thumb gently rolling them in her palm while her other hand grasped his now marble solid penis. He heard her breath catching her throat. "Holy fuck," she said.

He knew he was endowed on the happy side of adequate but his experience was limited and he'd never elicited this sort of reaction. "What's wrong?" he asked.

"Nothing. Not a damn thing! I love it. So thick, and the cool curves, I can't imagine what that would be like. I want that in me!" She stroked it slowly up from the base letting two of her fingers slip over the tip. "And I like that you're trimmed, not all that extra skin in the way."

He was panting now, almost beyond words. "I grew it just for you."

She bit his shoulder. "Bullshit! But I'll borrow it. Turn around."

He did. She smiled up at him. He grabbed her waist with one arm, smashing her against him, took a handful of hair and kissed her hard, thrusting his tongue between her warm lips.

She pushed him back with both hands. "Slow down!" She held his face between her hands. "What are we doing?" Before he answered she kissed him gently then sucked lightly on his bottom lip. She kissed his cheek softly, her lips barely touching. The spray from the shower trickling down her face, beaded on her eyelashes and earlobes. Then she kissed his chest while again holding his rigid member with both hands. She sucked his nipples, alternately sucking, nibbling, and circling them with her tongue. She kneeled and sipped water from his navel. Still grasping him with both hands, she sucked one of his balls into her mouth, rolling her tongue around it. Finally, she tenderly kissed the head of his throbbing rod.

In the course of three seconds the water turned ice cold. "Fuck!" They screamed in unison. He turned off the cold water, still cold, just less pressure. He turned the water completely off. "What the hell!"

"We ran out of hot water," she said, handing him a towel from the rack. "Come on in the bedroom. I'll warm you back up." She grabbed another towel from the cabinet.

On the very short trip to the bedroom he wondered if it was some karmic sign to be interrupted by circumstance. At least it gave his upper head time to regroup. "I don't have any condoms with me," he said.

"It's okay, I'm safe." She ran a fingernail down his chest.

"You're on the Pill?"

"No, but it's not my time."

"Famous last words."

"Seriously, DJ, it's not for you to worry about. I'm safe."

Kevin swallowed and stopped just outside the bedroom door. "I'm sorry. I'm a kind of a condom guy," he lied, just to regain his footing. "I want to do this. I do, more than I should, just not now."

"You're mean," she pouted. "You got me all worked up."

"I know. Me too. I'm sorry."

"Can you stay with me while I fix it?"

"What do you mean?" He pulled a pair of cutoff jeans and a T-shirt off the dresser.

"Go ahead, get dressed if you're scared. I'll fix my problem.

You can stay and watch if you want." Lydia posed on the bed, pillow under her shoulders with her head tilted back, damp raven curls strown across the pillow. She cupped a breast in her left hand while sucking on her right two middle fingers. When she removed the fingers from her mouth a string of saliva glistened on her lower lip. The fingers buried in the chocolate colored down between her thighs as she spread her knees apart. She thrust her protruding hipbones up against the effort of her palm against the still damp mound.

Tiny trickles of dampness formed on that lovely throat just below her earlobe. Kevin's senses were acute. He caught every detail, the circular rhythm of her wet fingers dancing at the edge of her aperture and the force with which the thumb and forefinger of her left hand pinched her swollen nipple.

Low sounds like an unbearable sadness escaped from behind the tongue skipping across her teeth. A loud wail erupted as she shoved the two fingers deep inside and ground her palm against her pelvis. She shuddered, whined, and pulled wet fingers out holding them up toward Kevin. She panted, "Want a taste?"

Kevin leaned over and licked the salty candy from between her fingers then sucked them like a popsicle. She put them back in service, circling her now protruding clit. "Please help me," she begged. "I can't nibble my own nipples." She sounded so desperate. He kneeled beside her and took her left nipple in his mouth while she grabbed her right breast with such force he thought the angry red nipple would explode. "Bite it!" she ordered, as she thrust three, then four fingers so deep inside that only her thumb and the back of her hand were visible.

"Harder!" He screamed, as she locked her left arm around his neck smashing his face into her breast. "Bite down, hard. Please, God. Harder."

He could hear the slurp - slap of her hand spanking her clit so viciously the headboard slammed against the wall. He was biting the nipple to the point he thought he might draw blood. "Harder please," she begged. Sobs were now racking her body. "Please, bite it hard, make it happen." She tightened the headlock, smashing his face against her chest. He could feel the wanton vibrations tremble through her desperation as the waves began to carry her to orgasmic oblivion. "Yes, oh please. Let me bleed for you!" A guttural inhuman groan began in the back of her throat as her whole body shook, arcing up from the bed as her slick fingers slapped and tugged at her clit. The intensity kept rising. Every muscle from her curled toes to the rigid tendons of her throat spasmed in ecstasy, like a long shapely twisted rubber band stretching to its snapping point. She thrashed so violently he feared she might injure herself. With a yelp and a rising howl she peaked, then collapsed in a trembling mass. She pushed his face off her breast and rolled away from him, curling into a fetal pose in the center of the bed. Sobs racked her body and tears streamed down her cheek. "I'm so sorry," she wailed.

He had no idea where that came from. "For what?" He asked.

"Not being what you wanted."

"No, it's not like that. You're amazing." His swollen purple appendage served as an exclamation point. He regretted his lack of participation.

"Could you hold me for a minute?" It was a tentative request spoken into the pillow without eye contact. He crawled into the bed and wrapped around her, replacing her pillow with his bicep. She sighed and snuggled deep into the curve of his abdomen. Within minutes the dainty wheeze of her exhausted, rhythmic snore was the only sound in the room. It took considerably longer for his raging hard-on to begin softening.

Julio spent the better part of the drive back from Dahl's ranch trying to figure out when everything had gone off the rails. The produce business had been profitable. It was a hard but honest living. Then he lost his wife. Carmelita had been his true love and his reason to succeed, her and his own strong work ethic. She had also been his greatest challenge and his most devastating failure, a puzzle he'd never been able to solve. Then she was gone and he'd done nothing to prevent it. Regardless of outside advice, he still blamed himself.

She left him Lydia. He promised to make it better for his daughter, an easier life; whatever she needed to be happy; to keep the world from hurting her.

It began by taking an occasional load off the books, a load from Laredo, tagged and sealed with a manifest he knew was likely bogus. Then farm workers, still this side of the border; just helping his people. Why should he care if they had papers? Now he was stuck. It was hard to justify smuggling the women. Maybe it was their choice. Maybe they just wanted better pay for the same job, but inside his conscience was screaming at him.

He was left with no alternative. He had to protect Lydia. He had to protect the business. He had to admit the money was good. Kevin Cash was the wild card. Could he be trusted? He seemed to be dependable and trustworthy, and fond of Lydia. Was that a good thing, or not? In the grand scheme of things it no longer mattered. He was stuck. He had to make this work.

Julio may have had his superstitions, but he didn't believe in ghosts. Still, as he approached the entrance to S I P he swore he saw Miguel's ghost stepping out of his old trailer; same tight white T-shirt, same baggy cutoffs hanging below his knees. The sun was playing tricks on him. When he looked again, there was no one there.

Kevin slipped his arm from under Lydia's head without waking her up. He pulled the covers up and kissed her lightly on that heavenly spot under her ear. "Manana, Mamacita." She sighed without opening her eyes. He picked up his work clothes from the bathroom floor and corked the remaining rosé, setting it back in the fridge. Just before he opened the door he thought he heard Lydia crying. He slipped out quietly. He was almost across the parking lot when he saw Julio's truck slowing to turn off the highway. With no way to explain the situation that wouldn't end up with him in deep shit, he sprinted for the shop and crouched behind a barrel of waste oil. Julio drove up the hill to the main house without slowing. After a reasonable interim, Kevin pulled his pickup out of the bay, locked up and headed toward town. Late again but counting on some sweet relief from Betty Lou.

THE CATCH

Carrie rolled into the parking lot of the Line Shack thirty minutes early. Bottle caps and pull tabs littered the expense of gravel. A dually, one of the two pickups in front of the low-slung clapboard building, looked vaguely familiar. She spent no time contemplating it. She had other things on her mind. After checking her Peacemaker to make certain it was fully loaded, she re-holstered it.

She entered the sagging building letting the screen door slam behind her. It took a moment for her eyes to adjust to the light of the neon beer signs. Looking up from the sports section briefly, the bartender saw her uniform, stood and placed his hands on the bar.

"What can I get you?"

"Got coffee?"

"I can make some, be a few minutes."

"Never mind," Carrie said. "I'll have a coke. Can I get a glass of ice?"

"No problem." He fixed her drink while she took in the surroundings. Two men played pool under a dim hanging light bar. The heavyset man wearing spurs reminded her of where she'd seen the truck before. She'd run his plates. Raul somebody. Rap sheet, mostly unruly behavior, assault, and something related to a chop shop. He'd done time. She knew he was probably breaking parole being here but it wasn't something she was ready to pursue at the present. He was doing his best to ignore her but failing. She took her soda to the opposite end of the room and sat facing the door. This seemed like a strange place for a meeting. Prickles of ominous discomfort danced along Carrie's spine causing tiny glistening beads of perspiration to spring from her temples. The stagnant smell of sour beer and whatever was in those jars on the bar caused her stomach to consider expelling its contents. She took a deep breath and told herself it was probably nothing. Fear and curiosity fought for control of her imagination.

Tall and elegantly coiffed like a high-end real estate agent, Aurora entered. Clacking high heels across the hardwood floor, she went straight to where Carrie sat and placed her briefcase on the table. Her unreadable deadpan expression formed into an unreadable platonic smile. "Good to see you again, Carrie. Glad you could make it." Aurora sat so close that her perfume was overpowering.

Carrie had to hammer down a spike of raw panic. "Aurora... hi," she stammered. "What's up?"

The bartender appeared with a rag over his shoulder. "What can I get you?"

"Lone Star longneck," Aurora said, never taking her eyes off Carrie. "So, girl. My old man giving you trouble?" The lilt in her voice was betrayed by the dark question beneath.

"Nothing I can't handle." Carrie took a breath, trying to adjust to the situation. "So what drags you way out here to the depths of depravity?"

The beer arrived with a glass. Aurora chugged a hefty swig right from the bottle and handed the glass back to the bartender. "I need your help figuring out some details," she said, opening the briefcase.

"Why the clandestine Spy versus Spy shit?" Carrie asked. "Are you hiding from Ross?"

" Not so much. I just wanted to keep this between us. It's out of his jurisdiction." She pulled two sheets of paper out of the briefcase and placed them side-by-side in front of Carrie. "You know what these are?"

"Not my area of expertise but they look like DNA profiles."

"Anything else?"

Carrie studied them for a moment. "They're very similar."

"Ninety seven point four percent to be exact."

"Okay, so?"

Aurora held up one of the papers. "This one came from a murder victim on a case I'm working, an ATF agent who was murdered in some bizarre sex act thing down in Corpus a few weeks back. Remember?"

"Yeah, he was supposed to teach a class I was taking. I was at the scene. Gruesome shit." Carrie didn't like the direction this was taking. "So what about his DNA?"

"I didn't say it was his. We found this under his foreskin."

"What?" Carrie felt her face go flush.

"His penis." Aurora was fixated like a cat stalking a grasshopper.

"I know, but... So what?"

Aurora held up the other sheet. "You remember how contaminated the scene was? How we had to do elimination samples on the entire team? You know where I got this one, don't you?"

Carries throat closed up. She couldn't answer. She couldn't even breathe. Her hand went for her weapon then she realized Aurora had a 9 mm from the briefcase aimed at her chest.

"Don't!" Aurora's expression had yet to change. "Reach across with your left hand and put it on the table. I just want to talk."

It had been years since Carrie cried but the hot tears were scalding her cheeks. She relinquished the Peacemaker.

"I don't have the manpower or the money," Ross explained, "and if the truth be known, I doubt I even have the authority." Real truth be known he didn't want to rock the boat. "I'll give you what I've got but this is bigger than one county." He was on the phone and scribbling notes. On the other end of the line captain Graham Putnam of the Texas Rangers had been pleading for assistance. "What about the truck?" Ross asked. "I noticed you released it. Find anything?"

"All the physical evidence is in the report I faxed over," Putnam said. "We're trying to follow the money but I'm not seeing anything so far. What can you tell me about Southern International Produce?"

"One-man operation. I've known Julio Ramirez since grade school. Good guy. Widower. His daughter's a little loopy, but she was 10 when her mom committed suicide so that's understandable."

"He hires ex-cons though, right?" Putnam asked.

"Yeah, but that's what's available here. The two prisons are our economy. He keeps pretty close tabs on them, even provides living quarters for some."

"Any chance he's working off the books?"

"Hell, Graham, anything's possible but it don't sound like Julio's style. I'll have a word with him but I'm betting this was an isolated incident put together by one of his workers."

"Since he knows you I'd sure be obliged if you could have a chat and get back to me."

Ross wrote a couple lines on the tablet. "Will do, Graham. Keep me posted. By the way, I've got a new deputy, a woman. Hard as nails far as I can tell. She packs a SAA Peacemaker, used to be owned by Bobby Paul Doherty"

"Son of a bitch!" Putnam said. "If she ever wants to sell it, let me know."

"You'll be in line right behind me. I promise."

After hanging up Ross looked over his notes, not much to go on. He put on his Stetson and went to make a visit he dreaded.

"Howdy stranger!" Betty Lou said, wrapping her arms around Kevin and tousling his barely damp hair. "You smell delicious. How was the trip?"

"Long," Kevin replied. "I missed you." It was true.

"How about a home-cooked meal to welcome you back? I bought some salmon steaks and fresh asparagus."

"Lovely! Sounds good. Got any beer?"

Betty Lou smiled her lightning bright smile. "Do I have any beer? You just sit your hunky ass on the couch and let me handle all your personal needs." She skipped to the refrigerator, knocking over a bar stool on the way. "Damn barstool's drunk. Let it lay." She brought him a pale ale and a frosted mug, poured the beer and sat on his lap. She let him take a couple of drinks before she kissed him under the ear. "How hungry are you?" she asked. "If you're really hungry dinner can wait." She nuzzled his neck and slipped her wet tongue in his ear.

He took a gulp of beer and set it aside. Grabbing her wrists, he rolled her onto the couch and kissed her deep as she wrapped her legs around him and grabbed his ass with her heels, grinding against him.

"Damn, that's what I'm talking about," she said. "You should go away more often if you're going to miss me like this." She whispered, "Let's hit the sack. We'll have more romping room."

He set the bar stool up while she turned up the tunes. They dove headlong into the bed. The reggae music wasn't the only thing making the walls thump.

"I need you," Aurora said, laying her pistol on the table by her beer. We're on the same side."

Carrie's brain jammed between gears. Both hands gripped her glass of soda as she stared down at the useless Peacemaker on the table. Glancing over Aurora's shoulder she noticed the stocky pool player with spurs observing the scene from a distance. Carrie struggled to focus on the main event. "What can I do?"

"Relax, for one," Aurora said. "You're not in trouble, at least for now. You simplified my job. Bernard had been leaking info to the Zeta cartel. Every stateside bust set up by the ATF involving them had come up dry. He was the leak. We'd just found out when he came up dead."

Out of the corner of her eye, Carrie watched Raul remove his belt. He held the buckle in his right hand and wrapped the other end around the left.

"I'm fine with letting the investigators assume it was Zeta," Aurora continued. "I consider you an asset."

Carrie was at a loss for words. She tried not to look directly at Raul as he eased up behind Aurora. He held up the belt with a question in his eyes. "How so?" Carrie asked Aurora.

"I'll explain momentarily." Aurora snatched the 9 mil from the briefcase and spun. like a rattlesnake in strike mode, she stood with the barrel inches from Raul's nose. "Stand down, asshole!" Raul dropped the belt and laced his fingers behind his head. "Spurs? Seriously, Cowboy, not exactly ninja equipment. Leave or die, your choice."

Raul jogged out the door, beltless. Aurora sat down for the first time broke into an honest to God grin. "You got me, girl! I didn't figure on you having backup. Nice move."

"That's on him. I don't know him from Adam. Maybe just doing his civic duty."

"Bullshit! He lives on your street."

Carrie froze. No words of explanation would be believable. Aurora placed the pistol back in the briefcase. "There are several ways this can go. I want to be friends, teammates. Otherwise, I can be God, you can be Job. Worst-case scenario, I bury you under the jail, or at least bury you." She rocked her chair back on two legs. "Your call."

Carrie's brain sizzled between fight and flight. Neither seeming to be an acceptable option, she took a deep drink of cola. "Okay, say we're sisters. What's the deal?"

Lydia made up the bed, flipping the pillow damp side down. Like the homemaker she was, she detailed the bathroom and made the rest of the rosé disappear before washing the glasses. Though physically satiated she felt a hollow need in her gullet. Never before had a man resisted her approach. Was she losing her magnetism? Was Kevin different on some moral or ethical plane? She stumbled through the heat up the hill to the main house, becoming slick with sweat in the radiating madness of the afternoon sun. She desired only to hide in her room and escape the humiliation of the day. Though she gave the heavy oak door her gentlest touch, Julio heard her enter.

"Is it done?" He asked.

"Is what done?"

"The trailer. Is it ready for Kevin to move into?" He came into the hall and saw his perspiring daughter in a T-shirt and cutoff jeans carrying a box of rags and cleaning supplies.

"Just like new." She briefly met his eyes. "I'm tired. I'm taking a nap."

"Did you see Kevin?"

"Yeah. He fixed the truck, I think, then left."

"Did you tell him the place was ready?"

"Nope. It wasn't when I saw him." She turned toward her bedroom.

"I think the boy has a thing for you," Julio said. "I see it in a way he stares at you."

"Whatever. I don't think so. Anyway, no fraternizing, right?"

"I might make an exception in this case."

"Why? Because he has a degree?"

"Because he has a future."

"Don't get your hopes up, Daddy." She went to her room and locked the door before taking her mother's Bible from the nightstand.

Ross wandered through the back roads in the unmarked blazer, though "unmarked" was probably a misnomer as it was painted the color of the other county vehicles and the wheels were stock interceptor issue. Still it didn't have government plates or visible radio antenna and the light bars were hidden behind the grill and tinted glass. He contemplated how he'd approach Julio. He didn't want to show his hand. They weren't drinking buddies or anything but there was a mutual respect going back decades that had benefited both of them on several occasions over time. Ross sincerely hoped that Julio hadn't crossed the line.

He'd promised Graham. Might as well get it over with. Wandering aimlessly through the countryside wasn't going to make it any easier. He knew a shortcut to S I P. On the way, he was surprised to see one of his county patrol vehicles parked at the Line Shack. It was the one checked out to Carrie James. He'd told her to familiarize herself with the locals but this was an odd take on the request. He looked over the parking lot: one pickup and a rental car, the bartenders old Chevy, not much happening. Maybe Carrie was meeting a boyfriend or something. He could ask her later. Right now he needed answers to other questions.

S I P seemed quiet, locked down for the weekend. Driving up the hill behind the shop he saw Julio's pickup parked in the circle drive. Standing in the shade of the high Talavera-tiled porch he let the iron knocker fall against the oak door. When Julio answered he seemed smaller and thinner than Ross remembered.

"Ross, my old friend, please come in. I didn't expect you."

Ross stepped into the dark, cool entry, his boots on the terrazzo giving a slight echo in the vast open space and tall ceilings. "I was out this way and thought I'd check to make sure Lydia was okay. Y'all seem to have had a run of bad luck lately. Anything I can do?"

"Come on back and have a drink. I could use the company."

Ross hadn't been inside since Carmelita died. The place was tidy but otherwise completely unchanged. "So, how is she? Lydia, I mean."

"I don't know. You know teenagers, moody one minute, giggling the next." Julio was attempting to make light but within a veneer of sadness lingered in his voice.

"She'll be heading off to college soon, I guess," Ross said.

"Maybe. We'll see how this thing with the vandalism charge

plays out. I'm not sure she can handle being away from home anyway."

"I'll bet they go pretty easy on her. People deal with grief in different ways."

"Yeah I guess," Julio said. "That was damn sure different. I'm wondering if she might need some professional help. I'm at a loss."

"It's an option. What do you think set her off? Was she involved with Miguel, or maybe Carlos?"

"Just friends, she says, but who knows what that means these days."

Ross followed Julio into the dim study. The curtains were drawn. All the light came from a crystal desk lamp. Julio filled two short glasses halfway up with Maker's Mark. Handing one to Ross he motioned toward a couple of high-back leather chairs near the window. When Julio sat he seemed to shrink into the chair, almost disappearing.

"Ross, I really appreciate your concern, and I know you mean well. We've known each other for long enough you can go ahead and say what's on your mind."

"You never were one to beat around the bush. I like that about you. So, straight up, what did you know about Miguel and his, uh, project."

"He asked to borrow a truck to move some furniture up from the Valley. I probably should've asked more questions,"

"I hope that's the last of it. There could be some civil repercussions but I don't see any likelihood of further criminal investigation. I assume you have insurance."

Julio seemed to have dropped out of the conversation. He stared blankly at the strip of sunlight oozing between the drapes. His drink, held loosely in his hand, hovered halfway to his mouth.

"Julio?" Ross coaxed.

"People died. Good people. I should have asked more questions. Now it's too late."

Ross leaned forward, causing the leather to crackle in the dead silence. "Too late?"

Julio's gaze shifted to take in Ross' concern. "I'm in a bad spot, Ross. If something happens to me or Lydia ,,, ." He recovered, stood, and refilled their glasses. "I've said too much. I'm sorry. It's out of my hands."

"Don't! If I can help, hey. I'm the sheriff here."

"Forget I said anything. It's bigger than us. I really think I need to get Lydia somewhere safe. I just don't know where that is."

The flaky pink salmon, lightly flavored with lime and toasted almond, was the perfect ending to an afternoon of horizontal ecstasy. Betty Lou had taken over the choreography of their extended encounter leaving Kevin to revel in her Tantric talents. He'd never experienced the level of carnal sensuality she offered, and all accompanied by the perfect soundtrack.

Since they were now at least partially clothed, Betty Lou pulled back the drapes, flooding the room with an amber glow. Long shadows of fence and umbrella reflected languidly over the mirror finish of the pool. Kevin watched Betty Lou navigate through the room as if her apartment was unfamiliar, taking careful steps to avoid collision with the furniture. How could this be the same girl who so flawlessly extricated every last morsel of natural pleasure from their frolic, leaving him suspended on a pillow of satisfaction?

She snuggled on the couch beside him. "So what about next weekend?" She asked.

"What about it? What do you mean?"

"Will you be in town?"

"I guess. I'll probably be moving but that won't take long. Everything I own fits in my pickup."

"Cool!" She reached under the couch and brought out a small wooden box. "I got us a mini-vacation."

Kevin furrowed his brow. "You go ahead. I don't smoke weed. Nothing against it if it works for you, but it just makes me confused."

"No, I know," she said. "You told me. But check this out." She unrolled some tissue paper to expose two flat buttons the diameter of ping-pong balls. "Peyote."

"Whoa! I've heard of it. What does it do?"

She held them between her fingers, lifting them up to the light. "Some say these hold all the answers to universal secrets. I don't know about that, but they make everything funny and sex is crazy-hot."

"Our sex is already crazy-hot. I don't know if I could stand any more intensity."

"Maybe next weekend we can find out."

"Maybe. I'll think about it."

Betty Lou stuck her lower lip out in an overwrought pout. "I hope so. I got them for us."

Aurora pulled a folder from the briefcase. "There's a lot of red tape when you're dealing with international criminals. My job is to cut through a lot of it. I'm not here to secure convictions. I'm here to solve crime." She kept a hand on top of the folder while she swirled her beer bottle by the neck. "I have a stable of specialists I've vetted. It's doubtful you'll ever meet one, but I've profiled you. I know your history. I won't give you any assignments you can't, let's say, enjoy."

"I'm not really a killer you know." Carrie's leg trembled under the table as she leaned on her elbows gripping her glass until her knuckles were white.

Aurora guzzled the last of her beer and set the bottle on the table with more force than needed. She opened the folder. "These four guys might disagree." In the folder were pictures of Bernard, the guy from the strip club, her first victim while she was still a college sophomore, and Coach Sterling.

"I didn't kill Coach Sterling. That was suicide."

"But you watched."

"I didn't kill him."

"I know. It was brilliant the way you handled that. How many others? I'm guessing three based on time lapse."

Carrie stood and turned toward the restroom. "I've got to pee."

Aurora put the folder in the briefcase, stuck a gun in the shoulder holster, and followed. In the bathroom Carrie spun around, slamming Aurora against the wall with her forearm. Before she could speak she felt the barrel of her own Peacemaker jab into her ribs.

"I thought we were going to be friends." Aurora's voice strained against the presence of Carrie's forearm on her throat.

Carrie melted into a mass of emotion and slid down to the floor, her face in her hands. "I don't want to talk about it."

"We have to. You can talk here or I can bring you to my office."

Carrie sat still while her mind raced through a half dozen scenarios, none ending on a positive note. She took a deep breath. "Are you wearing a wire?"

After dropping the guns in the sink, Aurora set the briefcase outside the bathroom door, took off her jacket, holster, blouse, shoes, and skirt. She posed before Carrie in nothing but a bra and panties. Carrie stood up. Aurora spun in a circle staying between Carrie and the guns. Carrie furrowed her brow. Aurora removed her bra and handed it to Carrie. It was far too sheer to hold a recording device.

"Only two," Carrie said. "There should have been one in Arkansas but I couldn't get to him without risking his victim."

"Interesting word choice, but I'm not surprised. What makes you think the so-called 'victims' don't have any control over their destiny?"

"I don't think that. They just don't realize it until it's too late."

"You're not giving these women much credit."

"These guys were predators, manipulators."

"Fine. So, say I know a guy who's manipulating hundreds of women, selling them for sex and making boatloads of cash. What about him?"

"He needs to die, a slow and painful death."

"Okay, I'm going to get dressed now. We're on the same page. Hand me my bra."

The middle of Tuesday, Kevin listened to his stomach rumble loud enough it got the attention of others in the room. He'd sat through preliminary interviews with potential parolees all morning. He had one to go before lunch. The parole board was made up of ancient community icons who, though friends of Judge Kendrick, had no criminal justice experience short of an obvious racist leaning. When Kevin mentioned that the federal government had begun keeping statistics on profiling and skewed racial numbers they dismissed his concerns as if he were speaking Arabic. The fourth guy might have a shot. Though his crime was the most severe, negligent homicide, he did possess a blonde crew cut and ivory skin.

Kevin just wanted to get back to the office. He'd spent Monday night at the ranch because he was out of clean clothes. He'd only shared a couple of brief chats with Betty Lou since Monday morning. Their assignments kept them apart. He was shocked by how much he missed her company.

The stooges, as Kevin secretly referred to the parole board, looked down their noses when they heard Kevin's stomach groan again. The blonde parolee tried smiling as he sat before the panel. It came off as more of a sneer.

Kevin took notes but asked no questions. It wouldn't have mattered. Twenty minutes later he was driving into town while arranging to meet Betty Lou for lunch at their favorite café on the square.

"What did I miss?" He asked Betty Lou as he glanced over the familiar menu.

"Same old, same old. Oh, except Julio Ramirez called several times. Doesn't he have your cell number?"

"Yeah, but I had to turn it off during the hearing. I saw his number. I'll give him a call after lunch."

Betty Lou scowled. I know it's not my business, but I wish you'd consider a different place to live. You may be able to watch him but he'll have you on a short leash too." She slipped out of her shoes under the table and slid her toes under the leg of his slacks.

Truth be known he wasn't comfortable with the arrangement either, but the problem had more to do with Lydia than Julio. "Don't worry. It's short-term."

"Oh yeah, I forgot. In two weeks, Labor Day, is the annual government employees appreciation barbecue. It's put on by the County Commissioners. We should plan to make an appearance."

"Together?"

"Why not? We work together. Probably won't stay long anyway. It's usually hotter than hell that weekend."

"What time?"

"Starts at 10AM on Monday."

Kevin hesitated, not wanting to drop this next bomb. "I can go early, but I've got a DJ gig that evening."

"No shit! Where you bustin' out?" Betty Lou's smile woke up her face.

"S I P company party. Julio rented the VFW Hall."

Her smile disappeared.

CARNIVORES

"**Not much happening on the courthouse square.** You told me to get to know folks and I shoot a pretty mean game of eight ball." Carrie needed to make the conversation brief. "From my experience the folks who live on the fringes hang around pool tables. It was just an idea."

"How'd that work out for you?" Ross asked.

"The Line Shack doesn't have coffee but they have these little non-reg quarter pool tables. I met a cowboy and a trucker who seemed nice enough."

"Trucker's name Raul?"

"Yeah, turns out he lives on my street. Know him?"

"I've got my eye on him. Rough guy when he was younger. Hasn't been in trouble for a while. Probably breaking probation being in the Line Shack."

"He wasn't drinking... far as I could see." Carrie took her purse off her desk. "I gotta go, Ross. Visiting with my mom tonight."

"Don't take the cruiser."

Carrie rolled her eyes. "Like it would even make it out there and back."

"Say hi to Lois for me."

Kevin was loading his last couple of boxes into his pickup when he saw headlights coming up the drive. Carrie's Civic blocked him in. "Lois isn't home and I'm leaving. Can you park somewhere else?"

"I know she's not here. The Jim Wells Democrats meet on the third Monday. We need to talk."

"I know. It's taking a while to get my ducks in a row."

"Distracted maybe? We need to focus. If we don't make a move pretty quick, all hell's going to break loose. I ain't bullshitting. The Feds and the Texas Rangers are sniffing around."

Kevin hiked himself up on the tailgate of his pickup. "Maybe we should back off."

"I can't." She folded her arms and stared toward the border.

"Why not?"

"Mainly, I'm already up to my ass in it,... And then there is the payback... And then, this should get you thinking, there's the pay off. I'm fucking broke living in a trailer in fucking Beeville. No!... Just no!" She was pacing now, spittle forming in the corners of her mouth.

"Whoa! Okay. Chill out. What do we know?"

"I know that my boss talked to the Rangers today right before he went to have a chat with your boss, Julio."

"How do you know that?"

"He doodles. I saw his notepad. Plus he saw me at a bar out near S I P. Where else would he be going?"

Kevin sniggered? "At a bar? You?"

She spun around, her fist clenched like it wanted to rip out his throat. "Shut up, God dammit! This is serious!"

Kevin put up his hands, "Oh...kay then." He wished he'd left an out. She was in his face and there was nowhere to go. "Let me think about it. I have inroads to all the players, maybe even the cash, or some of it. It's going to cause a problem in my personal life."

"Your personal life is the problem."

"Whoa! I'm closer than you are. Who do you have?"

"I have Raul, the muscle guy, and I'm working on Ronnie Dahl."

"Dahl? The fat man? You think he's involved?

Carrie continued to pace but her fists became hands again. "I think he's the fucking boss, at least on this side of the border. He's involved in some extreme money-making scheme and smuggling fits the bill. What about Julio?"

Kevin scooted to the side and patted a spot on the tailgate. "Relax, you may need to sit down for this." She leaned on the edge of his tailgate but kept her feet on the ground. Kevin continued. "If Julio's guilty it's by association. I get the feeling he trusts me. I've gone out on a limb to help his fucked-up daughter. I'm picking up a load of women from across the border this weekend, dropping them at a safe house in Houston. They'll end up in New Orleans I suspect."

"You're scum."

"It's me or Raul. They'll be safer with me. The border guards are covered. I'm not sure of the logistics but if I make my timed crossings I should be okay."

"So what happens in Houston?"

"Why?"

"Somebody needs to save these girls!" She sprang from the tailgate and resumed her frantic pacing.

"Focus, Carrie. That's not what we're in this for. Big picture, remember?"

"The fuck! We can't let these girls get to New Orleans."

"I'm out then. I'm not risking my life without a payoff. We have to establish trust. If my first load gets busted I'm dead meat. They'll know. I'm the new guy here."

Carrie kicked a rock so hard it skittered a good 50 feet down the drive. "Fine. I figure we have maybe two weeks to wrap this up. I'm meeting Dahl on Labor Day. I'll need another week to set him up. You need to put Julio out of business."

"Why? He's a victim here, too."

"Bullshit! Is he not the one trafficking in girls?"

"It's not his choice."

"He's getting paid, right? Has been for a while probably… One way or another."

"I'll see what I can do."

"You'll need to make yourself scarce. The shit will hit the fan. Just saying…"

"Fine. Can I leave now? I need to be somewhere."

Carrie jumped in her Civic, jammed it into reverse and cut a semicircular groove in the yard. Kevin was in his truck and gone before she was out of the car. She felt hot patches form on her scalp. Sweat from her armpit soaked through her T-shirt. A short circuit of her central nervous system dead-ended in her skull, creating a scream inducing migraine.

She rummaged frantically through the closet of her old bedroom. Nothing. In her mom's closet she found a tan sleeveless dress and a dust-colored shawl. Mom's jewelry box held a pair of pearl earrings. She laid it all out in her bedroom. Under the bed was a pair of 3-inch cream-colored stiletto heels; In her nightstand was a five-inch chrome plated switchblade she purchased for protection several years back. She checked its operation with the flick of her wrist. Perfect. Minutes later, as the scalding water filled the bathroom with a thick cloud of steam, coyotes across the parched ranch land stopped yelping and tilted their heads as an unearthly moaning wail vibrated through the cooling desert air.

At 80 mph, downtown Alice was only 15 minutes away from the ranch. As Carrie pulled off the main road onto Business 281 she stopped at a convenience store for a pack of Marlboro 100s. With her windows down she smoked a couple as she got her bearings. It'd been a few years since she'd been in Alice proper. It hadn't changed a lot but the booming oil patch brought some prosperity. On King Street she found a bar named Solace. The irony elicited a smile. She crushed out her second cigarette with the toe of her stiletto, draped the diaphanous shawl across her shoulders and checked her purse to make sure the knife was easily accessible. She lifted her chin slightly and strode slowly and confidently into the bar. Being Monday night, it was slow; no band, no door dragon. Good. She slid onto the bar stool at the darkened end of the bar, crossed her legs and waited. When the bartender finally acknowledged her she gave him a smile and ask for a premium margarita on the rocks, no salt. When he asked for ID she pouted but dug out her driver's license. She held it out to allow him to see her picture and date of birth though her index finger partially obscured her name. He smiled and left to prepare the drink. Other than one couple nuzzling in the corner booth the dozen other patrons were men. At the far end of the bar sat an Aryan-looking man with a close-cropped flattop, almost white in color. His pale blue eyes were fixed on her. She stared back, never breaking eye contact. He smiled. She raised her eyebrows but kept her other facial features neutral. The bartender brought her drink. Still making eye contact with Mr. Hitler Youth she picked up the drink and used her tongue to locate the straw and guide it into her mouth. He stood and ambled toward her.

"Hey," he said. "Mind if I join you?"

She glanced at the adjoining barstool, finally hinting at a smile. "Please do."

"I'm Darrell. You from around here?"

"Tonight I am," she said and smoothed the hem of her dress. "You?"

"On business, I'm in oil."

"I hear that's really good for your skin." She checked his left hand. He hadn't even bothered to remove the wide platinum band.

"You're quick." He motioned for the bartender. "You didn't tell me your name."

"I didn't, did I? What would you like it to be?"

"You pick. You have all the answers."

"How about Roxanne, like the Police song?"

"I'm cool with that. You're not with the police are you?"

"Can't hold a tune or play anything but the radio."

Darrell broke into a full-blown grin. "What do you do?"

"Lots of things. I could show you but not here. You have a room?"

"I'm at the Hampton, in a suite since I'm in town for a while."

"Why don't you buy me another drink so I don't get thirsty while you empty the ATM. Then you can show me your suite and I can show you my toys."

The exhaust noise reflected off the little metal house as Kevin backed his pickup in. The reflected brake lights gave the surface a mournful glow. He cut the engine and set the brake hoping that Lydia hadn't noticed his arrival from her vantage point in the big house. Still, a part of him wanted to touch her again, let her fire burn him just a little.

The tension flowed through him from his groin. He picked up a box.

Twenty minutes later he'd moved into his own little tin house in the desert, walking distance from one job, three miles from the other. Cheating distance from Lydia, three and a half miles from Betty Lou, a girl he may be falling for, if that were even possible.

The space was small, but a little bigger than the garage apartment, a castle to him. He grabbed a beer and stretched out on the couch, turned his phone off and closed his eyes, breathing and drinking, waiting for the edges to smooth over. Kevin drifted back to when his life had no ambition, simple and easy; make the grades, move the cargo, whatever; linear events that rarely intersected. Now women complicated his life, two of them downright terrifying and the third one he couldn't get a handle on. Betty Lou seemed to like him, even cared about him on a superficial level, but he couldn't reach her or maybe it was him. He felt his lack of experience hampering his efforts to connect. The beer slowed him, but his muscles unfurled. Lydia and Carrie faded into the background. He dozed off with his mind and heart wrapped around Betty Lou.

The sweet thickness of honeysuckle lay heavy on Carrie's porch. The bees dancing around the crimson blossoms of the Texas Hibiscus harmonized with a satisfying hum laced into her central nervous system. She'd only slept four hours but the deep repose left her energized, saber sharp, to thrive on her day. The thin vapor from her coffee mingled with the evaporation of dew as the morning began to warm. She was still in her robe. Having decided to forgo the shooting range, she was in no hurry. Beyond the arc of the lane she observed Raul glance toward her as he jogged to his dually. She raised two fingers and thrust her chin toward him. This morning, instead of avoiding her end of the loop, he turned the big Chevy in her direction and paused at her driveway.

He leaned out of the truck, chin on his elbow, "Hey, Chica, all is good? I was worried about you, that crazy puta at the Shack drawing down on you?" Raul seemed to show genuine concern.

"Nah, she was just showing off. I can handle my shit. But, thanks for the backup."

"No sweat. You need anything, you just holler." He pulled his elbow in the truck then paused. "You want to get a beer sometime?"

"You know I'm a cop, right?"

"You don't drink beer?"

"Okay sure, you're right. I shoot pool too. Maybe go to the Line Shack some evening. Straight up though, I don't date guys if that's where you're headed."

Raul raised an eyebrow. "Okay, whatever. Shouldn't affect your eight ball chops." He closed the truck's window against the warming morning as she pulled the Ray-Bans down over her eyes.

She reveled in the memory of the previous night. The interactions with the forensics team during cop school had changed her procedure. It wasn't difficult to convince last evening's companion to participate in a romantic walk in the desert. He'd have done almost anything to achieve his quest. Besides, it was a full moon night. A few whispers at his ear lobe about sweaty romp to the mournful tunes of coyotes and the suggestion to bring a blanket from the room while she acquired a bottle of red wine, he was hooked. "Follow me. I know just the spot. I live out that way," she lied.

It was unlikely they'd ever find the body. If so, they'd never tie it to her. In the back of her mind she hoped he would be found, for his stupid wife's sake. Most life insurance policies have double indemnity clauses for accidental or violent deaths. It wasn't accidental, but it was damn sure violent. The wad of cash in her purse would cover a couple months rent with a chunk to spare. The rings she'd have to meltdown. Everything else stayed with the body, for safety's sake.

She stood, stretched and went to refill her coffee cup, relishing the quiet peaceful morning, the slow constant beat of her satisfied heart. Her goal was nearer, even a plan to save those women became obvious in this perfect moment.

SETTLING IN

Lydia woke to a gentle knocking on her bedroom door. Outside her window the sky barely held color. The clock on her nightstand read 5:50 AM. Assuming she dreamed the noise, she closed her eyes. Another knock, louder this time.

"Lydia?" Julio's voice was weak through the door. "Can you get up. I need a favor."

Lydia clicked the light on her nightstand. "Give me a minute."

"I'll be in the kitchen," Julio said, his voice getting even softer as he walked away.

Lydia stepped into her bathroom and scrubbed the dried blood from her inner thighs with an alcohol soaked towelette. The sting freshened her with an ecstatic jolt of painful clarity. After making sure none of the cuts would resume bleeding she pulled on yoga pants and a sleeveless white T-shirt.

In the kitchen Julio handed her a cup of coffee. "Can you put together some breakfast tacos?" Julio asked. "I'm going down to the shop and see if I can catch Kevin before he heads into town. I have work for him this weekend. I figure if I'm getting him up this early I might as well feed him."

"Give me twenty minutes," Lydia said. "I'll get myself together, then another 20 and I'll have breakfast." Thirty minutes later Lydia had the kitchen steeped in the aroma of coffee, bacon, onions and cilantro. She looked even better than the kitchen smelled. She wore a burgundy gown with a black sash and her hair was tied back with a wide black ribbon. Kevin sat mesmerized as she handed him a mug of strong dark roast coffee. "Breakfast will be a few minutes but let me know if you need anything else." She hoped he caught the inflection in her voice. All indications confirmed he had. He stared until she disappeared into the kitchen.

"So," Julio interrupted, "there's a change of plans for next weekend. We're moving the load up to Friday night and you'll have to pick up about 40 miles south of Ciudad de Acuna. The good news is you just drop at Mirage Auto Shop and Raul will take over from there. You'll have the rest of the weekend off. You still make $900 but not as many hours. You'll have to be at the Amistad border crossing before 5 AM though. Any problems?"

"Any checkpoints?"

"There is one, but I have a deal with a rancher to avoid it."

"I hear that hasn't worked out too well."

"You'll have an escort. I'll give you coordinates to where you'll meet."

"Why the change?"

"The buyer wants to inspect the cargo. Not your problem. You'll be long gone by then."

Lydia brought the first of several plates of taco fixings in. "There should be plenty for your breakfast and lunch," she said. "I'll even wrap up a few for your coworkers if you like. It never hurts to make a few brownie points with the judge, right?"

Kevin saw a new side of Lydia, almost as if she were a normal person. "Thanks," he said. "I'll take you up on that, assuming we don't scarf them all down. They smell delicious." He left for work with a full belly, a dozen tacos, and a new perspective on Lydia. Still, in the back of his mind he couldn't completely dismiss other things he knew about her.

Carrie didn't relish the prospect of wandering around Beeville introducing herself to the crusty old curmudgeons who owned the local shops and businesses. Most saw her as an outsider taking a job that should have gone to a local boy just for the sake of some trumped up diversity program. Once she explained that her family had owned the ranch in the next county over for five generations it helped a little. They still couldn't understand why any young white girl would pursue a career in law enforcement. "I just want my neighbors to be safe," she said, obviously needing to avoid explaining that vengeance and profit were her true motives. It pacified most folks but the less progressive old farts still looked askance at the silver badge perched on her left breast.

When she stopped by the office to pick up her daily assignments, Ross caught up with her. "Got a minute?" He asked.

"Sure, what's up?"

"Come in. Shut the door." He took a seat at his desk. She stretched out in the chair across from him and propped her booted ankle across her knee in what she hoped was an indication of relaxed indifference. "

He watched her closely, letting her squirm a second. "I ran into Lois last night at the Jim Wells Democratic Party forum. I was on a panel to encourage cooperation between agencies," Ross said.

Carrie felt her ears grow hot, knowing she'd been caught in a lie.

"She asked how you were taking to the job." He paused, watching her for reactions that didn't appear. He continued. "I was aware you knew Carlos, the kid we found in the truck. I didn't know y'all were so close. What's your take on the situation?"

"I liked Carlos, but I knew the other guy, Miguel, too. He was trouble. I really haven't been around enough the last few years to keep up. I lived in Austin for seven years before I came to work here."

"Right, but do you think Carlos or Miguel could have set up this operation or why would they have just driven off into the desert like that?"

"The Carlos I knew would have never intentionally hurt anyone or break the law. He was one step away from being an Eagle Scout."

"What about Miguel?"

"Maybe. He loved putting on the high-roller front. He wasn't stupid but I don't know if he had the connections to set up this deal. I'm betting he had help other than Carlos."

Ross watched Carrie's nonchalant deadpan. No reaction. "So why'd they leave the road?"

Carrie shrugged. "No idea. Shortcut maybe. Could be they were avoiding a checkpoint?"

"Maybe," Ross said. "Depending on their destination. Lois said she and Carlos' mother talked to the girl that survived. She said Carlos tried to intervene?"

"Yeah, that's what I heard, for what good it did." Carrie put her foot on the floor and leaned forward. "We done here? It was a sad situation but I really don't have anything you don't already know."

"I was going to question the guy that found Carlos's body but he seems to have closed his business. I have his home address. Can you check it out? See what he knows?"

"Sure. You want me to bring him in?"

"Depends. If anything is quirky, I'd like to talk to him. Use your own judgment. Afterwards, call me on my cell. I might have another little assignment."

"Related to the case?" Carrie asked, happy to finally be on the inside track on this one.

Ross looked to Carrie and noted a slight indication of interest. He smiled. "We'll see. Just call."

"Good morning, Sweet Hottie Hot-a-Tot. I got a little something for you, Kevin said as he dropped two warm breakfast tacos on Betty Lou's desk.

"What the…. Don't come in here talking that trailer trash shit! Oh wait, how's the new box?" She unwrapped the foil from one end of the taco and inhaled the spicy aroma.

Kevin put on his best hillbilly accent. "It ain't a box darlin'. It's all rounded on the ends." Then in his regular voice, "It's okay but it was lonely without you."

"You know where I live."

"I do, and you have a pool, and a queen bed which by the way I hope to share this weekend. I only have to work Friday night. I should be back in town by midday Saturday."

"So we can have our little party?"

"Reckon so, sweetie."

Betty Lou jumped up, ramming her office chair into the shelving behind her, went over and leaned against the door, closing it with her muscular posterior, then reached behind her, locking it. She wrapped her arms around his neck and probed his mouth with her feverish tongue. "This is going to be so much fun," she squealed as she pushed him against her desk.

"It's pretty damn good right now." He said between wet kisses.

She ground her hips into his pelvis as she exhaled warm breath into his ear, flicking his earlobe with her lips. The intercom buzzed. "Seriously!" Judge Kendrick said. "This is a government facility, not the No Tell Motel."

"Would you like a breakfast taco, judge?" Kevin asked while Betty Lou quietly giggled in his ear.

"Sure," the judge replied. "Then we should probably get some work done."

With the vapor of burning oil and smoky exhaust causing her eyes to water, Carrie parked the clattering old cruiser near the ditch in front of the blue clapboard house. It was a shotgun style bungalow on a deep but narrow lot in the less prosperous side of town only a few blocks from her trailer. A late-model Ford Expedition sat in the gravel driveway, the rear hanging a foot into the street. As her dilapidated cruiser wheezed to silence, she noticed the front door of the house wide open. She unsnapped the safety strap on her holster and walked to the door. Standing to the side she knocked aggressively on the door frame. "Deputy Sheriff, James. I need to speak with you." She waited a second before a woman's voice replied, "Come on back. I'm in the kitchen."

With her hand resting on the stock of the Peacemaker, she eased through the small living space and into the kitchen / dining area. An overdressed plump woman with a clipboard peered into cabinets that were all standing open. "Hi. I'm Deputy Sheriff Carrie James. I need to speak with Lupe" (she glanced at her notepad) "Moreno. Is he around?"

"No, the woman said, "Just a minute. I'm counting." Carrie waited while the woman huffed around the sink, stretching to shuffle through a cabinet full of dusty canning jars. Finally she put the clipboard down and turned. The amount of makeup on the woman's face was comical as if every feature was painted on. "What did he do this time?"

"Nothing," Carrie said, "at least as far as I know. He may be in danger though."

The woman's expression almost changed. You could see the fear in her eyes. "He went to the East Coast to visit my Grandes neces. I'm his niñera. I'm also the real estate agent for selling this little gem. You need a house?"

"Not now. When do you expect him back?"

"Maybe never. What did he do?"

"Like I said, I'm not sure if he did anything. How can I reach him?"

The pudgy little woman grabbed the clipboard and sat at the table. "Give me your cell number. I'll ask him to call you."

Carrie rattled off the number. "Are you handling the sale of his shop too."

"No. The fool already sold it to some trucking company, not for shit. Such an idiot. I know it's an old building but I could have got him more than he sold it for."

Carrie looked around the kitchen. It was clean but decades out of date and cluttered with trinkets having no discerning theme. "I'd appreciate you letting him know it's important that I speak with him. He's not in any trouble with the law."

The woman reached into a clipboard and handed Carrie a Century 21 business card reading Juanita Renfro. "You should think about this house. It's a good starter house for a single girl. Good for catching a husband."

Carrie took the card. "How do you know I'm single?"

"So pretty, but working, and no ring."

Carrie smiled, not wanting to even try to explain her life to this clown-faced woman. "I'll think about it. Please tell Mr. Moreno it's important." She walked out to the car shaking her head, knowing she'd never hear from Moreno. She turned the key. The engine spun for a few seconds before it chugged back to life in a cloud of rancid black smoke. She grabbed the radio. "Unit 203, I'm wrapped up here."

Gina's static-riddled voice came through. "Ross wants you to give him a call but first we've got a 517 at the Fulenwider Dodge dealership. Could you check it out? It's not an emergency. Ask for Jack Talbot."

"Ten-four, I'm on it." She didn't want to sound like a rookie but she couldn't remember what a 517 was. She checked her cheat sheet of call numbers. Nothing. It must have been a mistake or some oddity she hadn't written down. At least it wasn't an emergency.

Raul lounged across the bench seat of his dually parked in front of S I P's shop/warehouse. Apparently he'd just missed DJ but the stop wasn't a total loss. At the main house he'd scored a couple of fat breakfast tacos and one of those strangely provocative looks of Lydia's. He could never tell if it was a look of desire or she was just toying with him. She never failed to get deep enough into his personal space that he could feel the heat she exuded. He knew better than to test the waters. He'd known several coworkers who'd gone down that road. None of them still worked there. A couple of them were dead. He had to admit as he ate, she made a bitchin' taco. He left the boss's house as soon as matters would allow. Julio had assigned his weekly tasks and gave him an envelope full of working capital. He saw himself as Julio's second-in-command. He often wondered if Julio saw it that way. Probably. He had quite a bit of free rein.

As he waited in the truck he tried but failed to get the vision of Lydia in her burgundy gown with the black sash out of his mind. How easy it would be to pull the end of that sash and watch the gown fall away. What exquisite pleasures it would reveal. He shook the image from his head just as the pearlescent Lincoln Town Car eased in off the highway. He sat back up in the seat when the driver parked next to him and lowered his window. He knew the fat man by reputation.

Dahl watched Raul swallow the last bite of taco. "Morning, son. How's business."

"Same old same old, Commissioner Dahl."

"Call me Ronnie?" Dahl said. His expression made Raul think of a monitor lizard waiting patiently for his prey to make a deadly misstep.

"So, Ronnie, what brings you by our little shop?"

"Big party coming up. Need fruits and veggies," the fat man said from behind his aviator shades.

Raul new Dahl had his parties catered and was full of shit. He chose to play along. "You came to the right place. I'm sure Julio can hook you up."

"You drive for him, right?" Dahl asked.

"On occasion, if somebody's out sick or we get real busy. I'm more into logistics. I'm officially the fleet manager, set up routes and runs to the broker, that sort of thing."

"Would you be interested in taking a couple of gigs off the books, for cash?"

"Depends."

"Yeah, right," Dahl was showing a lack of patience. "Money's good. This weekend, to Houston on Saturday on to New Orleans on Sunday. Bobtail back next week. $1500 plus expenses. There may be a couple of perks for above and beyond. We'll see."

"What's the catch?" Raul asked.

"Hauling workers, undocumented."

"This the deal Miguel was doing?"

"Yep." Dahl still faced down Raul.

"That didn't end well for him."

"He was stupid. You're not. You wouldn't be running the show if you were."

Raul smiled. "You're right. I'll need two grand."

The Commissioner snorted and broke into a grin. "Done. Be at the Mirage Auto Repair building by noon on Saturday. Here's a couple hundred advance to let you know I'm serious." Dahl held an envelope out the window of the Lincoln just far enough that Raul had to get out of the truck to retrieve it. "Bring five family meal buckets of chicken, a couple of army surplus cots and soap, shampoo, and towels. Keep the receipts. I'll have the rest of your money when you get there. In the meantime go out and spiffy the place up. I'll get a key from Julio."

"I've got one."

"Fine. I'll see you there," he said as he raised the window and drove up the hill to the main house.

Carrie's stomach reminding her she was missing lunch competed successfully with the clattering of the tired cruisers unnatural engine noises. As she turned into the gleaming Fulenwider Dodge dealership with its military grid of red, white, and blue Ram trucks facing the highway, she groaned, assuming that whatever this 517 call was would further delay her gastric satiation. She parked in the customer parking. A lanky cowboy bounded toward her with an unnatural level of gusto before she even stepped out of the car. Her natural tendency to tense up during such an approach was short-circuited by the Cowboys goofy grin. She unfurled from the car and found him already orbiting her personal space.

"You must be officer James?" He said. "I am Jack, Jack Talbot, the sales manager. I've been expecting you."

"It's Deputy James, Mr. Talbot, what can I do for you."

"Please, call me Jack." The man seemed as though he might put an arm around her shoulder. Upon seeing her tense up his hand chose to extend toward a handshake instead. "It's more like what I can do for you." He glanced at the ragged police car behind her. "Come on in. There's some pizza and brownies in the break room. It's almost ready, just a few details to check."

"What's almost ready? I thought I was here on police business."

"Well, yeah, I guess, although the business part has been taken care of. We just need to transfer the radio and gun rack. All the other fixtures are updated, the emergency light bars, lightweight, high tensile grid cage and remote security for the back passenger compartment. The paint job will blow your mind."

Carrie was beginning to get the picture. "A new cruiser? They didn't tell me. I thought I was here about a disturbance."

"No. You're to pick up this new Charger Interceptor. It'll take about an hour to put it together. Feel free to snack or chill. I'll need your keys."

She hoped this would mean she'd end up with a somewhat better vehicle. She'd at least get to drive this back to headquarters. She called dispatch on her cell phone. "I know what a 517 is."

Gina responded, "yeah, I do too. I made it up. What do you think of the Charger."

"I haven't seen it yet."

"You should check it out."

"What difference does it make? It won't be mine. I'm low man on the totem pole."

"That's not what I heard."

"It would just piss off the guys with seniority. Not going to happen."

"It's all politics and PR. You'll see."

"I hope not." From the corner of her eye Carrie saw a metallic gunmetal gray Dodge Charger pull out from behind the building. Red and blue strobe lights pulsed from behind the front grill. The engine rumbled low like thunder on steroids. Deep within the gray of the side panels the word "POLICE" shimmered in a dark charcoal.

Carrie finished the remaining two thirds of a large pepperoni pizza while the techs were finishing the installations on the new Charger. With her belly full, the previous night's lack of sufficient sleep was catching up to her. She didn't really believe she'd end up with this new cruiser, nor did she really care as long as she got some kind of upgrade. Her head was resting against the wall. Her eyes had no reason not to close. Consciousness had departed when it was abruptly reintroduced by her cell phone buzzing in her pocket. She checked the number, "What's up, DJ?"

"I'm keeping you in the loop, like you asked. I'm picking up a load tonight."

"Where?"

"Mexico."

"Shit, Dude. Don't get killed."

"No sweat. It's all preset. I'm just the driver."

"What are the details?"

"Can't say, other than my part ends Saturday morning at that auto shop in the desert."

"Women?"

"Hookers."

"Asshole! They're still women."

"Don't get your panties in a wad. They chose to come. Better pay. Probably better working conditions."

Carrie was wide awake and gritting her teeth. "You are one sick puppy. You know that?"

"And you're getting emotionally involved. That's against the rules, your rules, remember? I'm just sharing info."

"Fine. Where are they headed?"

"Not sure I should say. I can't afford for this to go south. It's my ass on the line."

"I'm sorry. You're right. I'll back off. So, you're safe?"

"Hope so."

"You don't know where they'll end up?"

"I know they'll be in Houston Sunday. After that I have no idea. The last group was supposed to end up in New Orleans, but who knows?"

"Thanks, I'll keep it quiet. Be safe." After the call disconnected Carrie realized she was standing, pacing back and forth across the customer waiting area. She plopped down on the vinyl chair with an exasperated sigh and stared at the screen on her phone. She stuck it in her pocket. She pulled it back out and scrolled through the numbers. She dialed Henrique Garcia.

THE RUN

The center of night hummed to him in the ominous blackness, the only light oozed from the Milky Way's gash across the sky. The steady low rhythm from the Kenworth's diesel soul failed to hypnotize or even soothe the edge of Kevin's observations. Still the yellow light fanning across Carretera 29 found only jackrabbits, snakes, and the occasional mule deer. Since leaving Acuna 10 miles back, he'd seen little evidence of human habitation. He was tempted to take the shortest route to Christales but, being out of his element, reluctantly made the turn toward Vieja de Palestina. Julio's instructions were specific, the directions scribbled on the notebook beside him on the seat. He wondered if Miguel had experienced this level of apprehension. At least Miguel had been fluent in the language. Julio assured him language wouldn't be an issue this near the border.

Rolling through Valle de Palestina Kevin finally saw lights dotting the landscape. At 1 AM they were few and in a mile or two he was again driving through total darkness.

Christales was an insignificant village on a crossroads, a half dozen buildings clustered in the desert scrub. One had lights on. A couple of late-model pickups were parked out front. He parked the Kenworth tight against the dark side of the structure, killed the engine, and rolled open the door to the cargo box.

Two boys in military uniforms met him at the corner of the building. Pistols in hand and rifles strapped across their shoulders. "¡Detener! ¿Tienes mi dinero?" The shorter one asked.

"No habla espanol. I'm supposed to meet Marcos Aguilar." Kevin held his chin high, chest out, trying to display a countenance of calm confidence. His neck and armpits were becoming damp from the sultry humidity.

The taller of the men broke into a grin. "Follow me, kid," he said, though he was several years younger than Kevin.

Inside the warehouse Aguilar lounged on a dilapidated office chair, his feet propped on a folding table. His shirt was unbuttoned and a doe-eyed teenage girl balanced on his lap with her short skirt bunched around her waist. He stood, rolling the girl onto the concrete floor as though she were a pile of dirty laundry he'd been sorting. "Bad timing, gringo. I was about to test the merchandise." He had a genuine smile as he reached to shake Kevin's hand.

Kevin looked around the dim room. Two dozen women were

scattered about in small groups, most appeared barely 18 years old. Some gathered around tables on folding chairs. The younger girls sat on the floor leaning against the walls or each other.

When Kevin reached inside his jacket for an envelope he felt the barrel of the pistol against the back of his head. He froze.

" Relax, chicos, funda sus pistolas. Él es uno de nosotros " Aguilar said.

After Kevin heard the guns return to the leather he gingerly handed the envelope to their boss.

"How was your trip?" Aguilar asked. He motioned to the women around the closest table to move. They scattered immediately and reconvened in a corner, their eyes never leaving Aguilar.

"Uneventful, until now," Kevin said.

"Don't worry about my boys. They're harmless. Have a seat." Aguilar produced a small flask from his back pocket, uncorked it, and took a sip. "Tequila? For the road?"

Kevin took the bottle and gulped a small amount. It was smooth for tequila. He took another and felt the warmth radiate from his core. He handed it back to Aguilar. "Gracias."

Aguilar smiled, extending a palm toward the women. "Pick one. There's a mattress in the back if you want to take a roll."

Kevin had no intention of going down that road. "I appreciate it, but I have to be at the Amistad crossing before five. I should load up and go."

"Your call," Aguilar said. He turned to the girls. "Consiga su equipaje, señoras, su destino está esperando."

The girl from Aguilar's lap sidled up to Kevin and wrapped her fingers around his bicep. "I speak English. Let me ride up front, I'll translate." She squeezed his muscle. "Maybe more."

Aguilar pushed her loose from Kevin. "Leave him alone. Get your girls together." He whispered to Kevin, "Watch her, Lina can't be trusted. She is fun though, but watch your back."

"They're cargo. Just another load as far as I'm concerned." Kevin felt the cringe as he said it, but it needed to be said. He needed to believe it.

Two hours later the slow steady rumble of the engine and the dry hiss of the truck's refrigeration system had lulled the women to sleep. They were curled together on the floor of the box sleeping so deeply they never felt the truck slow. Kevin saw the row of floodlights illuminating the Amistad dam. No other trucks were at the checkpoint. He slowed, as a border patrol agent motioned him into lane two, the wrong lane. He stopped at the line. An older heavyset agent trotted from the guard house. "El Jefe needs your assistance," he told the young guard who'd stopped him. The big guy walked up to the truck, hand on his pistol. "You work for Julio Ramirez?"

Kevin felt his veins ice up. "Yes, Sir."

"Step out of the vehicle." The guard said. "Keep your hands where I can see them."

Kevin obeyed. Two other agents joined them. One ran a mirror on wheels under the truck. The other checked the rollup door at the rear. "Ag seal," he hollered.

"Yeah, right," the large guard grunted. He stepped up to face off with Kevin. "Did you know Miguel?"

"No. I just started with S I P."

"He was my brother-in-law. My wife still cries every day."

"I'm sorry. I really am." It wasn't hard for Kevin to sound sincere. He knew Miguel should still be alive.

"I know what's going on here. I can fuck up your life you know."

Kevin knew this was true. That wasn't all he knew. "You could," Kevin said, "but you're turning a buck on this too."

"Sometimes I wonder if it's worth it."

Kevin felt his future flying south. The thought of his weekend with Betty Lou, how he didn't want to miss it, especially by 5 to 10 years. "Listen," he told the guards, "you and I are on the same side. Let this go. We both win and soon, very soon, the people responsible for Miguel's death will pay… And pay big time."

The guard glared until his eyes softened. "I'm counting on it." He stepped away and motioned the other guards back to the guard house. "Drive safe," he said and waved them on.

Carrie had to give Ross credit. The man must be the master of spin. After a brief talk from their boss every single one of the deputies supported Carrie getting the new Interceptor. They had to admit it was far less macho than the Chevy four-wheel drive SUVs they drove, not to mention their chivalrous tendencies insisted the lady gets the safest and sleekest vehicle. Ross tossed her the keys. "Now you have to get out there and make the payments. Ain't much that can outrun it. I need stacks of tickets. Get way out there on 77. I don't need a lynching from the locals. Pick off some of those rich bastards in the German autobahn toys. They can afford it."

The whole department laughed. Even Carrie smiled. These hi-rollers were the "father figures" she liked to see suffer anyway. It was a win-win. She grabbed an extra ticket book. Everyone was heading to their allotted assignments when Ross called her into the office.

"Close the door. Have a seat," Ross said. It wasn't a suggestion. For the first time Carrie felt her spine tingle. Little hairs on the back of her neck began to itch. She obeyed. He put a manila envelope on his desk between them but left his fingers on it. "What's going on?" He asked.

"About what?" There were so many topics he could be referring to.

"Raul Garza, SIP. What's your connection?"

"Connection? I'm not sure what you mean." She forced herself not to fidget. It took more effort than she'd anticipated.

Ross rubbed his chin with his left hand while thumping his right fingers on the envelope. "You move back to town after your friend Carlos died and immediately applied here. I know you were at the Line Shack with Raul who works at SIP. You have an interest in this renegade parole officer who happened to come to town at roughly the same time as you. In fact, he lived at your mom's house until he got a place and I assume a part-time job at SIP. Coincidence? Maybe. I don't think so."

Carrie squirmed in her chair. Her collar was damp. She tried to decide just how much to share. "What do you want to know?"

"I have some info that may help you," he said, picking up the envelope. "I need to know what you know and what you plan to do with the knowledge."

Carrie exhaled. "Okay. I'm trying to find out who's the big boss running the smuggling ring. It's not Julio Ramirez."

"I know," Ross said. I've known him since grade school."

"I'm trying to find out who pulls his chain and if it's one of the cartels."

"Do you have a theory?" Ross slid the envelope toward her.

"Maybe." She opened the envelope and found an 8 x 10 of Ronnie Dahl handing something to Raul in the parking lot of SIP.

"Don't ask me how I got that."

She assumed Aurora was the photographer. "No. I don't care, but it fits my scenario. I just can't prove anything. No way to follow the money."

Ross leaned across the desk and lowered his voice. "I might have a way. I have a buddy with the Texas Rangers. There's another photo in there."

She pulled it out. It showed her old cruiser and Raul's truck at the Line Shack. She knew Aurora hadn't taken this one. She suspected Ross took it and wondered if he knew who was driving the rental car in the picture. She looked back at Ross and waited.

"Give me a few days," he said. "In the meantime be very careful... And please, leave this alone, at least for now. I'm working on it."

"Is that an order?" Carrie asked.

"Would it matter?"

"I respect the badge, Sir. You know the folks involved. I want to know what happened to Carlos and I want justice, but I'll back off… As long as I know you're working on it. I still want to help where I can."

"What about this Kevin Cash guy."

"He's like, I guess, a confidential informant."

"Is that all?"

Carrie wondered how deep into her Ross was capable of seeing. "Yeah, that's about it," she lied.

Ross stood. "Cool. By the way, Aurora's in town for the next few days. Why don't you come by for dinner on Thursday if you don't have other plans?"

The guilt wrenched her gut. "I'd love to. Can I bring anything?"

"Just you."

Kevin considered how the aptly named auto shop shimmered on the horizon. Disoriented by sleep deprivation and the thick numbing ache between his eyes left by the tequila shots, he hoped the sand-colored building would stabilize on approach. The dually parked next to the dormant gas pumps confirmed his supposed hallucination. He parked in front of the building and honked the horn. Rustling commenced immediately in the cargo box. Raul walked from the entrance, pushing his long hair back from his receding hairline before hiding it under a black narrow brim Stetson. He'd obviously been asleep just moments before. They met at the rear of the truck.

"Let's see what we have here," Raul said.

"They're really young," Kevin said. "I doubt most of them are legal age."

"Funny guy! Ain't nothing legal about none of 'em. Nice and tight though, I bet. You try any of 'em out?"

Kevin felt a twinge of anger try to break through his exhaustion. He tamped it down. "Didn't have time. Had to make the border by five." He immediately realized his mistake.

"No longer a problem. There's plenty of time now. We'll get them fed and cleaned up. I brought some cots out. We can pick a few to play with."

Kevin cut the seal and unlocked the box. When the door rolled up the girls gathered on the tailgate. "Welcome to Texas," Kevin hollered. Several of the women smiled. Kevin gave them a hand negotiating the climb down.

Raul opened his arms and a few of the girls chose to jump to him. As he set them on the sand, he gave them each a rough swat on the ass. They were herded into the service bays where tables were set with fried chicken and all the sides. A case of Modelo Especial waited on ice in the air-conditioned office. Only two cans were empty so far. Raul grinned, showing his gold teeth. "Party time," he said.

Kevin went to the bathroom. He was numb from the trip. The only thing he desired was Betty Lou and a long uninterrupted nap, but he knew he had to play this the right way. He splashed water on his face, dampened his short-cropped hair, and became DJ Cash. He shook the cobwebs from his brain, burst from the john door, and hollered, "Hey, y'all hot little Chicitas. Who speaks English?"

More than half of the women looked up from their lunches. DJ filled the bucket with beer cans and ice. "Raise your hand if you want a beer." Several of the girls raised their hands. Kevin began passing out cold brews. He held each one just out of reach, where the girls would have to stand or stretch to grab them. Raul was getting a kick from the antics. A party atmosphere developed. DJ came to a particularly shapely woman who was obviously in her 20s. She sported long silky hair, pouty lips, and an athletic build with breasts that, though full, retained their youthful perkiness. He held the beer can high. As she reached for it he put a finger on her nipple, then jerked it back. "Ssst! damn, Mamacita! You're hotter than a two-dollar pistol!" He grabbed her around the waist as he let her have the beer. He pulled her to him and to his surprise she straddled his legs and ground into him. Her arm slipped around his neck and she gave him a deep kiss, shoving her tongue in his mouth. When she gave him a minute to breathe she pulled the tab on the Tecate, took a long chug, and set it on the table. To the hoots and calls of the girls and Raul she took his face between her hands and pulled it deep between her ample breasts.

In the few seconds this took, DJ noticed he'd developed a rock-solid hard-on. She'd noticed it too. She cupped it in her hand and massaged it through his jeans.

"What's your name?" DJ asked.

"Does it matter, hombre. I ain't your sister."

"Just curious."

She whispered in his ear. "It's Karla. I can make you remember it if you want."

"Oh, I want."

"I know you do," Karla said. She picked up her beer, took his hand and led him to the office, closing the door behind them.

From inside the air-conditioned office they could hear the wild whoops and whistles out in the bays. She backed him to the desk where he sat while she unbuttoned her shirt and unclipped the clasp at the front of her bra. She placed his hands on her caramel-colored breasts. "You like?" She asked. He replied by giving her erect chocolate nipples a pinch. She moaned and leaned into him while reaching for his belt buckle. In seconds his pants were around his ankles. He reclined back on the desk while she held his curved member between her ample breasts. A trickle of her warm perspiration provided just enough lubricant to slide the full length as he arched and thrust. Her hands tightened her breasts around him as her thick silky hair cascaded across his thighs.

"Unbutton your shirt," she said. She took his rod between her lips, then tongued a slick layer of spit on it before sliding it back between her breasts. He fumbled with his buttons, finally opening his shirt. She kissed his stomach and rolled his nipples between her fingers as he continued to thrust between her tits. He caught an organic whiff of something like river water flowing into the sea. He looked down to see her hand down her britches. She pulled it back out and smeared her juice across his chest.

"Sit up," she demanded. He obliged. She licked her juice from his chest, nibbling at his nipple nubs while holding his curve between her hands. She stood up and pulled his face back between her breasts. "Now you do me."

He tasted the salt of lust on her tits, licked the nipples, then held them between his teeth while batting them with his tongue. She moaned low and squeezed his throbbing hard-on with both hands. She kissed his ear, then his chin, his throat, his navel. Finally, she put her full dark lips on him, coating his rod in hot saliva, swallowing almost all of him. One hand cupped and gently squeezed his balls. The other hand slowly stroked the curve of his rock-solid member. Her tongue danced the perimeter of the head as she extricated it from the depths of her throat.

He felt a finger or two reaching toward his ass, massaging the prostate. "No! Don't rush it. I know the tricks. Make it last."

"Why? You want to fuck me?"

"I don't have a condom."

"Your loss," she said. "Mine too, with the shape of this thing, I think." She giggled under her breath. "I can take it in the ass, but I don't do that for free, not even for you."

"I'm good. Let's go with this. Just don't rush it."

She rolled her eyes and smiled. "Whatever you say, Boss."

Try as he could, he couldn't restrain, especially after the "Boss" comment. She had just taken the head into the back of her throat when he felt the juice coming from deep inside. She swallowed the entire length of the shaft as she squeezed his balls. Her tongue continued to slither around the rigid member as his juice pumped into her throat. He moaned. She swallowed. He groaned and yelled. She slurped and hummed, vibrating his skeleton. She stayed on him until he could no longer stand it. When she refused to relinquish his softening member from the depths of her gullet, he finally pulled her loose by her hair.

    Betty Lou searched the back shelf in her walk-in closet until she retrieved the long dormant lava lamp she'd saved from her college days. She thought of the weekend all-nighters between semesters when the lamp oozed and bubbled convulsively, throwing dim red shadows across her dorm room walls. She hadn't been a stellar student but she had mastered the art of weekends.

    Her apartment was spotless. Most of Friday night had been spent preparing for Kevin's return from the border. She cleaned because she couldn't sleep. In addition to the dull ache of desire in her abdomen, a greasy chunk of something like fear polluted her frontal lobe of reason.

    She turned on the lava lamp. As the sedimentary layer of color began to undulate, so did the dark lump of fear, heated by the desire building below. She didn't want to think about her heart wedged between. That little organ had run the show before, with disastrous results. Now was not the time.

    She didn't want to call him, she knew he'd show. She knew he'd be late, probably by several hours. Only a tragic death or an arrest would prevent his eventual arrival. Either of those outcomes were well within the realm of possibility. To tamp down her worry she walked through the apartment again, checking every detail. Then, extracting her carved wooden box from under the coffee table, she took the two plump peyote buttons and wrapped each one in colored cellophane tied with a white silk ribbon. She placed them in the center of her coffee table, stretched out on the couch, and counted her heartbeats.

    As much as Carrie admired Ross, as much as she respected Aurora, she wasn't one to give her trust easily. Truth be known she didn't fully trust Kevin. She barely trusted herself. Though she didn't like Garcia she did trust him on some level. Besides, she controlled the information he received. She knew he would rescue the women being smuggled, if only to gain credence with his superiors. She gave him only basic info, the truck owned by SIP on I-10 between Houston and New Orleans, Sunday or later. It wasn't much to go on but she could almost guarantee he'd run with it. She only needed to set the other side of the trap, keep the suspicion away from her and Kevin. She was at a loss.

It had been an interesting 48 hours. She was making a better world and it was taking a lot out of her. The aroma of the honeysuckle strengthened in her nostrils as the golden orb of setting sun warmed her shoulders from behind. Admiring the chameleon paint shimmering on the Charger in her driveway boggled her mind. Something was wrong. Things being this perfect had to mean a lack of balance. In her world balance and perfection were opposing forces.

Her fingers tightened around the ice cold bottle between her legs. She raised the beer to her lips and took a long frosty pull. Down the street she heard Raul's dually rumble to life. As he slowed to admire the new toy in her driveway she flagged him down.

"Who'd you bust to rate this shit," he said. Leaving his truck idling in the street, he walked a slow circle around the Interceptor. "Did you put a senator in jail?"

"Not yet. You'd best behave out there. We still have to pay for it." She motioned toward the other chair on her little porch. "Want a beer?"

"Sure." He reached in his truck and silenced the engine, tossing the keys on the floorboard.

She had a cold one waiting when he reached the landing. "I owe you one." She let the statement settle until he sat down and twisted off the cap. "This info is just for your protection, okay?"

"What info would that be, Deputy James?" Showing his gold teeth jittered her stomach.

"It's confidential, but, your company, the one you work for… SIP, is being investigated by the Texas Rangers. I thought you'd like to know."

"Why should I care. I ain't nobody, just a gofer. I deliver an occasional truckload of veggies."

Carrie caught his gaze from the corner of her eyes. Raising her bottle in his direction she stated, "Sure you are. Reckon you shouldn't be worried then. Just keep it to yourself, okay?"

"No sweat. Want to hit the Line Shack, shoot some eight ball."

She put her boots on the porch rail, stretching out her long legs. "I'm not going anywhere. I've had four hours sleep in the last two days. My butt moves out of this chair, it's hitting the sack."

She could see the gears clicking behind Raul's eyes. Just before he made a huge mistake he chose to back down. "Some other time then," he said. "Not the best day for shooting pool anyway. Got a load to Houston tomorrow. Better make sure it gets packed properly. I'm blocking the road. Thanks for the brew."

"You driving? I thought you were el jefe' these days."

Raul leaned against the railing. "Big load. The new kid was going to take it but he begged out. Woman trouble I think."

"Kids today, right? Be careful." She tipped the longneck slightly in his direction as complete and total exhaustion washed over her. He couldn't help but admire the Interceptor one more time as he walked back to his truck.

"Veggies, mostly greens, definitely some cilantro," Kevin said. "Hence the shower." He hated lying to Betty Lou but not near as much as he would have hated telling her the truth. "Anyway, I had to take Raul's truck back to the shop to pick up mine. I didn't want my truck smelling like cilantro, much less having you boot me out to the parking lot."

"I love fresh cilantro," Betty Lou said.

"To each her own. But please, don't try to feed me anything with cilantro in it. That shit smells like feet."

"Aw, Baby, you don't like feet either? That ruins my big surprise." She'd already cuddled next to him on the couch and supplied him with a cold IPA and a frosted mug. "Have you eaten?"

"Yeah, Raul had a bucket of chicken waiting when I dropped the truck at Mirage."

"Why Mirage anyway? That's kind of weird."

"Who knows. Save a few miles, a little less road time. Julio bought the place. I guess he plans on expansions. It's got a pretty decent shop."

"Isn't there a shop at the warehouse?"

Kevin, having poured the beer and leaned back, put his free hand on the soft magic of Betty Lou's inner thigh. "Yeah, but I left work at work." If only he could leave the guilt there too. "So, how does this party work?"

Betty Lou unwrapped one of the foil pouches on the table. Leaving the peyote buttons on the foil, she used her pocketknife to slice it into four pieces. "It's a lot like acid but more spiritual and without the body rush. You probably want to chop it into pieces you can swallow whole. If you chew it tastes really putrid."

Kevin stared blankly as she popped a chunk into her mouth and washed it down with a swallow of beer. "Okay I'm lost. You know I'm just an Arkansas hillbilly. I tried moonshine once. That's about as exotic as I get."

"Moonshine? Wow really? What was that like?"

"It tastes nasty. The hangover is brutal. I don't remember much else."

"You'll remember this."

"Is that a good thing?"

"Depends. You'll learn things about yourself you don't already know. If you can handle that you'll be okay. I bet we have fun."

"I can't think of anyone I'd rather bare my soul to." Kevin said. He thought he noticed a pink tinge lighten Betty Lou's cheeks.

She opened his foil. "How many pieces should I make."

"At least six. There's no way I can swallow a chunk like you did."

She grinned. "I could've swallowed mine whole but I didn't want to show off."

"Oh please, feel free to show off anytime."

"Maybe later," she winked, then chopped his button into eight small pieces. She swallowed another chunk of her button. "Better get busy, boy. I'm way ahead of you."

Kevin swallowed three pieces in rapid succession using small sips of beer to wash them down. I see what you mean about the taste. I hope this is worth it."

"Oh, one other thing," Betty Lou said, "some people get really upset stomachs. If that happens just go throw up in the bathroom. It won't affect the high but it will settle your stomach."

"Wonderful! What have I gotten myself into?" He gulped down a couple more pieces.

Betty Lou finished her button. "You won't regret it." She turned off the ringer on her iPhone. "Turn off your phone." She put hers on the dock and punched in a six-hour playlist she'd designed specifically for this experience.

Kevin reluctantly shut off his phone. "Why?" he asked.

"You're not going to want to talk to anyone on the outside for a while." Ambient piano jazz filled the empty spaces in the room.

Betty Lou brought two more cold beers while Kevin finished his button with the last of his first one. He thought about how the experience was similar to a communion except that he was actually in the presence of an angel, an angel of unconditional love who assuages his inherent guilt. He didn't think this peyote was going to have any effect on him. His stomach was a little queasy, but not anything to worry about.

. "When does it start working?" He asked.

Betty Lou smiled. "You'll know." Her smile was heart fluttering radiant, but then it always was. He hadn't noticed in a while because he'd become accustomed to it. The warmth of her cheeks against his shoulder felt like a low hum in the ether between his cells, setting the universe at rest.

He noticed the curtains over the front windows waving slightly. Looking to where the breeze came from, he noticed the wave of the curtains continuing into the wall and into the music, now the muted trumpet played in front of a string section. A dark-voiced woman sang *Our Love is Easy*. She had the most beautiful voice he'd ever heard. He wanted t ask who the singer was. When he turned to Betty Lou she was in the center of the room, her skin glowed with an amber gold hue. Her dreads, backlit by the window, floated around her face, sheaves of underwater stalks dancing in the sound waves from the muted trumpet. She swayed to the music, her arms above her head, boneless as if she'd become a water nymph caught in the aural undulation of the musical sea. She caught his eye and a surge of sensual energy passed between them, an invitation to join her in the dance. She tilted her head back and the woman's magic voice surged from her like the inviting heat of sun warmed stones on the high desert mesa.

When he stood, he felt 30 pounds lighter. He'd acquired the energy and coordination of a whitetail buck. Rather than wanting to avoid dancing he ached to join her in the waves of music and light. Yes, light had now paired with shadows in the sensual ambience of the inner space they shared. When she draped, her arms around his neck, his around her waist, they moved together with one body. They were inside the body of the giant classical guitar, the only light coming through the sound hole above, awash in the vibrations of the six strings sealing the space. Where their bodies touched, energy exchanged on a level below sentient emotion, like pack animals, or those flocks of birds that moved in perfectly choreographed formation. Now he understood. He gave himself to it.

The dance had no words, none were needed. Their communion, a hive mind intimacy. It lasted through a song or a day or some immeasurable time bubble. Finally she lay her head on his shoulder, lips to his ear, "I'm going to change into something comfortable. I have something for you if you want."

"Sure," he said. She vanished. He knew where she was. He knew she wouldn't care if he joined her in the bedroom but something, real or imagined, kept him in the living room encased in the pulsing music. He folded in on himself. The part he called self that stood outside and observed, judged, and directed all the Kevins and DJs he showed the world was putting away those movie poster versions of himself. He took over his own being. Those paper-thin versions of Kevin (DJ) Cash held no sway in the world of Kevin and Betty Lou. If any honesty existed in the world he had to face it. He could start in a new plane, be himself. It would take time, work, and insight. It was what he needed, but was it safe. Something to think about when he came back to the world. But with Betty Lou, at least with her, he owed her his true self, even if it wasn't pretty.

When she entered the room, in brilliant white yoga pants and a tube top barely containing those magnificent breasts, her smile almost stopped his breathing. "Here," she said. "I brought you shorts and a tank top. Eventually even these may be too restrictive. Get comfo"

She watched him slowly as he shucked his pearl-white western shirt, boots, and jeans. By the time he slipped the tank top over his head, she'd pulled his jockey shorts to his ankles. "No rush," she said. "It's all about the comfort." Her warm palms on his butt helped him realize how cool his skin had become. Her warm breath on his inner thighs gave him a hard-on that strained to burst. She caressed it and squeezed lightly. He felt the warmth of her hand. Never had he needed to be inside her so much. She stood and pulled her tube top down to her waist. She danced to the slow drumbeat and the haunting wooden flute, her breasts against his chest, his curved member throbbing against her fertility dome. Through the ecstasy of several songs their bodies slithered together as their tongues played hide and seek. He ached for her. "Please," he said. She led into the bedroom where they spent a naked afternoon sharing each other, becoming a single soul and exploding into radiant flares of sexual energy, both being inside the other in skin and spirit.

Lydia poured the carne guisada in a well-seasoned cast-iron Dutch oven. The spicy stew had likely increased its salinity from the stream of tears cascading down her cheeks. Before even closing the container she exorcised a soul wrenching scream and hurled the empty Dutch oven with sufficient force to shatter three porcelain tiles in the backsplash after ricocheting off the granite countertop. On a whim, she marched the container of artisan stew down the hill to DJ's trailer and slung it across the entrance and down the porch. She'd spent all morning seasoning and simmering the beef until it was the perfect rendition of a generation's old family recipe.

Vigilant observation had informed her that he'd arrived alone in Raul's truck. When she called to invite him to lunch his phone rang once and went to the mailbox. Figuring he was showering; she left no message. She would invite him personally. While the stew simmered, she'd walked down just in time to see him gun his own truck out of the driveway, wearing a fresh-pressed pearl snap shirt and his favorite beaver Stetson. She knew he was leaving to meet that hefty white bitch he worked with. She could not fathom what he saw in that hippiefied slut with the nasty tangled up hair.

What the fuck, DJ? How can you not see? If you just give me a chance! The tears started again, then the shakes and the swirling tornado of anger in her brain. She thought about chasing him down, but no, she refused to show desperation. Fuck him. She'd show him. He could never have her if she was dead. Then he'd see what he missed.

The elegant gowns in her mother's closet had been imported from Europe and custom tailored to fit her mother like a second skin. Lydia was built almost exactly like her mother, only an inch and a half taller. She picked an oyster shell white dress with a plunging neckline and bell half sleeves, a two-layer number; satin clinging to her skin draped with a diaphanous lace skirt. Her mother's words echoed in her mind. "Live fast, die young, leave a good-looking corpse." She checked her image in her mother's full-length mirror. Mama, am by doing this right? Her hands cradled her breasts, pushing them up and forward. She shook her hair until stray ringlets framed her face and shoulders.

As long as her presence was desecrating her mother's sacred bedroom she may as well check the medicine cabinet too. Four years had passed since Lidia had entered these spaces. It held mostly makeup and beauty enhancement tools required to meet the socially accepted definition of goddess. She tinkered with her face somewhat though few improvements could be made to one of nature's masterworks.

An amber plastic bottle of Prozac sat on the bottom shelf. Lydia doubted the four expired pills it contained would do the deed. She checked the other cabinets but found only vitamins and birth control, also all expired. The birth control pills were confusing as she had been told her mother couldn't have more children. No one here to answer that dilemma. Keep looking.

Her father's bedroom decor featured an elegant minimalism, unlike the excesses evident through the rest of the hacienda; one tall chest of drawers, a wrought-iron framed bed sporting white cotton sheets and a tan wool blanket, a nightstand with a lamp, a table and three framed photos of her and her mother; one each separate and one of them together in a classic pose. Lydia wondered if her mother waited on the other side and if she would be happy to reunite. The nightstand also held a pill bottle. It contained dozens of Percocet. She added five of them to the bottle containing the four expired Prozac. Now she was getting somewhere. In her father's bathroom she found nothing but basic body maintenance supplies. She wondered where he kept the Seroquel he routinely insisted she ingest. A few of those would complete the deadly cocktail. She checked the nightstand again. In the drawer she found her father's Ruger 38 pistol and beside it, her meds. She added half a dozen of them to her stash. All set.

Exhausted beyond words, all Carrie wanted was ten hours of sleep. She didn't even bother with a shower. Maybe that was the problem, probably not. She new Raul's record and reputation but he had come to her defense when he mistakenly thought she was in trouble.

She tried relaxation techniques, deep breathing even counting the stupid sheep. Sleep failed her. Finally she scrolled through her phone for Garcia's number. It went straight to voicemail. "Garcia, James here. That thing we talked about? It's been postponed. Call me when you get this message." She'd done as much and she felt comfortable with. She turned off her phone. Let him wonder. She switched off the remaining lamp and dropped immediately into a deep dreamless sleep.

Julio wanted alibis. He was all over south central Texas from Bandera to San Antonio to Victoria, anywhere that was nowhere near Mirage Auto Repair or the Amistad border crossing. He took a couple of his sales staff with him visiting clients, legitimate clients from bankers to baker's to restaurateurs; fourteen hours of making small talk while cooped up in salesman's sedans. Salesman he was related to in some extended way incapacitated him. He despised family outside of his own house, always wanting the inside scoop on his crazy dead wife and crazy outlaw daughter. They could all go to hell!

Lydia had mentioned her iconic carne guisada before he left that morning, a perfect end to a less-than-perfect day. He could almost taste it as he turned in the driveway. "I know you guys want to get home to your families. Just drop me at the shop. I'll take the four-wheeler up to the house."

In Betty Lou's magic apartment sleep was not a consideration. They had made love four, or was it five, times now. There had been tender sweet moments, playful moments of loud squeals and laughter, ferocious moments when all their energy was consumed in grab, grope, and thrust. Some screams of "Fuck me you beast" and fingernails tearing into flesh. Always there was an unspoken tactile communication that kept them on the same plane. There were breaks to catch their breath but each time, as the room danced and throbbed around them, a touch, a glance or an innocent kiss would blossom into ripe purple lust screaming from their hearts and loins.

This time they were leaning over the coffee table. Betty Lou's breasts sliding on the sweat soaked glass top while Kevin used all the power of his thighs to thrust deeper in her than he'd ever been. With every deep push he felt himself grow larger. Betty Lou felt him so deep in her she could feel it in her diaphragm. With every plunge she set free a little yelp of pleasure until they combined into a roiling orgasm at the center of her soul.

They saw their distorted reflection in the table top. Red skin pulsed like lava, eyes glazed with blue fire. He could feel her holy inner temple as her body broke free causing him to burst inside her once again. Aftershocks tremored from their universal center out to their extremities as they lay heaving on the slick hot glass.

"Let's take a break. Want a beer?" Betty Lou asked. Kevin untangled from her and fell back on the carpet rubbing his bloody knees.

Hanging out with salesman all day made Julio feel dirty. The 94° temperature on the darker side of dusk wasn't helping either but at least he had nothing to do with a truckload of professional women heading for New Orleans. He made sure of that. No connection whatsoever, if you didn't count the trucks and the guys driving them and the wad of crisp hundred dollar bills locked in his safe.

The headlamps on the four-wheeler weren't very bright but it didn't matter much putting up the hill to the hacienda. They were enough to illuminate a pile of black hair and white cloth at the edge of the driveway. He jumped from the cart and rolled his daughter on her back. Her face was crusted with vomit and caliche. Her lips and eyelids were blue. That's about all he could tell in the light from the cart. He dialed 911 and began looking for a pulse. He thought he felt something in her throat but nothing at her wrist.

"I think she's alive. God, I hope so! I'm not sure if she's breathing," he told the operator. "I'm starting CPR. Please hurry!"

After his wife died he'd taken CPR. That's how his logic worked. Even he realized it was shutting the gate after the horses had disappeared. He had no problem with helping Lydia breathe, even with the dirt and vomit. The brutal compressions needed for the heart massage was another story. He screamed in agony for her every time he crushed her delicate rib cage to help her heart pump the vital blood. He looked for a clue to what had happened but her mother's elegant formal gown was the only clue, a devastating clue, but why? Is there ever a reason? Breathe. Pound the delicate chest. Cry gallons of tears. Curse God. Rhythmically, incessantly, on his knees in the sweltering humidity. "Please, God, you heartless bastard, don't let her die!" Eons passed and finally he heard sirens in the distance. Breathe. Pound. Curse God. Are there ever any reasons? Are there ever any answers? Is this his punishment for his failures? Why does it have to be so damned harsh?

Under Pressure

Every joint in Kevin's body ached gloriously and his cranium felt as though it had been pressure washed from the inside. When he rolled onto his stomach his penis burst into screaming pain. He reveled in the discomfort, unsure he was the same person who woke up the previous morning. Betty Lou lounged next to him, snoring daintily. He opened his acid-washed eyes to the warmth of the butter-tinted sun cascading through the bedroom window ricocheting, off her dreadlocks. This was not a place in the mental landscape he was familiar with. It took him a few minutes to gather his thoughts. His recent adventure stretched time and space into shapes that made him question a reality he was no longer sure existed. Considering rolling out of bed, he reached over to run his hand up Betty Lou's warm thigh. Her dainty snore became a low moan and she rolled towards him. A smile came to her lips. "That was freaking awesome," she said. "What a way to spend a weekend!"

Kevin's phone lay dormant on the nightstand. He powered it up to see what time it was. "It's 12:30 in the afternoon," he told Betty Lou. "We missed church," he snickered, ignoring the 18 missed calls.

"I didn't miss anything," Betty Lou said. "I've got everything I need right here, with the possible exception of breakfast. How sore are you?"

"Too sore to be your breakfast, if you're on a high-protein diet. Besides, my extension is expended. I propose we go out for migas."

Betty Lou pried her head loose from the pillow, gave Kevin a juicy kiss on the lips, threw a little tongue in for fun. "You wouldn't have said that last night. Let's take a hot shower first so our funk doesn't clear out the restaurant. I'll wash your back if you'll wash my front."

"No problem. My fingers are working just fine.

They frolicked in the steaming shower for a good 20 minutes, laughing, moaning, yelping for so long that they didn't hear his phone ringing repeatedly. They didn't hear Julio's desperate voice. They didn't hear Carrie's exasperated message. They didn't hear Raul's threatening growl. They were the center of their own universe and apparently everyone else's too.

Carrie's eyes popped open barely passed dawn. She fixed coffee and took a hot shower. After drinking a smoothie made from leftover fruit salad, she prepared to run before the sweltering Texas heat made it impossible. This would be her first week on the night shift and the eight hours of sleep she'd just finished enjoying seemed to be enough. She stepped out on the porch, took a deep breath of jasmine and honeysuckle, laced up her running shoes, and trotted out of her little barrio shaped cul-de-sac. The rhythm of her feet on the pavement erased all thoughts from her mind. Breathing and gushing sweat, feeling the blood coursing through her veins, set her at peace. She finally felt centered and stable for the first time in her adult life. After jogging an hour, circling the downtown, she slowed to a walk for the last half mile to cool down. Once home she took her phone off the charger and powered it up. There was one text. It was from Garcia.
{Mission Accomplished}

"What mission? Then she remembered. "FUCK!" She looked across the street. Raul's dually was nowhere to be seen. She called Kevin. It went straight to voice mail. There was no one else she could consult without having to try and explain something she couldn't reveal. She didn't even leave a message.

Occasionally a case came along that had Dr. Morrison question his decision to become an ER specialist. As Sundays go, this one marked a new low. He stepped into the staff bathroom, splashed water on his face, and took a long breath. At the nurses' station he requested the charge nurse find Julio and bring him to the chapel. It seemed more appropriate than his closet sized, fluorescent lighted office. He stood until Julio arrived.

"Please, have a seat." He offered Julio a leather office chair and he sat on a wooden fold-out. "She's stable," Morrison said, "but she's in a coma and I can't promise she'll ever come out of it. I have no idea how long she was unconscious or how long her brain was oxygen-deprived. It's highly unlikely she will regain anything like a normal quality of life. Anything is possible. She's young and otherwise healthy. There's also the issue of kidney function. I'm afraid the general prognosis is not promising. If she's going to recover any cognizant brain function we should know something in the next 24 to 72 hours."

Julio sat stunned. He spiraled downward, gripping the arms of the chair to remain upright. "But she was breathing... when the ambulance came. Isn't there something we can do? I'll give her a kidney if that will help." He scooted forward, resting his elbows on his knees. "Please, isn't there anything we can do?"

"Pray," Morrison said, "and hope." I know you're not going anywhere so I'll have housekeeping bring a cot in for you. You can stay with her as long as you like. We'll take it day to day and see what happens."

The morning news on the local CBS affiliate out of Corpus Christi led with the story. Dozens of cars with emergency lights flashing surrounded the box van as it was hooked to a commercial wrecker. The sign on the side of the cargo box was out of focus, as was the face of the stocky cowboy being led away in handcuffs. His silver spurs reflected the pulsating lights of the various emergency vehicles. A number of Latinas dressed for the clubs were being transferred into two 14 passenger vans with Harris County Sherriff decals. There was one pale green Border Patrol vehicle with a young officer standing by the open driver's door. He answered questions posed by a windblown blonde reporter from KHOU Channel 11 in Houston. An expression between disgust and curiosity fueled her inquiries.

Reporter: So, Officer Garcia, how many women were locked in this refrigerated box van?
Garcia: Twenty-two.
Reporter: What made you decide to stop the vehicle and investigate?
Garcia: Fortunately, we received a tip from a concerned citizen.
Reporter: Do you suspect these women were smuggled in from Mexico?
Garcia: Most definitely!
Reporter: ...against their will?
Garcia: We're continuing to investigate the circumstances.
Reporter (turning toward camera): There you have it. Twenty-two women who may be victims of sex trafficking have been rescued by a joint operation of the Border Patrol and the Harris County Sherriff's Department. Back to you, Dan
Talking Head: Thank you, Angela. Texas attorney General George P. Bush has promised to form a task force to study ways to prevent these operations from putting the citizens of Texas in jeopardy. Stay tuned for more information as the story develops.

Well, shit! Carrie thought to herself. It's not like I didn't warn him. She turned off the TV and tried to decide her next move. This would certainly pick up the pace of the operation.

Kevin and Betty Lou were in the back booth at Taqueria Arandas nursing steaming cups of coffee while waiting on their migas. Kevin glanced up at the TV bolted to the wall across the room. The truck surrounded by police vehicles caught his eye, as did a few of the women. When he saw Raul being led away in cuffs it hit him. "Son-of-a-bitch," he whispered.

"Look! On the TV. That's our guy, Raul.

Betty Lou checked the TV. This channel had not blurred the box van. "Oh shit! Isn't that your side hustle?

"Not anymore!"

HELL!

Kevin and Betty Lou arrive at work a few minutes apart for the sake of appearance. Kevin doesn't even have time to pick up his coffee cup before Judge Kendrick calls him in.

"Close the door." Kendrick is not a happy woman. "I suppose you've kept up with the events of the weekend?"

"I reckon you're talking about Raul?"

"Of course. Strange thing is, he has already made bail, on the weekend, no less, or someone has on his behalf. I'm not letting that sleazebag go. As a favor, they are holding him for us on a parole violation, but we have 24 hours to pick him up. Sheriff Carranza said he would send a deputy but I want you to ride along since you seem to know him better than you should."

"No problem boss. Whatever you need, I'm at your beck and call."

"Don't be an ass. You've got 30 minutes to get your shit together. You'll head out with the deputy at 9:30. I want him booked and in the county jail today. Are we clear? There's some evil in the wind and I suspect he has knowledge of it. You need to find out everything you can. Dismissed!"

Kevin grabs Betty Lou's coffee cup out of her office and fills them both from the break room. By the time he returns she's behind her desk. "I'm headed for Houston," he says and buckles his government issue 9mil into his shoulder holster and his official county P.O. jacket.

"Today?" Betty Lou asks.

"Right now apparently," Kevin says. "Picking up Raul, parole violation."

They hear the front door open. Kevin peeks out and sees Carrie, still wearing her shades and a professional countenance, strolling into Judge Kendrick's office.

Kendrick picks up the intercom. "Kevin Cash, your ride is here."

Kevin steps into the judge's office, eyes Carrie and holds out his hand. "Kevin Cash," he says.

Carrie shakes it firmly. "Deputy Carrie James. Pleased to meet you."

"Let's roll." Kevin says and holds the door
"Really?" Kendrick says, to absolutely no response.

Ronnie Dahl watched the same newscast as everyone else. Having a minion with too much information in police custody greatly disturbs him. He must get this in check before word crosses the border, if it hasn't already. It's a matter of life and death, possibly his own. He has one contact in Harris County. Fortunately, he's a county judge. Before the sun rises Raul has made bail. That was the plan anyway, until Bee County got involved. They want him on a parole violation so he's back in custody. Ronnie's running out of folks he can trust.

The mercury-vapor floodlight in the hospital courtyard prevents discernable variation between day aand night. Julio tries to add consistency to mother nature's plan by using the blinds. There's not a whole lot else he can do to make life normal for his daughter. It's been over 24 hours and he swears he's seen her move, seen her smile, heard her mumble. The doctors don't deny it but they also don't see it as an improvement. Her kidneys are minimally functional but her liver numbers haven't changed. She's still in ICU getting all the care the rural hospital is capable of providing. Julio has contacted a neurologist in San Antonio. After looking over her chart he tells Julio the same thing he's heard from the local doctors. "Wait and see but prepare for the worst."

It's Monday afternoon and he's dozing in the recliner by the window. He hears the door open and Ronnie Dahl is standing just inside the room. Julio's despair flushes to anger. "What are you doing here? You need to leave." I'm done with you."

Dahl seems genuinely insulted. "Julio, mi compadre', I just stopped by to check on you and see how your girl is holding up We can talk about the other stuff later. So, how is she?"

Julio doesn't know if Dahl is concerned or just being careful. "She's in bad shape, Ronnie. If she recovers it's going to be a long road."

"I'm praying for her," Dahl says. "If you need anything just let me know. I'm serious. By the way, I hate to be the bearer of bad tidings but the Harris County cops seized one of your trucks and the cargo. Raul was arrested but I pulled some strings and he made bail. You can thank me later. Right now, just take care of your girl and let me handle the other crap." He walked around and patted Julio on the back, wrapped his arm around him and gave him a gentle squeeze. "Take care, old friend."

Though concerned, Dahl had confidence his problem would work out. He was too many degrees of separation from the problem for the cartel to risk their Texas-based ally. There was a problem left to solve but he had the answer in his coat pocket.

Kevin followed Carrie to the Interceptor maintaining an air of professionalism uncommon to his character. As soon as they were on Highway 59 he dropped all pretense. "How cool is this? It couldn't have worked out better if we planned ahead."

Carrie's expression hadn't changed and any discernible emotion hid behind those mirror-finished aviators. "Is it ... cool? See, that's the problem. There is no plan. You're up to your ass in this. If you don't get your shit together you'll be riding in the back seat on our next excursion!"

"I have a plan, kind of."

"Yeah, what?"

"I'm Julio's right-hand man. When he needs to vanish, who do you think he'll trust with his info?"

"Not you! Raul's already bailed out. How do you think that happened?"

"Wasn't Julio. He hasn't left the hospital."

"You're right. It was Julio's handler, Commissioner Ronnie Dahl. You're in the mix and I bet you didn't know that."

"Fat man in the blue Lincoln?"

"Yep"

"I've seen him around."

"He's putting on a huge event for Labor Day. I'm using the opportunity to get next to him, maybe bodyguard, protection, something that gets me in the inner circle. You need to do the same with Julio. It's the only way we'll bring down this nest of vipers."

Kevin felt as though he'd been relegated to the back burner. "What about Raul? Can we use him?"

"Don't know. Let's see where his loyalties lie. My guess is they're for sale to the highest bidder? You know him better. What do you think?"

"Not sure. He's pretty tight with Julio. This may be the chance we need to find out."

Ronnie Dahl waited at the elevator, his left hand in his pocket. A fat, diamond ring encrusted forefinger of his right hand pushed the button pointing down. A bell pinged. The door opened and he stepped in, alone. A few seconds went by as he fondled the envelope in his jacket. He pushed the button marked basement. He arrived in the florescent kingdom where machines hummed and the smells were ... different. He followed the rhythmic thumping to a row of dryers where a skinny Latina with twitchy eyes, blackened teeth, and lesions on her skin stood staring into the depths of a commercial dryer. "Hola, Juanita," he said. She failed to acknowledge his presence. He tried again. " ¿Quieres ganar algo de dinero?"

"Cuanta"

"Más de lo que ganas aquí en un mes."

She finally looked at him. Took in the rings on his fingers. Thought about taking a knife to his nasty hands and hocking the rings, maybe getting the fuck out of this basement. "¿Cuál es el trato?"

He pulled a hypodermic syringe from his pocket. "¿Supongo que sabes cómo usar uno de estos?"

She spit in his general direction. "Fuck You!", she hissed.

He chuckled. "I see you've been brushing up on your English."

"Yeah, so what?"

"So how does three thousand sound? Pretty decent traveling money I'd guess.

"Up front".

"Doable. The girl in 517, Lydia. This needs to go in her IV.."

"What is it?"

"Vitamins"

'Mierda"

" Okay, potassium. It won't show up on the tox screen. You'll be doing her a favor."

"I'll be doing you a favor. Give me the money.

"Wait until tonight"

"I get off at eleven. It will have to be before that."

"Fine, any time after dark. Make sure her dad is out of the room." He handed her the syringe and envelope of cash then left the way he came in. Stopping at the first restroom he saw, he scrubbed his hands.

"Pendejo!" Juanita whispered to his shadow then slid the cash down the front of her scrubs, inside her underwear. The syringe made her heart beat a little faster. Once emptied, the money would allow her to refill it with a short, sweet vacation before she hit the road.

Julio was a hollow shell. He could produce no more tears, no more anger, no more fear. He was beyond the point of caring what happened to him or his business. Raul was now a liability and Dahl's threats only made him consider the possibility of joining his daughter on the other side. He stood beside her watching her sleep. I should have been there instead of out gallivanting around with a bunch of salesmen. He thought. He could have made everything different. He reached out and caressed her cheek with the back of his wrinkled hand. He thought he saw her eyelashes flutter. "Lydia?" He whispered," Are you awake?"

"Daddy?" She opened her eyes, searching for him in the dark.

"I'm here baby. Talk to me."

"My head... it's pounding. I'm so hungry."

Julio had found a new fountain of tears. He held her by the shoulders, leaning down to kiss her forehead. "Oh, Lydia. I thought for sure I had lost you."

"I love you, Daddy. I'm so sorry. I'll be good from now on. I promise."

"I'm going to tell the nurse you're awake and have her call your doctor. I'll be right back."

"Can you bring me something to eat? I'm starving!"

"Sure, baby. Anything you want. I'll be right back"

"I might nap a little my head is really throbbing, but wake me up, okay?"

Julio felt like skipping down the hall toward the nurses' station. He asked to speak with the doctor or charge nurse.

"I'll send him down after he finishes rounds. He's teaching tonight."

"No problem. She's awake!"

The woman at the desk eyed him suspiciously. "Really? That's great."

Julio saw a thin Latina removing blankets from the warmer in the hall. "Could you please take one of those to my daughter in 517? She would love to curl up in a nice warm blanket."

"Por supuesto. o Problema."

"Gracias"

Julio waited a few seconds for the elevator then decided to

take the stairs down to the snack machines.

A tentative knock on the door of room 517 failed to rouse Lydia. The intensity of the headache pushed her back toward sleep. "Housekeeping." After waiting a few seconds, the woman entered the room and spread the warm blanket over the girl in the bed. Lydia moaned appreciatively but did not open her eyes. The housekeeper took a syringe from her pocket and found a port in the IV line. She slowly emptied the contents of the syringe into the port. "Sweet Dreams" she whispered. Lydia did not reply.

The housekeeper immediately pushed her cart back to the basement and exited the premises well before the end of her shift.
Only a few minutes later, shortly after Julio returned with an armload of sugar-based junk food, an unearthly howl echoed through the halls of Christus Spohn Hospital, one of those eerie guttural wails that creep from the depths of hell.

REDEMPTION ROAD?

The Interceptor ate the highway like a warm breakfast burrito, cruise control on 80, a low satisfying rumble emanating from the power train. The AC maintained a chill 67 degrees. Neither occupant wanted to open the conversation, though both thought the other had lost touch with the ultimate goal. Kevin studied Carrie's granite profile. Her eyes, hidden by the aviators, never left the center line. When they exited Bee County the digital clock on the dash read 9:08.

Taking highway 77 north they could avoid San Antonio but still take advantage of I-10. Carrie finally spoke when they hit the interstate at Schulenburg. "We'll be there well before noon if we don't make any stops."

Kevin looked out the window at the endless expanse of prairie. "And why would we do that?"

"Efficiency." That ended the conversation for the next 40 or so miles.

Betty Lou fidgets, drinks coffee, fidgets some more, paces in her tiny office, picks up the phone, puts it down. Her belief in Kevin teeters on the brink of confusion. He didn't even try to avoid the trip to Harris County. Part of her lives for the passion that brought them together over the weekend. A dark burning suspicion, supported by the obvious, gives her pause. Where is she in his list of priorities? She knocks on Judge Kendrick's office door.

"Come in."

"I skipped breakfast," Betty Lou said, leaning on the doorframe. "I thought I'd run over to the cafe and pick up a few kolaches. Any particular flavor you'd like?"

"Apple or blackberry, nothing with meat." Kendrick intently observed her star employee. "Rough weekend?"

"Just binge-watched a bunch of Netflix. Got my days and nights mixed up."

"Nothing good ever comes of those late-night rendezvous."

"Reckon not. Back shortly." Oh, if she only knew. Betty Lou thought. Then it crossed her mind, she probably somehow did. A shiver danced up her spine.

There was no longer any doubt. There was no longer any choice. Ross locked himself in his office to pick up the phone. He dialed his old friend Jake Tosh with the Texas Rangers. Morning rode his shoulders like a wet saddle blanket. This is not where he wanted to be. Jake picked up on the first ring. "Texas Rangers, Tosh here."

"Well, this is a call I'd hoped to never have to make. I need your help. It's out of my hands."

"Yeah, I saw the news. It looks like you have a problem," Tosh said. "What can I do?"

"It looks like my old friend Julio is up to his ass in the smuggling ring. I'm too close to this to handle it but I do want to be the one to go out and pick him up, if that's okay with you."

"Let one of your deputies handle it. You need to stay as far from it as you can, just for looks if nothing else."

"He just lost his daughter."

"Holy Christ, what happened?"

"ODed. Looks like suicide."

"I'm sorry, Ross. You still need to stay away from it. Nothing good could come from you being personally involved."

"Can you give me a couple of days? I'll have my guys pick him up but let him at least get his daughter in the ground."

"Fine, but if you want me involved, I need him in custody by Friday."

"No problem." Ross hung up and stared at the receiver until his eyes crossed. How had it gone from good versus evil to so damn many shades of gray? He remembered when he was younger when idealism flowed through his veins. Once upon a time he thought he had influence. Now it all seemed like politics, nobody wins, and everybody loses. He still couldn't believe Julio would have intentionally hurt anyone. That was not a call he was prepared to make. He decided to drive out and deal with it personally, totally against advice, but well within his ethical standards. He laid his badge on the desk and hung the keys to his police cruiser on the wall. It had been a while since his old Chevy pickup had been out of the county maintenance garage. He couldn't remember the last time he had interacted with anyone as a civilian. Truth be, he was looking forward to it.

Raul heard it to through the jail grapevine that he'd been bailed out. Then maybe not. Maybe he was in for a while. Maybe he had outstanding warrants. He honestly didn't know, but it couldn't be good. Human smuggling is no light sentence but maybe, just maybe, he could leverage some lenience. He'd spent the last five or six years trying to keep his nose out of other people's business, only doing what was necessary. Apparently, it had not paid off. When the two jailers came back in and unlocked his cell he knew something was happening. When he saw who was there to take him into custody he almost grinned. Kevin shot him a look that grounded him in his place. He decided to wait it out. No reason to play his cards yet.

THE DUES

Most of the year the desert appears crusted with death. What does live, moves slow and angry across the rough terrain. Ross knows this. Except for five years in the Marines he'd rarely ventured beyond the bounds of his county jurisdiction. He's fine living vicariously through Aurora and her international adventures. Truth be told, if it wasn't for her, he would likely be busting knuckles at some car repair shop or working at the prison like most of the local hombres.

He took the long way to SIP, in no hurry to confront his friend. How does one approach such a matter? Julio had supported him during the first three of his early campaigns for sheriff, back before he was such a fixture in Bee County politics that he usually ran unopposed. I bet that doesn't happen again any time soon, he thought. Having the hub of a major cartel smuggling operation located in the county seat is not conducive to an unopposed run for the local face of law enforcement. He passed the Line Shack, wondering how that decrepit bar figured into the story and why Carrie found the bar so intriguing.

Eventually Ross made his way to SIP and slowly maneuvered his pickup up the hill to the entrance of Julio's darkened abode. He sat in the cab, becoming part of the surrounding buildings seemingly frozen in time and space by the deceased desert landscape. The more he tried to gather his thoughts the less sure he was that he could make Julio understand the gravity of their mutual situation. Still, he had to try. He raised the cast iron door knocker and let it fall against the heavy oak door. Time slowed. Eventually Julio opened the door and, seeing Ross, turned and shuffled toward the dark interior, motioning Ross to follow. The brief walk ended in Julio's office.

"I've been expecting you." Julio's voice sounded as dry and brittle as the desert wind on an August afternoon.

"I'm not here as the Sheriff," Ross stated. "We go back a long way."

"I know. Make yourself at home, such as it is." Julio opened a cabinet and removed two glasses and a decanter of bourbon, pouring both glasses two-thirds full.

"I need to share something with you, completely off the record. It's not something you're going to want to hear. Please, though, it's important-- life and death important." Ross waited for Julio to lift his gaze from the floor and acknowledge his messenger. Julio's eyes were red and wet. The lines in the corners were deeper, more defined, than Ross remembered.

Julio took a deep swallow from his glass and melted into the overstuffed leather chair. "I can only imagine how deep the shitstorm is going to be. The thing is, I have no choice, and at this point, I really don't give a fuck. I've got nothing left to lose."

"What about the ones you take down with you?"

"I can try to warn them. That's about it. We all knew what we were getting in to." A look of sudden comprehension overtook Julio's countenance. "So what do you know about the shit hitting the fan?"

"In addition to the arrest and conviction with possible hard time, the government will seize all of your assets. The good news is, you've maintained a high enough degree of separation from the dirty side of the business that it's highly unlikely that you will do any time.

"Until that asshole Ronnie Dahl and his little love buddy, Miguel, started making runs behind my back, there was no dirty side of the business."

"Did they actually think they could get away with that? Everyone has to report mileage per job number."

"They didn't care. Once they completed a couple of runs, I was implicated. My company, right? So here I am, in hot water with the Feds, two good men dead, Lydia, ... My God, -- LYDIA!' ... That poor girl! How can we make her life count? and you here to arrest me on God-knows-how-many legitimate charges."

"I'm not arresting you today. But it will happen and I want you to be ready. You should put your valuables, money, and probably your house, since it sits on the same land as the business, in a trust or turn it all over to someone you can trust. Otherwise you'll end up destitute."

"Again, don't care."

"Here's the thing you might care about. You've already lost two loads unofficially, Maybe three depending on how it's looked at. You may already be in the crosshairs. It's a dangerous game and mostly when you lose it's over, if you know what I mean. You may not have much going, but when the cartel takes you out it's not pretty. If I were you, I'd cut my losses and disappear."

"And how does that happen. Everything is here!"

"I may have someone who can help you with that, but I'll tell you straight up, she's going to want something in return."

"How much?
"not money, -- information.
"This 'she', is it a good guy or bad guy?"
"I guess it depends on your perspective."

THE RULES
(and how to break them)

Raul seemed animated for a brown-skinned man being transported to a southwest Texas county to answer for a probation violation on a 5-year-old misdemeanor. Any criminal with street smarts would know that somebody was pulling strings just to keep him under control. Maybe he got lucky, but that wasn't the way things normally progressed in his world. When they locked him in the back compartment of the new cruiser, still handcuffed, he began to get the picture.

The Interceptor was incredibly quiet considering the number of horses under the hood. Not as quiet as the occupants of the front seat. There had to be a reason Carrie and DJ were the team sent to retrieve him. If something didn't happen soon it would be up to him to break the ice.

After 40 miles or so of silent travel Raul's patience took a nosedive. "Guy's, I really appreciate the ride. I know it's out of your way but I'm starving! If we can stop and eat, I'll buy, anything -- steaks -- I don't care. Nothings too good for my buddies. "Carrie looked to DJ and grinned. "How about it? Is it break time already?"

DJ stared into the fields of green. They were still in blackland prairie where greenery grew without any coercion. "I guess. We're only stopping once. We need to find a decent place."
"How about these handcuffs", Raul said.

"Pretend your auditioning for a porno," Carrie deadpanned. "We're required to keep you restrained. It's a rule." Carrie took the Brookshire exit. There were no restaurants visible, not even a convenience store. After a couple of miles perpendicular to the interstate Carrie turned off on a gravel road.

"I don't think you'll find a restaurant out here," Raul said.

"Probably not, " Carrie replied.

DJ grinned and leaned his seat back. As the road narrowed Raul grew more tense. When the gravel became dirt and the trees leaned over to create a dark canopy above the road, Raul let an almost inaudible whine escape his trembling jaw.

"Not much happening out this way," Carrie said. "Folks could get lost if they aren't careful."

"I reckon," DJ turned to look at Raul. "How about you? You know anything about this area?

Raul hoped it might open dialogue if he was helpful. "The Brazos River is somewhere around here. They grow a lot of melons out this way."

DJ caught Carrie's attention. "I hear that ole Brazos is treacherous—takes a lot of lives! We should go check it out."

This was not the direction Raul was hoping the conversation would take. "So, I guess the Labor Day party for the SIP employees isn't happening, what with Lydia's overdose."

"Yeah, that's not happening, but I hear Commissioner Dahl is throwing a barbeque out at the Special Events Center if you just want to eat and drink out in the hot sun." DJ said. "I'll probably go."

"I'm gonna stay as far away from Dahl as I can. He's the reason I'm here right now."

DJ chuckled. "I guess that's one way of looking at it."

ROAD TRIP II

Carrie pulls the Interceptor to the side of the dirt road and parks beside a crumbling concrete culvert. The grass is beat down around it where it appears a truck or tractor recently used the gap in the fence to access the hillside, sloping into the verdant valley below. She cuts the engine and rolls down all four windows. "I'd stay put if I were you." She adjusts the rearview mirror so her eyes can lock with Raul's.

DJ exits the car and follows the tire tracks to the point where the trail takes a sloping direction downward toward the valley floor. Carrie remains in the car. "Hear that?" She asks Raul.

Raul strains to take in the rural background noise. A disturbing rumble catches his attention, the sound of water, possibly rapids or a waterfall. "The river?" he asks.

"Must have been a good rain recently," Carrie says. She picks up her revolver and holds it high enough to show it off through the plexiglass partition and spins the cylinder. Raul is impressed by the shiny weapon but terrified to see brass in every chamber.

"Let's go check it out." She cracks open the driver's door just as DJ's head disappears below the valley's incline.

"I'd just as soon hang out here." Raul says, "not really a nature lover. You know, snakes and all."

"Not your call" she says, opening the back door and motioning with the Colt for him to climb out. "This can go one of two ways," she says, "depending on how convincing you are. You see, ole DJ thinks you're a liability, considering you know the extent of his involvement in your criminal enterprise. I'm on the fence, but you have done me a couple of favors. It's up to you to win him over. Might be a good idea to reassure me too." She waves the long barrel of the Chrome plated revolver again. "Let's go."

Raul's brain kicks into panic mode but neither flight nor fight seem to be a viable option. He turns toward the valley, head down and sighs.

DUST

Dust, the prevailing byproduct of the desert, covered everything. Ross could no more figure out how it covered the pristine interior of his 65 Chevy pickup than how it absorbed the illusion of liquid receding from the glistening two-lane blacktop as he meandered back toward town. Maybe everything was a mirage. He stroked the truck's dash with an index finger leaving a track of shining metal and dust on his finger. He wiped it on his jeans where the dust disappeared. He knew it was still there but there were many things he did not know, or in some cases, care to. He'd done all he could for Julio. It wasn't going to end well for his old friend, but possibly, just possibly, he might not serve any jail time. He could ask Aurora about the witness protection program but that would entail Julio flipping on his handlers, never a safe bet. Anyway, Ross thought, it's out of my hands. As he passed the Line Shack he saw only the bartender's vehicle in the parking lot and thought it might be a good time to engage in some police work. He parked by the front door. Bells tinkled as he entered. It took a few seconds for his eyes to adjust to the weak illumination of the neon beer signs. His sense of smell wasn't so fortunate as the odor of sour beer and pickled eggs swamped his olfactory receptors. The bartender had the taps disassembled. The parts soaked in a sink of diluted bleach.

"Mornin' sheriff," the bartender said. "What brings you out to the boonies?"

"Just passing by. Thought I'd see how your business was doing."

"You're looking at it."

"Little slow then?"

"Gets better after the sun goes down."

Ross sat on the bar stool and planted his boots on the rail, "I have a question about last Thursday. One of my deputies stopped by. Carrie James?"

"No kidding! What a hottie! Y'all doing some serious personnel upgrades."

Ross chuckled. It wasn't the first time he'd heard a similar reaction. "Can you tell me if she was meeting Raul Garza?" The bartender hesitated, then, "I don't think so. Not intentionally."

"What do you mean?"

"You don't know? Maybe I better not say then."

Ross looked at the faded, expired tax permit centered on the wall behind the bar. His demeanor changed to investigation mode. "Maybe you should!"

"She met with your wife." The bartender said.

"Aurora? Do you know what they discussed?"

"Not specifically but it got a little heated. Firearms were involved. Garza tried to intervene on Carrie's behalf. It didn't go so well for him, and he exited rather abruptly."

"Yeah, I imagine so," Ross said chuckling again under his breath.

"After that they took it to the lady's room. I heard some banging around like a fight and then eventually they emerged, cordial, with no blood showing."

"You didn't intervene?"

"Nope, too many firearms involved."

So, you have no idea what it was about?"

The bartender thought a minute. "It seemed to go south after your wife showed your deputy some photos. I didn't see them. I was right here behind the bar and they were at that first table over in the front corner."

Ross considered the interaction and felt the bartender was telling the truth. "One more thing, was Garza drinking?"

"Not that I remember ... I don't think so. Why?"

"He's on parole."

"Shit! He's not even supposed to be in here!"

"No, but I'm not gonna bust his chops over shooting a little pool."

KOLACHES

Betty Lou returned with a mixed-dozen fruit kolaches; Peach, Blackberry, Cherry, and Apple. It was way more than she and the judge could eat but, after her wild weekend, she was hungry and a bit indecisive. She felt the intimacy between her and Kevin growing, or so she thought. Then, his eagerness to go to Houston with that female deputy on a moment's notice unwrapped that feeling of security. There was something there she couldn't put her finger on. She didn't think it was lust, but it could still be dangerous.

She stepped into Judge Kendrick's open office door. "We've got choices."

Kendrick cleared a space on her desk and pulled a roll of paper towels out of a nearby cabinet. "What flavors did you get?"

Betty Lou rattled off the choices, grabbed an apple and a blackberry and turned to leave.

"Sit," Kendrick motioned to a chair. "We're not that busy today, let's chat."

Betty Lou sat, trying not to let her apprehension show.

Judge Kendrick smiled at the kolaches as if they were a trunk load of pirates' treasure. She took a cherry and a peach-filled and placed them on a paper towel. She picked up and examined the blackberry kolache before returning it to the tray. "I love these." she said, "but the seeds get stuck in my teeth." She picked it back up. "What the hell! You only live once." She took a large bite of the blackberry kolache.

Kendrick finished off the blackberry kolache then ask Betty Lou, "What's the deal with Raúl Garza?"

The twinge of nervous vibration shot through Betty Lou's abdomen. "I don't know. You'll have to ask Kevin. Garza is his client."

Kendrick took another peach kolache. "I'm asking you. I'm not sure I trust Kevin at this point."

"Why not?" Betty Lou asked.

"I think he has an ulterior motive, though I'm uncertain as to what it is. I'm hoping you can shed some light on it as you two seem to be close."

TARGET PRACTICE

Any other time the meandering trails, if it was a trail, through the native live oak and pecan trees would have lacked Raul's notice. He wasn't one to commune with nature. He considered himself more of a people person. However, staring down one's likely demise tends to heighten one's awareness of his surroundings, in this case to the point he realized the two parallel trails indicated an overgrown vehicular passage. So why were they walking? Well, there's another puzzle, one he hoped to work out to his advantage. The deeper into the wood they traversed, the quieter the traffic noise from Hwy. 290 but the rumble of the tumbling water maintained a constant volume indicating a path still running parallel to the unseen river. DJ was hiking ahead and no longer visible but he could hear Carrie's boots trudging just a few yards behind. He figured it best to try the friendly approach. "So, officer Carrie, when do you reckon I might get a chance to show you how my 8 ball chops shine? *The Side Track* almost always has a table open week nights."

Carrie holstered the Peacemaker but did not buckle the safety strap. "I reckon that will depend on how this little encounter goes."

"You mean this isn't just a romantic stroll through the woods?"

"Trust me. You'd rather not have romantic interactions with me. I pretty much hate everyone and I have my Peacemaker. You have what, better than average luck? Seriously, how did you rate a taxpayer funded lift home from Houston?"

"Had to be my looks and my charm."

"Or maybe several folks want to keep tabs on you in case you need to disappear."

"Do I?" Raul asked, "Need to disappear, because I don't mind. I can relocate in a heartbeat."

Carrie stopped, and unholstered the Colt. "I don't think your heart continuing to beat is a part of their plan."

Raul turned to face to face her, his hands still cuffed behind his back. "Is that why we're here?

Carrie motioned with the firearm. "Turn around and keep walking. I promise not to shoot you in the back. In fact, unless you do something stupid, I promise not to shoot you at all."

Raul obeyed. Carrie holstered the pistol. "So who do you think bailed you out and why?"

"It had to be either Julio or Dahl. Probably Dahl and you're probably right about why."

"You work for Dahl. I know that. So does Julio, am I right?"

"Not by choice. He got, what you call it? Entrapped."

"Riiiight, how so?

"Strange as it sounds, he was trying to protect some of his guys who worked there."

"That backfired!"

"Big time. "Now his neck is in the noose."

"So this is all Dahl's operation?"

"Maybe. Probably not. I don't know. Maybe on this side of the border, but Dahl knows I'll keep quiet. His handlers probably got nervous. It's why I got bounced so quick or maybe you and DJ are here to finish the job."

"No, too much of a paper trail. Whoever takes you out you'll never see it coming. If you work with us we may be able to offer you some protection, no promises, but I have a few connections."

"Why would you?"

"Couple of reasons. One, I'd feel more comfortable with you on my side. Two, like you, I have no loyalties. I'm here for the biggest possible payout. I think you have an idea where this money hides."

The trails, road, whatever, suddenly ended and in the circle of trampled vegetation DJ sat on a damaged plastic Coleman ice chest. Nearby were several plastic folding chairs featuring sun bleached canvas. A couple of the chairs seemed possibly serviceable. DJ focused on loading a full clip into his Taurus 9mm semi-automatic. Carrie and Raul silently observed the procedure.

"You've got to see what I found!" DJ said. "This is somebody's party spot. Ours today!"

Carrie looked around but noticed nothing beyond the broken chairs.

"Down by the river." DJ said. Check it out."

Carrie traversed the steep incline toward the water, motioning Raul to walk ahead. "You swim?" Carrie asked, looking at the course sisal rope hanging from a massive Cypress jutting over the river from the bank.

"Like a rock" Raul replied.

229

Carrie had already seen the sparkle in DJ's countenance. "So, we swimming or what?" Carrie continued.

"I didn't bring a bathing suit."

"We're not. Raul might be depending on his cooperation." DJ stepped near the edge of the crumbling riverbank using a long branch obviously left there to pull the rope swing back to the launch area. "This is not waterboarding; that's illegal, but I think we will get similar results. Cover me."

"I'm gonna give him a fighting chance."

DJ released Raul's left handcuff, brought his hands to the front of his body, and locked him back down.

"Come on guys." Raul was whining now. "Give me a break. You guys are armed and I can't even swim. Don't you think this is a bit one sided?"

DJ chuckled. "I didn't see the contract."

"What? There's a contract?" Raul is in panic mode now.

DJ just shook his head. "Not that I know of but apparently you think there's one somewhere assuring you that life is fair. Anyway, I've been contemplating while you two lovebirds ambled up the trail. Here's how we play the game." DJ pulls the rope swing over to Raul. "Grab it!" he says. Raul does. "Choke up on it enough that your butt don't drag the ground when you swing back but high enough you can get your footing without falling off the edge of the bank. If you miss that point you take your chances with the river. Got it so far?"

"Yeah," Raul says, "I'm mostly dead."

"Oh, don't be such a party pooper." DJ says. "You can do this. It's geometry. Here's where it gets good. There're only a few questions. Every time we ask one you swing out and back and catch yourself. If we like the answer we move on."

"If you don't?"

"That's where the fun comes in. See that big old knot holding the rope to the limb?"

'Yeah?"

"If you try to blow smoke up our asses we'll put a bullet in that knot. I've seen Carrie at the range. You don't have a chance for many wrong answers. There's no way to know how many bullets that knot can handle. I'd play it safe if I were you."

Raul grabbed the rope and tried to figure the best position. "I can't do this!"

"First question: Who does Julio answer to?"

Raul flinched "I don't know."

DJ turned to Carrie. "You buyin' this?"

"Nope!" she aimed the Peacemaker at the sisal knot there above their heads.

"Wait," Raul screamed. "He gets his assignments from Ronnie Dahl."

"Too late," Carrie said and pulled the trigger. The valley reverberated with the explosion and a chunk of the knot flew into the river. Raul is trembling. "Please, I'll tell you what I know. I can't do the swing!"

"Sure you can." DJ said as he put his boot against Raul's ass and launched the cowboy out over the river. The knot held. When Raul swung back over the bank he dropped to his knees and placed his forehead against the cool earth.

"Isn't this fun?" Carrie said. "Let's do another one. Your turn to shoot. Grab the rope Raul. This question is extra important to me because I considered Carlos a friend: Did Carlos know, when they went on that final trip, that they were transporting women?"

Raul shook his head. "I don't know. I imagine so. I know Miguel was aware."

"But you're not sure?"

"No, that's the truth."

"Next question: Is Dahl in bed with the cartel?"

Raul looked to DJ hoping for help. DJ released the safety on the nine mil.

"No." Raul said.

"Liar!" Carrie fired another round into the knot then kicked Raul out over the river. While the swing was fully extended out over the river, she put another round in the knot and the tangled sisal released about 10 inches of length. Raul came in dragging his knees on the edge of the riverbank and crying like a baby. When he tried to stand the red clay broke loose and splashed into the river below. Raul was left dangling thirty feet above the churning muddy river below. Every attempt he made to regain his footing only broke more riverbank free and put Raul farther from salvation.

"You're doing this all wrong," DJ instructed. "Think back to when you were a kid and you tried to make the swing go higher by kicking your feet and twisting? If you're lucky that might work here. Better hurry though. I have three shots due me just to catch up."

Raul hung too far down to grab the rope by his feet and the

handcuffs kept his hands too close together to gain any lift by climbing the knots. He started swinging and twisting desperately.

DJ aimed his pistol at the knot and fired. He missed. "Dammit! I need to spend more time at the range."

Raul twisted wildly and screamed, "¡Por favor! Estoy de tu lado. No me dejes morir."

DJ took aim at the knot then lowered the aim to center on Raul's chest.

"Wait!" Carrie said. "Think big picture here. Maybe he can help us . Besides, what deep shit will we be in if we lose him or bring him back dead? Besides, your target skillis are down-right embarrasing!"

"Okay, whatever. You're right, Ms. Buzzkill!" DJ said. "You gonna help us hang your boss? Probably some money in it and we might be able to keep you safe."

"Sure, I'll help you. I would have anyway. You didn't have to do this. Just get me down!" Raul continued to build momentum and was almost high enough to dive for the solid bank.

DJ grabbed the pole he used to pull the swing in and reached toward Raul. Raul reached for the pole just as the rope gave way. He caught the end of the pole and slammed against the almost vertical side of the bank pulling DJ over the edge. Both men tumbled toward the turbulent river. Just before being swept away by the current Raul grabbed hold of an exposed Cypress knee. The root held Raul but DJ was now in the rushing water held only by Raul's grip on the pole.

"Interesting turn of events," Raul said. "But since you were saving me, I reckon I could return the favor." He began pulling DJ toward the massive root, ever so slowly since he was still handcuffed.

Carrie looked over the edge of the bank at the two men hugging each other over a Cypress knee. It was all she could do to stifle a laugh. "Since this rope swing is too short to reach you and I'm the only one who came prepared, I'll get a rope from my trunk and save y'all's lame, hairy asses."

CEO

Ronnie Dahl doesn't usually worry. He runs a county the size of a Mexican state. He's lived here for every day of his 56 years and knows everything that happens, who it happened to, and why. His family spent years before his birth building a legacy. His connections are solid from Austin to San Diego, to Mexico City, to Washington DC. He hasn't been sleeping. He turned his phones off so he could get some rest. So far it hasn't worked. The motion sensors at the entrance to his ranch keeps alerting him to visitors but the security cameras seem to malfunction every time. He took a Xanax to keep from pacing. It's not helping. He tells himself there's really nothing to worry about. The visitor alert at the front gate beeps repeatedly. This time there is a voice, "Answer your fucking phone." He powers up his cell and it immediately rings. He lets it ring a couple of times before answering. He refuses to be intimidated but the caller ID says "Nightmare". Funny, he thinks. A joke, he hopes. He answers. "Hello?"

"Step outside."

"Who is this? Who do you think you are telling me what to do? Kiss my ass!"

The voice is silent for a bit then repeats, "Step outside." It's almost dusk. Dahl figures it won't be difficult to ID the wannabe intruder. He has dozens of cameras from the highway up the quarter-mile driveway to his door. He looks out the bay window in his formal dining room and doesn't see anyone. This must be someone pulling a prank. He steps out the huge oak door onto his porch and he immediately sees a red laser dot glowing just above his heart. He jumps back into the house. The man on the phone laughs. "We need to talk. Open the gate and no one gets hurt, at least for now."

Ronnie checks the camera at the gate and sees a black BMW 750i with heavily tinted windows. He knows who it is and why he's here. He opens the gate.

"What the hell, Aaron. The performance art was completely unnecessary,"

"Just reminding you who holds the cards."

"Come on up and have a drink. I'm sure we can work out a plan that satisfies everyone.

The gate opens. It's going to be another sleepless night.

POSSIBILITIES

Judge Kendrick has no trouble sleeping nights. She keeps her officers informed as needed and holds her cards close to her chest. She rarely considers intuition when approaching a problem but sometimes, like now, a problem exceeds the boundaries of logic. She's not 100% sure of Betty Lou's loyalty but she feels more confident in her than in Kevin Cash. Judge Kendrick decides to give Betty Lou the intake interview when they pull Raul Garza's probation and put him back in stir. She's fairly certain someone will come out of the woodwork trying to free him.

Bee County judge, being an elected position, there's little likelihood someone of consequence would run against her. Of course, the occasional underfunded Democrat will mount a single-issue campaign but it hasn't been a problem in the past and it's unlikely to be one now. There aren't any moldering skeletons occupying her closets. It may prove to be an exciting election year.

DOWN BY THE RIVER

Carrie drove the cruiser down to the party spot by the rope swing. She retrieved 100 feet of pristine climbing rope from the trunk and anchored it to the cow pusher above the front bumper. She looked over the edge of the embankment and broke into a grin.

"Either one of you Cowboys ever do any rappelling?"

"Not since Boy Scouts," DJ said, "and that was always going down."

"I climbed ropes in PE at school. I could climb a rope if it wasn't for wearing these bracelets."

"What's the world coming to," Carrie said as she tied the cuff key to the end of the rope. "I'm going to toss this rope to you. Bracelet keys are tied to the rope. DJ, you unlock one side of the cuffs and put the key in your pocket. You climb up first."

"What if I slip,"

"Then I guess you're fucked!"

"Raul, you hang on to that root. We'll get you next. Y'all need to pick up the pace I have a dinner date."

"And that's my problem how" DJ asked.

"I could just leave you both here to figure it out on your own."

"You wouldn't do that," Raul said.

"You obviously don't know me at all."

Once both men were on solid ground they looked like they'd lost a mud wrestling contest. Carrie pointed over the edge to the root that saved them. "Check that out!"

In a little eddy just upstream from the root languished a 9-foot alligator.

"That old Brazos, she holds a few surprises," DJ said. "Let's get out of here!"

"First I need an assurance y'all will be available first thing tomorrow to detail my cruiser." Carrie said.

Raul gave two thumbs up.

DJ just shook his head.

"Both of you in the back," Carrie said.

A SPECIAL GIFT
(just 4 U)

Ronnie waited on the invisible side of the door. The light illuminated the front porch but the inside entry hall stayed dark, allowing the outside to remain clearly visible through the peephole. Aaron was not alone. The gorgeous man with Aaron most likely spent his professional hours at the gym or modeling for GQ magazine. Aaron knocked lightly then let himself in. "I brought a friend. I hope you don't mind." Aaron, knowing the type of head turner Ronnie did back flips for, considered this announcement a mere formality. This was the first time Ronnie felt his blood flow since Miguel took the wrong turn in the desert.

"This is Axel," Aaron said.

"Pleased to meet you," Ronnie said. Axel smiled but otherwise didn't respond.

"He doesn't speak much. Skateboard accident when he was younger."

Axel opened his mouth to show his tongue, split down the middle, each half wiggling independently. Ronnie doubted the skateboard story but that didn't prevent his breath from catching deep in his chest.

"Please come in. Can I get you something to drink? I just scored some Glenlivet 21 ."

"Sounds good," Aaron said, glancing around. "Looks like life is treating you well."

"Family money. Somebody needs to keep the cogs greased." Ronnie noted neither of his guests so much as smiled at his attempted humor. "Well then, let me get those drinks."

Once in the kitchen Ronnie finally let his tension release a notch. Then a hand on his shoulder, "I can tawk," Axel said. Although his pronunciation was affected by the forked tongue, the voice was deep and lyrical. In any other situation it would have seemed soothing. Ronnie was startled.

Axel smiled. "I have hobed to meet you since Aawon toad me we might stob by."

Ronnie relaxed. I'm glad you were able to join us. I wish it could be under better circumstances. I think Aaron may be pissed off. We've branched into some new territory in our business and it hasn't worked out according to plan."

"Yes, he's toad me something aboud it. I thought I should warn you. He will ask you to keep me heaw on some buwshid excuse, to keeb an eye on you. I want you to know, I be no danger to you. I just "hang out. Axel took the hand from Ronni's shoulder and stroked the soft pink cheek. "… with benefits if you pwefer. I should go keep Aaron occupied. Just wanted to led you know.

Ronnie served the bottle on a tray with small glasses and sat next to Axel in the corner of the overstuffed white leather sectional. By the third short round of the Glenlivet single-malt Scotch, Axel and Ronnie sat so close on the couch the heat rolled from them in searing waves. The unbridled display of affection made Aaron jittery. "I can't fathom how two guys can be so… friendly." Aaron said. "It creeps me out."

"So don't do it." Ronnie said.

"I'd rather fuck a high school cheerleader" Aaron said.

Ronnie winced. "Now that's sick!"

"I wath a high schoo cheerleader," Axel smiled.

"Oh my God! I did not need to know that." Aaron reached for the Scotch and started to take a swig right from the bottle.

"Don't you dare!" Ronnie screamed.

Aaron fixed Ronnie in a stare that could have frozen the Rio Grande. Then slowly turned the bottle up, filled his mouth, and gargled backwash into the half full bottle of Glen Levitt. After wiping his mouth on his sleeve, he slammed the bottle down on the end table. His eyes still penetrating Ronnie, he said, "I think you have a severe misunderstanding of the hierarchy here… and very likely the depth of the shitstorm about to befall you."

Ronnie broke into such a sweat his cologne overpowered his olfactory sensors. "Can we take it down a notch? I realize mistakes have been made. I'm happy to cover the losses."

"You fucking jelly bean! It has nothing to do with the money, although, yes, you will take care of that immediately. It's the credibility. The Sinoans are crawling up our asses. If we aren't 100% they win – they win, we lose. We lose, you die, along with most of your useless fucking crew! Axel is my CFO. He's a problem solver and he's now your houseguest. You don't get any more chances."

Aaron picked up the bottle and headed for the door where he reached outside, grabbed a travel bag and threw it at Axel. "Don't fuck this up." The oak door slammed behind him.

"He gets a liddle emotional." Axel said. "Best to let him be and do his biddnas within boundaries.

"It's probably best if I take some initiative and fix some to these mistakes.

DINNER CONVERSATION

How can they, Carrie thought, just fall asleep like that with the end of the world is barking up their tree? Both men were passed out in the back seat before they were 10 minutes down the highway. The two mud-caked odorous piles of masculinity whose chainsaw snores assaulted at least two of her five senses. It would have been three had she not directed the rear-view mirror toward the roof. She turned on the AM radio to a call-in talk show to drown out their somnambulistic growls and fuel the residual rage keeping her alert and alive. The dinner date was not quite an exaggeration, but she kept it under wraps since, to her knowledge, none of the other deputies were invited to join the boss and his wife for dinner. It had been Aurora's idea. Carrie didn't seem shocked or confused. She observed the lack of communication within marriages to be the norm. It only meant she needed to be alert to keep the secrets in alignment.

It approached dusk by the time she booked Raul into county jail and dropped Kevin at his office to pick up his truck. She promised him that she would arrest him for defacing public property if he didn't come by before work in the morning to help detail the cruiser.

A THREE-WAY

"So, do we tell her tonight?" Aurora asked.
"Do we have to tell her at all? And is now even the best time to discuss this? Our liquid love is trickling down my butt crack." Ross made one more thrust of his softening member to try and seal the leak.

When he and Aurora were first getting to know each other, he found it fascinating she could only come when she was on top. As the relationship developed, nipple twisting and chest hair grabbing became part of the foreplay. He realizes now it's a control issue. He also realizes her question do we tell her tonight? Is already answered.

"She'll be here in less than an hour," Aurora said. "We should have our ducks in a row."

"Don't you think it's a little weird that we're discussing this while we're still naked?"

"Oh please! Don't tell me you don't fantazise about her when we're making love. She's hotter than a $20 pistol. Hell, I even fantasized about her and I'm 100% hetero."

"Really?"

"What? Which part don't you believe?" she rolled off him. As her feet hit the floor she said, "First in the shower!"

"Let's double up, times-a- wastin'."

"Since when did that speed things up?" she reached over and swatted his butt. "I drained you pretty well. We can give it a try, more time to discuss the issue at hand."

"What issue is that? The third possible fantasy you just laid on me? Pun intended."

"No! The new cartel info. Forget that other, ain't gonna happen!"

Aurora was blow-drying her hair so she didn't hear her phone. Ross answered when the caller ID flashed "Carrie James"

"I'm going to be a few minutes late. I had to book Garza and transfer his personal effects. He's a bit strange about those Spanish spurs."

"No problem," Ross said.

A brief silence, then "Oh, hi boss."

"That's alright," Ross said. Aurora is still in the shower."

"OK, see you shortly." Carrie still sounded a bit confused but no more confused than Ross was trying to discern why Carrie's ID was on Aurora's phone. It promised to be an intriguing evening.

"Damn girl, you shine up pretty," Ross said when Aurora

emerged.

"Regular rednecks dream," Aurora flirted.

"Anyway," Ross said. Reasons we should not tell her: We don't know what her reaction would be! She already promised to leave this alone but she obviously hasn't."

"And should she, considering? I have a pretty good idea how she'll react. But if she's in danger she deserves to know from where, don't you think?"

"And if she goes charging into the revenge goal?"

"We counsel her, work with her."

"She's just a kid, babe."

"You hired her. You said yourself she's one of your best patrol officers."

"But this is way above her pay grade."

Aurora began pacing. Ross saw the light at the end of the tunnel. He could hear the train. Aurora spun to face Ross, feet firmly rooted to the floor. "She deserves to know." end of discussion. Aurora tip toes to kiss Ross on the chin. "Want a beer?"

"I got em. Meet you on the patio."

Betty Lou rolled a significant blunt from a sticky sinsemilla bud she'd been saving for the weekend. It isn't the weekend and the way things were going she may be unemployed by the weekend. Judge Kendrick was questioning her interactions with her coworkers and her decisions. Now she's being tasked with the intake of that local boy, Raul Garza, who probably shouldn't even be going through this. She looked at her patio doors and noticed everyone had vacated the pool area. She decided to burn the blunt by the shimmering water of the pool. Stretching out on the plastic pool side recliner, she took a massive hit and held it as DJ's pickup parked in the visitors lot and a swamp monster crawled out.

"What the hell happened to you?"

"It's a long story," DJ admitted. "but I've got time if you do."

"Maybe take a shower first while I smoke this blunt. Then I'll listen to the details. Things are getting a little weird in the office too. I think there's some kind of outside action going down. Maybe cartel, and Kendrick thinks you're mixed up in it. Please tell me you're not!"

"I'm not!"

"That sounded too easy."

"You ask nicely."

"Truth?"

"You weren't specific there and I almost died today. I think I'm in too deep to back out now. I'm working both ends of the deal hoping to cash out. I don't want to put you in any danger. I need to tell you something but I also need you to trust me. I'm not going to be around much longer and when I go it will be like a disappearance, and I won't be able to contact you."

DJ stared into the crystalline water and considered diving in headfirst. "The deal is, I've got feelings for you. This close connection we have is going to be hard to break. I don't want to, but I can't risk you getting hurt."

"What the hell DJ? You're blowing me off?" Tears formed in Betty Lou's eyes.

"Not at all!" DJ reached to hold her.

"Eew! Don't touch me! Go home and get a shower and some clean clothes. Meet me for breakfast. We'll talk. If there are answers we'll find them. She went inside, refusing to look back. Her heart caught in her throat.

Once our illustrious prisoner transport team managed to convince Raul that they could change the shape of his fate any time, at their whim, he became much more cooperative. In fact, he was thrilled to be safely ensconced in the county lock up once he found out his Spanish spurs were included in his personal effects, and he would probably be released the next day. That only left a few details to be wrapped up. One was the filthy cruiser that DJ had no interest in helping clean up. Carrie would have to spring for a detail out of her own pocket because there's no way she would allow anyone to see her cruiser in its current shape. She left it at her house and took her little beat-up Honda to her dinner date. Dinner dates being what they are.

"I didn't think you dated?" DJ said.

Carrie gave him a sideways glance and rolled her eyes ever so slightly. "Not all dates have to do with intimacy. Sometimes you need to make your own plan.

"I thought we were partners, and we weren't going to keep any secrets." DJ appeared hurt.

"It's business but it's also personal. I'm trying to keep people that I care about out of trouble. I don't care how much trouble people that I don't care about get themselves into. That's why Raul's in the county jail and you're not." And with that she said goodbye for the evening.

As she pulled up to the little blue house on the corner of Eagle Street and 3rd, the first thing she noticed was the large number of succulents on the front porch, not a place you'd want to fall over if you cared about physical pain within the confines of your body. It was like a cactus museum. Otherwise, the house and yard were beautiful, well-kept and unexpectedly cozy. Carrie had envisioned a larger house with wrought-iron security panels over the windows and a rock wall around the perimeter for security's sake. After all, this was the county sheriff's house not to mention his wife who worked for the ATF branch of the federal government and probably had numerous well-armed enemies. She ambled up to the door. The porch light was a soft low-watt gold with small moths fluttering around it. Before she was able to ring the doorbell the front door opened and Aurora stood there dressed casually in an embroidered gauze top and tight high-waisted jeans. Her feet were ensconced in Huarache sandals. Before she could speak, Ross came up behind her, put his hand on her shoulder and welcomed Carrie in. "Welcome to our little love nest," Ross said.

Aurora rolled her eyes but smiled warmly at her husband. When we actually get a chance to enjoy it. We're almost never here at the same time anymore," Aurora said. "I keep hoping and praying and cajoling that he will retire from this silly job one day and just let the Border Patrol and the city take it over. There's not that much to do as the County Sheriff, it's more a position where you get your picture on the lamppost every four years and free coffee and donuts whenever you want."

"There's nothing wrong with free coffee and donuts," Ross said. "It keeps me happy and vibrant and permanently in a deep state of affection for my beautiful little wife. She could quit too if she wanted but she loves her job even more than I love mine. There's something personally satisfying about trying to make the world a better place. Sometimes it can get confusing however, and that's why we're here tonight. With formalities over though let's have some brisket, a couple of beers, and maybe a glass or two of wine. We'll figure this mess out."

Dinner was delicious but uneventful. It seemed no one wanted to dig right into the problem at hand. All three had a different perspective on what the problem was and myriad ideas on how to solve it, none of which would work without the others' cooperation. Ross has his childhood friend to think about who seems to be in a whirlwind of trouble not of his own doing. Carrie is still seeking vengeance for Carlos's untimely death and, since she'd seen the layout of the land here, maybe a little more revenge just because her own hometown is being overrun with criminals. And then there's Aurora, well Aurora just wants to kill the bad guys. There are dangerous people about, very dangerous people and they are threatening her way of life. She is not one for playing by the rules. She wants the quickest and most effective way of solving the problem with as little paperwork as possible.

Ross pushed himself away from the table and started clearing the dishes. Aurora pulled the briefcase out of the from under the table and removed a couple of folders Marked ATF top secret. Carrie didn't know what they contained but she knew that she would have some responsibility for solving the problem or she wouldn't be here. Aurora removed two thin folders and then put the briefcase back under the table.

Ross peeked over Carrie's shoulder where the photographs were displayed. One of the folders looked like a fashion catalog. Carrie called out to Aurora and said, "Who the hell is that? I didn't think we had good looking criminals in Texas.

Ross said "Yeah, we have good looking criminals and good-looking law enforcement officers. Texas is overrun with beautiful crime.

Aurora wanted to get serious but couldn't help releasing a brief snicker. "Will y'all quit horsing around. These are extremely dangerous people we're talking about here. Let's not take it too lightly." She pulled out a thin gray folder with a black and white 8 by 10 in it and explained what she had. "This guy's named Axel. He has several last names but the one he's using right now I believe is Sturtevant he's also gone by Jonathan Sturtevant, and he's gone by Axel Prince and Prince Axel."

"He's obviously got very good self-esteem. Take a long look at the photograph. My goodness. OK." Ross pulled the photo out of the folder took a close look at it. It was a black and white photo so he couldn't get a definitive eye color or any obvious hair color although he appeared to be dark haired with light eyes. "So, this guy's dangerous?" Ross asked. "How so?"

Aurora took over. "This guy actually has seventeen kills we know of. He's not just a hit man. He's known as a fixer. Something goes wrong in the hierarchy of the cartel, or somebody decides they'll take it over ---exercise some of their power, or if they think they've developed an internal power structure, this is the guy they call to straighten it out. He talks strange. He had an accident when was younger that split his tongue in half. He elected to not get it fixed. Who knows why. He thinks it's cute, maybe? Although he's good-looking and soft-spoken he is not to be toyed with. He is serious. He will kill you. We're not sure why he's here. Our local alleged cartel member and illustrious county commissioner, Ronald Dahl has now lost two of the cartel's loads of undocumented immigrants. We think this Axel is here to monitor and improve the situation. The oddity of this is who he works for." Aurora tuned to Carrie and sat down to share the folder. "We debated for a long time whether to share this information with you, so I need you to sit down. I need you to promise that you will not react until we've had a chance to calmly analyze the circumstances. Axel is currently employed by Aaron James, your father. We suspect Aaron James is the main domestic contact for the Zeta cartel. Aaron James has been sighted in this county in the last couple of days as has Axel, Prince Axel, or whatever he's calling himself these days. We're likely to have some bloodshed and we suspect the blood that's shed may be Ronnie Dahl's. In addition to losing two loads we suspect he is acting as an agent for the Sinaloa cartel while handling these Zeta migrant transports. That makes Dahl either very stupid, very greedy, or suicidal. I'm going with stupid with a side-order of arrogance. If that's the case it's going to put Bee County, Texas in the international headlines. We do not want this to happen."

YOU'RE NOT THE BOSS OF ME!

It had been a long, frustrating day. It was rare that Judge Kendrick regretted not driving her car to work. She loved the morning walk, listening to the birds, waving at the town folk she'd known all her life. Then there were days like this evening. She'd put in a 12-hour day. It was almost dusk, and she was dog tired. Not only had she been shorthanded in the office but she had to wait until Kevin returned from his assignment to debrief him and try to figure out what's going on with this Raul character. The streets were no longer peaceful; radio shows blasting the norteña music, the young guys in their loud cars racing up and down the street, people in their houses laughing, arguing, screaming. People she would see in her courtroom later this week. Just another day.

She put on her walking shoes. Tossed her judges robe over the back of her chair and set out for home. The streets of Beeville in summer burned too hot for most people to be outside——Janet Kendrick was not "most people".

From behind her she recognized one of those damned mini hot rods with it's a coffee-can mufflers sounding like loud metallic farts. It was coming from behind. When it got near her it slowed to keep pace. She couldn't see inside. The windows were all tinted illegally dark. Once it duplicated her speed the driver kicked it into neutral and revved the engine a couple of times. She glared at it. Another longer, higher rev. She checked the plates—Mexican plates. They pulled up beside her. The passenger window rolled down and one of those little skinhead punks greeted her with a sneer. He put his hand out of the window with his fingers in the shape of a pistol, aimed it at her head, and winked. She responded with a single-finger salute, but a cold shiver crawled up her spine as the window closed. The car took off leaving her in a whirlwind of noise and dust from its black-listed exhaust. She picked up the pace and once home she locked the door.

What a day, she thought as she ran a bath. Normally it would have been a shower but today she deserved this. As the tub was filling her phone rang. She ignored it, didn't even check the caller ID. A minute later her cell phone rang. Shit, seriously? This is getting ridiculous. This time she checked the caller ID. Blocked! She answered, "What!" As soon as she heard the voice on the other end, she regretted answering. "What the hell, Ronnie. I'm closed. I'm out for the day. I'm done. Whatever you have on your mind can wait till tomorrow."

"Just a minute Jjudge. This will only take a second. I have a friendly request."

"Like I said, it can wait till tomorrow. Nothing's going to happen tonight that I have any control over."

With his most friendly telephone voice Ronnie Dahl said, "I just want to make sure Raul Garza is released on personal recognizance as early as possible in the morning. I'd really appreciate your cooperation on this. It's important to me."

"Ronnie, I hate to tell you but you're not the Bee County legal system. You're a county commissioner. That's it. You fill the pot-holes and scrape off the roadkill." Judge Kendrick was getting a little hot under the collar. The bath was almost full and she needed this to end. "I don't know who is responsible for having Garza picked up in Houston and driven back here on this bogus misdemeanor parole violation at the county's expense. In my opinion, that should come out of your pocket."

"I have no problem with that if the money is the only issue." Kendrick was livid. "That's not the only issue. Jurisdiction is the issue. And you are out of bounds."

Ronnie Dahl gritted his teeth and poured more sweetness into his telephone voice, "We can't have criminals running loose. Garza isn't the only criminal that needs to be in custody. We have a much bigger issue here. I need your help with it. You know I've supported you in your campaign year after year even though you're a Democrat. I would like to be able to keep doing that."

"Ronnie, this conversation should not be happening. At this point let's say it didn't happen. If it does happen again, it will be made public and I will not be the one fighting for their position in the government of Bee County. Now, I'm going to hang up and take a bath and forget this intrusion into my personal space ever happened. Goodnight!" The judge was about to slam the phone down when she remembered it was her cell phone. "and lose this number!"

After a brief pause Ronnie said, "Be careful Judge Kendrick. It's getting more dangerous out there by the day!"

"Son-of-a-bitch!" Carrie whispered as her knuckles turned onion white from squeezing the edge of the table as she sprung up from her chair. "I knew he was a scumbag but I never suspected anything like this!" She paced fervently as the satisfaction from her recent desert conquest drained away.

Aurora blocked her path. "Sit! You promised to hold it together, remember." She wrestled Carrie back into the chair. A feral countenance overtook Carrie. Her hands and arms tremored as her fists pumped the table. "We hoped the family ties might offer some access. Is that even a possibility?"

"Doubtful," Carrie said. We are the definition of 'estranged'. We haven't said 10 words to each other since I was in high school. He banished me when I caught the philandering bastard in the act. If he keeled over dead tomorrow I'd celebrate."

CAN I HRLP YOU?
DJ & JULIO

Darkness rolled in with an unanticipated drizzle. Low clouds lent an aura of claustrophobia to the sticky summer night. The tires of DJ's truck hissed on the pavement like ominous snakes with an attitude problem. Betty Lou's reaction to his honesty left him without a solid footing. Truth though, he did still need a shower. "That old Brazos" had left a confused stench with no obvious workaround.

When he pulled into SIP it looked abandoned except for one flood light near the shop, where the bobtail produce truck would be when or if Harris County released it. He pulled up to his Airstream and walked to the porch where he saw a note taped to the door.

Great! More bad news he figured. Shower first, then a reality check. He stripped down on the porch and laid his stinky clothes across the porch rail. When he entered his space he inhaled the scent of Lydia's body wash. Had it only been three days since they spent that strange afternoon together? This was a utility shower, however. He had to make it quick. Still, he did briefly uncap her lavender body wash to enhance the moment. The memory flooded back bringing tears with it.

Once toweled off he pulled on some shorts and a tee-shirt, then opened the note.

Kevin,
please stop by the house.
no matter when you get back.
Important.
Thanks,
Julio

It was the least he could do with what the old man had been through even if it meant he was out of a job. By the time DJ walked to the main house the drizzle turned to a mist and the porch light was on. He knocked once and Julio opened the door. He appeared diminished, as if all his essence had drained away.

"Thanks for coming," Julio said.

"Sure, what's up?"

"Sheriff Carranza stopped by earlier today. We've known each other since grade school."

"That's good, isn't it?"

"Maybe but he said I'll probably go to jail - at least for a while."

"Why? You haven't done anything wrong!"

"I have. But I don't really care at this point. Everything that matters to me is gone anyway. I don't have many people I can trust. I hope you're one of them.

DJ looked around the kitchen. Lydia's influence permeated the space and the senses everywhere he turned.

"I miss her. She had such a powerful presence. Still does!" DJ was unsettled by how much influence she still held over him.

"I don't know how to go on without her."

"If there's anything I can help you with let me know."

"I hoped you would say that."

CONFRONTATION

"**This is bullshit!** How long have you known about this and why have these guys not been picked up yet?" The veins in Carrie's temples visibly pulsed as she stood and paced back and forth the length of the dining room and kitchen.

"Sit!" Aurora demanded.

Carrie grabbed the back of a chair, pulled it out, and slammed it on the floor. "There better be an immediate solution or I'll make my own!"

Aurora took Carrie by the shoulders and forced her into the chair. "You need to calm the fuck down! Now! Or this is going to take a direction you don't want to go!"

Ross put his hand on Aurora's shoulder. "Let's all relax. We're on the same side. We've got this! I've called in the Texas Rangers. Aurora notified the ATF." Ross sat in the kitchen across the table from Carrie. Now Aurora is the one who paced.

"Carrie, we need your help." Aurora admitted. "You have access no one else has. But you must be careful and keep your head on straight. These are evil, evil people with zero regard for human life."

Carrie assumed this access was Aurora's mistaken understanding of the James family's dynamics. Something she needed to clear up. "I haven't talked to my father in person since I graduated high school. I don't know how I can help on that."

"That's not the access I meant," Aurora said. "I was speaking more about your powers of seduction and the element of surprise you have displayed in previous encounters."

Carrie glanced from Aurora to Ross and back again, terror on her expression.

"He doesn't know," Aurora said.

"I don't think I want to," Ross admitted. "I trust Aurora and I know she's the best at what she does. There are "fixers" on both sides of the criminal enterprise. Rumor has it Aurora is the best on our side. Let's leave it at that."

"There is one thing you need to do, Darling," Aurora said. "It's important that you introduce her to Ronnie Dahl as soon as possible. Maybe at his Labor Day barbeque this weekend?"

"I can do that but be aware, He's very crooked and

dangerous," Ross said.

Aurora smiled. "Don't worry. She can handle him. She'll consider it a treat!"

"Wait a minute," Carrie broke in, "It's my understanding Dahl is gay. My magic powers may not work on him."

"I think you'll find him to be pansexual," Aurora said. He'll fuck anything he can exert control over. Just let him feel like he controls you until that magic moment he finds out otherwise."

Julio retrieved a bucket of ice from the refrigerator along with the bottle of Maker's Mark bourbon and a couple of small tumblers. "Let's retire to the office. I need to show you a couple of things."

DJ followed. He should have been elated. His plan to empty the coffers of the guilty were coming to fruition. Instead, all he felt was sorrow for this man who befriended him.

Like now, Julio had shared his good fortune with those around him. "Have a seat," Julio offered. "Since my time running the company may be limited, I want to show you some things I've put in place to keep this safe from the vultures who are responsible for its demise."

DJ wasn't sure his dreams should come true in this manner. "Are you sure you want to take this approach?"

"I do. Regardless of her eccentricities, Lydia was a good judge of character. She liked you and felt safe with you." Julio poured two bourbons on the rocks, handed DJ one, and began his story.

"I got wind of trouble in the ranks, from Raul, last Spring. We'd expanded our sales force, picked up additional commercial accounts, including the state jail and the Alice ISD. Instead of hiring more delivery drivers I let the guys pick up some overtime. I didn't think much of it when they wanted to borrow a truck here and there to move into better housing. Most of them were ex-cons who roomed together in those RVs parked over by the shop. It should have dawned on me when it was always Miguel borrowing the equipment. Even when Raul mentioned that anomaly I didn't immediately react. I finally confronted Miguel and within 24 hours Ronnie Dahl was on my doorstep. By then my company was already involved. I guess I could have gone to the authorities, but some fairly hefty truck rental checks were coming my way. What I did do was to squirrel away every penny that didn't cross the books. So, you see, I'm not golden either."

DJ picked up his drink and stirred the ice with his finger. "So, what happened?"

"First, the tragedy with that kid and Miguel dying in the desert. I tried to back out then, but Dahl already had multiple loads lined up with the Zetas. They don't take no for an answer. By then they had Raul in their pockets too, although he let me in on what was going on."

"Damn, Julio! This is some serious shit!"

"Yup, two choices. I can go to jail for a long time, or I can turn states evidence and, if I'm lucky, they will eventually find my remains in a barrel of sulfuric acid somewhere in the desert."

"Why are you telling me this?"

There may be a third option. I have a pretty hefty chunk of change stashed. Your connections put you in a good place to help me disappear. "I set you up for life. You give me a chance at a real life."

"I don't want to sound ungrateful or greedy but what are we talking about here."

"Behind you in that closet there's a gun safe with a hair over $880,000 cash in it. I've put the business in a trust worth $2.6 million. I did that before Lydia died. She insisted your name was on it with hers. Maybe trying to buy your affection. Maybe because she knew you had trucking company experience. Who knows? I was desperate So I went along. All I ask is I get some ice cream with my baloney sandwich on my birthday and a pile of Louis Lamour novels. Of course, witness protection would be preferable."

"This is very generous. How would we go about this?" DJ thought how this may possibly change Betty Lou's opinion. Not having to work for the rest of his life was another major plus. Julio smiled for the first time that evening. "It's all set up. We just meet with the attorney tomorrow at 10:00 AM.

"You seem pretty sure I would go for this arrangement!"

"I was young once."

"This sounds amazing. I'm going to sleep on it, but I don't see any problem." He bid Julio a good evening, turned off the ringer on his phone, and texted Carrie -*Meet at the ranch tomorrow after work. Big news!*

Carrie returned the text almost immediately; 10AM – I'm bringing Aurora. We need her help.

DJ's reply; *Must be 1PM. Meeting with savior @ 10AM.* DJ needed to make some phone calls. The ball was finally in his court, where he wanted it. If he could get everyone on the same page they would be safe, at least all those who deserve to be. Right now, things need to be aligned perfectly prior to tomorrow.

ADVANCED PROBLEM SOLVING & AVOIDANCE

Clouds still held the moisture close to the ground, trapped by a slow-moving tropical storm gurgling in the Gulf. Every breath swiped across the coastal plain like an unwashed armpit. No relief was visible from any direction, but experience promised an afternoon of blast-furnace heat. Judge Kendrick was barely dressed when her phone buzzed. This better not be Ronnie Dahl she thought. The caller ID said Betty Lou Spencer. I hope this is not a call-in. I'd be tempted to crawl back in bed myself.

"Good morning Ms. Spencer," the judge said. "Is everything OK?"

"Yes" Betty Lou said. "I may be a bit late this morning. I'm going to interrogate Kevin about Raul Garza over breakfast. I wondered if I could bring you anything."

"No, I'm getting a slow start myself this morning. I'll see y'all at the office. Don't be too late."

Bases covered; Betty Lou was primed for a confrontation.

Judge Kendrick stepped onto her front porch to assess the morning. Definitely a day for driving to the office. The street was quiet as usual. No one outside. She did notice the little mini hot-rod with the Mexico plates parked down the block. She made a mental note to call Ross when she got to work and have him check it out. In the meantime, she opted for an additional cup of tea. While the tea was brewing, she changed shoes several times. Shoes were her downfall. She had over 80 pair and many mornings started like this, with a lot of shoe indecision. No big deal, we all have our habits and our addictions. Shoes are about as harmless as it gets. As she was pulling out of the driveway, she noticed the little hot-rod was no longer on the street. It was probably nothing anyway. No need to bother Ross.

CALL YOUR MOMMA!

It had been months since Kevin had talked to his mom. It's not like he didn't want to talk to her, he just didn't want the possibility of having to talk to Jerry, who is still a dick to this day. That would never change. Still, today's conversation may alter the family dynamics in a way Kevin could live with. But before he could find that out, he needed to know where his mom stood. It took a while to build up the courage but once he did Doris picked up on the first ring. "Hey Kevin, I didn't expect to hear from you today. What's up?"

"Great to talk to you too, Mom."

"Oh, I didn't mean it that way. I'm just a little stressed out. Jerry's been trying to expand his business. It's hard to do without capital. He'll pull it off. He always does."

"So, you guys are still doing OK? Marital bliss and all that. I still have trouble seeing the two of you together in my mind, but if you're happy, I'm happy."

"Happiness is overrated." Doris paused. Kevin heard a door slam in the background. " So, to what do I owe the pleasure of this call," Doris continued.

"It seems I've stumbled upon good fortune. It's too much for me to handle so I thought I would share some. I wanted to let you know first. If you're not happy this could be your escape hatch. If you are happy this could be a team effort for you two to get success under your belt." Kevin was unsure if he should continue or hang up. There had been no response from the other side of the call. He elected to continue. Here's the deal: I have become the proud owner of an international produce distribution company valued at $2.6 million. It's in business and has been for a couple of decades. The owner wants to retire. He's had some bad luck lately, not financially, but his daughter committed suicide, his wife passed away recently, and a couple of his drivers are in jail. In order to prevent losing the whole company he put it in an offshore trust and deeded it to me with the agreement that I would give him enough money to live on and a new identity. I know this sounds a little sketchy but it's all being handled by attorneys and it's legal. My question is do you want me to sell it and give you the money or do you want to incorporate it into your existing trucking company?"

"I want $1.5 million out of the deal if I sell it to you guys. If I keep it and sell it on the market I'll keep the 2.6 million and you guys can go on about your business the way you're running it now. I figure you don't have the capital to pay for it outright so I'm willing to finance any part of it you can't get covered by the banks.

"Here's what I'm not telling Jerry. If you want out of the marriage and money is the only thing keeping you in it, I'll give you the money to get out and you won't owe me anything. You'll be able to live comfortably the rest of your life, not extravagantly, but comfortably." He could hear the hesitation in Doris's voice. "You still haven't reconciled the fact that I might love him."

"He's still a dick. That's not gonna change. If you want out, I can get you out.

"I don't want out. I do appreciate the offer. I'll talk to Jerry about it, or you can if you'd prefer. It sounds like just what we need right now to take this to the next level."

"There's one other thing. The guy that owns the company now, you keep him on the payroll under an assumed name. That's my only stipulation. I need to know by 10:00 in the morning, so you might want to give him a shout."

A moment of stagnant silence ensued. You could feel the cogs turning in Doris's head. "I'll let you know by 8:00 AM," Doris said. Don't talk to anyone else about this including Jerry or any of our employees. This is just between you and me, OK?"

"No problem! I love you, Mom. Be happy!

TIN CAN ALLEY

Kevin had to get up well before daylight to be at the restaurant to meet Betty Lou. It's a shame that misunderstanding had gotten to the point it had, they both had deep feelings for each other. Betty Lou knew there was something going on she didn't quite understand between Kevin and this produce company on the edge of town. She wasn't sure she wanted to know. This morning she was going to face the facts, whatever they were. Kevin was unsure about how much he wanted to share with Betty Lou. Her strong moral code may require her to turn him over to the law. He hoped he could put a spin on it that she could understand and maybe even benefit from. That's the direction he wanted to take. There were too many unknowns for him to guess. He'd share at least some truth with her even if it meant putting himself at risk. The streetlights were still on when he parked his pickup on the edge of the town square next to Betty Lou's lemon-yellow Jeep. Inside the café a smattering of crusty farmers were taking a morning coffee and generally spreading gossip about crop failures and the good old days. Betty Lou sat in a dim corner with her back to the front door scrolling through her phone looking for God knows what. DJ slid in the booth across from her. He noticed streaks of mascara below her eyes, an indication that she may have been crying. He hated to see her so upset over what surely was only a misunderstanding. He took her hand in his to get her attention. When she looked up at him, he said, "Are you OK?"

"Should I be?" She asks. "My best friend just told me he may be disappearing and not contacting me. I don't think I'm OK." DJ continued holding her hand and gave it a little squeeze. "Since we last talked I've got better news. I may be disappearing still, but I can take you with me if you care to go."

"So now the choice is; you can disappear and I can miss you, or I can throw away my career, leave my friends, and follow you like some bitch in heat because I'm a woman and that's what we do. Is that it? Did it occur to you that I've been here four years and you've been here four weeks and now I'm supposed to follow you because you're a misogynistic asshole? You know what, never mind. I have lost my appetite. I'll see you back at the office."

"I may be late," DJ said. "I have a 10:00 AM appointment. It might run long."

"Figures," Betty Lou said.

Judge Kendrick moseyed into her office at 8:45 . The phone was ringing. Since she had no receptionist on duty, she went ahead and took the call. As expected, it was Ronnie Dahl. He was less than thrilled. "Good morning, Judge Kendrick. I thought we were going to have an early morning bail hearing for Raul Garza."

"Mr. Dahl, I believe that was your fantasy. I don't have a bail hearing scheduled for a Mr. Garza this morning or this week for that matter. I see him as a flight risk. He was picked up in a jurisdiction beyond the boundaries of his required travel limitations, heading out of state with illegal cargo. I have recommended no bail until we get to the bottom of this situation at Southern International Produce." I'll need him available to testify as a witness. I don't want to have to chase him down every time I have a question."

Dahl found it exceedingly difficult to maintain his composure. " I don't expect him to be very forthcoming with information."

Judge Kendrick knew she had the upper hand, "I guess time will tell. Good day Commissioner Dahl.

Back at Hacienda Dahl. Ronnie had gone from worshipping at the crotch of Prince Axel to an uncontrollable rage. He slammed the receiver down. "That bitch! Fucking bitch! This has to end right here. No more Mr. Nice Guy! She's done.

"Is there anythig I cad do?" Axel asked. This is exactly what Aawon left me heaw for."

"I appreciate that but I want to handle this one myself. I've had a couple of guys on this bitch for the last week. I figured something like this might happen. I'm gonna let them have their fun. I'll save you for the big guns if I need them. I'd rather we just hang out and have fun like we've been doing .

He picked his cell phone up and hit a number on speed dial. The party on the other end answered almost immediately. *"Es la hora. Sácala y deja un gran lío. Esto necesita internacionalizarse. ¡Nadie jode a Ronnie Dahl!"* **

Ronnie hung up. "That should take care of it. Now back to some fun."

*"It's time. Take her out and leave a big mess. This needs to go international. Nobody fucks with Ronnie Dahl!"

Following Betty Lou's departure from the restaurant Kevin decided to wait for his mother's call. He ordered a plate of migas with cheese and opened his phone to a tab recommending offshore bank accounts. He was thinking Cayman Islands but after some research she found Belize to have the best deals for accounts his size and he could open it remotely, a definite plus. At exactly 8:00 AM his mother's name came up on his call log.

"Hi Mama! You are certainly prompt. The background noise sounds a little strange. Are you outside?"

For a moment there was nothing but this background noise. When his mother spoke, her voice was shaky. "I'm on my way to Texas. Jerry didn't take the news very well, not that I gave him all the info. He hasn't taken any info from me very well recently. I've spent too much time lately concerned for my safety. If you don't mind, I'm going to take this opportunity to become independent again. He will probably be calling you. I would prefer you tell him you hadn't heard from me. I left some red herrings around to throw him off the trail. It should keep him busy until I get established somewhere. You have no idea how grateful I am for this opportunity."

"Oh my God, Momma! Why didn't you let me know. I could have helped out sooner?"

"You had your own life. I didn't want to make it more difficult for you."

"When do you think you'll be here?"

"Probably tomorrow evening. I still have things to wrap up. I haven't told him everything yet. I want to make sure there's plenty of distance between us when I do."

"Be careful. Call me tomorrow with your itinerary. Don't text it. I love you. Borrow someone's car or take the bus to San Antonio. It's a big enough city to get lost in. Go to a convenience store to buy a burner phone for cash. Call me with that number but don't give it to anyone else. Leave your phone turned off with your car in some obscure parking garage in Little Rock. I'll buy you a car when you get here.

The Judge parks in her reserved parking space. It's rarely used and the illegibly faded J DGE   END ICK reminds her that she is well past her "sell by " date. When she takes her car to work, she usually leaves the space for those who may need it more. She's seventy-one and slowing considerably but what would she do if not this? Fact is, she loves this little town and she believes that a fair and impartial justice system can keep the town working properly. The temperature is already into triple digits and the town appears deserted. She spots Kevin's and Betty Lou's vehicles parked side-by-side over on the square and the little Mexican mini hot-rod a few spaces away. Maybe she will call Ross later about that. Right now, it's her turn to open shop. The idea of a justice "shop" makes her cringe. It's an idea folks like Ronnie Dahl would relish. Not in my town! She thinks.

She gets the coffee started and like always the sound of the water filling the carafe awakens her bladder, She runs into the bathroom and turns on the light just as a kid with a spider-web tattoo on his shaved head grabs her by the hair and pulls her over backward. Another kid with a shaved head hits her in the throat with a machete. Her head spins around to see her headless body fall to the floor, as the kid says, "Yep. You're fucked."

Betty Lou decided to go back to her apartment and clean up. She was done with DJ so the makeup wasn't necessary. A good clean scrub is what she needed. Work was going to be weird for a couple of days. Weird was her forte.

When she got to work she didn't see DJ's truck, but it seemed Judge Kendrick was already there. Not a problem. She had called in. She didn't see the judge, but the coffee had been started. The coffee was traditionally Betty Lou's responsibility. It seemed strange Judge Kendrick wasn't making herself visible. She checked the judge's office, no Kendrick. She checked the break room. No Kendrick. She knocked on the bathroom door "Judge, you in there?" No answer. She entered and saw Kendrick's legs in the handicap stall. "Oh, hey Judge?" No answer. That's when she noticed blood on the floor. She knocked on the stall, No response. She pulled the door open and nearly fainted. Kendrick's headless body was seated on the toilet. She pushed open the stall next to it. Kendrick's face stared up from the toilet bowl, eyes open and accusing! Betty Lou fell back against the wall. When shock turned to terror Betty Lou ran out of the building fumbling with her phone to dial 911.

DJ was out at SIP picking up Julio to shuttle to the attorney's office when he got the text from Betty Lou, Kendrick's been murdered. They decided to steer clear of the crime scene for the time being. They would continue to the attorney's office and get those papers signed before all hell breaks loose, if it's not too late already. The rest could wait. Julio needed his paperwork in order because he was going to have to bail out soon or so it seemed. DJ had an alibi but he needed to set up a safe place for his mom and he would need access to some of their cash. There is no safe place for any of them now.

DJ texted Carrie, can we meet at noon? Anywhere?

We will be at the ranch---noon. Came back from Carrie. We can trust Lois. Probably should let her in on this.

Bad news travels fast in the cartel. Kendrick's body was still warm when Ronnie Dahl got the word she was dead. He poured a drink to celebrate. He shared it with Axel in one of the quirkiest ways imaginable, but that's another story. Apparently, the guys that did it were proud of their work. Within minutes it got back to the boss man in Corpus Christi. Aaron James is livid. Aaron James calls Ronnie immediately. Ronnie sees who is calling and he is so happy. He picks up the phone without even a Hello and says "Did you hear, the wicked bitch is dead. We don't have to worry about that whore anymore."

Aaron James is not a fan of Ronnie Dahl. "What in the hell were you thinking. Do you want to bring the full force of the DEA down on us? How about the ATF? How about my wrath you dumb ass? You have a hornets nest and you decide to hit it with a stick, shoot it with a gun, and blast it with a firehose! We're trying to keep a low profile here. This is not what I wanted to see.

"But...,"

"Shut up! You better start figuring out how you're going to take the heat off us! Don't make a move unless you clear it with me or Axel. Give the phone to Axel.

Axel took the phone outside giving Ronnie reason to be terrified. After 20 minutes Axel came in and handed the phone to Ronnie. "It's for you. Boy is he pissed! Axel said.

Ronnie took the call. I'm sorry boss. I just wanted to get that thorn out of our side so we could get Raul back. He is such an asset." "Not anymore. Here's the deal; I want you to do exactly what you would do if nothing happened. Have your Labor Day Barbeque. Do something to honor the memory of that judge. Otherwise, keep a low profile."

"Yes sir."

The call ended. Ronnie stared at the phone in his hand as if he didn't know who's it was.

Betty Lou is devastated at her friend's demise. How could this have happened? A question the local authorities also need answered. After some preliminary questions they decide to take her in for interrogation. Once the authorities ask for her phone she knows they are considering her as a serious suspect. She makes one last text to DJ; *Please come fix this if you can.*

They take her into the interrogation room. She wonders who is on the other side of the one-way mirror. Is DJ there? How about that female deputy he has been riding with? She is terrified. She imagines the last minutes of her friend's life and bursts into tears. The thinly-veiled accusations begin almost immediately: Who made the coffee with a dead body in the bathroom? Why were you late to work? Was the judge angry about you being late? Where are your co-workers? Why no make-up? All her answers point to her guilt. *Please DJ*, she thought. *You know I didn't do this!*

THIS WAY OUT!

In the rural recesses of Jim Webb County a desperate group gathers for the sole purpose of putting a general crime wave to bed. The participants each have their priority but cooperation will be required if success is to be achieved.

Ross paces the front yard, his cell phone stuck to his ear, remotely directing the investigation at the courthouse annex. "OK as soon as I assemble my team they will be at your disposal. I have two state probation / parole officers that work in that office available, as well as an ATF agent with top level clearance in case there's a cartel connection which, as you know, I suspect to be the case. I appreciate y'all coming to work on this. It probably won't be easy but it should be productive. Anyway Jake, this is me officially calling you in. I hope the cargo and victims will be enough to close the deal. Is that going to be enough to make this work."

"Jake wants a head count," Ross says. "How many need to disappear? I know Carrie may need to disappear. Julio needs to disappear almost immediately. We will have to assess the other situations. There will be offshore accounts to set up as well. We need to work that out here now because we're not going to be able to get together again."

"This weekend we pretend nothing has happened?" Julio asks.

"Good question," Ross acknowledges. That's a yes for almost everyone. That said, I would advise keeping the lowest possible profile you can without raising suspicion. I don't know how far up the chain of command the cartel's awareness of our knowledge goes. Since we will be keeping Raul in custody through the weekend, how they respond to that will give us an idea."

"Wait!" Julio says, "You're going to use him as bait? Isn't that dangerous for him?"

"I don't know where he would be safer, and we have the parole violation and long weekend of government office closures to justify it. He'll be safe."

"Some of these fake IDs will just be that." Ross says. "We

won't need anything extravagant unless we are being hunted by the law or the cartel! "In other cases, we will need a complete new identity. I'd prefer to have the feds handle those if they will, and here comes the person who can tell us." Ross points to the highway where the new cruiser is turning into the driveway.

In typical Southern fashion, Lois whipped up a batch of brownies from scratch as soon as she found out she would be hosting a meeting of first responders. They come out of the oven at the exact moment Carrie and Aurora step from the car.

Ross makes one more call to his office. "This is Sheriff Carranza... Release Betty Lou Spencer on her own recognizance immediately... I know there's no judge to sign it... I'll take care of that next week.... I don't care, put me down as witness.... Do it now.... I'll get it signed.... And give her a ride to her car – tell her to call me as soon as she's released!"

Carrie and Aurora step out of the cruiser like they're on Baywatch, if Baywatch had no water visible for miles. As they walk up to the group assembled around the front of the house Aurora can't pass it up, "Hey boys, y'all solving the world's problems? I know we solved most of them on the way out here. We'll share the information with you if you haven't worked it out on your own." Carrie kicks a dirt clod out of the driveway with a full-quill ostrich boot, slips the keys in her pocket, and removes her aviator sunglasses. "They are so cute when they're stressed out like that. Think we ought to give them a hand?" Ross looked at the ground to keep from laughing. "We couldn't do it without you," he said.

"Sure you could," Aurora said. "There would be a lot more paperwork is all. By the way, did anyone think to get that poor little hippie-chick out of jail? She was pretty freaked out."

"Done," Ross said.

Aurora looked at the assemblage. "Well then, let's get this party started!"

"Y'all come on inside," Lois said. "I've got brownies."

"Nothing special about those brownies are there?" DJ asked. "I don't want this to be harder than it looks."

"Does anyone have any idea what he's talking about?" Lois asked.

"Another time, Mom," Carrie says.

The air conditioning was a welcome change from the brutal heat outside. Soon everybody had a chair under their butt and a brownie in their hand. DJ spoke. "Julio is safe, at least for now and the future of SIP is in good hands. He will need a new identity and hopefully he can go into witness protection, so he'll have a job and some income lined up. He's unable to liquidate most of what he owns on such short notice, but I'll help him. By the way, does anyone know who's responsible for judge Kendrick being murdered? If so, I want to be part of the team that removes them from the face of the earth, paperwork or not."

Check with me later," Aurora said. "We're gonna keep this on a need-to-know basis. If you get caught or captured by the cartel the less you know the better. Whatever you know will be extracted from you."

"Officially, Jake Tosh with the Texas Rangers will be leading this investigation. However, several of us have agendas beyond shutting down the cartel. I have no intention of preventing anyone from satisfying their vengeful fantasy, but realize it's dangerous and if you get caught the cartel will kill you. It won't be pretty." Aurora explained. "Since no one here is a Texas Ranger, Jake Tosh will contact you if he needs any information. Otherwise, share your information only with Ross or me. We want to keep this discreet as much as possible to prevent the cartel from acting against anyone not related to law enforcement. I want to personally thank you all for your participation. Be safe, be silent. Good luck. If you have any questions right now, we're here to answer them. In public, we don't know you."

As soon as the meeting broke up DJ called Betty Lou. "Are you OK?"

"Not sure."

"Can we talk in person."

"Yes please."

"Not at your house. Somewhere safe."

"There's a Starbucks at the HEB. How about there?"

"See you in about an hour."

Axel tries to admire his near-perfect face in the mirror, but it only reflects the face of dread. He tries to avoid getting into a personal relationship with his assignments, His MFA in theater arts usually makes it possible, if not always easy. Most folks are so distracted by his artificial speech impediment they overlook the clues to their impending doom and opt for compassionate empathy. Something about the alleged disability lowers the threat level. Unfortunately, he became enamored with this assignment. He never expected to take the road he's being required to take. He prides himself on his professionalism. If only he could figure a way out. He has to assassinate Ronnie Dahl. He has no choice. He doesn't have to do it today. He has until the middle of next week. Maybe someone will beat him to it. Right now he is going to enjoy curling up with his little cuddle buddy and enjoying the high life for a while. He could live like this if fate allowed.

Ronnie enters carrying two glasses of white wine. "We're having grilled shrimp kabobs tonight, figured to get an early start on the drinking part. Will you make it to my BBQ tomorrow? I'd love to show you off to my friends. You could even make some connections. This isn't a bad little town if you have the money and the power."

"I'm subbosed to keep a low pwofile. We've alweady pissed Aawon off enough. I bettow play by the rules."

"Fuck Aaron! What's he done for you lately. He doesn't even like us. I can show you a good life and you won't even have to work."

"I don't know. I've seen what habbeds to people that get on his bad side. Not something I'm intewested in doing. Maybe it's subthing we can tawk aboud for the future. Wight now I just wanna keep thigs simple."

As Kevin rushes back to town, the hypnotic hum of the V-8 powering his Silverado encourages introspection. Repetitive scenery and lack of traffic give him time to analyze his situation with Betty Lou. He considers his options. He's not supposed to have a relationship with anyone that could interfere with the goal of taking money and power from the cartel. He's left to question how this relationship has developed into his primary focus. If he's honest with her it may scare her away. If he's honest with himself that's not an outcome he can live with. Protecting her has become paramount whether she sees it or not! He needs to know what she wants from him and if he can stand to hear the answer. She's taken him to a place he's never been and it's both exciting and terrifying.

Then there's his mother, who he literally owes his life to. What will she need? Is there a safe place for Mom in this scenario? The solution to both challenges have a time element that can't be overlooked. If only this road went on forever, there may possibly be an answer. The way things are progressing there seems to be no solution in sight. All of this is above and beyond the goal that had become an international quest. A quest he initiated and coerced these folks into joining him on. A goal that will most likely put some of them in jeapordy.

After the passing of a very short hour, he pulls into the parking lot of the HEB and parks beside Betty Lou's lemon-yellow Jeep Wrangler. She's not in it.

"I'm going to enjoy having someone on the same team with the same goals as me." Aurora said. "We seem to click."

Without changing her expression, Carrie focused on the white line slipping beneath the cruiser. "I've always worked alone. I don't know how well a partnership is going to float. We can give it a try." Carrie leaned back in the cruiser and trounced the accelerator. At 110 mph she let go of the steering wheel. "See how this car seems to have its own plan, stays on the road without any coercion. That's how I work. We can work together as long as you don't get in my way. I'll try not to get in yours."

As the cruiser topped 115 mph, Aurora tried to remain calm. She looked at the steering wheel out of the corner of her eye but kept her hands folded in her lap. Carrie put her elbow on the windowsill and turned to talk to Aurora. "It's not just about removing toxic assholes from the face of the earth, at least that's not my only goal. I'm a blatant capitalist. I want their money." The speedometer read 120 mph. Aurora's hand was vibrating like a snake's head fixing to strike. At 130mph she lifted it from her lap.

"Don't! You'll cause us to lose control." Carrie said. "You have to trust the machine. In this case you also have to trust your partner. I know you think you have a handle on my motivations. I'm not so sure. Mine is a personal vendetta. It's not that I 'm insulted when I'm considered a conquest. It's more that I'm disgusted when someone feels they don't owe their spouse or children the honor they vowed. That's especially true if they have an extended family they pledged their devotion to. If a guy doesn't even attempt to play by the rules they don't deserve a place at the table,-- know what I mean?"

"Sure, I get that," Aurora says, "but isn't it worse if they do it on a larger scale? Take human trafficking for instance. Doesn't the for-profit angle make the act much more grievous?'

"That depends. Many of the supposed victims of those operations are part of the group trying to enter illegally. They're just trying to improve their lot in life. I don't really have a problem with that unless the coyote rips them off. Then the coyote needs to be eliminated, quickly and with malice!" Carrie takes her foot off the accelerator and lets the cruiser coast down to a healthy 60 mph before gripping the wheel again.

"Well at least we agree on that," she says. "Will you be at the barbeque tomorrow?"

"No. You'll be Ross' date. I have an investigation to wrap up in Corpus Christi, one that you're pretty sure you have a handle on but don't. If it all works out you'll be in the clear for that performance art in the No Tell Motel. Ross is planning to introduce you to Ronnie Dahl. Dahl is a sketchy guy. I'm pretty sure he's theh one that you're pretty sure you have a handle on but don't. Dahl is harboring this Axel guy and he's in business with your Daddy, I suggest trying to find a way into his inner circle. Be careful though. He's smart and well-connected. Also, he may not succumb to your regular lusty approach. He presents himself as gay. Sex is a power play for him, so it remains to be seen how that fits in, if you'll pardon the pun!"

"Don't worry. I can handle him," Carrie said, continuing their playful word game. "By the time I'm done with him he won't know which end is up!"

DJ charged into the HEB. There was no Betty Lou in sight. He ran back to the Jeep and noticed a folded page from a notepad on the floorboard. He unfolded it. "We need to talk" is all it said. No phone number, no address, but he knew. It was not the flowing formal script Betty Lou prided herself on. It was written in the hard block letters of a psychopath. There was no doubt the note was meant for him. He only had to figure out who wrote it. The answer came almost immediately as a mini rat-rod with loud mufflers and blacked-out windows pulled in behind the Jeep, revved the engine twice, and drove slowly away. DJ jumped in his truck and followed. Every plan, every thought, every idea, he had on the way back from Alice disappeared from his mind. His whole being was occupied with keeping Betty Lou safe. Only then could he allow his rage and obsession to manifest itself in the pleasure of slowly and methodically executing the bastards who kidnapped her. Tires cried as he tried keeping up with the little rat-rod on the two-lane road heading to SIP. It was extremely difficult to maneuver the pickup as he pulled the Beretta 9mm out of the console and stuck it in the back of his jeans. He covered it with the tail of his shirt. It was difficult but he had no choice. As he turned into the driveway, he saw the same truck he had put the U-joint in a few weeks ago was backed into the garage with the overhead door open. It appeared ready to travel. Two men exited the little rat-rod. They were both short and stocky, their heads were shaved, and they had tattoos on their faces, heads, and arms. In fact, almost every inch of their visible body was covered with tattoos; angular and tribal with a lot of sharp edges, blades, and guns represented. They each carried a machete. "The boss needs a driver. Today. Where's Julio?"

"I don't know." DJ said, because it was true, he didn't. "Have you looked up at the house?"

The shorter one swung his machete like a baseball bat stopping just millimeters from DJ's throat. "Are you calling me stupid? How much blood do you think your body holds, you idiot? Would you like to find out?"

"I honestly don't know where Julio is. What can I do for you?" DJ said.

"Are you deaf too. you cum sucking idiot? I told you I need a driver."

"I'm a driver. Let Betty Lou go. I'll drive for you."

"Who's this Betty Lou, cowboy? Is that your hillbilly girlfriend?"

"I want to see her.

"That should be easy enough." The guy not doing the talking got up in the cab of the truck, started the engine, and pulled the truck out of the bay.

DJ heard a muffled scream "Wait! Stop!" he said and started towards the back of the truck. The man not driving put the point of his machete in contact with DJs abdomen. The other man stopped the truck and motioned for DJ to move around back. DJ saw Betty Lou gagged and chained to the bumper by her wrists. She had fallen but stood back up when the truck stopped. Her knees and elbows were bleeding. Patches of blood we're dampening her raw skin. It was all DJ could do not to shoot the driver but the other man had his machete in contact with Betty Lou's throat. He kept his hands in the clear, waiting for a better opportunity.

"As I may have mentioned, I'm one of Julio's regular drivers. I'll get your load to its intended destination. I'm the only one of Julio's drivers who hasn't been in trouble with the law. I'm good, but I need Betty Lou left out of it."

The two skinheads conferred briefly. "Let me take it up with the boss." the one in charge said. He made a cell phone call and came back. "OK here's the deal. Hillbilly chick is gonna ride with you. We are going to shadow you. Anything looks the least bit strange, or you tip off the Border Patrol you don't have to worry about getting arrested. They don't arrest dead people. The good news is the cargo is already stateside. You'll be picking up 20 migrants at The Mirage Auto Shop and have them in New Orleans by midnight. You'll be doing a lot of driving. I would ask you if that would be okay, but you don't really have a choice. I'm hooking you up with some magic dust so you can keep up the pace. When you deliver and get the truck back here you get $1200."

DJ stared into the manipulator's eyes, "Bullshit! That run pays $2000 you skimming little bastard. I get the two grand. I could take it up with Ronnie but I'm pretty sure he doesn't want to be bothered right now."

The smaller skinhead chuckled, "Well ain't you a negotiatin' son of a bitch."

"You gotta do what you gotta do," DJ said. "Cut her loose."

"Done. Give me your phone. You better hit the road. You're burning daylight. Remember, I'm on your every move."

They were on the Katy freeway in Houton before the actual conversation progressed beyond tears and angry grunts. Heat threw waves on the molten blacktop. They almost spoke civilly at one point just before arriving at Mirage Auto Repair. As soon as Betty Lou realized what was occurring there, she shut herself back in the dark cloud she'd inhabited since the tiny Starbucks. The truck had no sleeper and the noise from the mini rat-rod's exhaust wasn't conducive to rest anyway. Betty Lou didn't want to sleep, or talk. She wanted to scream! She patched her knees and elbows with a depleted first aid kit she found behind the truck's passenger seat. She refused to get out of the cab. She watched DJ horse around with the skinheads while they loaded what was obviously a couple of dozen Latina sex workers into the refrigerated cargo compartment. Her stomach flipped in disgust every time one of these reprobates leered at her.

On the other hand, DJ rattled continuously an excuse or apology. His long-winded rambling only intensified after he spent an inordinate amount of time in the auto shop's bathroom coming out with a ring of white dust around one nostril. Finally, after a white Subaru with two kayaks strapped to the top ran him onto the shoulder while trying not to miss their exit, he sighed and eased back onto the freeway.

"I'm really sorry you're injured," he said. "But you know, I probably saved your life. You got that, right?"

"Fuck you!" she hollered. "If it weren't for you my life would never have been in danger. You got that, right?"

"Not sure that's true, but say, for the sake of argument, it is. How in the hell did you get from the Starbucks to the back bumper of this truck? My guess is they picked you up because you found the judge's body."

"Why do you clown around with these scumbags like you're their team captain?"

"That's just it. If I can get them to think we all have the same goals then we're safer. When we were planning to meet this morning, I know we both had a plan that included the other. Am I right?"

Betty Lou stared out the window at the dry brittle landscape. "Yeah, maybe. That seems like another time and place."

DJ sniffed and wiped his nose on his shirt sleeve. "I'm still the same guy I was then."

"If that's true I don't much like that person I'm seeing now, and I don't feel safe."

DJ reached for her hand but she yanked it away. "I'm working on that," he said. "I can explain some of it. The rest you'll just have to trust me. We're both alive and kicking. Right?"

"For now." she said.

THE MEAT OF THE MATTER

"**We have to manipulate the outcome** of the Kendrick assassination," Aurora stated. "Is there any believable way we can put this into perspective where gangs or the cartels are not involved."

"Not sure what you mean," Ross replied. "It has all the earmarks of a cartel assassination. You could spin it, but I doubt the public would buy into it. We have a Democrat running for office who will want to put it under a negative light, and he owns the local newspaper. All we can do is make sure nothing else happens. That will mean a virtual lockdown of the city. If we could get Ronnie Dahl's cooperation we might pull it off. I think our best hope on that is Carrie James, but I'm not sure what her hidden agenda entails, or if she even has one."

"Oh, she has one!" Aurora said.

"Really?" Ross asked. "What would that be?"

"She wants to shut down her daddy!"

"And how would that play out?"

"Not sure, but I bet she has a pretty tight plan. Aurora says, choosing not to enlighten her husband on the extent of her involvement.

Ross mansplains, "I'm also certain that Dahl won't, actually can't, cooperate. He's just a puppet."

Aurora gave her husband a sly smile. "I think you underestimate the power of a woman's influence."

DIESEL INTERMEZZO

The truth can be rare and undefined. It can also be easy to find. Some never find it. Some find it and never know they did. If fear is the opposite of contentment, and longing the opposite of satisfaction, where is magic? Pick one.

Julio wants to trust DJ. He seems like a good kid but who really knows? Trust hasn't served him well of late. He doesn't have a new identity yet, but he has a contact number for someone who can get him one. In the meantime, he may be in danger. He doesn't want to be in danger. He's not even sure he wants to be alive at this point. He lost everything, his wife, his daughter, his business. His reputation disintegrated in the wind. It's never too late to recoup. He takes a taxi to Corpus Christi then takes a plane to San Antonio. In San Antonio he must wait. That's where his new identity lives. He gets a taxi to the bus station because at the bus station no one asks for your ID. No one cares who you are. Maybe that's why the ID guy lives near the bus station; hard to say. There's a little bar three blocks from the bus station. Julio's taste buds express a fervent desire for good bourbon, but he realizes he probably won't get it at a bar three blocks from the bus station. He'll get something,---something that can take the edge off this horrible twist his life is taking.

Doris is tired. She's been on the bus 19 hours. It's about a ten-hour drive in a car. On the bus it seems endless. She's lost communication with her son, not sure why. She has faith that he'll reconnect with her. He's a good boy. He doesn't like her husband, Jerry, much. That's okay. She doesn't care much for him right now either. Her face is damaged beyond what makeup can hide. She's supposed to meet her son at the bus station. She gives him another call. There's no answer. He may be driving. He may be out of range. You never know with these cell phones. She can wait it out. He sent her $5,000 through PayPal. If she can just figure out how to get it off PayPal without revealing her location, she'll be in good shape. It's the last Friday before the Labor Day weekend so it needs to happen soon. She doesn't want to burden her son. She won't take the airline. It would make her traceable. She wants to escape. She doesn't want to die. She doesn't even really want to change her lifestyle much, just get rid of the husband. She's ready to try a different part of the country. She's tired of the Ozarks. Everyone's so backwards. While she waits, she looks for a place to eat. She finally settles on a little bar three blocks from the bus station. They have sandwiches. They have drinks. She sits on the stool at the end of the bar, orders a club sandwich, and a glass of iced tea. Nobody asks if she wants sugar. She gets it sweet because she's in Texas and that's how it works. She doesn't know that — a learning experience. She doesn't realize how hungry she is until she bites into that club sandwich. She inhales it in less than 5 minutes. She sees a sad little Hispanic man sitting at the other end of the bar sipping on a glass of bourbon. It looks like a glass of loneliness. When the bartender comes to refill it, she realizes it's a glass of how she really wants someone to talk to, just to have a conversation. So much has happened recently she doesn't want to talk to a confidant about. The little man looks sad. She's never done anything like this, but she decides she wants to buy him a drink. Whatever he's drinking she's going to have one too. She calls the bartender over thinking it's a little weird. You do things differently. You take risks. She has taken a huge one. Just tell him you're here. She thinks. It lets her know she's here too. They could share a little time together, strangers telling stories, passing time. Why not buy this stranger a moment in a life, maybe make a difference. It's not yet noon but the sky is getting darker and the wind is gusting. The future is fluid, not concrete. Moments are all they have. They can create a filler for this space, a choice between something and nothing. What's the worst thing that could happen? It may rain on their day. It doesn't matter, they're just waiting anyway.

The bartender goes to the other end of the bar and pours the drink. He indicates Doris at her end of the bar. Doris notices him looking. She makes a tentative toast from across the room. Julio smiles at Doris' gesture and joins her at her end of the bar.

"Thank you," he says.

Doris swirls the amber liquid with her index finger, "I just came in on the bus. I'm waiting for my son. I have no idea when or if he'll get here. I've lost contact."

Julio says, "I was at the bus station. I came here to get away from the smell of diesel. All these years running a trucking company. I can't stand the smell of diesel anymore. It used to smell like success. Now it smells like failure. If I never see another truck, it would be too soon."

Doris chuckles at the irony. "That's funny," she says. "My

ex-husband owns a trucking company." Interesting, she figures. She already referred to him as her ex-husband even though they haven't been apart for 24 hours yet. She notices Julio looking at her damaged face. "Yes, I did that trying to cover it up. I don't know enough about these things to make it work."

Julio looks out the window. The clouds are gathering. It seems like it might begin to rain soon. Fortunately, they are both inside this warm dry bar.

Doris considers telling him her name but decides there's really no point. "I've never liked the smell of diesel," she says. If I never smell another truck, it'll be too soon."

LABOR DAY

By 10:00 AM Saturday morning Beeville City Park feels like a sauna with temperatures approaching triple digits and clouds the color of bruises roiling on the southern horizon. Nine towable BBQ pits cluster at one end of the park. They have been smoking there since Friday afternoon. Every year the public wonders why commissioner Dahl chooses Labor Day weekend to sponsor his appreciation celebration. The truth is, he likes to observe his constituency suffering. He's good at controlling suffering. He looks forward to making Julio Ramirez suffer. He looks forward to making DJ Kevin suffer. All he wants out of life right now is to tangle up with Axel in his refrigerated bedroom. Since that's not happening, the more people he can make suffer the better. It always amazes Ronnie Dahl to discover how much suffering people will endure for free food.

Ross and Carrie do not arrive together. That would have fostered too much suspicion. Ross's wife is rarely seen in Beeville. Many people suspect he isn't really married. They don't need any more ammunition for their fantasies. Ross goes to the park early wearing his sheriff's uniform to brief his security team. He drives his restored '65 Chevy pickup. It's his pet project, drawing folks into admiring conversations. Carrie arrives in her recently detailed Interceptor. As she unfolds from the spotless vehicle, her brown deputies uniform appears to be painted on. She immediately begins searching for her boss and spots him near a polished gooseneck RV parked on the grass in the middle of the park. It has to belong to Ronnie Dahl. She ambles in that direction.

No matter how angry one is at another person, being ensconced in the cab of a refrigerated produce truck for 14 consecutive hours leads to some conversation. By the end of the trip, DJ and Betty Lou reconcile enough to attend the Labor Day festivities. Their primary goal is to use this event to give Judge Kendrick the honor she deserves. They feel guilty it's not them headed for the cemetery instead of Judge Kendrick. DJ's mom finally reaches him on Friday afternoon following his uneventful round-trip delivery to New Orleans. He's trying to convince Betty Lou to leave the area, maybe even the country, for good. At least to accompany him to San Antonio to relocate his mom. She's teetering towards that eventuality, but she has established herself in Beeville. It isn't a decision she has to make immediately. She wants to make sure people notice her because a certain faction of the town still holds her responsible for the judge's demise.

Betty Lou and DJ arrive at SIP exhausted. After finding his $2000 in the console of his pickup, sleep is the next priority. It's all DJ can manage to take Betty Lou to pick up her Jeep at the HEB.

"See you tomorrow?" DJ asks. When he parks next to Betty Lou's Jeep.

"Come on to my apartment," Betty Lou says. "You're exhausted and it's probably not safe for you to be staying at SIP right now."

DJ has yet to mention he now owns the company. He has yet to achieve total honesty, but he really does try. "As long as you're beside me I don't care where I sleep."

It's the first time Betty Lou actually rolls her eyes at DJ, but she almost smiles—headway, he thinks.

He follows her home. After a warm shower he calls his mom back "Hey mom. I've been up for two days mostly driving. I'll pick you up in the morning. Can you pay cash for a room? I'm sorry. There's just been so much going on."

"You have no idea!" Doris says. "But yeah, I'm OK. I already have a room, and I didn't have to use my ID. Just call this number when you're on your way. I'm fine. I even met someone to hang out with for a little while."

No mom. Do not under any circumstances strike up a conversation with someone you don't know."

"Don't be silly. I'm a good judge of character and this guy is in a similar situation to me. We're both just waiting on the next move. I told you; I'll be fine. Now get some sleep and I'll see you early tomorrow."

Doris ends the call just as Betty Lou comes out of the bathroom in flannel pajamas. DJ laughs. "I see how it's going to be."

"I'm too tired and sore to do anything but snore. Catch me in the morning - we'll see."

INTRODUCTIONS

"**This** is who I wanted to talk to you about," Ross said. "We have upgraded and diversified the Sheriff's Department since you and I last chatted. Meet Carrie James, a recent graduate in criminal justice from University of Texas at Austin, an incredible law enforcement official with roots in our county."

Ronnie stood speechless, looking over Carrie from head to toe. It wasn't that he didn't know what to say, more like there was so much to say he didn't know where to start. Being Ronnie Dahl, he jumped in anyway. "Well, this is just gonna cause a crime wave. People will break the law just to get next to you."

"They'll only do it once," Carrie said. I'm not gonna go easy on folks. For instance, I'm about to write you a big old ticket for parking on the grass and I'll bet anything the registration is expired on this vehicle. No telling what else I can find." Carrie smiled, Took the almost full beer from his hand. "Course you give me this beer I might look the other way I've been known to accept huge bribes from important people and I hear you're about the most important person in this county." She took a couple of deep swallows of the beer and licked the foam from her lips before handing it back.

Ross shook his head, looked out toward the people over by the BBQ pits. "It sounds like it's in my best interest not to be a part of this conversation. Y'all do y'all's negotiating and leave me out of it. I've got brisket on my mind."

Carrie waited until Ross was out of earshot and turned to Ronnie. "I don't know how much you know about me, but I know enough about you to know that you're in danger. I'm surprised you don't have your bodyguard here today."

"Why would I have a bodyguard?"

"You mean this Axel guy's not your bodyguard?"

"He's just a friend. I invited him but he said he'd rather stay home where it was cooler. Plus, he didn't really want to be seen here for some reason."

"And you didn't find that strange? I'm pretty well connected. In fact, you probably know my father. I'm just saying, I wouldn't want to be you right now. Word is; Axel is an assassin, and he may be looking to eliminate your space in the hierarchy. You should get a bodyguard—

other than him."

"I suppose you know someone interested in the position? Come into my air-conditioned office and enlighten me." He held the door so she could go up the steps ahead of him. This was not chivalry. He wanted a close-up view of that ass. She made sure he got one.

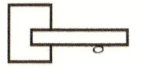

TRAVEL PLANS

"**That was beyond weird.** I didn't expect that kind of reaction." Betty Lou was having trouble with the public awareness that she was out on the economy and her boss was in the morgue. It was like they thought she was the murderer.

"They have to have someone to blame," DJ said. "When a public figure is killed there's a lot of guilt to go around. Don't take it personally."

It had probably been a mistake to go to their favorite restaurant on the square for breakfast, but he needed to get an early start. It wasn't yet 8:00 and he figured they could get to San Antonio and back before noon. They'd be there to honor Judge Kendrick and still have some brisket beforehand. Kevin had some explaining to do. He'd decided to pull out all the stops on the honesty and hope for the best.

Once he was on I-37 He opened the truck up to 75 and turned off the satellite radio. He said, "We need to talk."

"That's a scary-ass thing to say." Betty Lou said.

"Yeah, it is. You should see it from my end. I'm probably a high risk. You don't deserve to be stuck with me, but here we are., at least for now. I'm gonna be honest and lay it all out on the table for you and if you run away screaming I wouldn't blame you. I'll just say up front, I hope you won't."

"Well, you might notice that I do have my running shoes on. Let's hear it. I'll give you the benefit of the doubt."

DJ stared out the windshield, put both hands on the wheel and sighed. "I don't quite know where to begin."

"Start at the beginning."
I wasn't there at the beginning"

"You're going to have to do better than that."

"Why don't you tell me what you know and I'll fill in the gaps, okay?"

"I know you're somehow affiliated with that new deputy—the woman from Austin. I know she has something to do with that truck and the two dead smugglers they found in the desert southwest of here. I'm pretty sure you think Raul was involved. I don't know how it all fits together or even how you're involved.

"Okay, you've got the gist of it. I met Carrie James in Austin. I'd been studying criminal justice, but from the criminal point of view, making the most money with the least risk. It wasn't working out. Carrie was burned out at college. She was a roommate of my friend's girlfriend. They tried to do a matchmaker thing with us but Carrie is a militant asexual, at least that's my interpretation. I tried to recruit her for a caper. She wasn't interested. I figured that was the end of it. Couple of weeks later she gets hold of me, actually shows up at my graduation in Fayetteville. She wants revenge on these people that were smuggling humans across the border. Turns out a good friend of hers was killed in the operation. She said there was money involved. I needed money. I needed to get out of the house. So we collaborated. Once we got into it, I realized she was crazy and probably dangerous. I don't know what else she's into, but I suspect she's killed people, probably for money. As I infiltrated SIP I figured out someone from the outside was coercing Julio into taking these human smuggling loads. I suspect it's the county commissioner but I'm not sure. Anyway, to get into the inner sanctum of the operation I've taken several loads of produce and two loads of women—prostitutes. No one was harmed in my loads. I suspect Carrie set up Raul at least once to take the hit on a load of women. This is where it gets fuzzy for me. Was Lydia's suicide a suicide or murder? I also heard (and this is second-hand speculation) that the person controlling the border is Carrie's father, who she despises.

  Julio lost his wife and daughter, and two of his employees, and now the judge is murdered. He wants out but can't. My main reason for getting into this mess was to make money not stop crime or any other moral equivalent. I lost track of that for a while. Julio said I was the only person he could trust so he deeded his entire operation to me as long as I could arrange for his safety. Carrie has some kind of connection with the feds that she can procure new identities, like witness protection, except you don't have to testify in court, just to a special prosecutor. I'm hooking him up with that. I now own a trucking company worth $2.5M and I have $500K in a trust that's readily available and another$800K in cash. As far as I know I'm not on a hit list but I'm one of the few company drivers that can legally cross the border. I could run a trucking company, but I would have to get out from under these criminals forcing us to take these high-risk loads. We're working on that but that is not my department."

  "Let me get this straight; you're basically a scumbag wannabe thug that envisions himself as this kind of a Robinhood figure, maybe even a legend in his own mind."

"That's kinda harsh!

Dude! You sold women for sex. The thought of that totally creeps me out!

"You're right, and I realize that. But what was my option, or theirs for that matter. South of the border those women would be considered disposable. At least here they have a chance!"

Betty Lou shook her head and shut down. She felt rage bubbling up in her throat. She couldn't let this go unchallenged. "So, you pick them up, drop them off with people you don't know, in a place where they don't speak the language, where they don't have any control, and you're doing them a favor? That sucks! YOU suck. I don't even know who you are!

Kevin went silent. Nothing Betty Lou said was incorrect. What could he say? He had done a horrible injustice. "I didn't see it ... understand it. You're right though. Is there any way to fix it? What can I do?"

"You have to stop it at the source. I mean seriously, what would your mama say? Should I share this info with her? Icebreaker ...'Hey Ms. Cash, your son's really banking as an international pimp'."

It's called an awakening. It can be devastating. When you factor in death and dismemberment the stakes become extreme but the need to rectify the situation becomes imperative. DJ pondered the possible outcomes. "I can fix this," he said, and fully intended to end this horror.

"If I know one thing about Aaron James, it's that he's a vengeful bastard. If you cross him he will get retribution and it won't be pretty. How many loads have your guys lost? Do you think he's just going to write those off?" Carrie realized she could not see out the windows of the RV. They were completely fogged up . The temperature differential between the triple digits outside and the 65° inside was more than nature could handle. Carrie wasn't worried about being seen with Ronnie Dahl. She did, however, want to keep an eye on what was going on outside. It was approaching noon. DJ should be returning from San Antonio any minute.

Ronnie continued to visually undress Carrie. He had questions but for now he was enjoying the view. "Why does a luscious creature like you want to get involved in this seedy lifestyle? It seems to me you could enjoy a wonderfully comfortable existence without ever putting yourself at risk."

"Maybe, but where is the fun in that? I'll be straight up with you I'm in it for the money. The higher up the ladder you go the more money you make and the less risk you take."

"So, you want my job?"

"Au contraire. I want my dad's job, and I want you to help me get it. I can improve your situation as well."

"So why don't I just take your dad's job?"

"They will kill you. They already have a contract out on you and the assassin is living in your house. You're fucked. I, on the other hand, am not even on their radar."

"I seriously doubt Axel has any plans to eliminate me."

"See, that's where you're wrong. You're in heat and not seeing the big picture. I get it. I'm in heat too. I'm sitting here with the most powerful man in this county, possibly the state. I'm twitching to get in your britches, but I'm far enough removed from the situation I can see what's happening. You're less than 48 hours from pushing up the little daisies. Now, do you want my help or not? I think we'd make a pretty good team. With my training, connections, and your backing we could take over this whole border—Brownsville to San Diego. What do you say? Do we have a deal?"

"I'm intrigued." He went to the cabinet and pulled out a bottle of Scotch and two shot glasses. "Let's seal this deal." He poured two shots, leaned back in his recliner, and handed a glass to her. She swallowed the shot in one swallow, straddled his lap, and leaned in where he could rest his chin on her breasts.

"Now this is more like it," she said.

San Antonio traffic slowed even before they reached the loop. Kevin asked Betty Lou to dial his mom's burner phone and put it on speaker. It rang once.

"Hey Mom. We're running a bit late but should be there in about 30 minutes."

"We?"

"Yeah, I brought my girlfriend for you to meet."

"Wait," Betty Lou said. "I'm your girlfriend now? When did that happen? Nobody told me."

"She sounds lovely," Doris said.

"She is Mom. Whatever she is."

"I was hoping you could meet my new friend, but he had to

go pick up a package, so we said our goodbyes already. He seemed like a very sweet but troubled man."

"Sounds a lot like your son," Betty Lou said. "He's becoming more troubled every time he opens his mouth. I'll share with you shortly." She punched DJ in the shoulder. "I don't even like you right now, remember!"

Doris continued her story. "He owned a trucking company but wanted to retire. His family had all died so he gave it to one of his employees. That's decent of him, don't you think?"

"Wait a minute! Is his name Julio by any chance?"

"I don't know. Since we were both 'on the lam' we didn't share any names, but he said he was from Beeville."

Carrie slid off Ronnies lap, grabbed the scotch by the neck and topped off both of their shot glasses. "So how should we proceed?" she asked, holding out a hand to help Ronnie to his feet.

"I can't hurt him," Ronnie said. "We've been having too much fun together. I mean, yeah, I could probably slip him some poison but nothing violent or bloody."

"If we make it look like an accident we might get by without raising suspicions. It could buy us more time. Would an overdose be believable?"

"I've never observed any evidence of drug use. He's a health nut who works out constantly."

She contemplated the possibilities, amazed that this big pink tub of javelina lard would have any kind of relationship with an Adonis like Axel. "How about you give me some time together with him. I can make him disappear. I may need your help disposing of the body. You start thinking about that."

"So, when?" Ronnie asked.

"Is he home alone right now?"

"As far as I know."

"Okay. I got this. Don't come home until I call you on my phone. If he calls from his phone, don't answer but go home quick. We good?"

"We're good. You're sure he has a contract on me?"

"Positive! Here's the thing though. If you end up still alive, the cartel will send someone else to take you out. Removing Axel from the equation is just a temporary measure. We need to either fake your death or get you a new ID and residence, preferably out of the country.

That will mean liquidating your assets and finding a haven for you to grow old in."

"I hear some Caribbean islands are safe havens. In the meantime, are you my bodyguard?"

"It could happen. You might start looking into Grand Cayman, where it's easy to transfer money and no extradition treaty."

"My but aren't you a fountain of information!"

"If I'm going to be your bodyguard with benefits I'd prefer to do it somewhere with beaches."

When Kevin pulled into the San Antonio Greyhound terminal there were several forlorn individuals waiting on the benches. He recognized his mother only by the fact she was the only tall woman there. He got out to help her with her two overstuffed suitcases and saw the battered face and the bruises around her throat. "Oh my God, Mom! Did that bastard do this? I'll kill that son-of-a-bitch!"

"Let it go, Kevin. It's history. I have enough evidence to put him in jail for a year or two. By then I'll own the trucking company and with this one you own we can live well or sell them both and live comfortably off the proceeds. We can figure that out later. Right now, I just want peace and quiet long enough to heal. I can live comfortably in Beeville or south of San Antonio on just what I make now from my bookkeeping gig. Of course, I'd rather not have to work."

Betty Lou grabbed one of the suitcases and wrestled it into the bed of the truck. Doris grabbed the other one, but Kevin took it.

"I've got this, Mom. You need to take it easy for a while."

"I'm Betty," Betty Lou said and shook Doris' hand.

"I'm Doris. I'm not sure what happened to Kevin's manners. I thought I'd covered the manners thing with him pretty well."

"Don't worry. Now that I know I'm his girlfriend, I'll whip him into shape. Between the two of us we can probably get him dialed back in before he embarrasses the family too much. He's basically a good kid."

"Ladies, PLEASE! Let's hit the road," Kevin said. "There's some outstanding brisket and sausage waiting on us at the Beeville City Park. Let's go grab ours!"

CARRIE CALLS HOME
Carrie James

Oh my God, that was gross! *I can't wait to take that motherfucker off the face of the Earth. It was all I could do to keep from puking in his face when he was resting his fat little face on my chest. I've come up with a long-term plan that will make me rich and make him dead. It's time for self-control and planning. This next part should be more fun. I'll probably enjoy it. First, I need to pull in here and grab a pack of Marlboros. I'm not sure where the connection came from. I think it was the smell of my first victim. I say "victim", but he raped me. I remember him smelling like cigarettes. It was my second year at Sterling. I'd sneaked off campus so I knew if I reported it, it would be my fault. That's just how it is at Sterling. I didn't report it but I fixed it. The first of many. It always makes me feel like I'm making the world safer for young women, especially daughters.*

This Axel dude is supposed to be a hottie, according to Aurora. Since he's part of the cartel that participates in sex trafficking, that makes him a target in my book. I don't even need Aurora's permission. As far as I'm concerned, he shouldn't see another sunrise. I only wish I could take them all down. I will, but not soon enough!

This Better Homes and Gardens ranch looks like it's carved out of East Texas and dropped here in the West Texas desert. The damn gate cost more than a new Mercedes and it only gets fancier from there. I pull up to the control panel and punch in the code Ronnie gave me. It will let me in but not secretly and I don't know if Ronnie alerted him I was coming. It doesn't really matter. This is my specialty. I'll just roll up and knock on the door. I'm in my uniform and driving the Interceptor so no stealth is necessary. I get out, light my cigarette, and walk around the pool centered in the manicured front yard. I hear the front door open and look over just as he steps into the light. Holy Shit! Yep, he's a hottie alright.

"Can I help you officer?" He asks.

"It's patrolman ... patrolman Carrie James. I'm looking for Ronnie Dahl."

"He's setting up his festival downtown."

"I kinda figured. Interesting."

"How so"

"Well, you're not there. You've lost your speech impediment. You haven't completed your assignment. Should I go on?" *I spotted a darting of his the eyes as if looking for an escape route and wondered how powerful it must be to have people flinch at the mention of your name, not something I'd ever wanted to experience* myself, but here we are... thanks Dad!

"Come on in. The heat is brutal. I can fill you in." He walked back inside.

The fact he turned his back on me said volumes about his confidence. I unsnapped the safety strap on my holster and followed him. I'd barely stepped on the porch when I felt waves of refrigerated air roiling out the door. "I can see why you didn't go hang out in the triple digit heat today. Thing is though, my father wants to know why his assignment hasn't been carried out. He is ready to move on an acquisition and this is causing a delay."

I could almost hear the cogs turning in his head trying to figure a way to make everyone accountable without giving up too much. It wasn't working. I decided he may need some inspiration. "How about I call daddy Aaron and see how he wants me to handle this. Knowing him, I'm guessing he will give the assignment to me. He'll likely add you to his hit list and I can double my money." I pulled out my phone. "Let's check."

"Wait! I'll take care of it. I'll give Ronnie a call and get him out here. You can observe and report. Sound good?"
It might work. He's pretty pissed off but if you handle it with some class and ingenuity it might fly. He likes creativity."

He dialed Ronnie. No answer of course. He left a message. "Hey Won. Weeb god a pwoblem oud herw. Gib me a call whed you gid dis."

I explained. "This needs to be bloody and I need to be a place where I can record it. You need to be creative, so no guns. That's too easy. Do you have one?"

"I have a 22-caliber pistol."

"Where is it? Bring it to me."

"I'd rather hang on to it." he said.

I dragged the Peacemaker out of my holster and pointed it at the center of his chest. "I'm not giving you a choice." He went in the kitchen and took a small chrome-plated handgun out of the silverware drawer. "Leave it on the counter and step back."

"What are you planning to do."

"Not get shot." I put the gun in my waistband. "Is there a place I can stash my car where it won't be visible?"

"There's a stable out back. Follow the dirt road around the back of the house. There's no door but he won't go out there."

"Let's go," I said. After giving him a ride in the back seat of the cruiser and hiding the car in the stable house, we went into the house to await Ronnie's arrival. "Here's how it's gonna work," I explained. "I'm going to hide in that coat closet in the living room. You are to seduce him and then use whatever means you can to execute him. I'm a fan of the garotte myself but you're a professional, *use your best judgement. I will record it to share with Aaron so you will be golden in Aaron's mind. I'm only saving your ass because I need you on my side for some more in-depth work. If I have to bail you out again we'll have problems."*

STIRRING THE SOUP

When it is imperative that changes must be made, and mistakes cannot, you need someone with authority and experience. This group of reprobates are fortunate enough to have a few talented folks among them. The trick here is to have them all working on the same project with the same goal.

Packed tightly into the bench seat of DJ's pickup are three people who own 2 trucking companies. They are not comfortable. You would think with all those trucks they would have found a bigger one to travel in. Not so. Doris controls Acme Freight Lines of Fayetteville, Arkansas, or will soon. Her attorney assures her she can manage it however she wishes. She plans to leave most of the staff in place. She expects Kevin will end up running the sales department of both companies. It only makes sense since he's the world's biggest bullshit artist. Betty Lou knows absolutely nothing about trucking and prefers to keep it that way. She expects to temporarily run the county judge's office until the next election which is only nine months away. If they can just weed out all the corruption and put these companies on the straight and narrow, they could have a profitable enterprise. That would be fine with Doris, but she knows as well as Kevin that he will not be satisfied until he controls all the local freight in both regions. Getting all the bad guys off the payroll will be challenging but that's going to be someone else's department.

"It's unlikely that I'm in any danger." Doris said. "I don't have any desire to move back to Fayetteville. I have a good equity in my house. I can sell it or rent it. I wish I had the guy's number who paid for my hotel room and bought this phone. He seemed well educated in the trucking business."

Kevin looked over at his mom, slightly confused. "You sure this guy didn't drop a card on you or tell you his name?"

"No. We didn't share any personal information."

"If I'm not mistaken, the guy's name is Julio Ramirez. Was he a thin, short, but very regal Hispanic man?" Kevin asked.

"That describes him. Quiet and regal, I would say."

Kevin chuckles. "If I'm not mistaken that's the guy that just signed $3,000,000 worth of real estate and inventory over to me. I'm able to contact him. We still have some legal issues to work out but this also solves the housing crisis. There's a huge 4-bedroom ranch house constructed out of native limestone and oak. It's beautiful."

"Isn't he in danger?" Betty Lou asked.

"That's one of the things we're dealing with next week. He's receiving a new identity, birth certificate, passport, drivers license, everything, even the background information. Once that's done, he would be a prime candidate to run the Fayetteville operation if he's willing. I suspect he'll be bored soon and need something to do. There's going to be a major reduction in the criminal element over the next couple of weeks. If we can lay low for the next month, everything will be safe and above board. There may be a time or two we need to look the other way. I don't have a problem with it. How about you Betty Lou?"

"I won't do anything illegal. I don't see everything that goes on and I can wear blinders for the next week or two. I'm going to have my hands full anyway sorting out stuff at the office. Don't forget you are still employed there. You need to show up for work."

"No problem. You can count on me."

"That will be a first."

"Easy girl. Who brings you coffee every morning?" DJ noticed Betty Lou grow dark. She stared out the window, didn't say anything for a mile or two. He hadn't seen what she had seen, the one time Judge Kendrick went to make the coffee herself and…

She still had not reconciled with that final image.

The traffic faded away. It was less than a 2-hour drive to Beeville but barbecued brisket awaited them. The truck was crowded, and their mouths were watering, and there was a light at the end of the tunnel.

Carrie surveyed the room searching for items that could be connected to her. She didn't want to leave any obvious evidence. "So what's the plan, Big Boy?" Carrie asked. "Do you have a weapon of choice or some sort of a plan."

"I'm a professional, I've got this." Axel glared as he stomped into the kitchen and pulled a 12-inch serrated butcher knife from the cabinet.

Carrie pointed her Peacemaker at his chest. "Freeze bitch!"

Axel took the knife by the blade and held the handle out to Carrie. "Touchy much?"

Carrie refused the handle. Axel slipped the knife between two couch cushions on the back of the couch. Once he had Ronnie on the couch, he knew he could make him do just about anything. "Don't you worry about it girl, I've got this from here." Axel said.

The electronic gate sensor alerted them to Ronnie's arrival. Carrie made one last pass around the room then backed into the coat closet near the front hall. She had a full view of the rolling hills behind the house and the living area on the inside.

Ronnie blew through the front door short of breath. Sweat was pooling on his cheeks and forehead. He appeared disgruntled. "What's the deal?" he asked. He'd worked himself into a panic worrying about what could have possibly happened to make Axel drag him away from his soirée.

"The police cabe by looging for you," Axel said. "Id was dat female debuty."

"Fuck her!"

"I'b down wid dat. Thig she'd go for a two-on-one?"

Ronnie pushed his fat little hand through his receding hairline. "I think she would do whatever we paid her to do. Right now, I want to get back to my party. I hold this once a year to ensure my re-election. It's all it takes to retain my elected county commissioner position."

Ronnie began to relax as Axel removed his tee-shirt and slipped on an apron. "Led me fix you a sadwich before you head oud. I wis I could go wid you but I'b afraid I mide be pudding you in danger. Hab a sead on dee couch and I'll bwing id.

Axel delivered the sandwich and a beer in a chilled mug. He straddled Ronnie's lap and began grinding as he unbuttoned Ronnie's shirt and hand-fed the triangular sandwich. After Ronnie finished the first half of the sandwich Axel leaned in hard, thrust his tongue into Ronnie's throat, and curled his arms around Ronnie's neck. "I'b weawy goig to miss dis.

Ronnie smiled at his lover. "I'm not going anywhere."

Axel looked deep into Ronnie's eyes.

Before Ronnie could verbally respond, a knife was slicing across his throat.

Ronnie was so enthralled he didn't immediately grasp what was happening. As Axel was about to cut deeper, he heard the closet door behind him explode. The intense pain that followed stole his vision as he slid down Ronnie's bare chest, trickled with red rivulets of blood. Ronnie felt Axel's body go limp as Carrie smashed her Peacemaker into the side of Axel's head. Once was not enough. Carrie continued the destruction until the final twitches of life exited Axel's central nervous system and gray matter visibly mixed with the bone fragments of his skull.

"As far as I know they have one driver left, two if you count me," Kevin said. "That would be Raul, and he can't leave the country, can't even leave his cell right now."

Doris was squirming in the middle of the bench seat trying to find a comfortable place where she could show both Kevin and Betty Lou her attention. She didn't have any idea what was going on with the business side of the couple or the couple side of this business. "How about this guy I met, Julio? If it was his business. Maybe he could give us some pointers."

DJ shook his head. "I think he wants to get as far away from SIP and Beeville as he can possibly get. If he stays, his life is in danger. If we can hook him up with a solid ID he may be willing to help with the Fayetteville operation. I think we should consider combining the two businesses into one entity for the sake of simplicity and changing the name as well as ownership. I'm open to ideas."

"I'm fairly certain we can find more drivers from the jails once we get a few parolees back out on the economy," Betty Lou said. "I'm not certain how that is handled although I know that recommendations came from the judge and the parole board usually goes by her suggestions. If I can regain control of the parole board this may be fairly simple. We could also transfer some drivers down from Fayetteville, apparently they don't have as much work as they have drivers.

How's the equipment situation?"

"It's one of the things stressing out Jerry," Doris said. "Most of our equipment is well past its 'use by' date. Most of our drivers were owner-operators so they couldn't always be counted on to take a load. We do have competitive pay so we have some drivers we can count on."

SIP has newer equipment, but all the trucks are refrigerated box vans. We only have one long haul tractor, a three-year-old Kenworth sleeper. We have money, access to drivers, and good credit so equipment's not going to be an issue," DJ explained, "at least until the story breaks."

What did I tell you? You damn near died! He didn't get you this time. There *will* be a next time, unless I can intervene. I can. The guy sending his henchman to kill you... is my father. You're not safe here so you had better get your shit together and get ready to make your move quick. You don't have long." Carrie rolled Axel's body over on his back and gave him a final kick to the face with her cowboy boot. "Not so pretty now are you, you slimy bastard. Killing that turd made me hotter than a pistol. Any chance you could hang out for a while and toy with my affections? I didn't save you only for the money. I'm going to score some hot loving over this, if you think you can handle it."

"Challenge accepted," Ronnie said. He was grinning like a possum eating cactus thinking he had control of this luscious woman.

Carrie began to undress, starting with her T-shirt. "I need to fix that bleeding so you don't mess up anymore furniture or your clothes. And I need pictures. The damage to you and the damage to Axel after we finish doing it. Then I need to let daddy know we took out his guy and his guy failed. Grab his knife and sign that work. Make it messy. I'll take a picture of you beside him with the knife. You should be proud."

"As much as I'd love to hang out and diddle your twat, the smart thing to do would be to show up at my party so I'd have an alibi."

"You're not going to need an alibi," Carrie said.

"That remains to be seen. I'm not taking any chances."

Ronnie began cleaning up. Carrie began taking pictures.

After Carrie took pictures of the carnage to both men, appearing dead from their tussle, she put them in a folder on her phone and texted them to a rarely used number in her contacts. The name on the contact was James. The accompanying message stated: *8:00 PM Tuesday, Executive Surf Club. You only get one chance.* She sent the call *restricted.*

It's going to take more than a superficial disguise to fool Aaron. Even though they hadn't spoken in almost ten years, it's not like a family resemblance can be ignored. Possibly a hair color change, some drastic skin tone revision, maybe even blue contacts where the green eyes used to be.

This would not be a life ending meeting at least not only in the immediate timeline. Carrie does want to make him squirm, give him something to think about.

The recent update from Aurora explaining the consequences that would likely occur, would reinforce the fear and terror of being observed. She even considered not identifying herself as other than a concerned citizen but doubted that would work. Besides, she wanted to exert the power over him that he was always able to force on her even from a distance. The folder she transmitted earlier was probably enough to let him know his situation was unavoidable. Still, she wanted to be there to see his face when he realized his days were numbered.

The Immediate result was letting him think Ronnie was dead, saving her a lot of grief. She preferred to take care of that personally after having absconded with the bounty. Right now, she had to get Ronnie ready for the trip. He was having trouble giving up his Texas roots. She had to convince him that it was a matter of life and death. She had people to protect and she had people to sell out. It wasn't hard to discern who was in which group.

Once this was done she would just work for Aurora and her federal team of fixers. They suggested she run for County Sheriff since she will be credited with disassembling the cartel. At least that's the way the media will play it. Being an elected official will make a great cover for what she does as special agent for the ATF.

SHUFFLING THE DECK

Kevin will let the crime wave dissipate before he meets with Julio again. Aurora had agreed to put Julio in witness protection should he so desire. Maybe a new ID is all he needs. It is yet to be obvious. Lois suggested that Betty Lou run for County Judge. Any candidate who has Lois James's backing for political office will probably win in Bee County. Betty Lou liked the idea. Contrary to recent events it was generally a safe position, a position where she could make a difference in the lives of her fellow townspeople. She isn't sure how that will fit with DJ's plans, but he swore he was no longer interested in participating in criminal activity. He wants to run a trucking business, a legitimate enterprise.

"It's been an interesting turn of events.," Kevin said, as they sat in their breakfastI enjoying hot coffee and migas. "I've learned a lot. I'm not that guy. I'm not cut out for a life of crime. I hope you can see that and we can resume our relationship. I'm really sorry for what's happened between us. I never wanted to put you in danger."

"And yet you did," Betty Lou said. "I'm not ready to go through any of that stress and fear and danger again—ever."

Kevin reached out to hold her hand but she pulled it away. "No! I'm serious. We're not going through that again."

"I don't want to go through it again. I've learned my lesson. I'll be a good boy."

"I guess time will tell but it's going to take time. Anyway, I'm gonna be busy for a while. I have a campaign coming up. I have to reorganize the office and hire your replacement. I have to make this county a safe place to live again. This is my home. And you have a trucking company to run."

Doris agrees to Jerry's plea bargain. She won't press charges against him as long as he signs the company over to her. He will receive a reasonable payment over the next five years and abide by a restraining order. Failure to do that will result in immediate forfeiture of his company without any restitution. He agreed. Everything was done through attorneys, so they didn't even have to look at each other.

Aurora and Carrie meet at the Sidetrack to hammer out the final details of removing the cartel from the Texas borderland.

"I don't think this is the best move," Aurora said.

"He's not going to kill me. I'm his daughter. He's despicable. He's dangerous, but not to me. Besides, I have the upper hand, not just the upper hand, I hold all the cards." Carrie broke on the quarter table, a powerful break, then proceeded to sink 4 stripes before relinquishing the table.

"Impressive," Aurora said. She leaned over the table eyeing the angles, then proceeded to drop 6 solids.

"Damn Slick. It looks like I have my work cut out for me. This may be a short game." Carrie rested the cue stick on the toe of her boot and just shook her head.

Aurora ordered a round of beers. An iced metal bucket of Coronitas and a lime cut into eighths. "I've got all night. You know, the Sinaloans were keeping an eye on Bernard too. They knew Dahl was double-dealing with the Zetas. They were watching y'all the whole time. We found communication that implicates your date. They picked up his truck within 15 minutes of you dropping it off. If you hadn't eliminated him, he would have been dead within the hour of you leaving the motel. I'm convinced Aaron knew this, probably ordered the hit. You're the only reason he lived as long as he did."

"So all my art work was a waste of time?"

"No, you sped up the process."

"Glad I could help."

The beers arrived. Aurora opened two of them and handed one to Carrie. "You can help more by convincing him Ronnie and Axel are both dead even though we both know Ronnie is still breathing."

"I'll take care of that. I just need a week. I'm meeting with Daddy on Tuesday evening in Corpus. If you decide to join the fun. I may bring back-up. I have a guy who owes me a favor who may also provide cover."

"Don't get greedy. You're dealing with an evil empire. I'm not as convinced as you are about Aaron being unwilling to add you to the pile of corpses."

"You remember the guy who snuck up behind you last time we were here? I've spent time with him and I think I may use him as a back-up. He has a unique moral code for a criminal."

"Don't do anything yet. Let me vet him, okay? Let's keep this as close to home as we can. We don't officially exist, remember?

"Vet him quick. I want someone covering me when I meet with Daddy. I'm not worried about him but he surely has a crew and business partners who aren't too happy right now."

It took longer than he had hoped but Julio Ramirez became Xavier Vasquez complete with birth certificate (May 4, 1975, third gen native Texan born in Harlingen), Texas Driver's license (CDL w/ hazardous material endorsement), U.S. Passport, Visa, Mastercard, and Amex. No warrants. Registered voter. Bachelor of Business Admin from UT-RGV. He was prepared to start over. He called Kevin. "This guy's good!"

"What guy? Julio? Is that you?"

"Not anymore! The guy you hooked me up for an ID did a phenomenal job. He even set me up with a couple of bank accounts – totally legit! If you need to reach me, I'm at this number. My name is Xavier Vasques. I'm gonna chill out in Austin for a couple of weeks and regroup but I'll stay in touch."

Kevin felt a sense of relief he hadn't recently known, He took a deep breath. "Be careful."

NO WHERE TO RUN

Tuesday morning Kevin DJ Cash was elegantly attired in the gallery of Bee County courtroom #2. He served a steaming thermos of Costa Rican dark roast coffee and handed Betty Lou her Hoosiers mug. Betty Lou wore a black robe acquired from the Judge's chambers. It required no small amount of courage to wrap that respected garment over her shoulders knowing it had draped her mentor and close friend. Also present were District Judge Carson Elders who would perform the swearing in ceremony, and Artiss Pruitt, an ambitious crime / politics reporter from the *Bee Picayune*. The entire event required less than 15 minutes and County Judge Betty Lou Spencer called her first case, a DWI charge on a travelling ER nurse stopped on Highway 77 by Deputy Sheriff Carrie James. James appeared with the case prepared. The nurse was a NO SHOW. A warrant was issued, bail was forfeited, and the next case was called. Thus began a long day during which Raul Garza was released on his own recognizance. He walked out the front door of the courthouse and slipped into the front seat of Deputy Carrie James' Police Interceptor.

Ronnie Dahl was not there to celebrate at his own party. No one had seen him since Saturday morning, at least no one who admitted to looking for him. Most folks just ate the barbeque, drank the beer, and listened to the music. His phone remained unanswered, and his RV was still sitting in the Beeville City Park, plugged into city utilities with the AC fogging the windows. Dahl was running scared. Carrie James made sure she was his only contact. She'd saved his life but he didn't truly trust her. She rented a VRBO in the country near Victoria and dropped him there without his car or phone. "I stocked up your pantry and stuck a bottle of Scotch in the cabinet above the fridge. Here's a burner phone with my number saved in it. Don't call anyone else! I'll pick you up Wednesday morning. In the meantime, figure out how to quickly liquidate your assets. You'll have 72 hours to get as much cash together as possible. Can you trust your family?

"I can trust my parents, but they won't be much help. Mom's on hospice and Dad's dementia has progressed to where he's unreliable. My brother takes care of them but he isn't inclined to help me with anything that might put him at risk."

I'll be moving to Grand Cayman next week to get us situated. I know a real estate agent who can handle the sale of your ranch if that's okay. I'll book a private plane as soon as you have your ducks in a row. I've been looking at some property. I'll text you the info but just observe for now. We'll be down there soon enough."

I won't be able to come home? I hoped this would be a temporary relocation."

"Time will tell, but you should plan for it to be permanent. You've pissed off a lot of powerful people. They are not the forgive and forget type. You're safe here. Relax and use this time to plan our future. I'm looking forward to joining you on our permanent vacation." Carrie gave him a passionate kiss but almost retched when he slipped his fat, pink tongue between her lips. "Easy Big Boy! Let's consider Grand Cayman our honeymoon. Savor the anticipation! I'll see you on Wednesday.

NO WHERE TO HIDE

By the time Carrie rescued Raul from court it had already been a long day, but she counted on his help. She hoped Aurora could join in the party as well but it was a long trip. Their presence could be a matter of life and death. She dialed Aurora. "Can I count on you for backup tonight?" she asked.

"Hey girl, I thought we already had that figured out I've been in Corpus since Monday"

"Thank you so much. That's a relief. I'm bringing Raul too because I don't know if Aaron's gonna have back up or even if he needs it." Can Raul hang out with you at the restaurant? It will give you a chance to vet him. You were looking forward to that."

Aurora needed Carrie to relax. "Of Course! You need to chill, this is no big deal. You're not in any danger. Some of us maybe, but not you."

"I know," Carrie said. "It's just that I haven't seen him in over 10 years. I'm not sure he'll even recognize me. The only glimpse I've had of him was on the periphery of Carlos's funeral and that's been what, two years ago? The meeting is at 8. I plan to be there early just to observe and analyze the situation. He doesn't know either one of you by sight, so try to blend in. I'll see you there."

Carrie left the Interceptor at Lois' ranch house and took her Civic to Corpus. This was personal business even though many laws were broken in getting to this point. She didn't want to make an entrance, just be there. To be honest she wasn't sure Aaron would even show up. Surely, curiosity would get the better of him.

She dressed casually in blue jeans and a tee shirt so as not to stand out or get Raul's hormones worked up. She didn't want to be recognized from stopping by overly dressed two weeks ago, the night of the death of the federal agent. It had made local news. They pulled into the parking lot of the Executive Surf Club at 7:30 and looked for the familiar charcoal mist BMW. She didn't see it. She sent Raul in ahead. "You'll recognize Aurora. She's the red-haired woman who let you choose life or death at the Sidetrack a couple of weeks ago. She'll recognize you by the spurs. Go on inside so it's not obvious you're with me. Join her if she's here or get a booth in the main dining area if she's not."

Carrie let him get situated inside then put the folder of photos in her purse and went inside to wait at the bar. She saw Raul and Aurora sitting in a booth near the exit to the patio. Judging by the clutter and Lone Star beer bottles on the table she guessed Aurora had been here a while. She made very brief eye contact with Carrie but seemed deep in conversation with Raul.

Tuesday, after court ended, Betty Lou packed the robe in a small box. She dug through the closet in the judges chamber and found another robe still in the cleaner's bag and several pairs of shoes way to small for her. As she packed and organized the storage closet, she noticed tears forming in her eyes. As soon as she noticed, the trickle became a flood and deep sobs overtook her. Kevin tapped on the chamber door and started in.

"Go away," Betty Lou said.

"It's just me," Kevin replied.

"I know. Give me a minute. I'll be out shortly."

He went back to courtroom #2 and waited at the prosecutor's table. It was a good 15 minutes before Betty Lou emerged carrying a box full of shoes and garments. She seemed surprised to find him still there. "Can I help you with anything?" he asked.

"I just need some time to myself. Today was difficult. Go wherever you're staying and I'll see you bright and early tomorrow. We need to go over the docket for the rest of the week."

"Are you going to be okay?"

"Eventually." Betty Lou motioned toward the door indicating the conversation was over and he needed to be on his way.

As Kevin walked to the parking lot he realized he didn't have a permanent place for him or Doris to stay, or did he? He had put Doris in the trailer he lived in for the morning and called her during lunch to let her know he would be there when work was done. The logical thing to do was to move into the big house on the hill behind the shop. That felt invasive but it was what Julio wanted. Now that Julio was Xavier would he still want the same thing? He hoped so. It would have to work for now. He put Doris in the bedroom Julio's deceased wife had occupied. He didn't feel comfortable sleeping in Julio's bedroom and he definitely couldn't sleep where Lydia had lived. He grabbed blankets from the hall closet and stretched out on the couch. Sleep was a long time coming. He felt the ghosts judging him—harshly.

THE CONFRONTATION
Carrie James

It was almost 8:15 and I was getting ready to bail *on the project. Finally, his black BMW pulled into the parking lot. He parked a distance from the building even though there was ample parking nearby. I thought it strange but not enough to worry about. As he approached he appeared to be dressed in a three piece wool suit. This is the middle of summer you understand. He had to be incredibly uncomfortable. I assumed it was hiding a weapon. He had a folder with some papers randomly crammed in it and he strode purposefully towards the entrance to the Executive Surf Club. Once in the door he looked around. I was less than 8 feet from him at that point and he still didn't' recognize me. He had no idea who he was looking for or what I would look like. I saw Aurora get Raul's attention and point him out.*

I stood up and intercepted him. "Aaron James?" I spoke loud enough for him to hear me. He looked at me as if studying a statue in the museum. I let him do that.

He appeared momentarily confused. "Carrie?" I realized he may not have known that I was the one meeting him. I'd sent him a cryptic message but I never told him who I was on the phone. He acted like he wanted to smile and then his passion for control kicked in. "Let's get a table." He pulled the hostess aside and asked if there was space available in the dining room inside. She seated us without question. "I did not expect to see you here. What the hell is this all about? It looks like two of my operatives have been assassinated."

I did produce a smile. "That's correct," I said. "I'm fairly certain you already knew that, probably even before I messaged you. You can consider that a favor. One that I won't repeat for free."

"What do you mean favor? These two operatives were running my business on the Texas border. I need them and I need this trucking company that has obviously dissolved."

"You don't need these guys. They were ripping you off. If I'd let them continue, they would have probably gotten you killed. As deputy sheriff of Bee County, I'm in a unique position to help take care of family business. You're going to have to trust me, though. I can do one of two things. I can protect and assist you. Or, I have enough information to bury you and your associates under the jail for the rest of your natural lives. How do you want to play it?"

"What makes you think you have the talent to run this? I've been doing this for 20 years."

"You've gotten sloppy. I have your DNA on a dead federal agent. I have

a video of a company you own picking up that same federal agents' personal car within an hour after he'd been exsanguinated in a bizarre sex ritual, one that I set up." I have access to the federal government's special team that found that DNA and I made it disappear. OK, not disappear, but it's in hiding if I need it. That's just a sample.

"*And what do you want?*"

"*Ronnie Dahl's ranch.*

"*I want the ranch Ronnie Dahl owns free and clear, in my name. I'm OK with using it for collateral. I'll need it for legitimate business, equity, and money laundering. We will be dealing with only one cartel I don't care which one. You pick, you know them better than I do. We're NOT gonna be pitting one against the other. That's a recipe for disaster. We will be transporting NO MORE sex workers. That's non-negotiable. I've got the equipment. I've got the personnel. I've got government-trained operatives that make the Seal Teams look like kids in a sandbox. I will need protection but I will also offer protection. Together we can run the border from Brownsville to San Diego with minimal risk. You have 24 hours after which I'll be going dark for a couple of weeks. I'll need an answer. We're burning daylight. You can compete with me and we'll both lose, you more than me, or we can be a team. I'd rather be a team. What do you think?*"

"*I think it's doable but I doubt you grasp the magnitude of the operation. We'll have to establish a cooperation that we have not had for decades. I have your number. I'll call you tomorrow morning at 8:00. I'm impressed, Carrie. I never would have thought you had it in you.*"

"*The shit I've gone through in my life made me a very unique person, not someone you would like, but someone you can work with.*"

CLOSE CALL

Since he didn't sleep anyway Kevin figured he would get everyone up, make breakfast, and start the day. Then he realized everyone was just him and his mom. It was well before sunrise but he had bacon eggs and warm flour tortillas ready when he knocked on his momma's door. She was up and dressed already too.

"How did you sleep?" Doris asked.

"I didn't."

"Yeah, me either. I guess it will take some getting used to. It's been a weird few weeks."

" We'll figure it out. If you want to ride to town with me you can take my truck to go buy a car." He handed her $9000. "You can use this as a down payment or just buy a car that costs that much, whatever you want. You can't spend more than $10,000 at one time or it shows up on the bank records. We can't have that. I'm not set up that way yet."

Doris only took $200.00 and handed the rest back to him. "I'll just get some clothes today. We can go pick out a car this weekend. I'm not in a hurry."

"No problem, your call. I want you to meet up with Julio who is now Xavier. Y'all will be in charge of the trucking companies with my help where I can. You'll need to go to San Antonio for that. He can't come here it's dangerous. But I want you to be able to figure out how you want to run it. We will not be doing anything illegal." Kevin went to get dressed. He wanted to be at the courthouse by 8:00.

"Don't you find it stressful working with your girlfriend? " Doris asked.

"I don't think that's going to be a problem anymore." Kevin said." I've pretty much screwed that up beyond repair. Being in close proximity though, makes it possible for me to make amends. I hope so anyway. I really like that woman."

Betty Lou didn't get much sleep either. She missed DJ, but she knew it would be better for her mental health to keep it professional for now. Things had been too strange lately and she was scared. She was also a little angry and she had to get past that. Maybe working together would help. She went to the little I they used to frequent. She ordered a plate of migas to go and drove to work. It took everything she had to maintain a sunny disposition. She wondered if it was worth it. She had a backlog of cases to look at. Hopefully that would take her mind off other issues. She was looking forward to being a county judge, to making her county a better, safer, and more prosperous place. She arrived at the courthouse early and wolfed down the migas. She dressed in the black robe from the cleaner's bag. It gave her a feeling of authority, not something to which she was accustomed. She looked over the arrests from the long weekend who had yet to make bail, planning a way to empty the little county holding cells at the courthouse annex. She finished preparing a list for when Kevin arrived, just as he did.

He knew he was treading on thin Ice. "Good morning, Betty Lou. I made breakfast tacos this morning. I brought you a couple," he said, handing her a paper bag."

She put them on the edge of her desk. "Thanks, but I already ate. I'll hang on to them though. I may need to work through lunch. In the meantime, we need to clear out the cells at the annex. Can you check out this list of folks to see which ones we can let out with a PR bond?"

"No sweat. I'll get right on it."

"Thanks," Betty Lou gave him a cordial smile and handed him the list of perpetrators.

Aaron picked up the check. Isn't that what estranged Daddies do? Aurora and Raul had spent as much time together as they wanted to before Carrie arrived an hour ago. Aurora wanted to be outside before Carrie left in case Aaron had backup.

Aaron pulled out his phone immediately after leaving the restaurant. He spoke less than a sentence and stuck it in his pocket. Within thirty seconds a rat rod with blacked out windows pulled into the parking lot revving its nasty little engine. Aaron stepped over to the driver's side and handed a sheaf of papers through the slightly lowered window. The rat rod briskly departed. Aaron got in his BMW and left.

Aurora mentioned these actions to Carrie but had no way of knowing what they meant. Carrie offered Raul a ride back to Beeville.

Aurora had some business to finish in Corpus Christi. Before they split up Aurora ask Raul, "Are you packing?"

I have my knife and spurs, Raul said.

"I'm not sure what's happening here," Aurora said.

"I want you to have firepower. I have an extra gun in my car." She retrieved a 9mm Ruger and handed the case with clips and ammo to Raul.

Carrie's eyes widened. "I guess you vetted him."

"Obviously," Aurora had no concerns about the man at this point. "Better to be safe than sorry."

THE FLIP SIDE

Kevin and Betty Lou worked like well-oiled cogs, as if they had been working together without supervision for a while. By lunchtime six of the seven inmates in the county holding cells had been released on their own recognizance. They were local citizens without criminal records and with misdemeanor charges. One remaining inmate couldn't produce any suitable identification. Kevin suspected he was an immigrant from Mexico or Central America. Kevin's Spanish was minimal and the man would not talk to Betty Lou because he did not recognize her authority. Betty Lou decided to transfer him to the state holding cell the next day if he could not produce identification.

Kevin used his lunch time to contact his mother and Xavier. He was still having trouble with the new name but he managed to reach him on the phone. "Good afternoon, Xavier. I have a message and a possible job for you. First I want to know if you met a woman in San Antonio who owned a trucking company and was waiting for her son."

Xavier paused for a minute without speaking or breathing. "How did you know?"

"The son she was waiting for was me."

"I suspected as much but I didn't know how to ask her. That's part of the reason I was so generous."

"I appreciate you taking care of her. Would you be interested in running a trucking company in Arkansas? It's a little bigger than the one you have here but it's all legitimate, no back door loads. It's a business you're familiar with and it would pay better than the minimum wage jobs that the government would supply you with. Also, my mother would be available to train you in the specifics. I hear y'all hit it off OK. There may be a little more risk but we're working on cleaning up this cartel bullshit. The risk may be temporary. You don't have to decide right now. It's just something to think about."

As soon as he got off the phone with Xavier, he called his mother. "Hey mom. Did you find some suitable clothes?"

"I don't need anything fancy. I went to Walmart – got the basics. There's some cute little boutiques downtown I want to explore when I have more time, but I'm set for now."

"Did you get lunch?"

"I'm still working off those tacos you made this morning. I had no idea you could cook."

"Neither did I. I talked to the guy that you met in San Antonio. You impressed him. How would you feel about working with him to get these two trucking companies combined and running smoothly?"

I'm fine with it as long as Jerry doesn't give me any grief. I think I would enjoy working with Xavier."

"Let's see if I can get these criminal elements removed from our operation and we'll proceed with that plan."

It had been a long and stressful day for Carrie. She wanted nothing more than to get home to her little trailer and rest. With over an hour to drive back to Beeville, she was happy to have Raul along to help her stay awake and alert. She left Interstate 37 to take 181 to Beeville. It was a hard choice she was halfway between Beeville and her mother's house near Alice. She really wasn't paying attention after she left I-37. She was familiar with this two-lane road.

Raul was paying attention though. "Hey girl, isn't that guy following kind of close?"

Carrie looked in the rearview mirror and saw a little rat rod not much farther back than her license plate. She tapped the brake. The little rat rod pulled out to the left to pass. It was a 2 lane with oncoming traffic, bad idea.

"What the fuck! This shithead's asking for trouble. I'm in no mood. She slowed down to 50, 45, 35. The baby low-rider remained on her bumper. She pulled to the right to let the guy pass, deciding it wasn't a good time for a confrontation. As he pulled up beside her an occupant of the little car rolled the window down and pointed a rifle. "Shit!" She remembered she was in her Civic, a car she gave not a fuck about. "Get ready to rumble," she told Raul. She yanked the wheel to the left and rammed into the side of the rat rod then slammed on the brake. Fortunately, there was no one behind her. The little car had regained its position on the road but was in front of Carrie. She looked at Raul. He had the gun out and the window down. He leaned out the passenger door, shot out the back windshield, shot where he figured the gas tank would be, and shot the left rear tire which caused the car to slide back to the other side of the road. Just as it was directly in front of her she hit the gas and pushed it off the road. It went down an embankment rolled a couple of times and stopped in the ditch, right side up. She was still behind it but up on the shoulder of the road. She pulled the Peacemaker out from under the seat. Raul jumped out with the 9mm Ruger and they approached the little rat rod.

Carrie hollered, "Get your asses out of the car with your hands up!" She still wasn't sure how many people were in the car. The driver exited the car with his right hand up and his left hand still in the car. "Slowly show your other hand," Carrie screamed. The left hand came out of the car swinging a machete. Carrie shot the man in the knee totally against regulations, but effective. She would have preferred to kill him, but she needed information he had. She moved forward with the handcuffs, Raul covering her. Just then another man jumped out of the passenger side door and pulled a gun. Raul shot him in the face. He went down. Raul went to the passenger side to make sure the man was incapacitated. His face was gone. He was incapacitated.

"Hollow points," Raul said. "That Aurora girl you run with is a badass."

"Yeah, but you already knew that."

"Drop the weapon." Carrie said to the remaining punk. He did. Carrie handcuffed him. "You're lucky to still be alive. If you want to stay that way, you're going to answer these questions quickly and accurately."

He bent over against his car holding his knee with both hands. "No Habla Espanol, he said.

"Bullshit!" Carrie screamed. There was a violent explosion as Carrie shot his other knee.

Raul walked around the back of the rat rod and saw the Nuevo Leon, Mexico plates. " I'm gonna kill you too if you don't start answering the lady's questions. Comprende?" He dragged the body around the car on the side away from traffic. The living but injured tattooed punk spit toward Raul then his lights went out as Carrie slammed the Peacekeeper against his head. She slapped him back to consciousness with the back of her hand. Now! Start by telling me who you work for!

"Aaron James and Ronnie Dahl right now, but we hire out."

"To whom?"

"Whoever can pay."

"Even me?"

"What's the job?

"Ronnie Dahl. Did he pay for the hit on that county judge in Bee County?

"What difference does that make now?"

"Life and death... in your case."

"Ronnie Dahl paid for that hit and the method. It cost him a bundle to specify the method plus we had to sit on the target for a while. Now my brother is dead and my car is trashed."

"Tears the size of horse turds are rolling down my cheeks," Carrie said.

Raul went through the car and found the bundle of papers the brothers received from Aaron. "Check this out!" He tossed the folder to Carrie. It contained several photos. On the back of the photos were addresses, names, a dollar amount (all five or more digits), and a date.

"It appears to be a hit list," Carrie said. A couple of the pictures were X'ed out, including Lydia Ramirez and Judge Kendrick. Julio had a big red question mark on his face.

"Well lookie here," she said. "I'm in here. Axel's in here too! So is Sheriff Carranza. It looks like some major restructuring is going on. There's also a note to try and recruit you and Kevin Cash but just as drivers apparently. I'm worth a bundle! I wonder if I turned myself in, would they let me live long enough to spend the money."

"I'm not driving for those assholes," Raul said. "I think it's time for a hostile takeover."

"Just what I was thinking." Carrie held the barrel of the Peacemaker against the side of the punk's head. "Do you have any more information that could help us out."

"I ain't tellin' you shit!"

Carrie bent down beside the living punk and whispered, "I'm going to let you live, against my better judgment. You go back and tell your boss that he just made a huge mistake and the war is on. If you live long enough to be found here that is. If not, they'll figure it out pretty soon anyway. Here's something to remember me by." She slammed his head into the side of his car with her boot and left him lying unconscious on the shoulder of 181 with a trickle of blood running from his nose and left ear. "Oops, got a little out of hand there didn't I. Think he'll make it?"

Raul pointed at him with his gun, moved his body around with his foot, and ran the spurs across his chest without drawing a physical response. "Not looking too good for this guy."

"It's a shame. I really would have liked to run into him again." Carrie retrieved her handcuffs, went around to the front of her car, and looked underneath. "Nothing leaking. I hope she'll start. Looks like I'm gonna need a new car though. I think this one's totaled. It was only worth about $20 anyway." They continued home.

Carrie woke Wednesday morning to the phone ringing. She picked it up, saw that it was Ross and it was only 7:45 in the morning. "Damn." She answered. "Good morning, Ross, It's early."

"Yeah I was wondering if you could do something for me on your way into work this morning."

"I was going to call in. I'm up now though so what do you need."

Ronnie Dahl's damn RV is still sitting in the middle of City Park sucking city juice and I can't get ahold of him. I'm going to have it impounded and he can deal with it whenever. Could you go by and meet the tow truck driver, make sure everything's done by the book. I don't want him crawling up my ass later. I'll tell you what, after it's hooked up and hauled off could you go out to his ranch and see if you can make contact, find out what the hell's going on.

"Sure Boss." She started coffee. She was experiencing terminal exhaustion at this point and needed something to get her moving. This was the break she was looking for, however. It would allow her to get the story straight without any questions left unanswered.

No sooner had Ross hung up the phone with Carrie, than Jake called.

"Hey Jake, what's up?" Ross said. "Do you have any news on the situation we've got over here with the judge's murder and other issues of concern?"

"It looks like you've opened one hell of a can of worms over there. We picked up a couple of Mexican nationals off the side of the road who fit the description of the suspects in the judge's murder. They were quite dead. One was shot. One was shot and beaten to death, It's a mess. There's also been a lot of activity south of the border between the Sinaloa and the Zeta cartels. This could blow up if we're not careful. So what can you tell me?"

"Well since last I talked to you the owner of our local produce trucking company disappeared and one of the county commissioners has gone dark. The commissioner I suspect has cartel ties, but I can't prove it yet. I just sent one of my best deputies out to the commissioner's house to see what's up. I should know something in less than an hour."

"So Ross, old buddy, when are you going to come work with

the good guys. There's a polished mahogany desk waiting for you over here. Good benefits and a little action when you want it. We could use somebody with a finger on the pulse of this area."

"I think you overestimate me. I'm just an old cop waiting for retirement, not some adrenaline junkie."

"Well, there's a spot waiting for you if you want it. Just let me know."

Kevin took the day off early to move his stuff from the Airstream into the main house. Standing around the office with nothing much to do was making Betty Lou nervous. He figured he'd give her a break and call it a day. As he was loading some personal items in his truck, a small woman with caramel skin and piercing black eyes approached him with a glowing smile. He thought he'd seen her recently but couldn't quite remember where.

"Hi, I remember you from the swearing in the other day. You're the parole officer. I'm doing a series for the paper on the local legal system and the opportunities for employment. I was wondering, can I buy you lunch?"

Kevin could feel the energy exuding from this young lady and her smile was infectious. It helped that he was ravenously hungry. "Sure, there's a little I down on the square. We could walk there if you want."

"Sounds great. My name is Artis Pruitt. I work for The Bee Picayune. I've heard you go by DJ. So are you actually a DJ?"

"I've been known to spin a record or two. Working for the legal system doesn't give me a lot of time for that anymore."

"That's OK. I'm here about the legal system part anyway. Maybe if we hit it off I can hear more about your musical taste."

Kevin was enthralled with this woman from the start. He never even stopped to consider what her motives might be. We'll see what the future holds in that respect.

Ross put his feet up on his desk. He had not expected a headhunter call. He was in fact looking forward to retirement. Unfortunately, he was about 15 years too young. Jake had said "desk job," a very appealing position. He had questioned whether he was cut out for law enforcement work since he began the career. Mostly he was just following in his wife's footsteps. I wonder what she would think of my decision if I quit. He assumed she would be OK with it. It would make their dinner conversations a little less interesting but that's something he could live with. The more he thought about it the more interesting the idea was. This county wants diversity? He'll give them diversity, making sure Carrie James becomes the new sheriff. Not hard to do with her mom being a major political figure in the region. As he rested his boots on the desk and drifted into this neverland of never being an officer of the law again; never having to draw his gun again; never have friends being arrested again; never having to get up in the middle of the night again to chase somebody's cows back into their pasture. It sounded wonderful.

When the phone rang he was ready. He knew it would be Carrie. He wasn't prepared for what she had to say.

"Holy crap Ross! It looks like a war zone out here. There's a guy out here who's been beaten to death. It's been a while; he's starting to smell rank. This is the most violent crime scene I could possibly imagine. I don't know who the victim is but it's not commissioner Dahl. His ID says Axel Prince but it looks fake, and I don't think commissioner Dahl could have done it. This is too brutal of a job for a fat little fuck like him. There's no sign of him but his car's here. There has to be another person involved."

"Damn," I didn't need this on top of everything else today. I'll send out a forensics team. Can you hang out there till they arrive?"

Carrie hated lying to the one person who had always been nothing but honest with her. "I can, but I need to let you know that I need about a week to 10 days off so I can go back to Austin and tie up all my loose ends there. I lived there for seven years, and I just walked out one day. I owe some folks explanations and money and I have stuff there I need to bring home. When I get back I'll be 100% whatever you need, but I have to take care of this."

NO MONEY DOWN

The most qualified forensics team Ross had access to was in San Antonio and employed by the Texas Rangers. He called Jake mostly because he had the number on speed dial.

"Damn, that was quick," Jake said. "Was my offer that good?"

"You're not going to believe this! I had my deputy stop by this county commissioner's ranch and she found a body, somewhat decomposed. It wasn't the commissioner but he's in the wind. I'd like y'all's forensics team to handle this one. It's going to be in the media so it needs to be a spotless assessment. Can you get someone out there? I have my deputy sitting on it until I can get a team on site."

"It will take over an hour to get my guys out there but text me the info and I'll put a priority on it.

"Thanks, Jake. I owe you one."

" Consider my offer."

"Will do!"

At Dahl's ranch the AC was still pumping out frigid air. Carrie grabbed her notebook and phone, deciding to take care of business while she waited on forensics. First, she called the car dealership. " Jack Talbot, please," she told the receptionist."

He picked up in seconds. "What can I help you with?"

"This is Carrie James. I need a used four-wheel drive SUV in the $18K to $22K range. Low mileage, dependable. I'm paying cash so I want to have all the paperwork ready to sign. I'd like to be in and out of there in 20 minutes.

I can do that but wouldn't you rather have a new Ram truck?

"No, and I don't want pitched to. Here's a chance for you to make an easy buck or two. Don't blow it!"

"Gotcha! How about a three-year-old 4-Runner with 40K miles, and all the bells and whistles, leather, sunroof, 8-thousand-pound towing package. I can let you drive it off the lot for $18K."

"Why so cheap?"

"I'd love to say that it's because I'm enraptured by your beauty and you're a first responder. All that's true, but the real reason is because it's a weird color and I've had it on the lot for over a month."

"and what color is that?"

"Burnt Orange with a white top, had to be a custom job."

"Ha! No problem. I'm a UT alumni, so I'm your girl for this one. Detail it out and text me the bottom line. I'll have a bank draft sent to you. I'd like to pick it up this evening."

Will Do!"

"One more thing, and this is an odd but necessary request."

"I'll be arriving in an 89 Civic that's completely trashed. I have a clear title in my name, but I need the car to disappear and my ownership removed from the records. Crush it, bury it, I don't care. Please just make it disappear."

"Hmm. I don't know if we can do that.?"

"You can. You're a professional. Go ahead and mark it up $20K if you need to."

"You're right. I am a professional, so just give me the extra two grand in cash, so there's no record. I'm sure you understand."

"I do – I'll see you this evening."

Next, she needed to touch base with Ronnie. If he got antsy, he could screw up everything. She needed to keep him where she needed him. She dialed the burner phone she gave him.

"Carrie? Is that you? What's going on?"

"Chill out Ronnie. I've got everything under control. I just needed to hear your voice. I miss you. We're going to the Caymans Friday to get a place to stay, temporary but luxurious, like a honeymoon suite. I was thinking, we could go into Alice on Friday and get married. We'll have to be under the radar. It might be tough because everyone knows you. I can't wait to be Mrs. Dahl."

"I don't get to Jim Webb County that often. Not everybody knows me. I could take you out to dinner."

"That sounds lovely. We could spend the night together if you can decide on a temporary abode and we could get to know each other a little better," Carrie suggested. She needed to keep him needy. The best way is by being naughty.

"How soon before we travel?"

"I'm shooting for Friday. I've already set up the checking account and savings accounts. If you can tell me how much you think you'll be bringing or sending I can make sure everything goes smoothly so your money will be waiting for you when you arrive. In the Cayman financial system they don't ask a lot of questions, but you do have to have your paperwork in order. Once you get established down there you can start investing. I know you like to play with your money, and you're good at it. What better place to play with money than a beautiful Caribbean beach. I'll have to sign some stuff on your behalf to get your money down there, that's why I'm going this weekend. What I'll need from you is a power of attorney. I can't wait to be Mrs. Dahl. Have you had a chance to look at any property down there? I emailed you a couple if you can get to them through that burner phone. If not, whatever you do, don't go back to your house. I'll text you the account numbers as soon as we get off the phone you can put however much you want in whichever account you prefer. I wouldn't put more than $50,000 in your checking account though. People will try to scam you for your money if they know you're packing the big bucks."

"Well haven't you've been a busy girl?"

"I want us to have an easy life. You've worked hard and put yourself in a lot of danger. You deserve a break. And I can't wait to get you in the sack. I want to show you my secrets. I also want to find out your magic powers "

"I'm looking forward to that too. If we can get one free day where I can go to the bank and to my attorney's office I can probably come up with about $18,000,000 to transfer now. Later, when we sell the ranch, we'll have more. I was thinking I'd keep some in the United States."

"Bad idea Ronnie. Don't do it! They can trace you and they have the people to do it. They'll just seize it. You need to get out of the US—be somebody else. In fact, let me work on a new ID. You put all this in the Caymans under a different name, you'll be invisible. How does that sound?"

You could almost hear the pain in Ronnie's voice when he spoke; in his breath; even before he spoke. "I'm really not going to be able to ever come home, am I?"

"Not safely. It would be in your best interest to be an expat somewhere. It doesn't get much better than the Cayman Islands. I can help you make an amazing new life. Trust me. Now get busy rounding up that cash. We are going to live high on the hog." Carrie had no problem leading Ronnie on, making him believe that he had scored the golden ticket. The hard part would be when she had to cuddle up with him in the bedroom kissing his sweaty lips, when his pudgy pink fingers slipped into her private places, when his slimy little tongue parted her lips. But it was all for a compelling cause, her personal life of luxury. Now that she knew her father was willing to take her life, she only needed to figure out a way to eliminate Ronnie and Aaron in the most disgusting, devastating, and embarrassingly immoral way possible. It may take extended insight.

She began pacing, going through the rooms, peeking into closets. She found a set of keys in the garage. They held entrances to the outbuildings. She wondered what was in them, but waiting on the forensics team was a priority. She would have plenty of time to explore the ranch after it belonged to her.

She looked at the patio chairs. They were unpainted cast iron. Each weighed about 40 lbs. She realized Ronnie didn't spend much time outside. Those chairs would either be scalding hot or freezing cold 90% of the year. She chuckled under her breath thinking how she may need to find a suitable place for Ronnie's body. With 1600 acres it shouldn't be a problem. Little did Ronnie know he might never see the Caymans, would likely never even see the Caribbean, and if there was any way possible, none of his appendages would ever enter her body.

CHAPTER WTF

Carrie was into her second hour of waiting on the forensics team. There was very little she could do from Ronnie Dahl's kitchen that had not been accomplished. The scent from the body decomposing on the couch nearby was interrupting her train of thought, yet she persevered. Time was of the utmost importance. She felt like a prestidigitator working with hand magic, making things come true that should never have happened. As soon as introductions were made and the chain of evidence secured, Carrie was out the door and down the road. NONE. TO. SOON. She felt overwhelmed and needed someone to give her advice, someone with experience in these matters. She dialed Aurora.

"I'm a little concerned. Things seem to be going haywire." She could hear the desperation in her own voice as her confidence melted away.

"That happens occasionally," Aurora said. "Let's look at what we've got and what we need to do. Is this a secure line?"

"As far as I know the line is secure. It's my cell. My problem is I have Ronnie Dahl stuck in a VRBO out in the country. He's getting nervous and he doesn't like the way things are going. I'm afraid he's gonna crack and do something stupid."

"Judging from his background you should have planned for that. It was inevitable." Aurora chuckled a little under her breath. "Do you think he has the initiative to do something stupid?"

"Not sure. He doesn't have transportation, he has a phone, and he's nervous. But he has incentive."

Aurora contemplated for a moment. "I think we'll be OK. He's not known for taking the initiative. That's why he's somebody else's sidekick. And you're a pretty good incentive."

"I'm more concerned about Aaron. I now know he would have no problem stacking me on top of the pile of bodies he's accumulated. I might need your help with him. Somebody that he doesn't know needs to take him down. He would be hard to get to for someone he knows. To start with I need him to be distracted next Friday. I'm going to bring Ronnie into town to get a marriage license and he insists we have dinner. If I turned him down, he would know something was up. Also, I need a private plane that evening with a pilot I can trust who knows what's going on. Can you help me with that?"

"That should be doable. I tell you what, I'll give you backup if you need it, but this is your gig. I won't step in unless you are overwhelmed. This job you're going to be doing requires a lot of creativity. It's necessary to think on your feet. That's part of what makes it exciting. I'm certain you can do this, but since this is your first assignment, I won't let you fail. All I ask is that we don't travel to the Caymans together. I'll be there in the periphery when you land. Otherwise, you don't know me."

"Thanks Aurora. I won't let you down."

"By the way, Ross's birthday is in a couple of weeks. We're going to have a party when you get back from Austin. I guess it will kind of be a going away party for you too since you'll be moving to the Caymans (Nod nod wink wink)."

"I wouldn't miss it!"

THE DISAPPEARING I

Jack Talbot met Carrie at the door, not the door of the dealership but the door of her Civic. "Leave the key in it. It's fine where it's at. Join me in my office."

"Hold on a minute," Carrie said. "Let me check out this beauty you hooked me up with. Gotta admit that's one weird paint job. The burnt orange hood and the running boards give it a kind of interesting look. But it's a 4Runner, probably a good truck. Let's do this deal." She took a walk around it, kicked the tires as a comedic gesture. She led the way to the office, pulled an envelope out of her pants pocket, and handed it to Jack. He peeked in the envelope and ruffled through the money with his thumb.

"We good?" Carrie asked.

"We're good." Jack stuck the money in his pocket. "I put a new set of high-performance tires on it. It had the originals."

"Thanks," Carrie said.

"The papers are ready to sign. Let's set a new record." Ten minutes later Carrie circled the dealership in her new ride. The Civic was nowhere to be seen. She drove toward her mom's house enjoying the smooth, powerful drivetrain, knowing she was prepared for any terrain she might encounter. She briefly flashed on how convenient it would be when hiding bodies. That reminded her of something. She pulled out her phone and called her father.

"Hey Daddy, I missed your call this morning. Weren't you going to call at 8:00? You must have thought some unfortunate incident had befallen me. I guess you were wrong, very fucking wrong." She hung up before he had a chance to respond and chose not to answer when he immediately called back.

Betty Lou's premonition had come to fruition about saving breakfast nutrition to maintain her condition and work through lunch, or so it seemed. Partly she wanted to know what the brown woman who had observed in her courtroom all morning did when she dismissed DJ for lunch. As expected, the woman followed DJ out.

"Please be back on time," Betty Lou instructed.

"You can count on me."

"What, are you an abacus?"

DJ saluted her honor with one single finger. Artiss, a few steps behind him, snickered under her breath, barely loud enough for DJ to hear. She picked up the pace to join him. "Is that how you respond to authority? Aren't you afraid you're going to lose your job?

"I don't need this job. I'm just helping out until Betty Lou finds someone to take my place."

"Still, shouldn't you exhibit a modicum of decorum?"

"Yep, definitely somebody who plays with words. So how do you like working at the newspaper?"

"Honestly, there's not much happening around here. It's hard to find enough to write about."

"No that's where you're wrong. There are a lot of skeletons in a lot of closets around here, new ones popping up every day"

"Really? I haven't found much why don't you give me a clue?"

"I can't talk about it officially but if I were you, I'd look at the county commissioner and some of his holdings. You might also want to check out this prison system we've got around here. You might find that it feeds a lot of local businesses' employees. Not necessarily a bad thing, but it's ripe for corruption."

"Would this judge be a part of that?"

"Nah, she's as clean as they come. Worst thing she does is party on the weekends.

"We pretty much all do that," Artiss said. I've been known to crack open a beer or two.

"Yeah, that's kind of my thing too," DJ agreed. "She's more into the herb superb."

"I can't say I haven't tried that, but it just makes me sleepy."

"That's what I mean. I don't want to sleep through the party. Let's grab some lunch and maybe we can follow up on this party idea for this coming weekend."

Carrie appreciated the invisibility that the new ride gave her. She planned to stop by her Airstream and pick up some clothes, her passport, and some travel information before she reached her mom's house. She decided to play it safe and phone Raul before stopping by her house. He picked up on the second ring. "Hey Raul, I need to go by my house and get some stuff, but I figure since I'm still alive somebody's watching me. Have you seen any activity that's unusual and or directed at my house?"

Raul chuckled. "Well I haven't seen any tattooed guys driving rat rods in the neighborhood. I have seen a black Escalade that I didn't recognize cruising slowly through the circle, four times so far since I got home. So, no, I wouldn't recommend stopping by. You might die, and I would cry."

"Thanks for the update, weirdo. OK, you're right. I would cry if you died too. So, don't. I'm heading out to my mom's. First, I have to pick up a few items from my house. I bought a new car so I'm invisible, sort of, but if you could stand lookout while I get my stuff out, I'd owe you a favor. I'm going to be out of town for a few days. Not saying where I'm going but I'll be safe."

"I still have Aurora's Ruger. You want me to shoot this guy that keeps circling your house?"

"Nah, it would make too big of a mess. I'm in a hurry to get out of town and I don't want to deal with that sort of crap right now."

"How about if I just break his legs?"

Carrie snickered, "If it floats your boat, knock yourself out. Happy hunting. "You stay safe too and I'll see you in a week or so." She was in the Airstream for less than two minutes. She acknowledged Raul sitting on the tailgate of his dually; one hand on the Ruger and the other on a Bud Light. He saluted her with the beer hand. She nodded and put the 4-Runner on the highway, stomped on the accelerator, and let the horses run free.

~~CARRIE + RONNIE 4 EVER~~

It wasn't something she could explain to her mother. She had never intended to get married. Even now, the thought turned her stomach, killed her appetite, and caused a tremor in her hands. She had to hide for a bit. Rather than be honest with her mom, she decided to just show her the new 4-Runner and let that be the reason for the visit. Mom always asked questions. On the way out she stopped by Ronnie's ranch. Her intention was to pick up a suit for him to get married in. When she got there the gate was locked with a padlock. She wasn't walking a quarter of a mile to the house and back in this heat, carrying a dark polyester suit. She decided to go on without the suit, probably smell like dead people anyway.

She took Mama for a short drive to show off all the bells and whistles and the weird paint job.

"It's about time," Lois said. That Civic had seen its better days. This is definitely an eyecatcher!"

"Yeah, I got a great deal on it because of the paint job but I kind of like it."

"So what brings you out here to the boonies. I hardly see you anymore."

"Just keeping you in the loop. I'm going to Austin this week, probably staying for 7 to 10 days. I just need to tie up all the loose ends. I don't think I'll be going back to college anytime soon. I've got my life pretty well lined out here."

"Yes, you seem to have grabbed the bull by the tail."

"You have no idea. I think I may be the luckiest girl in the world. I've been offered a job with the ATF. I've also had my name thrown in the bucket for the Bee County Sheriff when Ross retires. It's not as exciting and it doesn't pay as much but I would be able to stay here locally. That's worth something." As she turned the 4Runner back into the driveway she stopped and looked at the house she was raised in and thought about Lois rattling around in there by herself. It brought a melancholy feeling. Lois had never been one to sit around and stagnate. Carrie was certain Lois would be in the middle of local politics as soon as she had a chance to take a breath.

Lois looked at her daughter and saw the grown woman she had become. "Somewhere in there I hope you have time to furnish me with some grandchildren," Lois said.

"Don't hold your breath. It's not on my agenda."

"Maybe someday you'll change your mind." Lois felt Carrie's urge to change the subject. Now didn't seem a good time to analyze Carrie's alternative relationship status. "Are you going to Austin tonight?"

"Tomorrow, but I mostly just came by here to show you my ride and pick up some clothes. Since I'm going to be gone a while I don't want to spend all my time at the laundromat. I'll probably leave sometime in the morning after breakfast. That was a hint by the way, the breakfast thing."

Lois chuckled. "I think we can handle that."

FALLING IS LIKE FLYING
WITHOUT THE WINGS

"**We have to take the course, Ronnie**. Otherwise, there's a 72-hour waiting period. I can't wait that long. I need you now." Carrie said, breathing heavily into the phone. "Besides I have a plane chartered for 9:00 tomorrow night. I can't wait for you to see the place I picked out for our honeymoon."

"So you'll be here when?" Ronnie asked.

I'll be there before 6:00 in the morning. Have your stuff packed up and be ready to go. We'll be on a tight schedule for the next couple of days. The course is 8 hours long, then we have to get the license, then we have to go to the Justice of the Peace. It's going to take a bit. We won't actually get to the Caymans until day after tomorrow but that's better than waiting 72 hours."

"I can't believe I'm doing this."

"We don't have to if you don't want to," Carrie moaned like her heart was breaking.

"No! It's not like that! I just can't believe how lucky I am. I never thought I'd be married to such a goddess."

Carrie giggled, not something she was good at. Hopefully she won't have to do it much longer. "Did you get those account numbers I sent you? I decided to go with two separate banks in the Cayman Islands. I opened the credit union account for our personal banking and the Cayman National Bank is for your business. They both had good ratings especially for business to business transactions. There's a Trust Bank in the financial center that you may want to talk to when you get there. They can handle larger deposits without too much scrutiny from government entities."

"It's not like I had very much to do here, so I've already arranged for 32.5 million worth of transfers. There's quite a bit more but I wanted to find out details before moving it."

"You're so good at this. You're going to have to teach me. Anyway, I've got a lot to do to get ready. This is a big move for me.

"For the sake of convenience I went ahead and kept Axel's name for domestic transactions." Ronnie said. "He has such an ambiguous ID."

You're so smart. We're going to have such a good life. I'll see you before 6:00 in the morning Be rested and ready."

Lois had breakfast on the table by 4:00 AM. Chorizo and egg tacos with extras for the road. Carrie was out like a whirlwind hugging her mom goodbye, hopping in the 4Runner and letting the horses fly. She backed up to Ronnie's vacation rental at 5:45AM. At 5:50 they were on the road. They were waiting at the courthouse door in Jim Webb County when it opened at 8:00. The course they had to take was an 8-hour DVD set. They did the first half and broke for lunch. Ronnie went to the county clerk's office where he'd picked up the DVD and talked to an intern there. "We finished this," he said.

"No way," the kid said. "It's an 8-hour course. You must spend the 8 hours watching it."

Ronnie whispered in Carrie's ear, " You said you wanted me to teach you how to make things happen with money. Here's lesson 1." Ronnie pulled out two $100 bills and handed them to the intern. "We watched the whole thing, right?"

The kid took the money and handed him the marriage license. They walked across the street to the Justice of the Peace and finalized the deal. Mr. and Mrs. Ronald J. Dahl went for steaks in Alice, Texas.

"I guess that takes the pressure off the time crunch," Ronnie said.

Carrie bolstered, "You're amazing!"

Carrie had just punctured her pink bloody steak with a steak knife when her phone rang. She looked at the number but didn't recognize it. It wasn't, however, blocked. She started to answer and thought better of it. "Ronnie, do you have that burner phone I gave you?"

"Yeah, why?"

"I need to borrow it back." He handed her the phone so she could punch the number in that had come in on her phone. A familiar voice answered, "Good afternoon Ms. Dahl. How do you like your new husband?" Aurora asked.

"What the hell. I've only been married for 45 minutes…"

Aurora interrupted, "33 minutes … and if I know, you can bet Aaron knows. You better get your asses moving. I have a plane waiting at Alice International Airport. It's paid for and the pilot has an envelope for you. Do not open it in front of Ronnie. It contains 2 pills; a 10mg Valium, a Rohypnol and some contact info for one of our operatives stationed in the Caymans. You'll know what to do, but only make contact if an emergency arises." The call disconnected.

"Shit!"

"What's wrong," Ronnie asked.

"We've been located. We need to pack this meal and hit the road."

Ronnie called for the waitress. "Something's come up. Can you pack this to go?"

They were on the run again.

DJ was entranced by the level of enthusiasm Artiss exuded. He was unsure if her energy was part of her job description or her true personality. In any case, he needed to be careful or he would end up neck deep in another relationship. He struggled with maintaining the one he had already. Complicating his life was not on the agenda. "Actually, can I get a rain check on lunch. I need to help my mom buy a car. She's new in town and I'm afraid somebody might take advantage of her."

"That's fine. I appreciate that you put your family first. I'll meet you back here for the afternoon session. Maybe we can talk about doing something this weekend, if you're up to it."

DJ was unsure if this was a challenge, a flirt, or just being friendly. He needed to tread lightly. "Sounds like fun."

When Carrie reached the private section of Alice International Airport she pulled her truck inside the one hangar that was open. Her pilot was waiting. She was struck by how small the twin-engine Cessna was, but you can't be choosy when you're in a hurry. The pilot jogged over to give her a hand with the baggage. "I'm Roger. Please, no jokes about the radio. I understand you're in a hurry. We can take off in 18 minutes if you're ready. I already have clearance from the tower." He slipped Carrie a small brown envelope.

Ronnie looked at the plane. "Oh, hell no! We can't go anywhere in that." Ronnie appeared as if he may cry.

"It's our ride, Babe. Either that or we die. Well, you die. Don't worry. It's safe. I take these all the time." Sometimes a lie is the easiest. "I have something that will help you relax anyway."

Ten minutes later Roger has gone through his pre-flight check and taxied to the end of the runway. Carrie opens the little brown envelope and hands Ronnie a small blue pill. "This is a Valium. It will help you relax. If this isn't enough, I have something stronger, but let's try to stay awake if we can. It's a four-and-a-half-hour flight, mostly over water. There's not much scenery. Our perfect new life is on the other end of the journey. It only gets better from here."

As they leave the ground, the engines surge and one wing tip dips toward the runway. Ronnie's butt clinches and his arms grab the armrests as if to break them loose. "You should probably just give me that other pill," Ronnie says.

Carrie sighs, "So I'll be here all by myself for the duration?"

"It's too loud in here to hear anything anyway," Ronnie hollers. "I'm with you in spirit. I'd just as soon not experience the flying part."

"Suit yourself."

"What's this?" Ronnie asked when she handed him the other pill.

"Does it matter? Just go to sleep."

"Since I may be driving back and forth to Fayetteville frequently. It would probably be wise to go with an economy car, don't you think?" Doris asked.

"You should get what you're comfortable with. What car have you always wanted? You're at a place in your life now where you can fulfill your desires."

"I've never seen the point of cars as a status symbol, and I don't need brand new. Something a couple of years old would be fine as long as it's dependable." It was over 45 minutes before Doris drove off the lot in a 2-year-old Toyota Corolla.

"You're set. I have to get back to work. I'm gonna be late."

"Now that I have transportation, I'm going to go do some shopping at these little boutiques downtown. I'll see you this evening."

RONNIE CONTEMPLATES
HIS GOOD FORTUNE

Is it hard to talk? *It seems difficult to talk. So loud. My tongue. ... dry! So rough. I can adjust. I need something to eat but I want to pick a place after we land. It's interesting to see all the agricultural grids from up here. Pretty squares of green and yellow. Roger said we would be flying at roughly 8000 feet that's more than a mile, I think. We are much closer to the ground. Whatever."* I look down at the water. Wait! Wasn't that land a second ago? It seems like a mirror finish. We're going to cook in our own house tonight. At least the one we'll be living in. I can't believe she agreed to be my wife. I don't care if she is marrying me for my money. Those pills are making me so confused. I know Carrie will take care of me. I'm a lucky man. She's taking off my seat belt, holding my hand, running her hand down the front of my chest lower... lower... Feels so good. It's hot in here. I don't think the windows open. Roger's not paying attention. Open the door. Let some air in. We are birds. Her warm breath chirps in my ear, "let's fly together." Roger banks a hard right, dumps me into the beautiful sky. I weigh nothing, The noise is dying down and I only feel the breeze. So beautiful. Carrie ... Carrie? Carrie, are you here? You have to see this. Where are you? Wait. Am I falling? What is this? It's getting so quiet. So quiet. Blue above and blue below. We'll be together ... somewhere in the blue.*

"He'll hit the water at about 475 mph, maybe a little less on account of wind resistance. Definitely not survivable," Carrie said.

Roger examines the instrument panel. "He won't be going near that fast., too many other factors. But you're right, not survivable. He'll have almost half-a-minute to contemplate it too. You'd be surprised how long a half-minute is in situation like that."

This guy is dark! Carrie thought. She shivered ever so slightly considering they were alone in an airplane 8000 feet above the Gulf of Mexico. He had never turned to look at her. He'd never even removed his cap or sunglasses. It may be time for some small talk to ease the tension. "So, how long have you known Aurora?" she asked.

"Who?"

"Aurora, the woman who hired you."

"I don't know Aurora."

"Well, who hired you then?"

"Aaron. Aaron James. I thought y'all were family."

Not the answer she'd expected. It left her no choice but to tread lightly. "Yeah, he's my dad but I didn't expect him to handle such a minor detail."

"Minor detail? We just killed a guy! Your husband if I'm not mistaken. If that's a minor detail, you're one cold bitch!"

Carrie was not used to fear as a reaction to even her most traumatic life events, but this caused her to flash into an ice-cold sweat. She barely succeeded at swallowing the rush of bile. "So, what's next. I'm obviously out of the loop here.?"

Roger was quiet for a moment. "I should probably stop talking. It seems I've already ruined at least part of your surprise."

DJ spent an inordinate amount of time picking out clothes for an evening discussing his favorite tunes, maybe because he wanted to experience the simplicity and raw energy of an earlier time, or maybe the energy was radiating from the young woman who had captured his fancy. Had he been honest with himself he would have realized his recent failure with Betty Lou damaged his confidence. He was living with his mother for Christ's sake! Sure, it was in a house that he technically owned, but STILL! But still, you can't go wrong with pearl-snapped shirts. he surmised, without even considering the racial connotations. A blinding white shirt with silver piping and black pearl snaps made the cut, offset by black Tony Llamas, polished to a mirror finish. He'd be in high style were he attending a cattle auction. He left his newly acquired compound looking clean and pristine, He had no reason to question his appearance until Artiss opened the door to her apartment, looked him over head-to-toe and asked, "Where's your Stetson. Son?

Before he had time to think, he answered truthfully., "In the truck."

The evening went off-track from there. He was surprised at the end of the encounter when Artiss asked if she could see him again. Assuming he had nothing to lose, he agreed. He was not known for thinking ahead in situations like this. "What the hell!" He was rich. Didn't that make up for a lot?

Artiss opened with a tease. "I'm writing an article about employment opportunities in the criminal justice system here in Bee County. It will be in the Sunday paper. It's my first op-ed piece. You should check it out."

With a little assistance from DJ, Doris was able to locate Xavier

Vasquez. It was a long drive to Austin, but she knew where to stay when she got there. She took some of the new clothes she bought at the boutiques in Beeville, hoping they would hold up to the style conscious crowds of Austin. When she arrived at the Driscoll hotel her first act was to check-in and take a shower. Once primped, she took a seat at the end of the Driscoll's elegant Victorian bar. She nursed a glass of pinot noir and waited. She'd timed it well. Within 30 minutes a man whose name she did not officially know sat at the other end of the bar. It was like Deja vu with a lot more class. She called the bartender and pointed out the regal Hispanic man at the other end of the bar and had a Maker's Mark on the rocks delivered. When he noticed her, he broke into a grin, enjoying her reenactment of their initial San Antonio meeting. This time she joined him at his end of the bar, "Two nameless truckers walk into a bar," Doris said. "It turns out one is named Doris Cash. That would be me. The other, I'm betting, is still trying on the much less commercial nom de plume of Xavier Vasquez. Am I close?

"All we lack is a punch line," Xavier said.

"Let's have another drink and work that out. It should probably have something to do with going truck shopping tomorrow."

"Should we get DJ's thoughts on this?"

"That's up to you. He wasn't directly involved in our business. He and Jerry didn't get along at all! Still, if he'll be driving, he should have some input."

Xavier contemplated the situation for a few minutes while staring into the amber liquid as if it held the answer. "He kept me alive, out of jail, and in business so I'd like to get him in the loop, especially since he's now the listed owner of SIP."

"Makes sense. In the meantime we should put together an inventory complete with values and depreciation. We have the money to upgrade but we should hold on to our assets and use OPM to purchase large items like trucks and logistics software."

"OPM?"

"Other People's Money. It lessens our liability and keeps our books in the black. Before we do anything as far as expansion or improvements we need to merge our corporations. You are incorporated, right"

"Actually, no. I never got around to it."

"No big deal. It might make it easier to just do a buyout. SIP is owed by my son."

"So, no truck shopping tomorrow?"

"We could look and get an idea of what kind of capital we'll need. It might be fun, get a handle on what we need. Tonight we drink to our future success."

"Amen!"

LARGER THAN LIFE

The apprehension building in Carrie's tormented psyche had her visibly trembling as Roger touched down and taxied to the private hanger at the north end of a small runway. With no reference to work from, her immediate goal was to reunite with her Peacemaker before her inevitable encounter with the local authorities. As soon as Roger cut the engines, she took a deep breath. "I know where I'm going once I get out of the airport but I assume I still have to deal with customs and immigration", she asked Roger.

He seemed like he would rather not be a part of her conundrum. "I have another brief jaunt leaving in about 45 minutes but I'll get you headed in the right direction. Let me secure my craft and I'll help load your gear in that Cushman scooter beside the hanger. Do you know how to operate it?"

"If it's like a golf cart I can most likely figure it out."

"Pull it inside and load it up. Take your luggage over to where that colorful flag is sticking out. You'll need your passport, destination address, and this manifest. You should be able to handle it from there but text me if you run into a snag. Leave the scooter with those others by the automatic doors. Good luck."

"Thanks for everything."

"Don't mention it. I mean seriously, ever!" Roger wasn't happy about his role in this event. Once Carrie's luggage was secured, he exited the hanger immediately and left her on her own.

Carrie breezed through customs and immigration due to her identification as a police officer. Aurora supplied her with an ATF badge as well, but it wasn't necessary. She continued to look for Aurora or anyone else she might know, even Aaron, without success. Self-sufficiency was her middle name. She took a taxi to the rental. She opened the digital lock, stepped inside, and nearly swooned at the level of luxury. She was pleased that someone had thought of turning on the air conditioner. Shaken and exhausted, all she wanted was to get a good night's sleep. Everything else she had to deal with could wait until tomorrow. The primary objective had already been taken care of, or so she thought.

In the kitchen Carrie found a bottle of bourbon and poured

herself a shot. She sat at the breakfast bar and contemplated the tiny lights from the fishing boats out on the bay. Her second shot put her in the frame of mind for some serious snoozing. She stepped through the bedroom door flicked on the light and heard a muffled "stop!" Right above the foot of the bed Aurora hung by her shoulders from a beam. She was bound in a sheet like a cocoon and gagged with a scarf, her hands cuffed behind her. She was screaming like a banshee. It only took Carrie a few moments to realize there was some sort of mechanical device on the beam where the rope was connected. There was also an unnaturally out of place rug below her. Carrie stopped to assess the situation.

Aurora was hanging with the rope tied through her armpits and knotted behind her head she couldn't choke but it would be very uncomfortable. The gag prevented her from speaking clearly. The device on the beam appeared to be some sort of pressure switch probably similar to the IED that was on the floor under the rug. Of course this was speculation. She needed to free Aurora safely. "Let's get you down from here," Carrie said. She started towards the rug. Aurora produced a scream through the bandana. "OK that's a bad idea. Let's MacGyver this shit." She went off to find some chewing gum and tinfoil. She returned shortly with two dining room chairs, the headboard from one of the other bedrooms, and a box cutter. She placed a chair on each side of the rug and laid the headboard across it, climbed up on the headboard and cut Aurora's gag loose. "Don't change your weight placement. Don't stand on the headboard. We're just going to communicate right now."

"Water," Aurora whispered. "I've been hanging here since yesterday morning, not sure I can even move my arms anymore. This trigger is plugged into the wall over there. I think it's pretty simple. It's supposed to set off the IED if I manage to wiggle loose and fall on the rug. There's a 50/50 chance it can be disarmed by unplugging it. It only took the bastard about a minute to set it up."

"The bastard?"

"Your fucking daddy!"

"He did this himself? That doesn't make sense. He's an attorney. His knowledge of explosives is rudimentary at best."

"I get the impression that he's running out of minions. Or this is a personal vendetta for him. That seems more likely. He didn't get where he is by being stupid. Trust me."

"It's probably a control issue. How long do you think we have before he returns?" They heard the digital alarm beeping and the front door open. "About that long" Carrie said. She pulled the headboard off the chairs and slid it under the bed, took the chairs and put them in the bathroom's majestic walk-in closet, then stepped into the shower and closed the door. Lying down made her almost invisible in the frosted glass. As she lay there hugging her Peacemaker, she remembered she forgot to put the gag back on Aurora's mouth.

If only Jerry could see her now, dressed to the nines, taking in a concert at the Paramount Theater. But he can't. He wouldn't know fun if it bit him square on the ass. She's doing this on her dime and treating her friend to the experience. She's living large and it feels so good. Yeah, tomorrow they'll be tromping around on dusty dirt lots full of second hand 18-wheelers and box vans, taking notes on price, getting to know salespeople way better than they want to. But that's the game. She needs to give her son a call, but it's a little late now, just after midnight. That's OK, tomorrow will do. She takes Xavier's arm as they stroll down Congress Ave. And stop for a late dinner at an upscale steakhouse. Isn't this how you're supposed to live? It definitely works for Doris. It's almost 2:00 AM when Xavier accompanies Doris to her room. As much as he kindles the desire to become intimate, she realizes at this point it is not in anybody's best interest to mix business and pleasure, especially when both the business and the pleasure are in their infancy.

Xavier is just beginning to find his way. He has never known a woman like Doris who had both feet on the ground. The thought of being able to communicate with someone so attractive and not having to deal with psychological issues made the world a beautiful place. He did not want to jeopardize this relationship. He's okay with it being strictly business if that's what she prefers. He's also open to a romantic interlude if she feels the attraction like he does. He pads softly to his room so as not to wake the other residents, slips the key card in the door, and looks up to see her following with a demure countenance and a small overnight bag.

"I've been lonely far too long," she said. "Do you mind if I hang out?"

DJ rattled around in the large house on the hill. He finally stripped all the sheets and blankets off the beds, washed, dried, and folded them. His mom was on a business trip, as she called it, with Xavier to look at trucks. He could have gone if he wanted to but he preferred hanging out at the courthouse with Betty Lou and Artiss just to see what happened there. Today, however, was Sunday morning. He expected to sleep in. He was bored to tears, but at some point he had to get his company rolling again. He wasn't sure where all the legitimate business was but he knew it existed mostly selling to the prisons, the schools, and a few restaurants around town. Hopefully he could rekindle some of that good will. Since the word went out about the connections to the cartel and the death of one employee and the arrest of other drivers it was difficult to be competitive.

He did like hanging out with Artiss. They had intelligent conversations. He saw her as a challenge, not as a conquest but as the key to understanding the economic drivers in the food service industry and other logistical factors of the trucking industry. Unfortunately, he hadn't had a chance to spend time with Artiss this weekend as she was completing her op-ed article. He wanted to give her plenty of room to work. He didn't want to make the same mistake he made with Betty Lou. Anyway, it gave him an opportunity to settle into his new space and contact some old accounts to see if he could get back in their good graces. He was dozing off when the phone rang. Since he'd left it in the kitchen, he decided he would just call them back later, whoever it was. He figured it was his mom anyway. He could do without a play by play of their "date". In less than five minutes it rang again. The only problem with having a large house was trying to reach his phone before it gave up on him. He almost made it. He just missed the second call from Betty Lou.

Damn! I wish I had answered that. Maybe she's forgiven me. He didn't want to be too available on a Sunday morning, but he figured if she didn't call him again soon, he'd give her a call later in the morning. He took his phone with him and started breakfast. Sure enough, ten minutes later she called again. He picked up on the second ring.

"Hey Baby. What's cookin', other than my love Jones?"

"Your ass! Have you seen the morning paper?" She didn't sound happy---somewhere between a growl and sobbing.

"No. I'm homeless remember? What's up" DJ joked.

"Get one and check out the front page. You'll then understand why You're Fired! And don't call me back!

BEE COUNTY CRIMINAL JUSTICE PARTIES HARDY
by Artis Pruit

With Beeville being the County seat of Bee County, a significant portion of local jobs are funded by the criminal justice system. The small town has larger-than-life employment opportunities as peace officers and other incarceration related jobs. In this four-part series we will examine each of these organizations. Individually we have the state jail, part of the Texas Department of Corrections G. McConnell Unit, the Bee County Jail and Criminal Court system, the City of Beeville has its own jail and court system. There's also a strong presence of Border Patrol due to the local geographical intersection of major trafficking highways.

Today we'll investigate the county court system and the holding facility. Recently a county judge was assassinated. Speculation has it cartel assassins were involved and that county employees were part of the conspiracy. Although it's unlikely that the county judge was responsible for any illegal activity, this reporter's investigation has unearthed some disturbing facts pertinent to the case. Unnamed sources have confirmed that several members of the judge's staff used illegal mind-altering drugs regularly. And also, that a local county commissioner who has vanished may have been involved in human trafficking. Investigations will continue until the answers are found and the commissioner has been located. (continued on page 6).

Such was the text above the fold on the Beeville Picayune newspaper when DJ checked out at the local convenience store. It occurred to him he may be one of the staff being investigated. Had Betty Lou warned him? More likely, she was just angry. This is not good news. One thing is obvious; he'd been set up and knocked down by Artis Pruitt.

"So she's here?" Aaron picks up the scrap of gag from the rug without avoiding the rug. Nothing explodes, or even clicks.

"I chewed through it."

"Liar! This has been cut." He uses all the force he can muster in slamming an elbow into Aurora's kidney bringing tears to her eyes but she maintains without a sound. "Why are you being such a little shit? I trained you, got you this gravy train gig and this is the thanks I get?"

"And how many times have I saved your ass lately? When it comes to your daughter you act so stupid. You have no idea what an extremely talented asset she could be. GET ME DOWN!"

Aaron locks his fists together for another kidney punch, but Aurora is quicker and kicks him in the face with a steel-toed boot. He goes down and comes up bleeding from the mouth with a couple of missing teeth. Rage sets in. He flicks open a nine-inch switchblade, screaming, "Where the fuck is she!!"

"Right behind you!"

Aaron raises the switchblade, "I'm not stupid!" ... just as the knife bursts from his hand and pain shoots through his right arm.

"I beg to differ," Aurora says. "Now sit down and shut up." Aaron turns to stare down the barrel of Carrie's Peacemaker.

Carrie smiles "Y'all need to play nice. You're messing up my pretty house. Daddy, you need to calm down. Close your knife, drop it on the floor, and kick it towards me. Don't do anything else." Carrie picks up the knife and sticks it in the back pocket of her jeans. "Is that an IED under the carpet?"

"Yes"

"How about the beam she's suspended from?"

"No, it's a dummy."

Carrie unplugs the mechanism from the wall. With the Peacemaker still aimed at Aaron she asks, "Can you disarm this IED?"

Aaron looks at the rug and says, "I'm not sure."

So what are the tricks?

It's spring loaded, no electricity. We could pile several mattresses on it and give it a try."

"You do that. We'll watch. In the meantime we will discuss our partnership. I'm offering you an opportunity. It's more than you offered me, and no I don't trust you, so don't even consider that. However, you have knowledge that I need to make this takeover work. If you're willing to share that information, it will make our job easier. We're going to do it anyway, with or without your help. So basically, you can profit or you can die." Carrie has been pacing in circles around the bedroom. She suddenly stands still, peering into her father's eyes without saying anything for longer than is comfortable. I'm only going to make this offer once. If you do not accept it or if you do accept it and decide to usurp my authority you will die. I know you would have killed me given the opportunity. There's not a doubt in my mind. I shouldn't even give you this opportunity but, like I said, I need information you have to make this takeover successful. You need to get busy dragging some mattresses in here. There's also a headboard under the bed there, And two chairs in the walk in closet inside my bathroom. Don't fall in love while you're in there it's an amazing bathroom. It's mine.

    "You can use whatever you need. We're going to stand over here behind the kitchen counter in case you blow yourself up. I'd prefer you didn't do any further damage to this house though, I love it the way it is"

EPILOGUE
BECAUSE WELL ... CURIOSITY?

Apparently in a close-knit community like Beeville having the county judge smoke a little pot on the weekends isn't nearly as bad as having some college-educated smart-ass come in and try to disrupt the systems that have been working for decades. So, Betty Lou became County Judge Beatrice Louise Spencer, and she ran a tight ship as far as courtroom decorum goes. She never rehired DJ Cash or Kevin Cash or any other Cash. However, some nights as she lay alone in bed with a slight buzz on, she sure did miss the warm skin and the lack of consistency DJ had added to her life. Doris Cash became a *very* close business partner with Xavier Vasquez. One thing DJ Cash did find out while researching the best trucking company options was that fresh seafood from the Gulf of Mexico was a much more profitable load with significantly less risk than hookers, regardless of what the cartels thought. Since most of the trucks owned by the merging trucking companies were refrigerated, it seemed a perfect natural product with which to pursue the resurrection of a trucking company. DJ liked driving up and down the Gulf Coast from the Mississippi River all the way to South Padre Island in his new pearlescent AMG Mercedes. Not only did he sell seafood to every restaurant, bar, and bowling alley, but by night he would come back and DJ at those clubs where there was space for a stage or dance floor. In some of the larger venues he would hire a professional Cajun chef to provide an extravagant boiling pot using produce from his company's trucking business. He was very successful at both quests, and he seemed amazed to find out that it's a lot easier to make a lot of money if you already have a lot of money.

DJ never spoke civilly to Artiss Pruitt again. He returned the house his mom and Xavier should have kept to start with. They put it in Doris' name to keep Julio / Xavier safe. The rest of the property, trucks, and buildings became part of Cash Logistics Incorporated where he served asPresident of the Boaed of directors.

DJ purchased a three-story beach house with a widow's walk and windows facing the Gulf on Surfside Beach near Freeport, TX.

where most of the shrimpers and fishermen came into port. He almost became the legend he had always dreamed of. He had money, friends, and the affections of many women. None of them ever took the place of Betty Lou in his mind or in his heart, but he believed he was happy and he made sure everyone else believed it too.

Obviously, Xavier Vasquez did not want the authorities to look too deeply into his background and identification. That improved the situation because when you're looking for other people's money to spend on your business it's an advantage to be a woman-owned business. Cash Logistics Inc. turned out to be a woman-owned business, at least as far as the paperwork was concerned. Sometimes you win without even trying.

Although sharing the elegant house on the hill behind the trucking company's facility, Doris and Xavier maintained separate bedrooms for almost a year, just long enough for both to put their fear of the opposite sex to rest. It turned out neither of them were very scary.

Carrie ended up with her husband's ranch, two apartment complexes, A contolling interest in all the Valero convenience stores in a 12 county area of southwest Texas, and that fancy RV she'd had towed to the impound yard. None of this property enticed her to move back to Texas. She loved the Cayman Islands. However, she did deed the ranch to Lois as it's necessary to live in Bee county if she's going to run for local office. The day after she moved in, she began campaigning for the County Commissioner's seat. She handily won even though being a Democrat proved a challenge in that part of the state. In addition to the name recognition, and her background in local politics, Lois had the newspaper's owner firmly behind her.

Carrie is still waving her Peacemaker around, making sure everyone knows she's the one in charge. "You need to wrap this up, Pops. I just booked you a flight back to Corpus Christi, leaving at 7PM."
Aaron pulls the last of four mattresses into the bedroom and leans it against the bed. The idea is to ride the four mattresses down flat to set off the IED.

"I thought I'd stay here tonight and go back in the morning," he states.

"Nope," Carrie says. "That's not gonna happen. She points the Peacemaker at the center of his chest. "Jump, while you still can." There's a muffled thump and the mattresses dances briefly prior settling.

"Lame!" Carrie says. "Get your shit and we'll take you to the airport."

Aurora driives so Carrie can keep her weapon trained on her bio-Dad. She pulls the rental car all the way into the hanger.

The pilot meets Aaron at the plane. "I'm Roger," he says. "Please, no jokes about the radio. I've heard them all. We can leave in 22 minutes.

Aaron gives the plane a once over. "We're gonna take this puddle jumper all the way to Corpus Christi?"

"Yep." Roger says.

Carrie looks at her father. "What goes around comes around."

Do I have to wear the seat belt? It seems so claustrophobic."

"Of course not," Roger says. "Your plane – your call."

The women wait in the hanger until the plane lifts from the runway. As it takes off, the right wing briefly dips toward the asphalt.

Aurora shakes her head and turns away. "He's never going to set foot on land again, is he?"

Carrie pulls her shades over her eyes. "Nope."

Another woman-owned business will be contracting with the DEA and ATF—under the radar.

THE END
Or is it?

tony burnett

ABOUT THE AUTHOR

A former board president of the Writer's League of Texas and the current managing editor and CEO of Kallisto Gaia Press, Burnett brings decades of storytelling craft to his work. His previous books—*Southern Gentleman* (short stories), *The Reckless Hope of Scoundrels* (poetry), and *Watermelon Tattoo* (winner of the Water Tower Press Novel Prize)—reflect his lifelong commitment to portraying humanity as it truly is: flawed, damaged, yearning, and resilient. He is also a writing instructor, workshop leader, and advocate for writers finding their authentic voice. Burnett lives in rural central Texas with his wife of 32 years, Robin, where he enjoys wandering backroads, poking metaphorical (and sometimes literal) wasp nests with short sticks, and fending off a pack of unruly Chihuahuas that claim his land as their kingdom.

With *Mirage,* Burnett delivers his most ambitious and explosive work yet—a border-crime thriller driven by trauma, vengeance, corruption, and the desperate longing for justice in a world built on exploitation.

Excerpt from
Suitable For Framing
a Cash & Carrie Adventure
Chapter 1
STORM

DJ reclines in his brightly colored gaming chair facing the floor to ceiling glass wall overlooking the Gulf of Mexico. He sips a warm tumbler of Maker's Mark while watching the Gulf with interest. He refers to this glassed-in space as the Widow's Walk, a technically inaccurate but descriptive term describing the third floor of his "mansion-on-stilts. Besides, it's his house, he can call it what he wants.

Little lights seem to flicker offshore. Not from electrical failure, but the fishing and shrimp boats are dropping in and out of sight between the massive hurricane swells. On land there are almost no lights visible. All his neighbors have packed up and gone inland. He has faith in the structural integrity of his house. It's engineered by Carrie's architect friend, Violet, who has designed several government buildings in the coastal Central American cities in Belize, Guatemala, Brazil, and Panama. His house can supposedly withstand 250 mile-an-hour gusts or a class four tornado. He never rode out a hurricane.

This will be his first. Not just a hurricane, really. There are three hurricanes currently in the Gulf. The meanest one was given the name Crazy Rhonda by the TV meteorologists. After cutting a devastating swath across the Yucatan peninsula, she crossed the Gulf and rebuilt, danced awhile with hurricane Teresa off the west coast of Florida, then wandered back into the Gulf where a low-pressure system, having recently been tropical storm Olivia, planned a late-night seduction in Rockport, several miles southwest of where he relaxed on Surfside beach. It's going to be a show. No worries, he thinks to himself. He isn't one to worry. His whole life shattered two years prior and he's already bounced back stronger, richer, and maybe a little less stupid. That, of course, is open to interpretation.

Xavier called earlier in the week, probably at his mom, Doris' suggestion, and offered him a place to ride out the hurricane inland. He did take his beloved AMG Mercedes and drop it off in Beeville where he picked up a box van to contain his patio furniture. It's most likely the only way he'll ever see those accoutrements again. He really wants to see the hurricane from the inside.

As far as he knows phone service is still working. He's contacted most of his friends and clients to let them know he's OK. He can't reach Joelle. It worries him. Joelle is a bit odd. Although he's a well-known regional artist, and journalist, he resides in an old AMC postal truck from the 60s he's refurbished into a camper. That was only one of his many eccentricities but he's become close friends with DJ. They both like reggae and ska music, love the beach, and they don't like anybody telling them what to do or how to do it. DJ is only slightly disturbed when Joelle doesn't answer the phone. It's common for him to drop out of sight for a day or two when he's working on a project. Maybe he's as curious about the hurricane as DJ.

The power goes out. He has never seen Surfside as dark as it is tonight. He can't see the hand in front of his face.

He starts counting backwards from 10. By the time he reaches 4 the lights come back on. His backup generator works perfectly, however the rest of Surfside is onyx black. The silent darkness brings on a howling depth of loneliness. A feeling he's tamped down for several months. He wraps himself in work and quick entertainment to fill the empty space. Tonight, there's no hiding place.

It's easy to occupy his time most evenings. When you're 27 years old, a multimillionaire, and live in a small community, everyone wants to be your friend. He usually has a beautiful woman on his arm when he goes anywhere important. If not he'll meet one when he gets there. No problem! But that isn't real. He tries to tell himself it is. Everyone else believes him, but he doesn't believe himself. Anyway, now the power is back on, thanks to his generator, but he has no cell or Internet service. He could watch a movie or play a game that doesn't require interaction with other people. Whatever…

When he tries his phone, he sees a text from Joelle. It says, "You're not going to believe this!" and that's all it says. When he tries to respond, he has no phone or Internet service. He'll just have to wait patiently, or as patiently as possible, until a connection returns.

www.ingramcontent.com/pod-product-compliance
Lightning Source LLC
LaVergne TN
LVHW040039080526
838202LV00045B/3399